PRAISE I

"Quick-witted, flirty and delicious.

— STACEY MCEWAN, *LEDGE*

"Expertly capturing the glamour and mayhem of wedding photography, *Shooters* is a debut romcom brimming with sex, sisterhood, and spice!"

— AMY BEASHEL, *SPILT MILK*

"I am hotly anticipating the sequel."

— MELISSA LOVE, PROFESSIONAL PHOTO MAGAZINE

"Humour, romance, complex characters, luxury locations and a sprinkling of sex seduce the reader into wanting more."

— ANGELA ADAMS, *IMAGEMAKER MAGAZINE*

Shooters

Julia Bosson

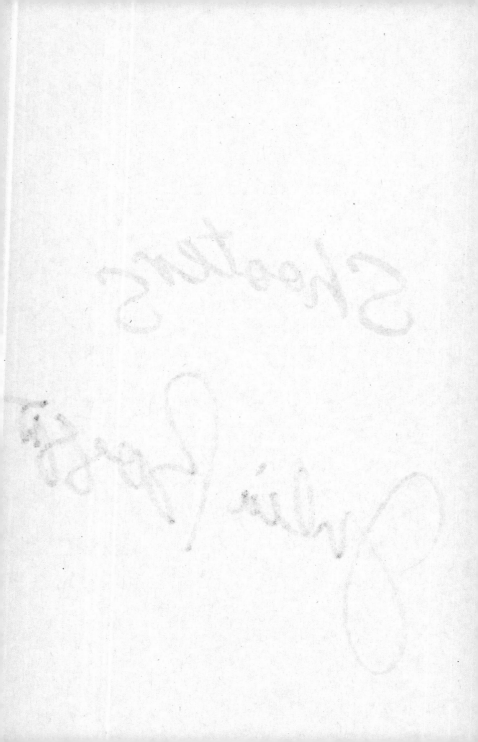

Shooters

A Novel

Julia Boggio

HOME BY MIDNIGHT PUBLISHING

To request permissions, contact the publisher at hbmpublishingUK@gmail.com.

Paperback: 978-1-7392151-1-8

First edition.

Cover design: Bailey McGinn

Library in Congress Cataloguing-in-Publication has been applied for.

To all the people who feel naked
without their camera

ANNUAL BAPP CONVENTION (BRITISH ASSOCIATION OF PROFESSIONAL PHOTOGRAPHERS)

THE ROOM SIMMERED WITH TALENT: those who had it, those who wanted it, and those who would always suck no matter how hard they tried.

Stella Price wondered where she fell on that scale. Was this new career the right choice, or was she about to make another big mistake?

Taking a deep breath, she retreated further into the corner of the busy hotel lobby, hugging the convention guide to her chest. It was one of those bland corporate hotels that existed solely to host conferences. Stella bet there would be a stereotypical Irish Pub on the ground floor and a bar named something insipid like *Whispers* or *Secrets*. It reminded her of a past life. She shuddered. Through her earphones, she absorbed the calming sound of Dolly Parton singing *'Love is Like a Butterfly'*, the tinkling notes soothing her nerves.

She scanned the room for her friend, Claudia. Late as usual. Their chances of sitting anywhere near the front, or even getting seats together, dwindled as the foyer filled with eager bodies.

'Ohmygod, hello! It's been so long!' A few feet in front of Stella, a brunette woman threw herself into the arms of a muscular bald man. The woman immediately started flirting with him, touching his chest, biting her lip. Claudia had warned Stella that these photography conventions were a hotbed of sexual activity, but so far, she hadn't seen anyone that would tempt her out of her self-imposed dry spell. Stella was strictly there to learn. She had one job, and nothing would get in her way.

Idly stroking the small cleft in her chin—one of her many nervous habits—Stella took another step back, away from the couple as though flirting was contagious. At the same moment, Dolly began singing 'Jolene' and Stella hastily switched off her music, tore the headphones out of her ears, and shoved them into her bag. The last thing she wanted to think about was a flame-haired marriage wrecker. She took another anxious step backwards.

Her heel kicked something behind her. Turning, she saw a roller banner that read 'Discover your potential with Connor Knight' above a picture of a thirty-something man who could've stepped out of an action film. He clung to the side of a helicopter with one hand, powerful muscles straining against the sleeves of his tight, white t-shirt. With his other hand, he held a camera in front of his face, only his chiselled jaw visible, but she didn't need to see his features to know his kind: arrogant and self-involved with an allergy to commitment. Exactly the Old Stella's type.

Next to her, a woman stopped and commented to her friend, 'It should be illegal to be that hot.'

'I'd like to discover *my* potential with Connor Knight,' sighed the second woman.

'I heard he doesn't get out of bed for less than £50k.'

'Why would anyone want him to get *out* of bed?' Laughing, they continued into the hall.

Stella crinkled her nose. Was this really the respected wedding photographer whose talk Claudia insisted she attend? Stella had researched his work before booking, studying blog post after blog post showcasing his wedding images, but she hadn't seen a picture of him. Standing this close to a life-size replica, she could practically smell his cologne: something expensive, arousing, its key ingredient milked from the glands of an obscure Bolivian rodent. Hopefully this wouldn't be a waste of time.

She snapped a photo of the poster on her phone, making a mental note to send it to Tristan—her oldest friend and ex-dance partner. Connor Knight was exactly his type, as well. Unfortunately for Tristan, based on what those women were saying, she suspected Connor wasn't gay.

Smiling to herself, she paused as she saw the time on her phone. Claudia was officially half an hour late. Stella couldn't wait any longer. The talk started in five minutes.

Clutching the guide to her chest, Stella inhaled deeply and plunged into the labyrinth of people. She hunched her shoulders to make herself small. As a slim redhead with green eyes and a healthy dose of freckles, she was used to attracting attention, usually from men, but today she wanted to blend in.

She brushed past a young tattooed girl talking to an older woman in a floral kaftan. Sidestepping a Sikh gentleman and a Hell's Angel comparing cameras, she narrowly missed getting crushed between a large bearded man leaning in to hug a Goth. Wedding photographers were a varied bunch. She yearned to belong among their ranks.

Stella pushed into the vast conference hall, scanning the packed room for free seats. Two chairs lay covered by a greedy brown raincoat. 'Sorry—are those...?'

'Taken.'

Swearing under her breath, she straggled up the aisle, her gaze sweeping over the room. There! Two empty seats. She snapped into action, dancing around the bodies between her and her goal. A yelp of triumph, Stella flung her bag onto the chairs, only to realise another woman had also been heading for them.

'Sorry!' she said automatically. The woman she'd beaten had elfin proportions, her white hair cut short like a pixie. Stella estimated her age at mid-to-late fifties. The woman leaned on a closed umbrella, using it as a walking stick.

Stella couldn't take the seats. Her Italian mother would be livid. *'Il rispetto che ricevi é pari a quello che hai dato,'* she always said: 'The respect you get is measured by the respect you give'. Stella had been hard-wired to do the right thing, even if she failed more often than she succeeded. 'You take them. I'll find somewhere else,' she said, picking up her bag.

'Oh, love, I only need the one. You can sit next to me,' the woman said with a strong Welsh lilt.

At least Stella had given the seats up for a compatriot. 'I have a friend coming. It's okay.'

'Do I detect a hint of Cardiff in your accent?'

'Good ear! Most people can't pick it out.'

'Yes, I'm a regular Sherlock Holmes, me,' she laughed, a warm, tinkling sound that complimented her fairy-like stature.

'Well, I better...' Stella slung her bag over her shoulder and re-started her search.

'Thank you, lovely,' the woman called after her.

Eventually, Stella found a pair of seats together at the back—middle of the row, behind two giants. She texted her location to Claudia and pulled out her new notebook and pen. *Connor Knight Talk* she wrote at the top of a clean page, underlining it twice. She drew a box around it for good measure.

The lights dimmed.

A tingle of excitement ran up her spine. The hubbub of conversation petered out as the opening drumbeats of Robbie Williams's *'Let Me Entertain You'* exploded from the loudspeakers. Heart pounding to the music, Stella couldn't believe she was here, finally starting her new career as a professional wedding photographer.

Two ceiling-height screens on either side of the stage flared to life. A figure appeared, black against the white digital backdrop. As the music galloped towards the first chorus, the silhouette swaggered down the centre of the stage. Whoops and screams filled the air. One of the giants in front of her wept. Stella huffed and shook her head.

The figure reached the front. Arms held wide, Connor Knight

4

struck a pose in the spotlight, tapping his foot to the beat and twitching his fingers, inviting the crowd to scream louder.

Stella's jaw fell open and she leaned forward in her seat. She stared at the screens, where his face was magnified. If Michelangelo had worked with blood and bone instead of marble, he might have created something like this man. Sharp, high cheekbones curved down into a stubbled jawline. His eyes were green-grey. Or blue-grey? Either way, his eyes were grey, like a stormy sky. And the hair...rich, chestnut locks cut just long enough to allow some curls to start showing at the ends. Her eyes finally came to rest on his mouth: full lips, now quirked in a cocky, lopsided grin that reminded her of Matthew McConaughey in every role he ever played.

She realised she was leering at him.

No! Bad Stella. She crossed her legs and built mental walls against his charisma.

The crowd clapped along to the music. 'Thank you! Thank you.' Connor's voice rolled into his Madonna mic, deep and slow, like he was in no rush to get his words out.

Behind him, a slideshow of images started scrolling. Remembering the reason she was there, Stella's heart thrilled at a dramatic portrait of a couple kissing on a rocky outcrop, the infinite ocean crashing behind them. Who said romance was dead? It oozed from every picture.

On the stage, Connor warmed up the crowd, bringing out his favourite bad one-liners from best man speeches. But Stella was distracted by a commotion to her left.

'Coming through.'

'Ow!'

'So sorry. Was that your foot?'

Stella squinted into the dim light, already knowing what she'd find: Claudia, causing chaos as she navigated toward her seat, her bag bouncing off the heads of the people in the next row. Disorder and Claudia went hand in hand. Stella had come home to the mess at their flat at the University of Edinburgh often enough. Pans caked in burnt food. Paintbrushes in the sink, covered in gobs of acrylic. A used condom floating in the toilet. She loved Claudia, but living separately in London had saved their friendship.

'Hello!' No apologies for being late as Claudia fell into the seat next to Stella. As usual, Claudia appeared to have been styled by Mary Quant herself in an orange jersey dress.

Settling in, she shrugged off her cream faux fur coat and slung it over her chair, throwing the man behind her a flirtatious smile. Her bag covered her knees, impinging on Stella's. A cap-less lipstick stuck out through a layer of crumpled receipts.

With affection in her voice, Stella whispered, 'You know you can be a complete cow sometimes.'

'Yes, but I'm *your* cow.'

Stella's attention snapped back to Connor asking: 'Why do you want to be wedding photographers?'

The million dollar question. Stella chewed her lip. She had always loved photography and had wanted to study it at university. But her father insisted it was a stupid idea and guided her towards a practical choice. '*You'll never make any real money taking pictures,*' he told her. He was less than thrilled about her recent career change.

After graduating with a degree in biology, Stella became a copy-writer in medical advertising and she was good at it. Until things went off the rails, she believed that's where her future lay: a lifetime of spin-ning data to sell medicine to doctors. Ugh. In hindsight she had been a glorified corporate drug pusher. Compared to that, photography had a nobility that she quite liked, uniting people with their past.

Besides, the idea of working alone appealed to her at the moment. Nobody to steal her sandwich out of the communal fridge. No one to gossip about her around the water cooler. No boss to screw.

'You want to be a wedding photographer,' said Connor in his unhurried, low drawl, 'because you like a challenge. Because you want to see how far you can push yourself to be your very best. There are no do-overs in wedding photography. You get the shot first time, or you don't get the shot at all.' Stella felt a squeeze of nerves, even though she hadn't actually shot any weddings yet. 'How many people in this room want to become better wedding photographers?'

Stella raised her hand self-consciously: not too high, not too low.

'Great. Can anyone tell me the most crucial ingredient in creating a beautiful wedding image?'

Love! Stella wanted to yell. *Or maybe romance?*

She had this idea that becoming a wedding photographer would be tantamount to pickling herself in passion. Surely if she spent all her time surrounded by people in love, some of that would rub off on her? Help her make better life choices in the boyfriend department? Maybe there was a single, successful, relationship-ready best man out there just waiting for her.

But not until she'd established herself in this new career. She'd allowed her bad relationship choices to derail her plans before. New Stella didn't have time for romance.

A few braver souls screamed their answers.

'A good camera!'

'A great venue!'

'A hot bride!'

Connor chuckled. 'All those things help, but the most important ingredient is *you*. The photographer.' He pointed into the crowd. Stella imagined he was pointing at her and her heart beat faster. 'You and your talent...your *experience* is more fundamental than anything else: the weather, the couple, even *love*.'

Stella sat up in her chair. *Really?!*

'In fact,' Connor continued, 'I'm going to prove to you that the couple's love isn't as important as your skill. I need two volunteers please.'

Hands shot into the air. Stella kept hers down. The last time she'd been on a stage, it hadn't gone well.

He invited his choices to join him: a scruffy man with thick glasses, greying hair and a t-shirt declaring *Nikon rocks!* and a stunning brunette with figure-hugging jeans. A more unlikely couple, Stella could not imagine. While he introduced them to the audience, another man set up lights, tested the flash, and handed a camera to Connor. Of course, Connor Knight would employ an assistant that looked like a Bollywood film star.

'Do you two know each other?' Connor asked. His models both shook their heads. 'When I'm done, these strangers will look like they've loved each other since primary school.'

He directed the man to stand in the middle of the stage, facing front. The woman, who towered inches above him, giggled as Connor took her hand and led her behind the 'groom'. From the hungry way she gazed at Connor, it was obvious which man she'd prefer to wrap herself around.

'She's taller, so I'm going to pose her behind him.' Connor gave her some instructions and she shifted her weight, leaning in towards the man. Connor asked her to throw her arms around her 'partner's' shoulders.

'Now they're in a pose. But do they look in love?'

No, of course not, Stella thought. *Because this is ridiculous.*

'No,' barked the audience in trained seal mode.

'Right, so now what they need is *animation*. A pose is just a pose. It's the emotion that elevates it into an impressive picture.'

He sauntered up to the woman and gave her an instruction the crowd couldn't hear. She giggled again and waited while Connor got into position, camera raised and ready. A nod from him and she turned towards her 'groom', whispering into his ear. They both laughed. The flashes fired, and a portrait jumped onto the big screens.

Stella's lip curled with disappointment. Connor was right. The photograph portrayed a couple in love.

'Do you want to know what she said to him?' Connor asked after the applause died down. 'I told her to list breakfast cereals in a sexy voice.'

Breakfast cereals, Stella thought. *You can fake love with breakfast cereals?!*

Perhaps there was more to this wedding photography business than she'd thought.

Connor demonstrated another three poses with the couple, just to drive his point home. By the time the coffee break arrived, Stella's thoughts were a whirlwind of self-doubt.

'I'm not sure I'm ready, Clauds. I can't do what he just did.'

'Of course you can't. Yet. He's one of the top wedding photographers in the world. That's why everyone wants to learn from him. He's like the photographic Yoda...except I bet he has a bigger dick.'

'Claudia!' Stella tapped her on the arm even though she thought it was funny.

'Actually, do you think Yoda even has a dick?'

'You really do have sex on the brain.'

'Well, what happens at convention stays at convention. We're finally single at the same time, so I'm counting on you to be my wing-woman.'

'I need to concentrate on building my business.'

'All work and no play—'

'—makes Stella a successful girl.'

Claudia pretended to gag.

Suddenly serious, Stella said, 'You know my situation.'

'I know. I know. Hey, how was that shoot you did last week? Chickens, wasn't it?'

'It went...well.' The cousin of an acquaintance needed some pictures taken of chickens for his breeding website. It had been a complete disaster. Not only was the pay miserable, but the owner wanted a dark background for a fine art look instead of natural shots. The chickens kept jumping off the crate where she posed them. Then her camera started flashing some cryptic error message. The final egg in the basket, so to speak, was when she found one of the chickens had done its business in her camera bag. She'd learnt lessons that day. Ultimately, the client loved the shots, but she never wanted to shoot chickens again.

Claudia chuckled. 'I remember the days when I couldn't afford to say no to a job. So glad I'm past that.' She ran a profitable family photography business. At Uni, if anyone had told Stella that her friend would end up working with children, she would have laughed long and hard.

The lights flickered, signalling the second half of the talk.

Another slideshow of Connor's portfolio played, exhibiting photograph after photograph of glamorous couples posed in grand locations around the world. As he spoke, Stella scribbled his advice in her rapidly-filling notebook. Posing, lighting, marketing—he covered everything. She panicked as she realised only ten minutes remained. She could listen to him all day long, and not just because he had a voice that should introduce movie trailers. Everything he said highlighted how much she didn't know about shooting weddings. Apparently, it would involve a lot of yelling to tell guests where to go and how to stand....she didn't have the confidence to yell at all those strangers! A dribble of sweat curved down the side of her face.

'Before we finish,' Connor said, 'I have an announcement.' An image appeared on the screen that made Stella cringe: a wedding photo, but a terrible one with unflattering light, so poorly exposed that the couple could barely be seen.

He continued, 'This was taken by one of my students on his last wedding *before* coming on my one-week course.' A new image flicked onto the screen. 'This is from the first wedding he shot *after* he studied with me.'

Stella's eyes widened as she took in the stark contrast between the two, the difference between a child's doodle and a Picasso. The lighting flattered the bride. The pose connected the couple without seeming forced. There was a black point and a white point and all the tonal shades in between. Altogether the second shot had a more professional finish.

'Who wants to see more?' Connor teased.

Before and after shots flooded the screen, all revealing the same level of improvement as the first. Stella's desire grew with each picture. Connor Knight really could help her discover her potential.

The next slide materialised: *Do you want to study with Connor at a French Chateau?*

Yes! screamed Stella in her head. She slid to the front of her seat and concentrated on what he was saying, along with everyone else in the room.

Except Claudia. Filing her nails, she said, 'Watch out—you're getting that glow in your eyes that people have at Tony Robbins conferences.'

Connor was showing pictures of a French chateau surrounded by fields and forest. 'Ten lucky people will get the chance to spend five days with me, learning everything we did today plus a whole lot more.' His eyes glittered with promise.

Stella nibbled her thumbnail, another nervous habit her mother had lamented since always. Only ten people. Should Stella do it? Should she jump on the Connor train and see where it led her?

Her foot tapped rabbit-fast, and Claudia stepped on it to make her stop. Those spaces would go in a snap. How would she beat everyone else in that room to snag a spot?

In her head, her father piped up. She remembered him pulling her aside before she won the British Open Youth Latin dance championships, aged eighteen. *'Winners visualise success.'*

Although Stella didn't feel like a winner lately, this course would point her in the right direction.

She narrowed her eyes. *I want this.*

The next slide popped up: £5000 per head. Her shoulders slumped. She couldn't afford that. The hush money from Bastion Communications was almost gone. Actually, everyone in the industry knew about the affair, so maybe *pay-off* was more apt. She'd already spent a hefty sum upgrading her camera kit. What had seemed like a decent package in the beginning had proved a pittance. She should have bargained harder, but she had been keen to draw a line under that chapter of her life. Photography needed to make money for her soon, or she'd be waiting tables by summer and living with her parents by winter. She shivered. Either way, she couldn't fork out five grand.

Slouched in her chair, Stella pinched the bridge of her nose.

Sometimes everything that had happened to her in the last six months felt so unfair. She was only half listening when Connor said, 'And here's the most exciting part: I'm giving away one free spot on this course to somebody in this room.'

A morsel of hope sprang to life in Stella's chest.

'Taped underneath one chair is a single red rose.'

The conference hall thrummed with the rustle of excitement, of cloth rubbing against cloth and people grunting as they leant over to explore under their chairs.

Stella closed her eyes and visualised winning, just like she used to do as a teen in her competitive dancing days. Without even looking, she knew. It was her. She had won. With a deep breath, she reached between her knees.

2

STELLA FELT UNDER HER CHAIR, flinching as her fingers landed on a glob of chewing gum. 'Ew!' She shook her hand and checked again, avoiding the disgusting, hardened mass. No rose.

Claudia also came up empty-handed.

'Yes!' a woman shouted.

Heads swivelled. Stella spotted a red flower held aloft with black gaffer tape stuck to it. Her gaze followed the person's arm to her face.

No, it can't be, she thought. The white-haired pixie to whom she had given her chair ran onto the stage with a spring in her step.

'We have a winner,' said Connor as the pixie attacked him with a hug, burying her head in his pectorals. As he peeled her off, she reached up and squeezed his arm muscles in the unashamed, I'm-old-enough-to-be-your-mother-so-I'm-definitely-not-lusting-after-you kind of way. But she didn't fool Stella. The woman was definitely lusting after him.

Stella seethed in her seat. She couldn't believe the prize had been within her grasp. She'd let it go. Poof. Respect for elders indeed. She focussed her anger on her mother, for every piece of Italian-Catholic mumbo jumbo she had drilled into Stella's head. Being the daughter of a morally perfect parent was hard.

Ha, mother, if you only knew. Upon further consideration, Stella didn't deserve to win the prize. Penance came in many shapes and sizes.

'What's wrong with you? Your skin's gone blotchy,' said Claudia.

'I gave that woman my seat.'

'Ooh, I bet that burns. Hey, you should challenge her to a thumb war to win it back. '

Claudia was referring to Stella's party trick. Stella had freakishly long and strong, graceful thumbs. Thumbs that moved like tiny dancers. Thumbs that could flick the top off a beer bottle with one smooth pop. Twisting, bending, physics-defying thumbs. Three things in life were guaranteed: death, taxes, and Stella winning a thumb war. But Stella's thumbs wouldn't help her right now. 'I want to go on that course. I need to go. That man is a photographic magician.' Her finger drifted to the cleft in her chin as she thought about what to do.

'Hmmm. I was afraid of this.'

'What?'

'Well, I know how you get horny around authority figures. I can't let you go to France in good conscience.'

'Oh...piss off!' Stella crossed her arms.

'Too soon?'

'I'm not interested in *that*. I'd learn a lot from him.'

'Pay the money, then. You can still go.'

'I don't have enough.'

'Ask Tristan to borrow some. He's got plenty.'

'I can't. I already pay a pittance to him in rent. Besides, I have no idea where he is right now.'

'Then do what I'd do. Stick it on a credit card.'

The temptation to do exactly that unfurled in Stella. She had two cards in her wallet. If she used both, she could cover the cost, although it would max her out.

Her foot started tapping again. While the rest of the audience clapped as the prize-stealing Welsh pixie leapt up to plant a kiss on Connor's lips, Stella considered the numbers. If she brought in £3k per wedding, she'd need five, maybe six to pay off the debt. But going on the course would get her those bookings. It was a catch-22.

'Okay,' she said.

'Okay what?'

'Okay, I'll put it on my cards.'

'Are you sure? I mean, *sure* sure?'

'You're the one who suggested it.'

The winner finally left the stage. Connor thanked the crowd and reminded them to buy his instructional DVDs and other merchandise. 'You can book France at the kiosk.' He pointed at the rear of the room. 'My last course sold out in ten minutes. Can we do it in five?'

Stella wished he hadn't said that. Now everyone would race for the spots. Her heart pumped faster.

She stood, along with thirty or so others. Their eyes pin-balled between each other. At the same time, they all sprang into action. The game had begun.

As the crowd broke into applause, Stella called out 'I'll meet you in the bar' to Claudia and began scissor-legging down the aisle between people's knees and the next row of chairs. 'Sorry. Excuse me,' she said to no one in particular, as she squished toes beneath her heel. Five of her nemeses had already reached the centre and were scurrying towards the kiosk.

The handle of a bag grabbed her foot like a needy toddler as she emerged from her aisle. She shook it loose, leaving the bag where it fell and shouting an apology to the owner. No time to be Polite, People-Pleasing Stella. The clock stopped for no one.

Those who weren't taking part in her personal video game exited their rows. All dancers had a keen sense of spatial awareness, developed to avoid banging into others while performing. Stella employed that skill now, navigating through the congealing crowds, dodging as gaps opened or closed. Up ahead, two competitors disappeared around the corner, heading towards the queue. Just then, a man blocked her path. She stepped left. He stepped left. She stepped right. He stepped right and laughed. She did not. They did the Get-The-

Hell-Out-of-My-Way dance enough times that she had to wonder if he was doing it on purpose. Dropping a shoulder, she pushed past him with another throw-away apology.

She skirted the last row of chairs and rushed to claim her place in the queue, just seconds before another man. As she caught her breath, she counted the bodies between her and success. Six, which made her the seventh. How many people had already paid? Minus the Welsh pixie, that left nine available spaces.

'Pardon me,' she said to the woman ahead of her. 'Do you know—'

The woman tutted and aggressively pointed to the phone against her ear.

'Sorry,' Stella mouthed.

At the head of the queue stood the man from Connor's volunteer demonstration. He paid for his spot and punched the air so enthusiastically that his glasses tumbled off his nose. Eyewear reinstated, he reached into his pouch and handed a business card to each person still waiting. 'Call me if you want to share a ride. I'm driving.'

Stella dropped the card into her bag, 'Do you know how many spots are gone?'

'There was at least one booking before me, I think.' He shrugged and smiled wide. 'Good luck.'

She did the math, bouncing on her toes. The final spot should be hers.

Even so, she couldn't relax until she had a receipt. She regarded the line with growing impatience as each student filled in the forms and paid. She could've watched all six episodes of the BBC's *Pride and Prejudice* in the time it took to move up a few spaces.

At long last she slid into second position. She allowed herself a momentary daydream about shooting models in the French countryside, Connor Knight praising her because no other student had ever advanced so rapidly. She'd return to England armed with everything she needed to make her new life work.

'I'll take two spots,' Phone Woman said to the sales assistant. 'One for me and one for my husband.'

It took a moment for her words to penetrate Stella's thoughts. 'No! No! No!' she yelped. Both women looked at her. 'Sorry. I mean, is that even allowed?'

'I'm afraid so,' the salesgirl said, wrinkling her nose as though she shared Stella's disappointment. Her false sympathy made Stella want to scream.

Her French daydream disintegrated, replaced by a vision of her working at Starbucks in central Cardiff. How much more ill luck could she handle today? Perhaps someone could walk by wearing her ex-lover's wife's perfume to trigger one of her shiny new panic attacks. That would be the proverbial cherry.

'Better luck next time,' said Phone Woman with a smirk before stuffing the receipt into her wallet with an air of triumph.

Stella opened her mouth to make a pithy, cutting reply—something that Oscar Wilde himself would want printed on a fridge magnet. But no words came out. She just wasn't a pithy, cutting reply kind of person. Stella sighed. Claudia would have known what to say.

Shaking it off, she stepped up to the desk, praying that maybe she had miscalculated.

But she hadn't. 'Those were the last spots.'

Her face fell. If only she had been quicker. If only she hadn't dated her married boss. If only she hadn't been shut out by the entire medical advertising industry. Then she wouldn't be at square one, trying to learn a new trade, failing at the first hurdle.

Unwilling to let hope die, she asked, 'Is there a waiting list?'

'Nobody ever cancels.'

'Okay, then…will he be offering another one soon?'

'Next one is in the autumn.'

That was ages away. Stella needed to be up and running by the summer. 'Thanks, anyway,' she said, turning sorrowfully towards the exit.

. . .

VINTAGE GUINNESS ADVERTS adorned the walls of the pub. Next to a framed poster of a half-naked leprechaun asking them to 'Turn me over and kiss me clover', Stella and Claudia sat in the corner, a bottle of champagne chilling in a bucket between them. They had a tradition regarding bubbles. During their third year at Uni, Stella had broken up—or more accurately, been dumped—by the professor she'd been dating. She had wanted more and he had wanted the new, blonde transfer student. That night, she and Claudia splurged on some Moët, deciding to celebrate the positive things they had in their lives. They toasted Claudia's new vibrator and the five pound note Stella found while running (which went towards the cost of the champagne).

At this moment, Stella didn't feel like celebrating. She slouched onto the table, the picture of despondency.

'What should I do?' she asked the gods, but Claudia in particular.

Claudia sipped her champagne. 'I was reading this article about PTSD—'

'I don't have PTSD because I didn't get on Connor's course,' Stella mumbled.

'—that said it's very treatable with therapy. And duh, I know that's not where you got it.'

Head popping up, Stella said, 'Does he have any online courses?'

'Have you gone to see that therapist I recommended?'

Leaning back in the armchair, Stella rested her head on the stained leather. 'No. I can't afford it.'

'You want to spend five grand on a course with Connor Knight, but can't afford a therapist? Priorities much?'

'Claudia, for the millionth time, I don't have PTSD. They're just panic attacks. And can we please focus on getting me to France?'

'Panic attacks are symptoms of PTSD.'

'Oh, for fuck's sake.' Sometimes Claudia could get her so angry. Stella scrutinised her friend—always so self-assured. Even her hair was unapologetic. Her black bob and fringe had been cut to severe, perfect angles, as though she'd gone to a geometry teacher with a razor-sharp protractor instead of a salon. But Claudia being Claudia, she introduced her own brand of mayhem by tussling it, giving her a perpetual post-coital bedhead vibe. If Stella tried to do that, she'd just look like she hadn't brushed her hair.

Stella downed her glass of fizz.

'Hello, ladies, mind if I join you?'

A long, lean man with foppish dark hair stood next to their table in a tweed jacket with matching flat cap. Either he was going to hit on them or embark on a pheasant shooting expedition. His eyes bounced between Claudia and Stella.

'Fuck off,' said Claudia.

Ignoring her, he pulled up a chair.

'Aren't you going to introduce me to your friend?' he asked as he settled into his seat.

Claudia rested her head on her fist, feigning boredom. 'Stella Price. May I introduce you to Magnus Fiennes, the biggest twat in photography.'

'Ebullient as always, Ms Monroe,' he said and then, to Stella, 'Really nice to meet you.'

She stifled a laugh despite her mood; his accent would have sounded at home in a Merchant Ivory film, pronouncing *really* as *reel-eh*. And who used *ebullient* in conversation like that? Posh people. That's who.

Refilling her glass, Claudia explained, 'She's being dramatic because she wants to go on Connor Knight's course, but it's sold out.'

He snorted. 'Personally, I think you've had a lucky escape. He's overrated in my book. I remember when his courses cost £500 and he held them at a Premier Inn.'

Claudia flicked the back of Magnus' hand. 'Thanks for your unsolicited opinion, you cockwomble.'

Aside from a degree in art, Claudia had left the University of Edinburgh with a deep and abiding love for Scottish profanity, even if her Essex accent stripped away their Gaelic heat. Usually Stella would laugh.

'Apologies,' he said to her, not unkindly. 'But it's true.'

19

'You're just jealous because the magazines keep naming him the world's best wedding photographer. Remind me... where are you on that list?' Claudia steepled her hands and rested her chin on top, batting her eyes at Magnus.

'Pah. Those "best of" lists are all based on advertising spend. You shouldn't believe them.' He lifted the corner of his mouth in a disarming smile and said to Stella, 'I'll teach you whatever you need to know. Free of charge.'

'Oh, fuck off, Fiennes. What could you teach her? How to kiss arse with the upper crust?'

'It's a surprisingly handy skill. It's called charm. You should try it sometime.'

'I do quite well just as I am, fuck you very much.'

'Out of interest, have you ever dropped the f-bomb during a family shoot?' he asked, leaning towards her with exaggerated concern.

'Of course not! I'm a professional.'

'I bet you have.' He winked at Stella.

'Do your parents ever worry they pissed their money against the wall sending you to Eton?' she shot back.

Their arguing provided background noise while Stella debated how to get on the course. Maybe she should call that man who gave her his card and beg him to transfer his spot? Offer to pay above cost to sweeten the deal?

A loud cheer went up at the front of the bar, near the entrance. The three of them looked up.

'Speak of the devil,' said Magnus without warmth.

Connor Knight sauntered into the pub wearing his signature jeans and white t-shirt, a size too small, to show off his muscles. Before he took two steps, friends and fans surrounded him. Stella watched him work the crowd, smiling, high-fiving, greeting women with kisses on both cheeks, hugging the men with that double back slap. Somebody gave him a bottle of beer. Stella wished she had that kind of reception when entering a room.

'Hey,' said Claudia, leaning towards Stella with a conspiratorial look in her eye, 'why don't you just go over there and ask him?'

Stella's entire body cringed. 'What? Me? No. No way. I couldn't do that.' *Could I?*

A memory nudged her. Twelve-year-old Stella had recently started competitive ballroom dancing. On a family trip to London, she couldn't believe it when she spotted Arlene Phillips, the famous choreographer of Hot Gossip, dining two tables away. Stella's father encouraged her to go over (*'Opportunity knocks only once'*), but she was so shy. It took her until dessert to work up the nerve. As Stella made her move, pen and paper shaking in her hand, Arlene excused herself from her table of glamorous friends, crossed within feet of Stella, and left the restaurant.

Would Stella let Connor be another Arlene?

'Okay. I'm going to do it,' she announced, hoisting the champagne bottle out of its icy tub and refilling her glass. She downed it in one before the bubbles had settled, which made her cough as they fizzled up her nose, causing people at nearby tables to look at her like she had some contagious disease.

'Slick, Stells.'

Magnus handed her a tissue. 'So what's your plan?'

'Thanks.' She wiped champagne off her face and the table, considering his question. 'Persistence?'

He shook his head. 'Comes across a bit desperate, don't you agree? Like—' Magnus mimed holding a dagger and stabbing it up and down, except his wrist was slightly loose, so it looked more like he was wanking off a small airborne penis.

'You're such a bloody muppet,' said Claudia before turning to Stella and saying, 'Flattery. Men love it when women talk about how great they are.'

'That's rich, coming from you.'

Claudia swatted him on the arm.

'Wish me luck.' Stella refilled her glass one more time, drained it, and stood, reaching out to rub the bare arse of the leprechaun on the wall.

'Don't forget to stick your tits out!' Claudia called as Stella marched towards the bar, where Connor held court with a small group, three men and two women. Stella insinuated herself into the outskirts.

'What can I get you?' the bartender asked.

'Er, um. Nothing. Thanks. I'm just...waiting for a friend.' She turned so her back rested against the counter.

She clamped her teeth down hard in an attempt to still her trembling. In situations where Stella pushed herself out of her comfort zone, she always pretended to be somebody else—like when she competed in dance competitions, she pretended to be graceful and in control like her mother, whose own dancing career had been cut short by marriage. 'If you act like a winner, then you'll be a winner,' said her father. Having a character to play just made it easier.

Right now, Stella needed to be somebody with no fear. Somebody unapologetic. Somebody with a razor-sharp bob and the tongue to match.

Cracking her neck to the left and right, she closed her eyes and channelled Claudia. She settled her body into a confident, unconcerned pose.

The minutes ticked by. She wished he would hurry up; her bravado would only last so long. Worried that she might look like an eavesdropper, she made herself appear busy by searching for something in her bag. Among the contents: her phone, knock-off Gucci sunglasses, a Phillips head screwdriver, her wallet, a room key, a copy of 'The Little Book of Calm' that Claudia had given her for Christmas, and a cheap blue pen emblazoned with *Bonera*™ —the erectile dysfunction drug she had been working on when she left Bastion.

Ten minutes later, her confident, unconcerned pose had melted into boredom. Arms crossed, she glanced at Claudia and Magnus for a sign that she should stay the course, but neither of them was paying attention. Was Claudia twirling her hair?

Stella yawned and turned her body toward Connor and his gang. Only one woman and two men remained. They were laughing at a story involving a groom who lost his wedding ring during a snowball fight.

It was now or never. She had to get his attention. As her father would say: *'Do or do not. There is no try.'* Actually, that might have been Yoda. The memory of Claudia comparing Connor Knight and Yoda's dicks popped into her head. Heat flooded Stella's cheeks.

'Can I help you?'

Snapped out of her trance, she looked towards the bar, but it wasn't the bartender speaking. It was Connor Knight.

'Sorry. Are you talking to me?' she said, a little more breathily than she would have liked.

'Yes. You. I noticed you hovering like you wanted something.' His grey eyes dropped lazily towards her mouth, and she swallowed hard. Her pulse quickened. Then his gaze continued its downward journey, stopping at her hand. 'Autograph?'

Surprised, she realised she still held the *Bonera*™ pen and had been repeatedly pressing the plunger. The nib was darting in, out, in, out. From his raised eyebrow, she could tell he knew the brand. For a second, she wondered if he used the drug, which returned her thoughts to his dick. Her gaze involuntarily flicked downwards. Yup, from the bulge at the front of his jeans, she could see he definitely had one. She swallowed and raised her eyes, only to find him considering her with an amused expression.

Clearing her throat, she said, 'Um, no. Sorry. Actually, I was hoping you could help me with something.' She flung the pen into her bag.

'What did you have in mind?' He leaned on the bar, a warm tone entering his voice.

What *did* she have in mind? Stella almost forgot why she was there. This man seemed to steal all the air in the room with his tight shirt, shiny grey eyes, and sexy mouth. She sucked in a deep breath and jiggled her head to snap herself out of it.

Be Claudia.

Mirroring his body language, she flipped her hair over her shoulder and quoted his advert. 'I'm ready to discover my potential with Connor Knight.'

Only after the words left her mouth did she realise how they could be misconstrued. 'I-I mean, I want you to take me to the next level.'

He raised an eyebrow. Even to her, it sounded like she was asking him to improve her orgasming skills. She felt the blood rush to her cheeks.

'Sorry, that came out wrong.' She needed to get back on track. What had Claudia told her to do? Flattery! 'What I'm trying to say is I attended your seminar today and you're the only person who can help me. Those before and afters... they were genius. I mean, you must be the best teacher in the—sorry, is everything okay?'

As she spoke she noticed that his brow had furrowed with concentration, but not because he was enthralled by her words. Instead, his attention was on her face, his eyes darting from forehead to chin and cheek to cheek like she had spattered chocolate all over herself.

Self-consciously, she raised a hand to wipe her mouth.

'Butterfly lighting,' he said.

'Excuse me?'

'Butterfly lighting. That's how I would light you.'

'W-what?'

'Sorry, it's a habit I have whenever I meet a beautiful woman. I think about how I would light her face. And butterfly lighting would really emphasise your exquisite cheekbones and chin. Do you know what butterfly lighting is?'

'Um, no.'

'It's the style they used in old Hollywood photos, where the key light is positioned directly above and in front...'

He continued talking and she nodded like she was committing his words to a mental notebook, but really she was trying to ignore that this talented Adonis of a man had called her beautiful and that it was causing her lady parts to overheat. Connor Knight was the best wedding photographer in the world and, aside from being obscenely good-looking, his massive talent was a massive turn-on, especially when standing this close to him.

She remembered when she had a brief rebound relationship with a drummer in Uni. During the month they'd dated, she'd gone to see him play a few times. She'd watch him on stage, bashing those drums and stroking those cymbals and the sex afterwards was intense. In her mind he was Tommy Lee and she was Pamela Anderson. For a second, she allowed herself to imagine what Connor Knight would be like in bed, with his eye for detail and appreciation for the female form.

Bad Stella!

Then another thought occurred to her. Was this how he always put the moves on women? The old this-is-how-I'd-light-your-beautiful-face line? Huh. Anger bubbled up inside of her, aimed at both herself —for being so easily taken in by it—and him. He had another thing coming if he thought she'd fall for that one. Did she appear easy? She was the new, improved Stella and the new, improved Stella was harder to enter than the royal family.

'Excuse me,' she interrupted his impromptu photography lesson/pick-up attempt, holding up a finger for emphasis.

His eyes focussed on her finger, then on her.

Clearing her throat, she said, 'I'm sure that line works on most women, but I'm not here for *that*. I'm here because I want you to teach me. I want to come to France.'

She watched his lip curl up with arrogant amusement. 'You thought I was hitting on you?'

'Weren't you?'

Connor leaned in towards her, close enough that she could smell the woodsy aroma of his soap—not at all the pungent designer cologne she had expected him to wear. His grey eyes held hers in a vice. Seriously, would it kill his DNA to choose blue or green? His irises made her think of storms and rocky beaches and wolves. Definitely wolves.

Wild. Elemental. Sexy.

She held her breath.

'I promise...' he said, flicking his eyes down to her lips and back up, '...that if I were hitting on you, you'd know it.' He lingered a moment and then abruptly stood up straight, breaking the spell. 'And France is sold out.'

Refilling her lungs, she tried to ignore the heated prickle of embarrassment all over her body. Her face must be crimson by now. This was not going well.

'Sorry. I-I know it's sold out, but—' She looked around to check nobody could hear. 'What harm will it do to add one more person?'

'No.'

'Why?'

'Because I don't want to.'

'That's not a very good reason.'

'I think it's the very best reason.'

'Please.' She could feel her Claudia-inspired resolve beginning to waver as tears thickened around her eyes. 'I can't go on photographing chickens.'

He laughed with a tinge of confusion. 'I'm sorry?'

'You know. Orpington. Sussex. Silkies. Legbar.' Inside she was screaming, *Shut up! Shut up! Shut up!* 'Pekin Bantam.'

'You photograph *chickens*?'

'Just once, but it was enough.'

Sighing as though she might be getting through to him, he asked, 'Why's it so important to you? I'm running another one in the autumn.'

She paused a moment to gather her thoughts. 'Because...I only have until June to make a success of this new career. I don't have time for trial and error. And...' —whether she liked it or not— '...you're the best.'

He considered her, his face softening. 'June, hmm? That's a pretty tight turnaround in anyone's estimations. It usually takes at least a year to get a full season of weddings booked in.'

For a second, she thought she had peaked his interest, appealed to the part of him that relished a challenge. She'd be a compelling case study for his training business if this worked. She smiled, hopeful.

'No, I can't help you.' Her heart plummeted. 'It wouldn't be fair to the others who missed out.'

'But I was next in the queue!'

'Sorry.'

He turned and rested his back on the bar, hand in a pocket. She felt dismissed, but she couldn't give up. Was this her punishment for not falling for his stupid butterfly-lighting line—which she still thought was a line despite his assurances to the contrary.

She sensed her chances sliding away. Desperate times...

'I challenge you to a duel!' she blurted out, pushing away from the bar and facing him square on.

'A duel? What—like pistols at dawn?'

'No. Yes. Sort of. If I win, you let me come on the course. If you win, then I'll find someone else who can help me. Magnus Fiennes has already offered...'

'Has he now.' Connor paused for a moment. 'I'm not saying yes, but what did you have in mind? I'm intrigued.'

'Thumb Wars.'

'Sorry?'

She leaned in as though telling him a secret. 'It's sort of my super power.'

Connor cocked an eyebrow. 'So you want a Thumb War right here? Right now? With me?'

'Why not?' She gave her head a shake, like a lion fluffing its mane. 'Are you scared?' God knew she was. She had to hold her hands in her pockets to hide the tremor. The stakes had never been higher. It added a frisson of danger, making her stomach feel funny. Or maybe it was standing too close to this man. She remembered what that woman said before his talk: it should be illegal for anyone to be so hot. Stella had to agree. Maintaining eye contact with him felt like trying to force north magnets together.

'Of course not. I'm just trying to spare you the embarrassment of losing.' He said it with surety. With arrogance. With the conviction of somebody used to winning at Thumb Wars. 'Okay, I'm in.'

He held out his hand. Steady. Ready.

She slit her eyes at him. Was he psyching her out? Attacking her confidence by having more confidence? She shook her head to dispel the worms of doubt. Instead, like an elite athlete, she visualised the pleasure of beating him, stapling that shadowy projection of euphoria into her brain.

Shifting her bag to her back, she stepped towards Connor and locked her fingers with his. The shock of contact was immediate, sending an electric pulse up her arm, straight down to her belly button. Her eyes zipped to his, to see if he felt it, too, but he seemed completely nonplussed, focussed on the task at hand.

His fingertips pressed against hers in an intimate embrace. She concentrated on the small calluses on his palm from long hours gripping a heavy camera, and breathed deeply: in through her nose, out through her mouth.

'Ready?' she asked. Her thumb swaggered, a snake ready to strike.

'Ready.' His thumb stood straight and still.

'One, two, three, four,' she said, their digits alternating from side to side, 'I declare a Thumb War.'

He exploded into action. She ducked left, then swung in a wide arc to the right. He chased, always a second too late to pin her down. Connor had her on the defensive, but if she wanted to win, she needed to attack.

After feinting down then up and around like Neo dodging bullets, she clipped his thumb under hers. The hold wasn't secure enough; he wiggled free.

At an impasse, their thumbprints kissed, both waiting to see the other's next move. She could do this. If she jumped to the base of his thumb, she could pin him. With lightning-fast reflexes, she did just that. She savoured his surprise as he tried to wrench himself loose. She mouthed the words, 'One, two—'

Before she hit three, his thumb leapt for freedom. *Shit.*

Both were breathing hard. Connor's mega-fans started chanting, 'Connor! Connor! Connor!'

They had an audience. She felt like he had stolen home-court advantage.

Concentrating, she tried to slide over his skin and trap him. But he flicked his thumb back and up, crashing it down on hers. Right on the knuckle! She couldn't move. *One, two—*

Channelling what Claudia would do, she pretended to sneeze on his hand. He startled. While he struggled with his disgust, she pulled her thumb free and crushed him.

'Sorry,' she said, for once not meaning it at all. 'Do you concede?'

He tugged his digit, trying to dislodge it one last time. 'That was a dirty trick.'

'What are you talking about?' She blinked, releasing her grip. He wiped his hand on his jeans.

Somebody clapped Connor on the back and his semi-circle of supporters melted into the crowd.

Connor picked up his beer bottle and took a long drink, regarding her with his direct, unflinching gaze. 'Okay.'

'Okay what?'

'Okay, you won, albeit dubiously. I'll add a space for you. Email my assistant, and he'll sort payment.'

'Really?' She jiggled up and down on her toes.

He put his bottle down on the bar with a thud. 'But just so you're aware: I don't enjoy losing.'

The moment seemed to stretch as their eyes locked, taking the measure of the other like adversaries in the ring.

A hand unexpectedly appeared on his shoulder and they both jumped. A sylph-like blonde woman appeared next to him, the kind of woman who could roll out of bed and be catwalk ready.

'There you are. I've been looking for you everywhere,' she purred, her accent exotic. Maybe Scandinavian? 'Our reservation...' She tapped her watch, a white Chanel number that Stella had seen in *Vogue.*

'Yup. Coming.' He finished his beer. Stella watched his Adam's apple bob up and down with the effort.

With a cursory, unthreatened glance at Stella, the woman turned to leave, but before he followed her, Connor leaned in. Stella froze. His breath tickled her neck as he hovered over her ear, making the delicate skin explode in goosebumps. 'See you in France, Mademoiselle Chicken.'

3

MADEMOISELLE CHICKEN?!

Of all the nicknames Stella had earned in her life, that one had to be the least flattering.

She spent the next twenty-four hours alternating between elation that she managed to get on the course—all booked and paid for with two credit cards—and embarrassment. She'd accused him of hitting on her when he had a super-hot model girlfriend the whole time. When Stella told Claudia about it, she said, 'Oh yeah, I'm always studying people to figure out how to light them. It's a photographer thing. You'll do it, too—eventually.'

Stella felt like a complete arse. Of course, Connor Knight hadn't been interested in her. He was the king of wedding photography and she was just some insignificant serf. She'd made a fool of herself. Again.

The thought of spending a week with him after what happened…it made her frown deep in her stomach.

She had to stop replaying their conversation. It didn't help that his name and picture were everywhere at the trade show: the album supplier used by CONNOR KNIGHT, the print lab of choice for CONNOR KNIGHT, the chosen camera brand of CONNOR

KNIGHT. They should just rename the conference The Connor Knight Experience.

Still, deep beneath the withering shame, she was excited. After attending more seminars on the Saturday, she realised just how much she didn't know. Being a wedding photographer required more than aiming a camera and snapping the shutter. She needed to learn everything from where to position a family for portraits in bright sun to how to compose a workable shooting schedule. The next month couldn't go quickly enough.

As she exited her fourth seminar of the day (an in-depth retouching workshop), she rang Claudia. The dim corridor was thick with people rushing to their next course, so she dived into an empty doorway while she waited for an answer.

When they'd parted the night before, Stella had headed back to her room for an early night, while Claudia decided to stay in the bar and catch up with friends. Stella's call went straight to voice mail, which either meant Claudia was hungover or she'd pulled, possibly both.

'Thank you so much for reaching out to Claudia Monroe Photography. I'm on a shoot right now, but your message is important to me. Please—'

Stella hung up. Claudia's voice message always made her chuckle. It sounded so formal and professional, unlike the woman herself. Thinking back to Magnus' teasing, Stella did wonder if Claudia found it difficult to keep her language clean when dealing with children. The probability of the odd slip-up seemed high. Stella headed back toward the lifts.

Her phone vibrated.

SRY. Head throbbing. 630 at hotel bar? Awards night!!!! Cx

Wincing, Stella replied with a terse **OKx**. Her palms grew moist as she dropped the phone into her bag. With the day so full of activity, she had forgotten about the awards ceremony. Or maybe not forgotten...more like packed it into a padlocked chest and buried it deep.

She did not want to go.

Every day for the past six months, Stella thought about the last award ceremony she'd attended, rerunning the events like a horror film where she was the stupid character that stumbled headlong into a haunted house. She would've found an excuse to avoid tonight, except for one problem: Claudia was up for her first major award in the children's portraiture category. Stella wanted to be there for her.

Stabbing the lift button, she swapped the heavy canvas tote full of trade show brochures to her other shoulder. This was going to be a long night.

'VESTITI SEMPRE COME SE FOSSE DOMENICA' or 'Always dress like it's Sunday' Stella's mother said, earning herself the nickname 'the Sofia Loren of Penarth'. She always looked immaculate: her frocks crisp, clean, and never above the knee. She even dressed to do the vacuuming, just in case someone popped over mid-hoover. Stella briefly wondered what her mother would think of her present outfit: a strappy green dress just a tad shorter than cocktail length with a long slit up her thigh. Perfect for dancing, rubbish for hanging out with priests.

She crossed and uncrossed her legs as she waited at the hotel bar, a more modern space than the Irish pub from the previous night. Low lighting and large potted plants between the tables made it the perfect place for a clandestine rendezvous of the type that Stella no longer partook. She swirled the straw in her frosty glass of cola. She rarely had soft drinks, but needed the caffeine boost to survive the night ahead. Alcohol would be a bad idea in her present state of mind. Plus it was cheaper not to drink.

Claudia was late, of course.

The front of the bar opened onto the hotel's main thoroughfare, where photographers strutted towards the lifts in their finery, outfits ranging from casual to LBDs to full-on Hollywood glamour. Stella barely registered them. Memories passed behind her unseeing eyes. Scene one: Nathan's hand secretly resting on the small of her back. Scene two: Going home in a taxi, blood streaming from her nose.

Stella destroyed a napkin, tearing it into ragged pieces. Rolling the shreds into a ball, she sipped her drink. The exclamations of friends greeting each other made her look up and then sharply away. Connor Knight stood ten metres from her barstool, talking with an animated group of fans while his statuesque girlfriend held his arm, a bored expression on her angular face. Swivelling her body towards the back wall, Stella brushed her hair forward to hide herself. She added 'avoid Connor Knight' to her To Do list for the evening, right under 'survive the night without having a mental breakdown'.

An insistent finger tapped her shoulder.

She startled. In the space of a second, she schooled her mouth into a casual smile and spun around, expecting to be skewered by cocky grey eyes. Instead, Magnus Fiennes lounged against the bar with all the menace of a baby panda, running his fingers through his floppy hair. He had changed out of his tweed and now cut a more dapper shape in a tailored dinner suit.

'Oh, thank God it's you,' she said, slapping a hand over her frantic heart. She stole a glance towards where Connor had been and saw he'd moved on. Relief warred with a feeling she was loathe to label as disappointment.

'I can't leave a beautiful lady sitting at the bar alone, now can I?' he said, holding up his finger to get the bartender's attention and ordering a whiskey. 'Can I get you another, uh...?' He looked at her mystery drink.

'It's just Coke. I'm fine, thanks.'

'Staying off the booze? Probably a good idea. These nights can get messy.'

You have no idea, she thought.

'Cheers,' he said, raising his glass and clinking it against hers. He took a slow sip, his eyes wandering around the bar. 'Is your charming, foul-mouthed partner-in-crime joining us tonight?'

'Ha. Yes, eventually. She's on Claudia Time, which is normal time plus at least fifteen minutes.'

'Magnus! Are you coming?' called a man near the lifts.

He turned his puppy-brown eyes on Stella. 'I'm happy to stay...'

'No, please. You go. She'll be here soon.' She would actually have loved him to stay and keep her mind off her personal ghosts, but she didn't want to inconvenience him.

'All right, then, if you're sure. See you downstairs.' He knocked his closed fist twice on the bar and made his way towards his friends.

Her eyes followed him until he disappeared around the corner. As her gaze swept back through the nearly empty bar, her attention snagged on a potted plant that had sprouted a triangular black haircut. Claudia's kohl-lined eyes popped over a large banana leaf, like a comedy detective in a B-movie.

Stella stood up and approached the plant. 'Clauds? What are you doing?'

Her friend startled and dropped her bag. 'Shhhh!' she said, holding both pointer fingers over her lips.

Whispering, Stella asked, 'Why are you hiding?'

'Is he gone?'

'Is who gone?'

'Magnus!'

'Yes, he's gone.'

She straightened, returning to normal speaking volume. 'Thought he would never bloody leave.' She picked up her bag, tucked it under her arm, and stepped out from behind the plant.

'Why are you hiding from Magnus?'

Claudia wrinkled her nose and averted her eyes.

'You didn't!' Stella said.

'I need a drink.' Claudia strode to the bar and Stella followed.

'I thought you hated him?'

'It's a very thin line, Stells. A very thin line. And we were exceedingly drunk.'

Stella laughed. 'What was he like?'

'To be honest, I don't remember much. I have a vague memory of him honking like a goose. I've always wondered what noise posh people made when they jet their juice. Now I know.'

'At least he didn't say "Mother".' Stella referred to a psychology student that Claudia dated in Uni.

'Small blessings. Oh god!' She grabbed the bar for support.

'What?'

'Another flashback. His tongue—'

'Please stop.'

'Bartender! Two shots of tequila.'

'Just one,' corrected Stella. 'I'm not drinking tonight.'

Claudia's eyes blinked wide. 'Oh my god! Are you pregnant? Shit. You're pregnant.'

'No, of course, I'm not pregnant. I haven't had sex in six months!'

'Then why the fuck aren't you drinking? It's party time.'

'You know...' Stella raised her eyebrows, not wanting to say the words.

'Oh, *that*. Yeah. Okay. Sorry.' She paused for a few seconds, thinking. 'Although you aren't winning any awards this evening and that bloody bawbag isn't here with his repugnant wife.'

'Still.' Stella shrugged.

'And the biggest difference of all? If anybody attacks you tonight, they'll have *me* to deal with.' Claudia downed her shot and wiped her mouth on the back of her hand. 'Shall we?'

'AND THE WINNER IS...'

Stella stared. Her hands mechanically found each other and clapped without hearing the name, subconsciously understanding that this was the required response.

Aside from Claudia's disappointing loss early on, most of the evening passed without Stella absorbing any of it. She didn't see the happy winners collecting their prizes or hear the tedious speeches. Her finger had practically rubbed away a layer of skin on her chin as she absently worried her cleft. No matter how hard she tried to block the ghosts, they found their way into her head, squeezing through cracks.

Next to her, Claudia drowned the sorrows of her loss in red wine, seemingly oblivious to the maelstrom of angst sitting to her left. Giving up the fight, Stella's thoughts travelled back to another night.

SIX MONTHS ago

'I don't know how I'm going to keep my hands off you until later.' Nathan lowered his voice, so the other people at the bar couldn't overhear. His hand, masked by the press of bodies behind them, found her bottom and squeezed through the flowing silk.

'Nathan...' she warned him. The last thing they needed was to have their relationship exposed at an industry awards show. She moved away even as she inhaled his intoxicating cologne—a musky scent, bespoke to him, hand-mixed by an exclusive perfumologist in Paris.

The event space at Grosvenor House sparkled with the good and great of the UK medical advertising industry. Polite, early evening laughter drifted over the bar. People were on their best behaviour now, aware that their bosses were in attendance, and some clients, too. It was easy to distinguish the account executives from the creatives; the former wore mostly black, a stark contrast to the taupe interior of the hotel. The creatives provided the flavour, showing off colourful ensembles like peacocks on parade. Stella felt every inch the catwalk model in her bright yellow Gucci dress, an extravagance that wiped out half her savings. It was so worth it.

Nathan swore when the bartender handed him the bill.

'It's for a special occasion,' Stella reminded him. He normally didn't splurge on niceties for his employees. 'That's why I'm rich,' he said to her once over dinner.

At this year's awards, Bastion reached the finals in an unprecedented five categories, including the highest accolade of the night: Ad Campaign of the Year for Stella's erectile dysfunction client—and she wanted to win. She could already imagine her dad, bragging to his friends that his daughter had won a major award. Although, to her face, he'd probably just nod his head and pat her on the shoulder.

It was exactly the kind of honour that could help her achieve Head of Copy in the next year. Her creative director believed their achievement was due to his inspiring guidance, but he spent most of his time snorting coke in the toilets and made no sense on the best of days. Once, he told her 'the best solution is a solution that's a good solution'. He was currently in rehab and, therefore, absent tonight. One day, she'd have his job.

'Can you get that, babe? Thanks. You're a star.' Nathan winked at her and walked back to the Bastion crowd, leaving Stella with multiple trays of champagne and glassware to carry.

'Sure. No problem,' she replied to his retreating back, eager to please, and tried to make eye contact with somebody in their crowd for help. Eventually, the receptionist noticed. She sent a few boys from the Studio over in their ill-fitting suits, all keen to earn their keep and help with the free alcohol. In other years, Nathan only bought tickets for the nominees and senior-level staff, but Stella encouraged him to open it up to everybody. Make it a morale booster.

When all the employees had a full glass, Nathan toasted, 'When I started Bastion ten years ago, I had no idea what I was doing. You all know me, so you know that's a hard thing for me to admit.' He smiled, flashing his white teeth. Everybody chuckled. 'I wanted to build an agency where strategy met creativity. Where the best of the best competed to work.' His eyes met Stella's and her stomach flipped. Under her dress, she luxuriated in the feeling of lace on her skin from the new *Oh! Paulina* lingerie she'd bought especially for the occasion. 'Thank you to each and every one of you for making my dreams come true. You are my heroes. To Bastion!'

Glasses raised in the air among cries of 'Hear, hear!' and 'Fuck, yeah!' from the younger staff. Stella took a sip, watching Nathan over the rim of her glass. He looked handsome in his tuxedo, his salt and pepper hair giving him a distinguished air. He was a successful, intelligent, powerful man who, for some reason, had taken an interest in Stella and her career. He told her all the time that he saw great things in her future.

Stella admired him. More than that, she thought she might love him. She hadn't felt this secure in a relationship in a long time. And the best thing was that *he* had chased *her*. He made her feel special for once, praising her at work and in the bedroom, telling her she must be the easiest woman in the world to fall in love with. At his side, she felt confident and sexy, like the winner she'd always wanted to be. In the past, she had a talent for choosing men who were commitment-phobic and emotionally unavailable. Nathan was neither.

No, commitment definitely wasn't his problem, for Nathan had a wife—from the stories he told her, a crazy wife, but a wife nonetheless —and Stella didn't have to worry constantly about whether he would ever commit to her because he couldn't. He was already committed to someone else. She was strangely at peace with the idea. In a way, it freed her. Whenever he intimated that he might leave his wife for her, Stella just shrugged as though the thought had never occurred to her. If it happened, it happened. That's what she told herself, anyway.

To Stella, his wife was just a character in a story that had nothing to do with her. His wife belonged in a book about Nathan's homelife and Stella kept it firmly on the shelf. If sometimes she felt nauseous or her fingernails were peeled to bloody stumps or her newfound self-confidence floundered beneath self-loathing or she withered when-ever her mother asked if Stella had bagged a husband yet...well, that was the price she had to pay. Out of necessity, she had become adept at boxing up uncomfortable feelings and tucking them away.

What mattered was that Nathan craved Stella. She was the one that occupied his fantasies, not his wife. He told her so often enough.

Plastering a smile on her face, she found her art director, Jezza short for Jeremy—a cheeky chap with grey hair despite being in his thirties. He threw his arm around her shoulders, giving her a friendly squeeze.

'There's me old mucker.' He made a face and sniffed at her. 'What's that you're wearing? Eau de Grandma's Garden?'

'Stop it.' She swatted at him, knowing he was poking fun at Nathan's taste. He had given her the perfume after his last business trip. Yes, the vanilla and gardenia scent might be considered old fashioned, but she preferred to call it classic. Jezza's teasing made her wonder if confiding in him had been a prudent idea. He'd sworn on the Sacred Bond Between Creative Partners that he wouldn't tell anyone. He told his wife, of course, but promised not to tell anyone else.

She and Nathan were careful to stay separate at work events in the interest of keeping their affair secret. Despite this, she noticed he'd edged closer and was standing directly behind her, conversing with his circle of account managers. He was close enough that she could reach backwards and grab his hand. Lost in her daydreams, she didn't notice when the chatter around her suddenly died, all eyes looking towards the door. Somebody jostled Stella from behind, and Jezza caught her by the elbow as she stumbled forward.

'Surprise.'

The high nasal pitch of that voice was hard to mistake: Jeanette, Nathan's wife.

Turning, Stella saw Jeanette kissing Nathan as though the entire company wasn't watching. Stella's thoughts scrambled, making it hard to think. What was Jeanette doing there? Had Nathan known she was coming?

Did she *know*?

Stella's pulse galloped. Blood raged in her ears.

Watching the scene unfold, one of her hidden mental boxes fell open and some self-loathing slipped out. She couldn't help but compare herself with Jeanette. Her short, figure-hugging sheath dress was covered in black sequins, hanging like tiny daggers. Stella had no doubt that it cost a lot of money.

Jeanette's hair and make-up looked professionally done, meaning her sudden appearance had been premeditated. As she pulled away from Nathan, she left red lipstick all over his chin.

But the thing Stella noticed most was the smell. Vanilla and gardenias.

In a moment of clarity, she realised Nathan must have bought

Jeanette the same perfume. 'Got you something, babe,' he'd said when he tossed the unwrapped package to her on the bed, an expedient booty call on his way home from the airport. It must have been a two-for-one deal at duty free.

Nathan took a step back from his wife. 'Jeanette. What are you doing here?' He did a good job of sounding pleasantly surprised.

'Oh, honey, I know it's a no-partners thing, but what kind of wife would I be if I didn't come to support you on your big night?' She laughed staccato machine gun bullets.

Stella only half-heard. She was too busy noticing the eyes of every single Bastion employee flicking between Jeanette, Nathan, and her.

They all know.

The taste of acid filled her mouth.

Some managed to hide their interest behind their champagne flutes while others, like the junior copywriter, looked like they were expecting popcorn to be handed around.

Stella froze on the spot, her thoughts pinballing around her head. What should she do? What would her *mother* do? (Aside from never getting into this situation in the first place). Acting on autopilot, Stella took an empty glass off the table and filled it with champagne. With as much grace as she could muster, she played hostess and held out the fizzing flute to her lover's wife.

'What a lovely surprise, Jeanette. So nice to see you.'

The woman turned towards Stella and skewered her with black-lined eyes. Her gaze slid down to the glass in Stella's hand and back up to her face. The air stilled as forty people held their breath.

'Thanks…' Jeanette's features pinched together in a dramatic parody of confusion. 'Sorry—what was your name again?'

Fair enough. They'd only met once before. 'St-Stella,' she answered, but Jeanette had already grabbed the glass and returned her attention to her husband.

A bell tingled, slicing through the tension and calling the crowd into the main ballroom for dinner and the awards presentation.

Stella glued her gaze to the ugly hotel carpet, feeling like she'd been slapped. *Does she know? Everybody else seems to.* What must they think of her? She could guess. They thought she was sleeping with Nathan to get ahead. That her promotion to Senior Copywriter was earned with sexual favours instead of hours of hard work. That she went on so many trips abroad not because she added value, but because she gave a good blow job. Her skin itched with embarrassment. A rash of guilt.

What if Jeanette was there because she suspected? Stella didn't want to ruin the night for everybody else by sticking around as a source of tension. Nor did she want to be the main player in the Bastion soap opera.

She took a step towards the exit.

'Not so fast,' Jezza said, taking her arm and leading her towards the stairs. 'This is our night. We've worked hard for it. Harder than she has in her entire life. Don't let her take it away from us.'

'But everybody knows. I didn't...' She couldn't even finish the sentence.

'Fuck 'em. Who cares? You have terrible, and I mean, *terrible* taste in men. But you are one of the most talented copywriters I've ever worked with. *Do not let him take this from you.*'

He was right. She was good at her job. If she and Jezza won Ad Campaign of the Year, it would give them an open ticket to work wherever they wanted. Any agency would kill to have them. Lord knew she didn't want to work anywhere near Nathan Bastion anymore. She was worth more than bargain-bin perfume. What had she been doing for the past year? Her self-esteem dipped along with her stomach, like they were riding the same rollercoaster.

She wiped a tear from her eye, careful not to smudge her mascara. 'I've been such an idiot.'

Jezza rubbed her back as they descended with the crush of bodies into the ballroom. 'Nobody's perfect, Stells. Come on. Sit next to me.' In the original seating plan, her spot was at Nathan's table.

Up ahead, she could see Jeanette, arms linked with her husband, navigating their way through the crowd. He hadn't looked at Stella once since his wife arrived. With Jeanette on his arm, he appeared comfortable, as one would after fifteen years of marriage. She thought back to all the things Nathan had told her about Jeanette: the drinking, the depression, the jealousy, the constant drama. As an ex-actress, his wife loved being the centre of attention and rarely in a good way. But here, now, Stella thought what a handsome couple they made. Perfectly matched.

She was the outsider.

Maybe he made up all that rubbish just to get into Stella's pants. He seemed to have a sixth sense for getting her to do what he wanted in the boardroom and the bedroom. Lord knew she'd sucked him off in both, acting like a porn star because he told her that his wife wasn't very adventurous sexually. He praised Stella all the time, convinced her she was special, told her that she made him feel things that Jeanette never could. And Stella was such a people pleaser that she'd fallen for the whole thing. *What did I ever see in him?* It certainly wasn't his taste in gifts. She wished she could run to the toilets and scrub the perfume from her skin. Jezza was right; it did smell like an old lady's garden.

In the ballroom, a stage rose from the centre of the white-linened tables like Pride Rock. Bastion was assigned to a cluster of tables only four rows back. That could be a good sign. Winning was the only thing that could redeem this night.

Jezza held out her chair and she collapsed onto the red velvet, abandoning her jewelled clutch on the table next to her cutlery. The receptionist sat on her other side and grabbed Stella's arm, forcing her to make eye contact. 'I'm so sorry,' she said.

'For what?' *You're not the one fucking the boss*, she thought. And then as an afterthought: *Are you?!*

The young girl raised her eyebrows and nudged the top of her head towards Jeanette, who had draped her arm over Nathan's shoulders in a possessive way. 'I think it's my gaffe she's here. She calls up this morning, wanting Nathan, but he's in that Pfizer meeting, you know? Then she starts asking questions about the awards and I say there's an extra ticket because Gary's in rehab. And now...'

Stella shrugged, trying to seem unconcerned. 'I'm not sure why you think I'd mind.'

The girl looked at Stella like her nose had grown an inch.

Breaking the awkward silence, Jezza stood and held up his glass. 'I want to make a toast to my partner, Stella...'

She cringed, wishing he'd just leave it. With a deep breath she forced herself to meet the eyes of the others at the table. She couldn't read their expressions. Mostly polite, masking that they thought she was a giant whore.

'...The person singlehandedly responsible for giving more middle-aged men erections across Europe than probably any other woman.' The table erupted in laughter, the kind that makes other tables jealous. The fact that they were all laughing made her feel forgiven, like she was one of the gang again, even though her face was flaming. Nothing like naming the elephant in the room to take away its power. She relaxed just a little bit and reached over to squeeze Jezza's hand. He responded with one of his winks.

A cadre of waiters appeared to place plates of salmon terrine nestled on beds of limp lettuce in front of each guest. Stella exhaled and tucked into the meal. If she could just win this award, everything would work out okay. She set up a mental wall to block out Nathan and Jeanette on the other table, although her laugh made her hard to ignore.

After desserts were cleared away, the ceremony began with the MC, TV star Joanna Lumley, taking the stage. She started with a joke about how her character from *Absolutely Fabulous*, Patsy, was a huge supporter of the pharmaceutical industry. The room loved that.

Stella wanted to meet Joanna almost as badly as she wanted the award. She'd promised her mother that she would try to get an autograph, a mutual love of *AbFab* being one area where mother and daughter were in agreement. Thinking of her mother conjured one of their oft-repeated conversations: '*I want grandchildren. Do you have any boyfriends?*'

'*No, I'm too busy,*' Stella always replied. And when that stopped working, she made up love interests: the doctor who joined Medicins Sans Frontieres. Her environmentalist boyfriend moved to a remote town in Norway to save glaciers. Now, her mother thought Stella was dating a Spanish sculptor. Alas, he would soon be heading off to Greece to restore ancient art.

The lies ate at Stella. Her mother would disown her if she knew, in fact, that Stella was dating a married man, her boss. It went against everything her mother had taught her, but her need for his approval was stronger.

Stella was a home wrecker. A liar. An adulteress. A neglecter of friends and family. A bad person.

'And the winner is…Bastion Communications!' After losing out on two of the five awards, Bastion finally landed a win on the third.

A knife stabbed through her heart as Nathan leant over, planting a kiss on Jeanette's cheek. Stella felt betrayed, even though that woman was his wife. So much for her mental wall. Stella slapped a smile on her face and clapped with the others. Jeanette jumped up and down with such exuberance that her £20,000 breasts were in danger of escaping her dress. Some hair slipped free of her beehive. When she stopped bopping, she refilled her glass and downed it in one.

Stella dragged her eyes away when she realised she was staring. Part of her was waiting for Jeanette to point a manicured finger at her and brand her with a scarlet A. But the more time passed, the more Jeanette appeared solely interested in getting drunk and pawing Nathan. She didn't know. She was on her own planet.

Only three more awards to go until the big finale. Not long until Stella could go home to her cosy Fulham flat, hopefully with a trophy in tow.

Bastion missed out on the fourth award. Jeanette's voice rose as she commiserated. 'Aw! Such a shame, honey. Such a shame.'

Amused looks flew around Stella's table. She was grateful for her colleagues' loyalty, even if it was misguided. She was the bad guy, after all.

Finally, the last award of the evening rolled around and Joanna Lumley announced the finalists: a statin, an anti-depressant, a herpes treatment, and Bastion for Bonera™. Jezza and Stella squeezed hands, hoping.

'And the winner is...' Joanna paused long enough for the entire room to fall into silence. A few nervous coughs punctured the stillness. Hearts beat faster. Jezza and Stella squeezed harder.

'Bastion for Bonera™!'

Screams ripped through the air. Stella hugged Jezza and he lifted her off the ground, despite being shorter. Before they headed to the stage, Stella glanced at Nathan. He was finally acknowledging her. Pride shone from his eyes and he was clapping as loud as anybody else.

'Well done,' he mouthed at her.

She glowed. Perhaps everything would be all right.

But then Jeanette put her arms around him and kissed him with tongue.

Jezza took Stella's hand and pulled her onto the stage, followed by the two account managers and one of the boys from the studio who prepared the artwork. Nathan brought up the rear.

The six of them crowded around Joanna Lumley. She looked every inch the star in her white suit and perfectly coifed blonde hair. Stella felt a thrill as she reached out and slid her palm against Joanna's. She seemed genuinely pleased to give Stella her congratulations. The photographer told them all to pose and Stella smiled brightly, puzzling out a way to ask for the star's autograph.

As Stella turned back towards Joanna, somebody knocked her from behind. Not a small excuse-me-for-bumping-into-you knock, but an intentional knock, meant to make her fall—which she did, straight into Joanna Lumley's arms. And because Stella was Stella, the prevalent thought in her head at that moment was: *I hope my make-up doesn't rub off on her white suit.* She stammered an apology.

'Stop her!' she heard just before somebody's hand tangled in her hair, tugging her back.

'You fucking slut!'

Pain mingled with confusion. Did Joanna Lumley just call her a slut? The smell of vanilla and gardenia enveloped her, along with understanding.

Reaching back, Stella yanked herself free, grimacing as strands of hair ripped out of her head. She pivoted to find Jeanette glowering.

Her expression was savage. Her beehive had flopped and one of her false eyelashes had flipped upwards, reminding Stella of the psychopath from *A Clockwork Orange*. Jeanette grabbed the mic stand and screamed so the whole room could hear: 'Stella Price is fucking my husband, Nathan Bastion,' like she was revealing the murderer at the end of an Agatha Christie novel. Nathan had been right; Jeanette never met a spotlight she didn't like.

This can't be happening. Stella's vision wobbled and she stumbled sideways as though the earth had tilted, hands clasped over her ears. She didn't want to hear the gasps from the audience, as they shifted in their seats to get a better view. Some even stood, phones out, recording video. *No, no, no!* Their judgment thickened the air, making it hard to breathe.

'Ow!' Jezza cried, snapping her back to reality. He held Jeanette by the arms, trying to subdue her, but she skewered his foot with her stiletto and slipped free.

As she advanced, the only thing Stella could think to do was apologise: 'I'm so sorry, Jeanette. It was a mistake. I never should have done it.' Her voice echoed through the sound system.

Before Stella realised what was happening, Jeanette wound back her arm, and—pow!—hit Stella straight on the bridge of her nose. The world exploded into jagged crystals. Jeanette pulled her arm back again, but this time her aim was off. She slugged Stella in the jaw.

Her face throbbed in pain. Her heart was numb.

Through the haze, she saw Nathan. He wasn't even looking at her. He had his arms wrapped around Jeanette protectively, hugging her to his chest and soothing her. Stella could just hear the words: 'Jeanette, babe. She means nothing to me. You know that. It's always been you.' Then they kissed.

After that, Stella lost track of what happened. When she tried to remember it the next day, it flickered like a slideshow.

Jezza pulling her from the stage.

Someone handing her a bag of ice.

Outside, vomiting into a potted plant.

Flowers of blood blossoming on the yellow silk of her Gucci dress.

Her, in a black cab.

Her heart in a vice, making it hard to breathe.

Shock set in, as did the trembling. What just happened? Was she really attacked and outed as an adulteress in front of the entire pharmaceutical advertising industry? Had her lover just publicly betrayed her? What would she tell her parents when they asked about tonight? More lies?

On her lap, she discovered a large black box weighing her down. She had no idea how it got there. Removing the top, she found her delicate glass trophy nestled in dark, die-cut foam. She read the inscription.

Stella Price. Bastion Communications. Ad Campaign of the Year.

If no one knew who she was at the beginning of the night, they did now—for all the wrong reasons.

In her kitchen, she put the trophy on the table and stared at it, before picking it up and smashing it on the floor. As she cleaned up the sharp pieces the next day, a shard of glass cut her hand, leaving a bloody reminder of the worst night of her life.

4

AS IMAGES from that night assailed her, Stella started shaking. Her fingers automatically flew to the permanent scar left by the trophy, located at the joint of her left thumb. She had to get away.

The audience burst into laughter over something the MC said and Stella excused herself to Claudia, saying she needed the toilet. Claudia waved her off, not noticing the sweat glistening on Stella's brow. She squeezed out of the room.

Stella could feel it starting. Her breath coming in fast huffs. Her limbs growing heavy with adrenaline.

Time was short. There had to be somewhere she could meltdown privately. The last panic attack had lasted roughly ten minutes from beginning to end. If she could just lock herself away in a cubicle, then she could ride it out. She followed the signs for the toilets down the dim hallway.

Left. Her palms began to itch.

Right. Her chest tightened.

Right again. A tear slipped down her cheek.

Left. *I'm going to die.*

Ten feet away, the door to the ladies' toilets beckoned. So close, yet so far.

She wouldn't make it. She was a fairy tale statue turning back into stone, muscle by muscle. Propping her body against the wall, she clung to it, rolling her fevered forehead onto the cool maroon paint. Heartbeat. Heartbeat. Heartbeat.

A phantom smell flooded her nostrils. Sugary vanilla mixed with nauseating gardenia. The scent of confrontation and betrayal and bad decisions. The scent that triggered her first panic attack.

Most of the time, she could think about the events from the past year dispassionately, as though they had happened to somebody else. But once in a while, something would trip a switch in her brain. For example, she might feel embarrassed about something completely unrelated and find her thoughts returning to the night she was dumped by Nathan and attacked by his wife in front of thousands of people. The sheer magnitude of the emotion would sneak up on her, resulting in *this*.

Her heart stepped up a gear into full fight or flight mode, wondering which direction the blow would come from. Sweat poured down her forehead and pictures flashed behind her eyes: Nathan, her co-workers, Jeanette, faces of strangers, all looking at her like she was scum. And afterwards, the interview rejections. Lying to her parents about why she wanted to change careers. She choked on her own breath.

How could she have been so stupid, stupid, stupid?

Somewhere far away, a door swooshed open.

Somebody was whistling tunelessly. A pause. 'Looking for a rematch?' It was the last voice she wanted to hear. Shame at their encounter yesterday heaped itself on top of the panic. She'd accused him of hitting on her! How mortifying. She turned her face further into the wall.

'Hey, Mademoiselle Chicken, are you okay?' Connor asked.

She couldn't even shake her head.

What would he think? She wished she could run away from this whole situation, from her life. Her thoughts swirled: he must think her some sort of idiot. She had made a bad impression before she even began. She didn't belong in this industry. She would never make it as a photographer.

His tuxedoed chest appeared in front of her. 'I think you're having a panic attack,' he said, reaching out to put his arms around her rigid body, pulling her towards him. He manoeuvred her head to rest against his shoulder. Part of her worried about getting make-up on his tailored suit, just like she had with Joanna Lumley. The bigger part was grateful for the comfort, even if it came from an unexpected source.

He held her for a minute, arms tight, giving her boundaries she could feel. She appreciated that he didn't try to talk or coach her through it and wished somebody had realised she was having a panic attack the first time: Claudia was treating her to a post-break-up, post-losing-your-job lunch at Harvey Nics. An American woman sitting at the next table was wearing *Tempestuous*, liberally, and the cloying grandma-garden odour wafted towards Stella as she ate her mushroom risotto. Now, she didn't even need the perfume to send her spiralling.

Usually calm in any situation, Claudia had no idea what was happening when Stella froze. That day, they learnt what *not* to do when someone is having a panic attack, like *don't* crowd the person or shake her, screaming, 'Stella! What's wrong? Snap out of it!' And *don't* call an ambulance, because the attack will likely only last minutes and there's nothing a paramedic can do about it, especially when he arrives after it's passed. Stella had wanted to die from embarrassment as she came to, the restaurant staff swarming around her and the maitre d' fanning her with the dessert menu.

Her breathing began to slow.

'Can you walk?' asked Connor before pulling back, moving his strong hands to her arms. Supportive. Sympathetic. So different from the arrogant rockstar she believed him to be. Where had *this* guy been earlier? 'There's a sofa around the corner.'

Grateful, she allowed him to move her to a more private location. She didn't want anybody to catch her sobbing in Connor Knight's arms. She could imagine the gossip, and if there was one thing she couldn't handle right now, it was becoming the subject of industry gossip again.

He guided her to a velvet loveseat in an out-of-the-way alcove.

'S-sorry...' She struggled to get the words out.

'What are you apologising for? It's fine.' He kneeled next to her and rubbed her quivering back.

She'd been alone for the second attack. It happened at the V&A. She'd thought she was the only person in the room, but then she surprised a couple making out behind a display about geishas. Something about their tryst reminded her of how she and Nathan had conducted their affair in dark corners. She stumbled to a bench, where she gripped the edges of the seat and waited for the lightning inside her to subside.

She realised she was squeezing Connor's hand. Hard.

'Sorry,' she rasped, releasing her fingers.

'It's okay. They're insured.' He flexed his hand to encourage blood flow. They both laughed. It was a good sign. Normal function returning.

Stella didn't know what to say. What could she say to the man who she accused of hitting on her before forcing her way onto his course? It wasn't exactly the kind of scenario covered by a greeting card.

'How did you know?' she asked, avoiding his eyes.

'My brother has them.'

Distantly, the MC announced, 'And the winner is...Connor Knight!' followed by intense applause and a snippet of a rousing pop song. A few moments later: 'Has anyone seen Connor Knight?'

'I think you won something,' Stella said, trying to stand and failing. She didn't want him to miss his big moment because of her.

'Mm-hmm,' he agreed thoughtfully while their eyes locked for a few seconds.

Snapping out of it, he took her hand and eased her back onto the sofa. 'It's fine. I already have plenty. My assistant will collect them for me.'

She noticed how he used the plural: them. He expected there to be more than one. She thought about how happy her father would be if she could win an award for her photography, even though he disapproved of the about-face in her career. He loved bragging about her achievements which were, unfortunately, thin on the ground lately. She wondered if Connor's parents were proud of him.

Her nose tickled and she sniffed.

Connor reached into his back pocket and pulled out a handkerchief. He shook it open and handed it to her.

'Thanks.' She wiped her nose and face, her runny mascara leaving streaks of black on the fine white cloth. She shuddered to think how she must look like right now. She wasn't one of those women who got all dewy when crying. Her fair skin tended towards continents of red patches.

She held out the ruined fabric to him. 'Sorry,' she said again.

'That's three times you've apologised. Really. It's fine. You keep it.'

Now that the panic had passed, humiliation set in hard and she felt that familiar drop in her stomach. She twisted the handkerchief in her lap. It had beautiful embroidery around the edges, the name 'Grace' sewn into one of the corners. *Who's Grace?* she wanted to ask, but didn't. Probably one of his girlfriends.

'How long have you been having these attacks?' He motioned her over and sat down.

'Too long,' she said. She closed her eyes, wishing he would just leave her alone now, climb back on his steed and gallop away. Job done.

'Have you seen anyone about it?'

Stella studied the carpet. Claudia had urged her to get help, even giving her the name of a psychologist. 'No. I thought they'd go away. Like a cold.'

'How's that working out?' Connor leaned forward, and angled his head towards her. She found it more difficult to avoid his gaze now that he was in her line of vision. 'How many times have you had these?'

This was excruciating. Like that time she got called into Father Paul's office for skipping assembly, but worse. She cringed as she admitted, 'Four...maybe five in the past six months.'

'Tell me if I'm overstepping.'

She wanted to, but the people pleaser inside shook her head.

'You need to sort this out. Soon. Imagine being in the middle of shooting a wedding—'

'All right,' she said louder than she meant to, and then more gently, 'Sorry. I get it. I'll see somebody.'

'Promise?'

She sighed. 'Prom—'

'*What's going on here?*' said a voice Stella recognised. Her head whipped up. Connor's blonde bombshell date stood at the bend in the hallway, skinny arms propped on her hips as though posing in front of a step-and-repeat board.

Inga. The woman looked like an Inga. From her angry pout, Stella could tell that his girlfriend thought something nefarious was going on, but Stella's 'other woman' days were over. She didn't want anyone connecting her name with Connor Knight's in a romantic way.

'Nothing!' Stella said with the enthusiasm of a camp councillor. 'Nothing is going on. He was just...I was just...' She took a deep breath, trying to get her thoughts in order. She pushed away from the couch, the light of one of the wall sconces catching her face. Inga winced at Stella's blotchy complexion and puffy eyes.

She ploughed on. 'See, I'm not interested in men. I mean, I'm interested in men, but not right now. And *certainly* not Connor Knight. Ew! Can you imagine? He's a bit too Brad Pitt in *Legends of the Fall*, if you know what I mean.' She didn't even know what she meant. She looked back at Connor, who was now standing, arms crossed. 'No offence.'

'None taken.' He was giving her a bemused look.

'So he's all yours! I'll just get out of your way.' She tiptoed past Inga, glad to get some distance from Connor. Stella turned back to give a thumbs-up sign, but then she worried that it would remind him of their Thumb War. She dropped her hands.

Connor joined his date and she threaded her arm through his. They really did make a striking couple. With a twinge of unexpected jealousy, Stella knew they'd probably be butterfly lighting the shit out of each other later tonight.

'They're looking for you,' Inga said to Connor. 'You won some trophies.'

Ignoring her, he said to Stella, 'Are you sure you're all right?'

'Absolutely fine,' she said with too much intensity. She needed to get away from them both, backing away in the direction of the toilets. 'Anyway, have a great night. Thanks again for your help, Connor. And congratulations! And sorry. And good night.' With that, she leaned backwards on the toilet door. It gave way more easily than expected, and she tumbled into the ladies' loo, the door calmly closing behind her. She could hear Inga asking Connor as they walked past, 'Is she on drugs?'

Exhaling, Stella slumped against the wall for a second before ducking into a cubicle. She sat on the toilet lid and dropped her head into her hands. Her heart thumped against her ribcage again, but it wasn't another attack. She felt like an idiot. How could she spend a whole week with him in France when he'd witnessed her like this? What must he think of her? The anxious Mademoiselle Chicken. What a ridiculous box to occupy in anybody's brain.

And now she'd promised him to seek help. She'd been putting it off because she didn't want to accept that panic attacks were a permanent part of her life. The thought of telling a stranger the whole story…it filled her with dread.

She realised that she was still fiddling with Connor's sullied handkerchief. *Grace*, she read again, written in neat hand-stitched script. It must mean something to him, this piece of cloth. She held it to her nose and inhaled deeply. It smelled of a man, not a woman. Spicy and warm. His scent. For a moment, she allowed herself to recall the comforting feeling of her head against his chest, his arms around her body.

Nope. None of that. She shook her head and stepped out of her safe haven as a group of girls entered the toilets, 'YMCA' leaking in after them. In front of the mirror, Stella kept her head down, hair shielding her face until they'd all filtered into their own cubicles. Looking up, she was glad to see that her skin wasn't as bad as she'd thought. The blotchiness had subsided and most of her mascara had been wiped off.

The door swooshed open again. 'Stells?' yelled Claudia. 'Oh, there you are.'

'Sorry. Funny tummy.' Stella washed her hands, hoping she didn't look like a liar.

'Yeah, that salmon was fucking dodgy.' She belched and laughed. 'Ooh, fishy. Come on. I've requested "The Birdie Song" for you.'

'Ha ha,' Stella said, flicking her wet fingers towards Claudia, who pretended to flap her wings and cluck.

Yes, a spell on the dance floor with her best friend was exactly what she needed. Checking her face one last time, she saw the handkerchief sitting next to the sink. She folded it and tucked it into her bra, out of sight, out of mind.

5

STELLA'S ALARM clock went off at 9AM.

She reached over and hit snooze on her phone, not ready to face the world after her long, emotional evening. Checkout wasn't for another hour.

'Hello? Hello! Stella?' A tinny voice called her name, as though transmitted through an old radio. 'Hellooooo?'

Pushing herself onto her elbows and wiping spit off her mouth, she glanced at the clock. 8AM. *What?* She picked up her phone and found an active call with her mother. She yanked her mobile off its charger.

'Sorry, I'm here,' she croaked brightly.

'Where are you? You sound horrible,' said Angela.

'I'm at that photography convention I told you about.' Stella flinched, well aware of what was coming.

'Oh. Are you still doing this crazy thing? I don't understand why you left Bastion, especially after winning that award.' She made an Italian noise of disappointment. 'At least remember to go to church. It *is* Sunday.'

Stella sighed. 'Of course, I will.' *Forgive me, father, for I have sinned,* she thought as the lie slipped off her tongue and her stomach clenched.

'Make sure you do. *L'amore della ricchezza è una trappola, che tenta le persone a ogni sorta di peccati.*'

The love of riches is a trap that tempts people to all sorts of sins. Her mother obviously didn't know a lot about wedding photographers. Rich? Ha.

'You never know what God has planned for you. Don't forget, your father and I met—'

'—As you were coming out of church.' Stella had heard the story a million times: on holiday in Venice, her father saw Angela outside of Santa Maria dei Miracoli. It was love at first sight. Stella's mother insisted it was God's miracle. They married a week later.

'Your father wants to speak with you.'

'No, mamma, I have to go!' she said pointlessly. Covering the bottom of her phone with her hand, she turned her head and screamed into her pillow before returning the mobile to her ear.

'Stella? Everything alright?' her father asked.

'Fine, dad. Fine. You?'

'Great! I have news. I got the role of Prospero in *The Tempest.*' He had joined the local Shakespearean society as a retirement project and was acting like it was the RSC.

'Well done!'

'Show's in August. I expect you to be there.'

'Great—I will.' And because she was still half asleep, she made the mistake of adding, 'As long as I don't have a wedding booked for that weekend.'

He grunted his disapproval. 'Stella girl, I'm disappointed to hear that. Are you still insisting on doing this photography thing? You know, you'll never be able to support yourself from snapping pictures. It's a vanity project and the sooner you realise that, the better. Look, I'm sure Bastion would take you back...'

Turning onto her side and curling into a ball, Stella listened to her father berate her for her life choices. He then moved on to his other favourite topic: comparing her to their neighbour Dilwyn, whose Taff Man and a Van business 'could be the Welsh FedEx', with Bill's mentorship. He sounded prouder of Dilwyn than he'd ever been of Stella. For a moment, she resented Dilwyn. He was painfully shy and had an obvious crush on Stella, manifesting in his inability to speak around her. Even as her father's praise made her prickle with jealousy, she felt bad for Dilwyn, whose gentle nature would bend like a sapling in a hurricane under Bill's forceful tutelage.

By the time they hung up, Stella felt emotionally battered herself. Maybe she was living in a fantasy. Maybe she should just give up now and look for a more practical job.

But then she remembered: she was going to France with Connor Knight. She'd be learning from the best wedding photographer in the world. She could do this.

Fully awake now, she flung herself out of bed and packed her bag. The conference finished today and she just wanted to go back to her flat. She rang Claudia. It went to voicemail. Stella didn't want to leave without saying goodbye, so she grabbed her suitcase and went down two floors to her friend's room.

Poised to knock, she heard noises on the other side of the door. Noises that definitely wouldn't welcome an interruption.

'Well, well, well,' Stella chuckled all the way back to the lift.

TWO HOURS LATER, Stella arrived at the flat she shared with Tristan.

She fancied a Sunday roast, a glass of wine, and a chance to regale her oldest friend with stories about the weekend's emotional roller-coaster. If there was one thing that Tristan loved, it was schaden-freude. Unfortunately, his schedule placed him in Milan until Wednesday. He travelled constantly, jet-setting across the globe for fashion shows and photo shoots.

The front door swung open. Tristan's portrait, the same image that had once graced a billboard in Piccadilly Circus, greeted her with his brooding eyes, dark hair, and pouting lips. It had been his first big job for Calvin Klein, his stomach so ridged it looked like someone had slipped a loaf of knotted bread under his skin. This portfolio piece was one of many framed portraits of the flat-owner on the walls. Sometimes it felt like living in the Tristan Hughes Museum.

Throwing her keys into the bowl under the picture, she turned the corner into her bedroom. The entire flat was decorated in a minimalist style without feeling empty, a delicate balance only an expensive interior designer could achieve. Still, Stella had tried her best to make the room her own. The first thing she'd done was remove the long picture above the bed of Tristan lying on a beach, water lapping around the bulge in his Fendi swimwear. She'd replaced it with a landscape picture she'd taken in the Brecon Beacons.

Her suitcase landed with a thud and she threw herself onto the bed, face down. As her body sunk into the memory foam, she considered staying there the rest of the day. The convention and the chat with her mother had left her drained. Her eyes fluttered closed, a lone seagull calling out as it flew past her window.

Her phone rang, shattering her peace. She really needed to keep it on mute when she was sleeping. She checked the screen to make sure it wasn't either of her parents.

'Hello—'

'Those bloody tadgers,' Claudia said.

'Nice to hear from you, too.'

'I just had that meeting about the ambassador role. They decided to go with some paunchy middle-aged twat from Coventry despite the fact that my business is miles more successful than his.'

'Did they say why?' Claudia had mentioned wanting to work with the German lighting brand, not just for the prestige but also for the free equipment.

'The usual sexist bullshit. When they asked if I had any suggestions to, you know, help them do more business in the UK, I was honest. I said the fifty percent of professional photographers who are female would appreciate it if they stopped using half-naked girls in their brochures and demos.'

'Let me guess: they didn't like that?'

'No. They want someone like Roger from Coventry who won't blink a fucking eye at their misogyny.'

'Their loss.'

'You still around? I could use a drink.'

Stella winced. 'Sorry. No. After last night's episode, I just wanted to come home.'

Claudia paused. 'What episode?'

Right, she hadn't told Claudia about the attack. If only Stella were a good liar. She was one of those people who couldn't fib. Whenever she tried, her face took on an odd expression, as though the weight of the lie hung on her features, dragging them down. Her father called it 'Melty Face'. Over the phone, it was just as bad.

'Nothing,' she wheezed, followed by a cough.

'You're a big fat liar. Was it that godforsaken perfume again? *Incestuous?*'

'*Tempestuous*. And no. Just…a lot of memories circulating last night. The award ceremony…' Stella squeezed her eyes shut, not wanting to think about any of it.

'Jesus. Sorry, I didn't realise.'

'It's not your fault. I could've pulled out if I really wanted to.'

'You need to get help.'

Stella hugged her knees to her chest. 'By the time I saw you, I was fine.' Wanting desperately to change the subject, she said, 'Anyway, how did you sleep last night? Anything you'd like to share?'

Claudia snapped her tongue. 'Oh my god. How did you know?'

'You can't get anything past me. Is this a thing or a fling?'

'Please. I can't date him. He's a Tory, for fuck's sake. My parents would love him.'

Stella laughed. Since knowing each other, Claudia had dallied with tattoo artists, struggling musicians, gangsters, and even a traffic warden. Her parents would think it was Christmas if she came home with someone like Magnus.

They made a plan to meet the following weekend and hung up.

Stella was about to close her eyes again when the ululating cry of a woman having an orgasm echoed through the flat.

Stella sat up and perked her ears. In normal circumstances, this would be cause for concern. She had heard of people breaking into the homes of famous people to have sex in their beds and Tristan did have a lot of dedicated female fans.

But Stella knew this was not the case.

'Ula?' she shouted. 'Is that you?' Stella kicked off her shoes and padded towards the open plan kitchen/dining/living room.

A buxom thirty-year-old woman with a bob that started platinum and ended bright pink was buffing the metal balcony handles with a toothbrush. A thin cord connected her headphones to a yellow Sports Walkman at her belt.

'Ula?' Stella tried again, louder. No response.

She walked up behind the cleaner and tapped her shoulder.

'*Kurwa!*' Ula shouted, the metal arch of her headphones slipping as she turned. 'You scared me.' She switched off the cassette player.

Stella said, 'Sorry! What are you doing here? It's Sunday.'

'I texted Tristan to ask if it is okay. He said yes.' She shrugged. Ula usually cleaned some time between Monday to Friday—though exactly which day or time changed every week depending on Ula's other job. She only accepted clients who could be flexible.

'Dare I ask why you were making those sounds?'

'Oh, I am practising for filming.'

'Again?' Stella dragged her hands over her eyes and rubbed her temples. From what Stella could piece together, Ula worked as an actor, cleaning houses as a side hustle when she wasn't making films. Stella had suspected for some time that when Ula said she acted as an extra in 'movies', what she really meant was 'porn'.

And with a body like Ula's, Stella wasn't surprised. Statuesque, with breasts so globe-like that they probably had their own gravitational pull, Ula had the physique of a sex goddess. Stella just hoped that Ula knew what an incredible person she was, above and beyond her many physical assets. She was a woman of many talents. On one occasion, Stella came home to find that Ula had taken the pipes under the kitchen sink apart to sort a leak. On another, she'd rearranged the living room furniture to create better Feng Shui (and it really was better). Stella didn't like to think of Ula selling herself short or being used by shady directors or doing porn because she needed money. That's why Stella convinced Tristan to pay Ula twice the going hourly rate, so she could have more choices.

So far, Stella's plan didn't seem to be working.

'Don't worry. I am going soon. I have a cousin's birthday party today.'

'I didn't realise you had family in London.' That eased Stella's mind slightly. At least Ula had support.

'Oh, *tak*! Many! Fifteen cousins. I just finish this.' Ula smiled, revealing her deep dimples. She was about to turn back to her work when she narrowed her eyes at Stella.

'Something bothers you. Your aura...it is like mud.'

Stella shook her head in confusion. 'What are you talking about?'

'I research auras for my psychology degree. Every person has an aura. Yours usually is bright yellow. Creative. Friendly.'

'You have a psychology degree?' said Stella in surprise. Ula was an onion, but the more Stella peeled off, the more onion there was. An infinite onion.

'Yes. In Poland. But I can't use here.' She shrugged, as though that was that and there was no point discussing it. 'So tell me problem. I listen.' Moving to the white sofa, she sat and motioned for Stella to join. Ula put her toothbrush and dust cloth aside and crossed her legs. The session had begun.

But Stella hesitated. There were very few people who knew the whole story of the awards ceremony. In fact, aside from those who were there on the night, the list had two members: Claudia and Tristan. If Stella could keep it contained, then perhaps it would eventually disappear. Poof! Like it had never happened.

On the other hand, she obviously wasn't dealing well. The panic attacks were increasing in frequency, and Claudia had begged her to see somebody. Now Connor Knight had commanded her to get help. Well, Ula *did* have a degree in psychology...

'I'm having panic attacks,' she began, sitting opposite Ula.

'Do you understand why?'

'Yeah. I'm pretty sure it's because I have PTSD.' And she told Ula the whole story.

Ula nodded and made sympathetic sounds throughout. She offered to have one of her cousins beat up Nathan, but Stella declined. At the end, Ula leaned back, her eyebrows scrunched in concentration. Like a cork popping out of a bottle, she suddenly leaned forward. 'There is Hungarian folk tale I want to tell you.

'Once upon a time there is a dead bride,' she began. 'Poor woman who died of broken heart. Her father—he is king—posts many guards outside her...how do you say? Place under church where body is kept?'

'Uh...crypt?'

'Yes! Crypt. And every night, she wakes up and kills them.' Ula strangled the air violently. Stella flinched. 'She piles their bones in a corner. It becomes the job nobody wants to do...like cleaning toilets. So a solider from far away, he hears this king is offering huge rewards of gold to the person who survives a night guarding his dead daughter. So this man thinks, "I can do this thing." First night, he hides inside the bell. She searches for him but cannot find him. At midnight, she loses her power and returns to her coffin.'

Stella wondered where this was going. Perhaps she'd made a mistake expecting their cleaner to fix her. Then again, it couldn't hurt.

'The soldier, he gets his money. But now he thinks, "I did it once, I can do it again." So he does. This time he hides under a pile of bones. Very gross, but she does not find him. He gets more money. He wants to do it again, but he is becoming very anxious whenever he goes to crypt. Palms wet. Head sweating. You know how it feels, yes? He realises he cannot keep doing this thing. So he decides to break curse. It is a strange part of story. He meets old man who says soldier needs to survive night *inside* coffin. Do not ask me how he knows this. It's folk story. They agree that if it works, old man gets half the gold.'

Stella's polite smile of engagement wavered. This story was going on.

'So! This is what he does. There is, um...high thing where priest makes speeches?'

'Uh...pulpit?'

'Yes! A pulpit with stairs on both sides. The soldier stands at top and calls to this bride. She runs up one stair, and he runs down the other, jumps into coffin, holds the lid shut as she bangs on top. At midnight, her screaming suddenly stops. He lifts the lid and finds the princess, alive, not dead. They have a beautiful wedding and everybody is happy.'

Stella nodded thoughtfully, squinting at a picture of Tristan half-naked in a Hugo Boss ad. She played with the story in her mind, like a ball of dough, stretching it and rolling it up, and then stretching it out again, trying to discern its meaning.

Finally, Stella said, 'So you want me to get in the coffin?'

'Yes! This is the best idea.'

'What does that mean?'

'What do you think it means?'

'Sorry, but I have no idea.' Perhaps it meant she'd just wasted half an hour.

'You think about it. Its meaning will come.'

'I was hoping...I was hoping you might have some advice that was more...practical? Like, what to do when I actually have an attack?'

'Oh, yes, this is easy. It's called the "STOP method". I'll write it down for you.'

She went directly to a drawer under the kitchen counter and grabbed a piece of paper and pencil. She scribbled something down and handed it to Stella:

Stop

Take breath

Observe feelings, thoughts, and physical symptoms

Continue (I cannot remember word with P, but is the same thing)

Stella grunted. Ula made it sound so easy. 'I'll give it my best shot.'

Ula picked up her cleaning tools. 'I must finish before my cousin's party.'

Dismissed, Stella returned to her room. Confusion puddled in her brain, but she also felt lighter, as though she'd eased her burden by telling the story. *Get in the coffin.* What did it mean? Should she confront Nathan? Or apologise to his wife? Relocate to a funeral home? All options filled her with foreboding.

'I go now!' shouted Ula.

Stella heard the front door open. 'Wait!' she yelled, grabbing her wallet and pulling out her last £20. She ran to the entranceway and handed it to Ula.

'What's this? Tristan has already paid me for this month.'

'A little something extra. You know...a bonus! For the therapy session.'

'You're always so kind. Thank you. One day, I'll do something kind to you. Maybe put you on a date with my cousin who is a bodybuilder. We can be family!' She planted an exuberant kiss on Stella's cheeks.

'Please. It's my pleasure.' Worried about Ula's possibly pornographic extracurricular activities, she added, 'Just...take care of yourself, okay?'

With equal concern, Ula said, 'Remember: it's only adrenaline. Next time it happens, separate physical reactions from emotions. Observe how it makes your body feel, like a scientist. Remove its power.' And with that surprisingly sage advice, she stuffed the money in her bag and left.

6

ON SOME LEVEL, Stella knew she was dreaming. She was in a yoga class, stretching. The teacher, who happened to be Magnus Fiennes in a royal purple onesie, instructed her to flow into Embryo Pose. As Stella and Magnus transitioned into Baby Cobra, Connor Knight walked into the room in nothing but an apron printed with chickens. He held a tray of camera lenses, arrayed like coffee cups. 'Thumb war?' he said, stopping in front of her, in the perfect position for her to look straight up his—

'*Nous sommes arrivés!*' shouted a loud voice in badly accented French.

Stella rubbed her eyes as the car turned onto a gravel lane flanked by two regal stone lions. She glanced at Alan, Connor's volunteer model from the conference, as he pushed his thick black glasses up his nose for the millionth time.

She yawned, even as her heart beat faster. Without thinking, she started nibbling her cuticles.

Part of Stella was dreading this week. The last time she'd seen Connor Knight, she had been a mess. How could she look him in the eye after that? Every time she thought of meeting him again, her mood dropped. She hoped he wouldn't bring up the panic incident. She really didn't want to talk about it, especially with him.

The car broke free from the tunnel of trees revealing the chateau: a grand mansion made of tuffeau stone, glimmering sandy yellow in the mid-afternoon sun. Verdant creepers snuggled into the lower walls. Stella counted five turrets with grey tiled roofs like witches' hats. It looked so picturesque. So romantic. A shiver of excitement ran through her body, despite her apprehension. She imagined how she would photograph this place: in the early morning light with the sun's first soft rays making the building glow.

Signs directed them to a parking area hidden by a row of cypress trees where they pulled into a space between two rusty Renaults. Stella chipped a nail in her scramble to open the car door and unfold herself from her foetal prison.

'Sorry about all my stuff,' said Alan for the hundredth time as he watched her struggle to stand upright.

'It's absolutely no problem. I'm fine.'

Alan had packed every piece of photographic equipment he owned into the vehicle, leaving barely enough room for Stella and her bags. As it was, she'd had to put her small suitcase in the footwell, meaning her legs had been bent into her chest for over eight hours. She was grateful for the lift, but it would take a while to regain all the feeling in her limbs.

Blood rushed to her extremities as she stood and stretched, cricking her neck left and right. The countryside air filled her lungs. Its sweet-smoky smell of pine and warm earth made her think of childhood camping holidays in the Dolomites, the only time when her parents shed their high expectations of her and they could just be a family of three, exploring the woods. Eager to get to the privacy of her room, she tugged her suitcase out of the footwell and hoisted her camera bag. She crunched over the gravel towards Alan, who had already unpacked half of his gear.

'Are you sure you should bring everything inside? Maybe leave some of it here until you need it?' she suggested.

He glared at her like she suggested he leave a puppy in the car on a hot day. After reinstating his glasses, he said, 'I couldn't possibly do that.'

'Okay, well, I'll check in and come back to help you.'

When she got to the chateau, she found Connor's assistant sitting at the top of the stone stairs, clipboard in one hand, beer in the other. Krish, if she remembered correctly. He pushed his shiny black hair out of his eyes and said, 'Stella, right?'

She liked his face. Handsome, but with a boyish openness. He looked like he'd laugh easily. Stella gave him an enthusiastic greeting and started to climb.

'Wait,' he said, jumping up. 'Let me help you.' All six foot something of him pummelled down the steps to lift her suitcase out of her hands. He attempted to take her camera bag, too, but she held onto it.

'Oh, don't worry. I can carry it,' she objected. She didn't want to inconvenience him.

'Do you want to settle this with a Thumb War?' He winked, and Stella blushed. Connor had told him about the Thumb War. What else had they talked about? How she'd accused him of hitting on her? The panic attack?

She laughed to cover up her inner turmoil and followed him into the house. Inside, she stopped to let her eyes adjust to the light.

An opulent hallway blinked into focus, straight out of a BBC period drama about Napoleon. The marble staircase curved down into a shiny black and white chequered floor. Paintings of various long-dead French people hung on the walls: one feeding apples to her lap dog, another carrying a brace of expired grouse, a third sneering out of the frame, as though thinking, 'Who are these peasants in my house?'

Inhaling the soothing scent of lavender, Stella walked underneath an imposing chandelier, crystal drops hanging like rain, refracted light falling across the floor. She followed Krish up the stairs, her hand gliding along the ironwork balustrade.

'Has everybody arrived?' she asked.

'Three more *en route* to make an even ten.'

'Oh. Aren't there eleven of us?'

'Someone dropped out due to a death in the family.'

'That's great!' He looked at her with surprise. 'Sorry, that's not great. I mean I'm glad the numbers aren't uneven anymore. Um, please pass on my condolences.'

She snapped her mouth closed, even though she really wanted to ask after Connor. Was he in the chateau? Best not to say anything, in case Krish read something into the question.

He stopped in front of a wooden door that looked 300 years old and turned a skeleton key. 'This is you.' Shouldering it open, he placed her suitcase on the floor and motioned her inside.

Her jaw dropped. A solid wooden four-poster bed dominated the room, its carved column supporting a heavy canopy, also made of wood. In contrast, a delicate cream quilt covered the mattress. Plump white pillows, more than any one person could possibly need, lined the headboard. As her eyes wandered the room, she noted the afternoon sun pouring through the lattice shutters, creating slits of light. Past an antique wardrobe, she spied another door, which she assumed led to the en-suite.

Krish continued, 'We're all meeting downstairs at seven, so you have some time to kill. Feel free to explore. Just don't get lost in the woods.'

He left and she placed her camera bag on the floor. Flopping backwards onto the high bed, she ran her fingers over the detailed stitching of the handmade quilt, exploring its tiny craters and bumps. Smiling, she imagined the stories that quilt could tell. With a squeak of joy, she grabbed one of the fluffy white pillows and screamed into it, kicking her dangling feet against the side of the bed. She couldn't believe she was actually here. Forgetting her anxiety for a minute, she cuddled the pillow to her chest and laughed.

And then she remembered poor Alan waiting for her downstairs.

. . .

It took them five trips to get Alan's things to his room, Krish reiterating on every haul that Alan wouldn't need any of it. After they finished, Stella paused to wipe the thin sheen of sweat from her brow.

Still no sign of Connor. Or anyone else, for that matter.

After sitting still for over eight hours, Stella decided to explore the grounds. The chateau was quiet as she pocketed her skeleton key, disturbed only by the muffled sound of voices behind a closed door and the clink of pots and pans in a distant kitchen. Somewhere, a man laughed. Could that be Connor? Stella hurried out the front entrance.

Skirting the chateau towards the back, she found a swimming pool reflecting the fluffy spring sky. She dipped her fingers in the water to check the temperature. Freezing. Past the pool and through a stone archway, she emerged into a garden of cherry blossom trees in full bloom. She laughed in delight at the cotton candy landscape and the sweet floral smell. Checking that she was alone, she twirled as a slight breeze caused the light pink petals to rain down around her. On the edges of the walled garden, wildflowers nodded under the buzz of happy bumblebees. It was paradise. For the first time in ages, she felt free: no thoughts of Nathan or Jeanette weighing on her mind. No fear of judgment from her parents. Just the gentle stroke of the wind, the sound of birdsong, and a feeling of great potential.

She exited the garden through another archway into a fairy tale forest. Three different paths led into the trees. She imagined she stood in a real-life choose-your-own-adventure book: 'To the left waits a sabre-toothed tiger, to the right, a wicked elf guarding a magic sword. Which do you choose?'

She chose the middle one. Wandering deeper and deeper into the forest, she checked the time on her phone. Ninety-minutes until dinner. Plenty of time to explore and then freshen up before she met the other course delegates. And Connor.

Nearby, she heard the swoosh of ducks landing on water followed by quacking. She parted the hanging branches of a weeping willow, revealing a Monet-esque pond, complete with a small green bridge.

Lily pads dotted its surface and wisteria was just starting to bloom on the far edge. Could this location get any cuter?

'Oh, oh, oh, don't stop!'

Movement on the bridge caught her eye. A woman sat on the railing, her yellow skirt pushed up around her waist and the white of her thighs reflecting the afternoon sun. Her blonde lover stood in front of her, thrusting away.

'Harder!'

Squinting, Stella recognised the woman who had been in front of her at the convention. The one who bought two places. The pondscape didn't feel so cute anymore.

'Spank me!' shouted the man.

The sound of hand meeting flesh echoed around the water. A duck quacked.

Stella released the branches of the tree and turned, ready to find her way back. Had she come from the left? Or the right? It all appeared the same. Tree, bush, tree, bush. Recalling a documentary about a tracker, she bent to examine the ground for footprints, but a fine layer of dry pine needles lay on the dusty path, obscuring any marks she might have left. Next, she scanned for broken branches. Unsurprisingly, that turned up nothing. Her shoulders slumped. She should have brought some breadcrumbs.

'Harder!' the man roared.

Ugh. She would just have to wait for them to finish, then ask to tag along back to the chateau. This must be what Krish meant when he said don't get lost in the forest.

They continued to grunt and groan, in no hurry to finish, so she leaned against the rough bark of the tree and waited. She sighed and closed her eyes.

Stella remembered sex. She remembered it being fun. Not always satisfying, but fun. Nathan had turned out to be a big mistake, but he had a 50/50 success rate with helping her reach climax, better than most of her ex-boyfriends. She wondered how long her self-imposed drought should last. A year? Maybe two? Long enough to establish herself as a photographer. And whomever won the role of Stella's Next Boyfriend would have nothing to do with her new career. Maybe a plumber. Or a carpenter…somebody who was good with his hands. In the meantime, her vibrator would have to work overtime. Too bad she'd left it in London.

'Enjoying yourself?'

Her eyes snapped open to find Connor Knight in front of her, camera bag against his feet with arms crossed and an amused half-smile on his face, as though reading her mind.

Horrified, Stella realised she'd been sketching sensuous figure eights on her chin while she daydreamed. She pushed herself off the tree, her finger to her lips.

'Shhhh. There's a couple bonking on the bridge,' she said, even though he had ears and could hear for himself and *Oh my god, did I just say* bonking *to Connor Knight?*

The couple's cries were getting louder, increasing her discomfort. She moved to step away from the tree, but her trainer caught between two raised roots. She yanked on her leg. The shoe stayed put. Her foot, however, slid out, surprising her and causing her to hop forwards and lose her balance, despite her dancer training.

She hopped right into Connor. His hands found her waist to steady her, but then his legs tangled in the straps of his camera bag. He tripped backwards, pulling them both down with an emphatic oomph.

Her palms landed on his chest and her body pressed into his. A sudden rush of heat flamed to life between her legs. Perhaps it was the show on the bridge. Or her many months of chastity. But she found herself wondering what it would be like to have sex with Connor Knight on the forest floor, surrounded by the primal thrum of nature. Would he take her up against a tree or would they lie entwined among the moss and leaves, birds singing overhead as their voices rose in intensifying need?

The pictures flying through her mind made her burn brighter. Her lips hovered just above his mouth. He was close enough that she could smell the hint of citrus on his breath. Her hair hung down around his face, making an intimate room for just the two of them.

It took her a moment to realise Connor was saying something. 'Price? Are you okay?'

Did he just call her Price? She kind of liked it—better than Mademoiselle Chicken anyway.

She shook her head. What the hell was she thinking? Intimate relations with Connor Knight were not going to happen. She fixed a picture of Nathan in her head and all sexual feelings shrivelled. *Focus, Stella, focus.* 'Sorry. I'm...I'm fine.' Wanting to separate herself from him immediately, she pushed herself up and stood.

'I can't believe I tripped. Are *you* okay?' she asked, extending a hand, but then retracting it, thinking it would probably be a good idea to maintain some distance.

'All good.' He rolled to his feet with the ease of a man who sometimes hung off helicopters.

She hopped on one foot back to the tree, wiggled her errant shoe free, and slid it back on.

Swatting at his clothes to dislodge bits of forest, he shook his head and said, 'Do you do anything like normal people?'

'What do you mean? I am normal people. *Person.* I'm a normal *person.*'

He arched an eyebrow, as though she'd just made his point. 'Since I've met you, I've had Thumb Wars, a panic attack, and tumbling in the woods. What next, I wonder.' She didn't like the laughter glinting in his eyes.

Nor did she like the casual mention of her panic attacks. The fact that he'd helped her through her episode at the convention didn't give him carte blanche to bring it up whenever he wanted.

She crossed her arms. 'Sorry, but I'd appreciate it if you didn't tell anybody about the awards night.'

'Don't worry. I wouldn't.'

'Did you tell Krish?'

'No, of course not. Did you get help by the way?' he asked, his voice turning serious.

'Yes, I kissed a magic frog and suddenly all of my problems disappeared. It was amazing.' Whoops! Her inner Claudia sometimes came out of nowhere. This man seemed to have that effect on her.

He raised an eyebrow at her.

'Sorry. Yes, I talked to someone. Thank you.' She didn't mention it had been her cleaner. And she wasn't sure why she'd thanked him.

'Good.'

With an impressively loud climax, the couple finished their auditory show.

Not wanting Connor to think she'd been spying on them for her own pleasure, she said, 'I got lost and I thought I'd just wait for them to finish and ask them to show me the way back. You know, safety in numbers.'

'Ah, yes. It can get a bit confusing back here, what with the signs that say "Chateau".' He pointed towards a sign stuck into the ground that she'd missed, probably because it was half covered by moss. Well, at least a quarter covered. A red arrow pointed left. How did she miss that? Now he thought she was an idiot. Again.

'I'm heading back if you want to come along,' Connor said, settling his bag onto his shoulders.

She lifted her foot and hesitated. Old Stella would have said yes and gratefully followed him out of the woods like a human-sized breadcrumb. But New Stella was her own woman. New Stella could save herself. New Stella was going to ignore the dirty thoughts she'd had moments earlier.

'I'm fine,' she said. 'You go ahead. I just want to...' She cast around for an excuse to stay, but nothing came to mind. Listen out for more sex? Go mushroom picking? Something she used to do by herself on camping holidays popped into her head. '...build a fairy house.'

That look again, like she was a puzzle with a piece missing. 'A fairy house?'

'Yup. Out of moss and twigs and leaves. It's very relaxing.' *Shut up, Stella.*

He studied her for a long moment and then crossed his arms, tilting his head to the side. 'I applaud your independence, but it would be irresponsible of me to leave you out here, lost and on your own in a forest, with the light disappearing, knowing that you suffer from panic attacks. Call me old-fashioned, but...'

She grunted. He had a point.

'So shall we...?'

'Fine,' she said, hating that he was right. She motioned for him to start walking. With a smug grin, Connor set off in front of her. They walked in companionable silence and she tried not to notice how good his bum looked in a pair of jeans. She contemplated whether this had been more or less embarrassing than their last two encounters. Why couldn't she act like a normal person around him? He wasn't wrong about that either.

Twisting his head over his shoulder, he said, 'You know, I looked over the portfolio images you sent through. You have a good eye. You see light and make use of it in a way that's rare in newcomers.'

Almost stumbling on a root, Stella swelled with pride, but then tamped it down again. She had literally paid him to build up her confidence. Ergo, it didn't mean anything.

All the delegates had been asked to send in ten images that best represented their work, so Connor could assess their level. She chose some practice photos that she'd shot with a bride and groom, as well as some of—

'The chickens...' he said, stopping to let her catch up.

Stella groaned as she drew abreast of him and they continued to stroll, side by side. 'I know. They aren't great.'

'I disagree. I thought they were really *hen*-some. Dare I say even—'

'Don't do it.'

'—*egg*celent.'

'You went there. So *fowl*.' Her mouth widened in a self-congratula-

76

tory grin and he chuckled, the deep, warm sound causing her to shiver.

'Sorry, I couldn't resist,' he said. She flicked her eyes towards him and found he was already looking at her. His voice turned serious. 'I thought you did a good job. Animals can be a handful and you executed it well. You captured something in them... they each had *personalities*.'

Turning his words over in her mind, she searched for any sarcasm, but didn't find any. 'Well...thank you,' she said, allowing herself a small smile.

'Have you studied photography before?'

'Just at A-levels. I wanted to pursue it at Uni, but my father convinced me not to.' She deepened her voice. *'You'll never make any money at that, Stella girl. Do something practical, like economics.'* She laughed.

When Connor didn't join in, Stella glanced over and saw that his brow had drawn down, his jaw tight.

'What's wrong?' Had she said something wrong? She replayed their conversation in her head.

'He should have encouraged you. Anyone with eyes could see you've got talent.'

Connor Knight thought she had talent? Her heart flipped. She could float the rest of the way back to the chateau. Even so, she managed to avoid embarrassing herself and asked, 'How about your father? Was he supportive?'

He huffed. 'In a way. He didn't mind what I got up to, as long as I stayed out of jail and didn't get anyone pregnant.'

'Ah.' That explained a lot.

Turning the conversation back to her, he asked, 'What about your mother? Did she support you?'

'Not really. My mother is...complicated.' Stella remembered a scene, after she and Tristan had failed to place at a dance competition. During the car ride home, Angela said, *'I gave up my dreams for you, Stella'*—implying that quitting dancing, getting married, and having a baby had somehow been a choice Stella made for her. A classic case of the mother pushing her desires onto her daughter. And then when Stella and Tristan *did* finally win, instead of being happy, Angela got worse. She pushed harder, picked at Stella constantly with her tiny criticisms and endless proverbs to guide her behaviour. So Stella quit. Just walked away. It was the first time she truly defied her mother's wishes.

But she didn't want to go into that with Connor Knight.

'Both my parents are very... strong-willed. It was like growing up between two bricks. My dad was CEO of his own company and ran his family like a corporation. As his only child, I was expected to perform well. Hit targets. Be the best. Although I usually missed the mark. I bounced between trying to please either my father or my mother at any given time. If I could do both, that was the sweet spot—although that was rare.'

Stella stopped herself and pursed her lips, realising that she had completely overshared with a man she barely knew. Something about the security of his solid presence made her chatty.

Connor regarded her, forehead furrowed. 'That must have been hard.' They walked a few moments in silence before he added, 'The only person you need to please in life is yourself. That's my belief, anyway.'

She'd love to see him withstand the double onslaught of Angela and Bill Price. 'Don't you like to make other people happy?'

He shrugged. 'If you live your life trying to make other people happy, you'll fail.'

For some reason, she felt like he was attacking her personally. She knew she was a people pleaser—Claudia reminded her of it often enough— but she also knew she didn't want to ignore the needs of others. It seemed selfish. 'You don't have to do it *all the time*. But, you know...*once in a while* won't kill you. You can't go through life not caring—'

'I care plenty. What I said is that I don't worry about pleasing others. There's a difference.'

They entered the cherry blossom courtyard and she opened her mouth to reply, but Krish was striding towards them. 'Hey, Boss! Hey, Stella.' Even though they'd been doing nothing wrong, Stella blushed. To Connor, he said, 'The chef wants to go over the menu for the week. Are you free?'

'Coming now.' Before he hurried off, he turned to her and pretended to tip his imaginary hat. 'Price. Pleasure as always.'

She bit her tongue.

As he disappeared through the arch with Krish, Stella kicked a pile of blossoms on the ground. What an infuriating man. In one breath, he made her feel ecstatic—Connor Knight thought she had talent!— and then in the next, he criticised her.

Nice. Only five more days with the man.

Footsteps sounded behind her. 'Did you enjoy the show?' The couple from the pond strolled past and the woman snickered, hips swaying. She peered over her shoulder at Stella like they'd both been vying for the captain of the rugby team and Stella had lost. *Ha!* As though she would be interested in Lanky Spanky, as she'd christened him, due to his sexual proclivities and tall, slim build.

Even so, she grimaced with embarrassment. Great way to start the week.

7

STELLA TOOK A HURRIED SHOWER.

In front of the bathroom mirror, she flicked mascara onto her lashes, worrying about the roomful of strangers downstairs. She hated that feeling when she first walked into a crowd of people she didn't know. It always took her a little while to settle, figure out how she fit in the group. Would people think she was the annoying one? Every group had one of those. Who would be the star? The know-it-all? The arse-kisser? She preferred to be The One Everybody Liked.

According to the antique clock on the mantelpiece, it was 7:00 on the dot when Stella rushed into the ornate drawing room, hoping she wasn't the last to arrive. She searched for faces she knew: Alan, Krish, the bonking couple. Connor was in the far corner conversing with a man dressed head-to-toe in athletic gear. He glanced up when she came in. Their eyes met and held for a handful of heartbeats before he tipped his chin in silent greeting, returning his attention to the athlete. Her belly did an unwanted flip and she reminded herself that New Stella didn't make eyes at men with girlfriends. It would help if he didn't clean up so well, wearing a pair of black slim-fitting trousers and a grey V-neck jumper that brought out his eyes.

A circle of ten plush armchairs had been set up in the centre of the room, although only a few were occupied. An undulating wave of small talk shifted through the air. Stella hoped to slip in quietly, perhaps find Alan and stand next to him until she could meet some of the others.

'That's her! That's the woman who gave me her seat,' cried the Welsh pixie. The entire room hushed as she sprang out of her chair and made straight for Stella, taking her by the hand and pulling her towards the circle with a surprising amount of force for her height. Stella's cheeks burned. 'Heavenly Anthony Hopkins, I was just talking about you. Were your ears ringing?' Raising her voice again, the woman addressed the room, 'Can you believe it? I wouldn't be here if it weren't for her.'

Stella could feel everyone's eyes, especially Connor's. She dared to look his way and found him standing with arms crossed, an inscrutable look on his face. She wished she could disappear through a crack in the floorboards.

'Come, sit next to me.' The woman pulled her into a chair. 'I'm Liliwen.'

'Stella Price.' She shook the woman's hand. To her relief, the others quickly lost interest and the buzz of conversation returned.

'I did try and find you after I won. But you weren't anywhere. If I'd've known you wanted to come, I would've tried harder.' Liliwen swatted the air. 'Never mind, you managed to get a spot all right.'

Behind a smiling mask, Stella thought about the Thumb War and her two maxed out credit cards. 'Perhaps it's fate we're both here.'

'I love a course, I do. Husband thinks I'm addicted to them. I did a flower arranging one in Amsterdam. That was lush. And pasta making in Tuscany. And now this! I have this idea I could photograph anniversaries and weddings for the Saga set.' She laughed, an engaging tinkling sound that made Stella laugh, too. This woman was too cute for Stella to hold a grudge.

A young man in black entered the room, carrying a tray of fizzing champagne flutes. The man, who couldn't be older than 18, offered Stella a glass. As she grasped the stem, he said something in French to her and winked. She didn't understand him, but she understood flirting. Stella realised it was the first real French she'd heard since she'd arrived. She loved the sound. A man who could speak French...*très sexy.*

'*Iechyd da!*' Liliwen said in Welsh, clinking her glass against Stella's. Taking a sip, she continued, 'I wonder what it would be like to screw a French man. Always wanted to, but never got round to it. Shame.'

Almost choking, Stella wiped a dribble of champagne from her lips. Did almost sixty-year-olds still think about sex?

Apparently so. 'I mean, they have a completely different attitude to it here, don't they? Not as uptight as the British. Anyway.' Liliwen slung the rest of her drink down her throat.

Regaining her composure, Stella said, 'I haven't tried it myself, but my friend said it was the best sex of her life.' Claudia had been so broken up when her Parisian returned home after one semester. *Quelle dommage.*

With a suggestive wink, Liliwen pointed her chin towards the Frenchman. 'Well, this could be your chance. Alas, I'm an old married woman. Too late for me.'

Shyly, Stella confessed, 'I'm on a strict diet of no men at the moment.'

'Ah, love, don't make the same mistake I did. Wish I'd had a lot more sex before saying *I do*. The wisdom of age...'

Stella had to admit this made a nice change to discussing Nikon versus Canon upon meeting a fellow photographer.

'Shall we get started?' Connor moved into the circle of chairs. Within moments, everyone had found a seat.

Stella admired how he commanded attention. Her heart began beating faster. She could see him deciding where to sit, as all the seats were occupied. His eyes met hers and he did that half-smirk thing she found both sexy and exasperating.

'May I?' he asked, gesturing towards the wide arm of her red velvet chair.

'Be my guest,' she said, although what she meant was no. She squashed herself as far to the right of her chair as she could to put space between them. Finishing her drink, she wondered how to get another. At just that moment, Krish reached over her shoulder to refill her glass before doing the same for Liliwen. Stella loved Krish.

'Hello. I'm Connor Knight.' A few people clapped and whooped, but he motioned for them to stop. 'No need for that. It's me who should be applauding you for taking this step. I know this is a big investment, but let me assure you: I'm worth every penny.'

Stella bit her tongue so she wouldn't roll her eyes.

'Just kidding,' he continued. 'With the greatest humility, thank *you* for choosing me as your teacher.' He put his hands together and bowed his head.

Watching him, Stella got the distinct impression that she knew two Connors: the teacher who performed for his fans and the annoyingly cocksure man whom she regularly embarrassed herself in front of. When he stood before a crowd, he was a sight to behold: confident, experienced, totally in control of the room. She could be his student. That was easy: listen, learn, absorb.

It was the other Connor that made her nervous. The one who made her pulse speed up. If she was going to survive this week, avoiding that second one would be a necessity.

'You're the best, C Dawg!' shouted an American from the other side of the room.

Acknowledging the compliment with a wave, Connor continued, 'I always start the first session with introductions, so we know who's in the room. If you could just say your name, where you're from, how long you've been photographing weddings, and one thing about you that's unique. You already know who I am, so...' Stella held her breath. Her mind raced for something to say if he chose her first, but all she could think was, *Don't pick me. Don't pick me.*

Connor turned left, towards Alan, and Stella exhaled. She hated being first at these group icebreaker games. They represented a delicate tightrope, each player keen to reveal something that made him sound interesting without being boastful, fascinating without seeming nerdy, entertaining without trying too hard. What could she say?

She ran her finger over her chin as though, if she rubbed hard enough, a genie might appear and give her the answer. She barely listened as Alan talked about his signed collection of Terry Pratchett novels.

'My name's Gunner Hurst. From the New Forest,' began the dark-haired man next to Alan with the penchant for athletic wear. 'I shoot fifty weddings a year...'

Stella's attention phased out as he went into detail about some of his favourite venues. She flicked through her life, remembering and discarding past achievements. Nobody wanted to hear about winning the school spelling competition in year five.

As Gunner wrapped up with his ability to play guitar left-handed, Stella settled, as usual, on her dancing days. Winning the Latin title was big, but she always used that one in these situations. Was that the only noteworthy thing she'd done in her life? There must be something else.

The bonking couple, real names Lisa and Mark Young, came next. From a quick glance, Stella saw that his eyes were too close and he had an unattractive, arrogant curl to his lips—as though he thought he was more talented than everyone else in the room. *He'll be either the Know-It-All or the Arse Kisser*, she thought.

She found it difficult to look at them after listening to their performance that afternoon. It made her remember lying on top of Connor. She finished her champagne and caught Krish's eye, jiggling her glass with a pleading smile. He came over, poured more luscious bubbles into her flute and even left her the rest of the bottle. She put it on the floor, next to her feet.

Mark Young, aka Lanky Spanky, came from Oxford and had been shooting weddings for ten years already. His wife, Lisa, became a photographer a couple years ago. He mentioned that he'd won some awards and they were really there to help Lisa learn how to shoot. By the time he finished, Stella had discounted Arse Kisser and settled on

Know-It-All. They finished with a lengthy description of their 'mind-blowing' festival-themed wedding at Glastonbury Tor. Stella looked over at Liliwen who rolled her eyes and pretended to smoke a joint behind her champagne flute. Stella already loved her.

The American was up next. 'My friends call me Flash—handy, being a photographer and everything.' He laughed, an echoing hearty laugh that made Stella like him instantly. 'I'm from Philly, but I came over for the BAPP convention and decided to join the course. France is awesome so far. I even tried frogs' legs. Did you know it's an actual thing?' Stella giggled, his earnestness endearing. 'Anyways, I'm twenty-seven, and I've been a photographer for three years. I used to shoot concerts and stuff, but the money wasn't so good. So I'm expanding into weddings because I hear that's where they flash the cash. Can't wait to learn from the master.' He made a little bowing motion towards Connor. 'Oh, my interesting fact—Denzel Washington is my distant cousin. And I'm single, ladies.' He winked at Liliwen and she flapped her hand towards him.

Next to Flash, Karen, a recent divorcee from Oxfordshire, talked about her two children currently back home with her mother. She'd been a chef, but had given it up for photography so she could work from home while expressing her creativity. In the middle of her introduction, her phone rang. She ran off to take the call.

Stella counted only three more people. *Shit.* She still didn't know what she was going to say. Her heart beat so loud in her ears that she thought everyone could probably hear it, especially Connor whose presence burned next to her as he readjusted his seat.

A pretty blue-eyed girl with perfectly straight blonde hair went next. 'Um. Hi. I'm Hannah.' Stella missed the rest, partly because the girl spoke so softly and partly because Stella was in a spiral of indecision.

She flipped through a few more possible fun facts. She was scared of dogs? No. Not really unique. She once played Orphan No. 3 in an amateur production of *Annie*? So what? Or she went to primary school with Catherine Zeta Jones's cousin's daughter? No. No. No.

Not unique. Not impressive. Maybe she should just go with the dance championship.

Then suddenly, she had it. Something memorable, funny, and also mildly impressive that didn't involve dancing or tenuous celebrity connections.

Her fingers tapped her knees in anticipation. Now that she had her fact, she wanted the whole experience to be over. She finished another glass of champagne and refilled Liliwen's, then her own. Her head floated.

Jared, an ex-actor-turned-photographer from London, told them about the five-star reviews for his turn as Cinderella's evil step-sister in the *Chichester Observer*. Liliwen revealed that she came from Cowbridge, not far from where Stella's parents lived. She'd been the runner up for Miss Wales in 1972.

All eyes gravitated towards Stella as her turn came around and Connor shifted in his seat to look at her.

'Hi! I'm Stella Price! Um. So, I live in London. Putney, to be exact. I used to be a pharmaceutical copywriter, but, um, I'm retraining as a photographer. No weddings under my belt yet, so I'm a completely blank slate but looking forward to becoming a better shooter under Connor's, um...under his, um. Under him.' Bad choice of words. She couldn't get the image of being under Connor out of her brain. He stuck his tongue into his cheek and his eyes twinkled in a way that made her uneasy. Time to get this over with, fast. 'And as far as my unique fact goes, I am singlehandedly responsible for giving more middle-aged men erections across Europe than probably any other woman.'

The tick of the clock became the only noise in the room.

Her introduction out of the way, Stella smiled with relief, while everyone else blinked at her collectively. The American's eyes resembled baseballs. The divorcee, who had returned from her phone call just in time, covered her mouth with her hand. Lisa Young was nodding with grudging approval.

Stella replayed the introduction in her head. What did she say?

She'd told them she was a copywriter and then made a joke about one of her ad campaigns. They should be laughing! Maybe they didn't know what a copywriter was.

Or maybe she hadn't made it clear enough. Did they all think she had just confessed to being a continental hooker?

She had to clear this up. 'Because I was in advertising! I wrote the campaign for *Bonera*™ – the erectile dysfunction drug!' She scrambled for more words. 'You won't have seen the advert. It was only in the medical press. But, um, anyway...'

Finally the laughter came.

'I thought...' Gunner tried to say, 'I thought you were going to say you were a – a – a porn star!'

'Totally!' added Flash. 'I was like, "Hey, thought I recognised you." But only for a second. I don't actually recognise you.'

Next to her, Connor's body vibrated with mirth. He clapped her on the back and said, 'Way to go, Mademoiselle Chicken.' Back to that again. Wiping tears from his eyes, he said, 'I think Price wins that round, with a close runner-up to Miss Wales and Denzel Washington's cousin.'

Liliwen joked, 'Ah, well! Always second place, me.'

As the students broke into animated conversation again, Stella slumped backwards, wishing she could disappear into the upholstery. She looked at her full glass of champagne, but perhaps she had drunk enough. She put it on the floor. Across the room, Krish caught her eye and gave her an enthusiastic thumbs up. She slapped her hands over her face, shaking her head: *Stella Price has done it again.* Krish shrugged and smiled.

The chic French man from earlier re-entered the room, beckoning to Connor. The man began to speak rapidly. Stella could only pick up a word here and there, despite her ear for romantic languages.

When he finished, without missing a beat, Connor responded. *In fluent unaccented French.*

Forgetting herself, Stella's jaw dropped open.

Liliwen said, 'Of course, he speaks bloody French. Do you think he also fosters kittens or plays football with orphans in his spare time?'

Snapping out of it, Stella laughed. 'I'm sure he's too busy dating models and cavorting around the world.'

'If I were twenty years younger. Or even just ten...' Liliwen sighed.

'Dinner's ready,' Connor announced, waving them toward the dining room.

Liliwen threaded her arm through Stella's and said, 'Shall we, *cariad*?'

Stella covered her new friend's hand with her own, vowing to sit far, far away from Connor Knight at the table.

8

TWO DAYS INTO THE COURSE, Stella couldn't be happier. Her skills were improving with every snap. Each day, a pair of models would appear after breakfast, resplendent in their wedding clothes, dressed to perfection by the styling team. Day two's 'bride' had an obvious crush on Connor and laughed too loudly every time he gave her instruction, flirting with him in sensuous French. Stella pretended to find it funny when Liliwen wagered, 'Five pounds says she stays the night.'

By the end of the second full day on the course, Stella had settled into a flow and developed a rapport with most of the other delegates. Jared, the ex-actor, always had something funny to say and was a terrible gossip. The double act of Gunner and Flash provided constant entertainment with their good-natured banter, the two having bonded instantly over their shared worship of Connor. They also flirted with everyone, male and female.

'How's our sexy Welsh cougar this morning?' Flash asked Liliwen at breakfast.

'Is that a 70-200 mil lens on your camera or are you happy to see me?' said Gunner to an oblivious Alan.

Both made overtures towards Stella on the first night, but she made it clear that she wasn't interested in anything past flirtation.

'I've revirginated after finding salvation in Jesus Christ,' she told them, which they thankfully didn't take as a challenge.

They refocussed their efforts on Hannah. Understanding that she suffered from severe shyness in social situations, Stella included Hannah in conversations as much as she could, trying to draw the quiet girl out of her shell. It must have taken Hannah a lot of courage to come on this course. But even with Stella's efforts to include her, Hannah rarely had anything to say.

Karen, the divorcee, seemed nice enough, although it was hard to know because she was always on the phone with her mother. Stella worried that Karen wouldn't learn anything if she kept disappearing to hear about 'Stu-boo' and 'Jonny Bear'.

The only people Stella hadn't befriended were the Youngs. Lanky Spanky's high opinion of himself manifested in his need to show off at every opportunity. Whenever Connor demonstrated a new skill, Lanky Spanky would challenge him in some way, either by questioning his lens choice or offering up contrary thoughts on the pose. The rest of the group, save Lisa, exchanged eye rolls and yawns every time Lanky Spanky opened his mouth. Stella admired Connor's patience when dealing with the Know-It-All, letting him speak and then calmly explaining why he was wrong.

Worse, the Youngs persisted in waking Stella up at 6AM with their headboard-banging, vocal sex. Just her luck they'd got the room next to hers. The way Lisa Young looked at Stella over breakfast, she had the feeling that Lisa enjoyed seeing the darkening circles underneath her neighbour's eyes.

If there was one shining result of the course so far, it had to be Stella's growing fondness for Liliwen. In a short time, they'd become close, to the point where Gunner started calling them Thelma and Louise. When the group broke into pairs for assignments, the two women stuck together most of the time, which is how Stella discovered that Liliwen, bless her, was a Very Bad Photographer. If she could learn to stop cutting her subjects off at the knees, then she'd have done well from the course. Stella wondered if Connor would include Liliwen's Before and After photos at the next convention.

Stella's respect for Connor as a teacher had grown considerably since their first session. He had an innate eye for light and posing, but the fact that he could also explain the concepts to others in a way they'd understand elevated his talent to genius. She could see why he had a worldwide following and people paid him upwards of £50,000 to photograph their weddings. He had a gift.

On their daily one-to-one image reviews, Connor complimented Stella on her composition, noting that she had a natural instinct for posing women. Stella would be lying if she said his words didn't make her feel a warm glow inside. But a completely professional warm glow. Not any other kind.

So far, she had managed to avoid encounters with the other side of Connor, the one that made her toes curl with naughty thoughts. Thanks to the other keen classmates, she didn't have to try too hard. At meals, Gunner and Flash always claimed the seats next to Connor, eager to hear anything their hero had to say. Lanky Spanky also liked sitting nearby, mainly to goad Connor with questions: what did he think of *PhotoLife's* recent 'Top Ten Wedding Photographers in the World' article? Did he agree that Blake Romero from the US deserved the number one spot?

Stella stayed out of it, eating at the far end of the table with Liliwen and Jared.

Her plan was working perfectly.

Until the third night.

As they all sat down, Connor walked up, pulled out the chair to her left and asked, 'Is anyone sitting here?'

Stella gracefully replied, 'Please, sit down.' *Oh, shit.*

She had no choice but to be civilised about it. She managed to keep things light all through the starter, letting Liliwen on Connor's other side do most of the talking. Thinking it was safe territory, she encouraged Liliwen to tell Connor the story of how she'd met her husband. It should take them at least through the main course. 'It's so romantic,' Stella said. 'You have to hear this.'

Liliwen launched into the tale. 'Well, I first noticed him in maths class, when the teacher made a terrible joke about parallel lines and we were the only two who laughed.' She then told the joke and it really wasn't funny. 'We started dating soon after, but then he went to *find himself* in his gap year. We both knew he wanted to screw his way across the planet, so I said good riddance. We lost touch; I met someone else. A trainee doctor, no less. My parents were gagging for him. He proposed, and I said yes. He seemed a nice enough fellow and treated me well, so...' She stopped and took a long drink of wine and a bite of chicken. 'Anyway, a few weeks before the wedding, Gareth arrives home like some returning hero. Confesses he still loves me but too little too late, I said. He'd probably contracted some venereal disease in Thailand and I wanted nothing to do with him. Besides, I had a dress bought and a wedding paid for. But you know what they say: *wrth gicio a brathu mae cariad yn magu*.'

They waited for Liliwen to translate. She didn't. 'On the Big Day, Gareth turned up outside the church, went down on one knee as I was climbing out of the car and made this whole speech about how he couldn't live without me and he'd give me the life I deserved if only I'd let him. I'd just seen *The Graduate* and it all seemed very romantic and I said, fuck it! Why not? I left my fiancé at the altar, much to everyone's dismay, but especially my parents, who really enjoyed bragging about their doctor son-in-law. Well, the long and short of it is: Gareth and I've been married over thirty years now. And to prove my parents wrong, he used his smooth-talking ways to start a recruitment business, which I helped him run. Now it's sold, we're semi-retired, and I entertain myself by trying out different hobbies.'

Stella sighed. It really was the perfect story. That's when Connor dropped his opinion on marriage:

'Marriage is obsolete.'

She almost choked on her disbelief. 'But you're a wedding photographer,' she said.

Connor shrugged. 'I photograph a lot of football players as well. Doesn't mean I want to be one.'

'Oh, Saint Dylan Thomas,' said Liliwen. 'Here we go.'

'You're obviously the exception to the rule,' he said, bowing his head towards her.

Stella cringed, but tried to keep her tone relaxed. 'What does that even mean? My parents have been married for almost forty years. So that's two exceptions.'

'I'm sure there are lots of exceptions. But in my experience, marriage is over-rated.'

'How so?' She narrowed her eyes at him, calmly stabbing a piece of meat with her fork.

'Fact: monogamy and marriage were constructs created by the Catholic church to control society in the eighth century, give or take. Today, there is no good reason for a couple to get married, except maybe a few minor tax breaks. Especially for the man. All that piece of paper does is make it more difficult when the marriage eventually falls apart.'

Stella couldn't find words.

'Another fact: half of the weddings I've photographed have ended in divorce, which mirrors national statistics on divorce rates. I mean, some of them even had me photograph their *second* weddings, which are even *more likely* to end in divorce. And then the man goes to court —loses his kids, loses half his money. Just loses, full stop. I've seen it happen to friends of mine. Not for me, thanks.' He sat back and took a triumphant sip of his wine, as though his point had been well and truly made. Conversation closed.

Recovering her power of speech, Stella asked, 'Are your parents divorced?'

'They aren't together,' he said without explanation, the muscles around his eyes going tight. He poured more wine into his companions' glasses.

She frowned and shrugged. 'It just seems like you have a very narrow view. And why do you assume it's only the man who loses?

Plenty of women make more than their husbands. And anyway, it's not just about money.' She shoved the carrots around her plate before spiking one.

'Just wait until you've been in the business a while. You'll be cynical too.'

'Sorry to disagree with you, but I won't.'

'Okay.' He smiled. 'You won't.'

She glared at the mischievous twinkle in his grey eyes. 'Now you're just being condescending.'

'Me? Never,' he said, clapping his hand to his heart.

Deciding to try a different tack, she said, 'Let's make a wild assumption that you met the love of your life.' He raised a single eyebrow at her and his eyes roamed lazily up and down her face. Her heart stuttered. 'What is more romantic than you getting up in front of all the people who mean something to you to declare your love for each other and your intention to share your lives. It's beautiful.'

He shook his head and his lips lifted in that arrogant half-smile. 'There's no such thing as The One. Just The One For Now.' Having finished his meal, he wiped his mouth on a napkin and leaned back in his chair, resting his wine glass on his stomach. 'Sometimes it works. Sometimes not.'

She could feel the back of her neck itching with irritation. His calm really irked her, especially when she wanted to raise her voice at the confrontation, a tendency she shared with her mother. Leaning in with a rigid smile, she struggled to keep her voice even as she said, 'Maybe you just don't like being vulnerable.'

'Maybe.'

'That's an awfully sad way to live, don't you think?'

'Don't worry about me. I have plenty of love in my life.'

'There's a difference between sex and love,' she mumbled into her napkin before throwing it onto the table.

Liliwen pushed her chair back. 'I'm going to the toilet before you both start throwing food.'

Connor laughed. 'Who said anything about sex?' A wolfish grin spread across his smug face. 'I meant friends, family...'

'That's not the same thing.' For a moment, she wondered who she was. She never normally argued like this with anybody. Old Stella would have just pretended to agree with him and seethed inside. But New Stella seemed to be more sparky, standing up for her beliefs. Connor was obviously having a positive effect on her. The realisation made her uncomfortable.

He sat back in his chair and tilted his head, studying her, as though aware that he was making her behave out of character and liked it. 'I had you pegged all wrong, Price. With the way you forced your way onto this course and told us all about your penchant for erections, I took you for the strong modern woman type. Someone with opinions, who wouldn't subscribe to all the antiquated traditions of marriage. A father to give you away. A white dress to represent virginity...'

Her cheeks flamed as she said, 'Who says I want my father to give me away? Or to wear white?' She wanted both those things. 'Or that I'm a virgin?' Two could play at this game. She impaled him on the end of a hard stare. The seconds ticked by.

He grinned at her. She was suddenly aware that his knee was resting against hers under the table, soft heat coming off his leg. She moved away. 'Maybe...maybe my dream is to get married in a polka dot dress in front of Richard E. Grant doing *Withnail & I* impressions.'

'Well, that conjures quite the picture.'

She could feel her Italian side coming out as her hands leapt into the air to emphasise her words. 'My point is that what you've mentioned isn't marriage. It's just the wedding. The *relationship* is the marriage: the decision to work on your commitment to one person throughout your life—it isn't easy.'

'Speaking from experience?'

She bristled, a picture of Nathan and his wife fleeting through her thoughts. She pushed it away. 'Yes actually—first-hand experience of watching my parents do it. And maybe half your couples have divorced, but at least they tried. It's easy to sit here and criticise when you're too afraid to get in the ring.'

'Who says I'm afraid?' His eyes held a challenge that she didn't want to acknowledge.

'What did I miss?' Liliwen asked as she sat back down in her chair. 'Have you two put the world to rights yet?'

'I think we've agreed to disagree,' Connor said, relaxing in his chair, all nonchalance.

Stella emitted a snort. 'I have *not* agreed to disagree. You're a hypocrite!' She poked him in the chest.

'How so?' he asked, looking down with unconcealed amusement at the spot where her finger had bounced off his button.

She thought back to the marketing seminar he'd delivered to them that afternoon. 'How can you go to these weddings and say all those things to them about how it's their "special day", and this album is their "first family heirloom"'— she flinched as she realised she was carving quotes in the air with her fingers— 'when in your head, you're making bets on when they'll break up?'

His eyes narrowed, suddenly unsmiling. 'That's not fair. I take my work very seriously and I am happy for them. Truly.'

'How can you say that? You're just some sort of...of Love Scrooge!'

He paused a moment, letting her words float on the air. And then he barked with laughter. 'Hah! Love Scrooge! I like it. You have such a way with words, Price.' He toasted her with his glass.

Stella could feel her face burning. This wasn't funny! She opened her mouth to continue her tirade, but Liliwen jumped in. 'Hey ho! I think it's time to separate you two before somebody says something regrettable. Come with me, lovely.' She pulled Stella up by her arm. As Liliwen led her away, Stella noticed that the entire room was silent and all eyes were on her. What had she just done? Shame flooded through her.

'Love Scrooge. Can I put that on my business card?' Connor called after, chuckling.

In that moment, she really disliked him.

'Are you okay?' Liliwen asked in the foyer.

'I don't know why I let him get to me.'

'I can't imagine,' Liliwen said, her tone implying that she imagined quite a lot.

'What? No, it's nothing like that. I'm not attracted to him.' *Liar.* She swallowed. 'Don't you think it's hypocritical that he makes money out of love, but thinks so little of it?'

'Honestly? No. Doesn't bother me, really.'

'Why not?' Stella asked, incredulous. That just increased her embarrassment. Maybe she'd been misguided on top of being vocal.

New Stella was getting this all wrong. New Stella wanted to go to bed.

Liliwen offered a kind smile. 'Life is full of contradictions, love. The cleaner whose house is a mess. The lawyer who breaks the law. The wedding photographer who doesn't believe in love...'

'I suppose.'

'Instead of getting angry, you should probably give him the benefit of the doubt. He must have reasons. If there's one thing I've learnt it's that we all have our own story... I'm sure you have yours.'

Indeed, she did.

Liliwen took Stella's hand. 'You know what you need? A night of charades. Come on.'

Stella pulled back. 'I think I'm going to turn in early. I... haven't been sleeping very well.' The idea of spending the night listening to Karen talk about her kids or watching Gunner and Flash competing to see who could get into Hannah's pants first made her feel exhausted. And she most definitely didn't want to talk to Connor Knight.

Her new friend looked at her with deep concern. 'You sure, love?'

Stella nodded, keen to get to her bedroom and sort out her feelings alone.

. . .

UPSTAIRS, Stella slammed the door too hard and immediately apologised to it. She climbed onto the creaky bed and bounced on it a couple times. Now, in the quiet, alone, she realised that she didn't want to be in her room at all. The walls seemed closer than they had earlier. Standing, she threw open the window and leaned out, taking a deep breath. The earthy smells of the forest calmed her nerves as she inhaled through her nose and exhaled through her mouth. Sounds of merriment floated up to her through the fragrant spring air, and she regretted having excused herself.

'What is *wrong* with me?' she said out loud.

Connor Knight. Her conversation with him had left her feeling irrational and irritated. Why was she letting it get to her? Who cared if he didn't want to get married? What was it to her? He was just another commitment-phobe, just like all the others before him.

Except…he had also been kind to her on more than one occasion. The panic attack, the woods…

She bit her lip. Maybe there were reasons closer to her heart for despairing that Connor seemed hell-bent on being single. She dismissed that thought.

In some ways, he reminded her of Nathan. Handsome, egotistical, charming… a womaniser. However, while those traits defined Nathan, Connor was also funny and sensitive. Creating photographs like his required at least some level of emotional intelligence, a quality that, in hindsight, Nathan lacked completely.

How could she have missed it? She remembered how Nathan used to phone her on weekends for a quick booty call, telling his wife he was meeting a friend at the tennis club or running errands. And she, being an idiot and so eager to please, spent most of her weekends waiting in case he wanted to come over. All she needed from him were a few words of praise—'*You're so special, Stella*', '*You're so talented, Stella*' —and she neglected her friends and her own mental health. She put her life on hold and was stupid enough to believe him when he said he would leave his wife for her, even as she pretended she didn't care. It was obvious now that he'd been using her. Shame rose inside, as it always did when she thought about that period in her life.

Then it hit her, realisation dawning as unhappy memories of Nathan trampled through her head. She wasn't mad at Connor Knight. She was mad at herself.

What kind of hypocrite was she to argue for marriage? She'd *known* Nathan was married when they started the affair. Jeanette wasn't perfect, but she was the one with a ring on her finger. Stella *deserved* the panic attacks. She deserved everything that had happened to her since she had made the decision to be Nathan's bit on the side. Who was she to dream about a happily ever after? Her mother had raised her better. Her mother...she'd have a fit if she ever found out what Stella had done.

In autopilot, she picked up her phone and dialled Claudia. She answered on the sixth ring.

'Stella! *Stop it! Shhh!* What's up? How's France?'

'Um...is now a good time to chat?'

'Yeah, great. Not doing anything.'

'*Or anyone,*' rumbled a deep voice in the background.

Stella narrowed her eyes. 'Are you sure?'

'Yup! Just me. Watching TV. Some ridiculous cop drama. Tell me, are there any hot men there, aside from Connor, of course?' Stella heard what sounded like a spanking noise.

Stella ignored the question. 'Am I a bad person?'

'Whoa! That came out of left field. Why would you even ask? You're one of the best people I know. On a scale of one to ten, you are an *eleven.*'

Sighing, Stella said, 'I'm in a guilt spiral.'

'You have to stop doing this to yourself. He was a bad man.'

'I know that. I'm feeling guilty about *her.*'

'Listen, you know you weren't the first for him. He had cheating down to a fucking art. She stayed with him for her own reasons. Money. Security. Nice holidays in the Caribbean. Who knows? But she's a grown woman and can make her own choices.'

'I know this all. But I still don't *know it*. You know?'

'I know.'

'I got into an argument with Connor Knight about marriage.'

'Why were you fighting with him about *that*?'

'He was saying he never wants to get married and thinks it's...*obsolete* was his word.'

'Well, marriage *is* pretty stupid. Cursed to fuck one person for the rest of your life? Besides, he's not known for his monogamy.' Claudia yelped and laughed, which seemed like a strange sequitur, but Stella was too tired to make a witty remark right now.

'I don't know why I was fighting for it so hard. You know me. I'd usually just—'

'Sorry, Stell. Um...food delivery. Going to have to stop you there. Have fun. Stop feeling guilty, okay? Bye!'

The call died. *Weird,* she thought. Blowing her breath out in a long, slow exhalation, she laid down on the bed and stared at the canopy.

'Indecent Proposal!' came Liliwen's yell through the open window followed by hysterical laughter. But all Stella could think was *get in the coffin, get in the coffin, get in the coffin* until she finally fell into a troubled sleep.

9

STELLA AWOKE JUST BEFORE SIX, expecting to hear the Youngs at their usual routine. Silence. Closing her eyes, she tried to go back to sleep, but couldn't get comfortable, flipping left then right and tangling the sheets. Memories played, keeping her from slumber, as they had all night.

She imagined what her mother would say in this situation. Something like, *'Se vende i suoi figli per il formaggio, non puo riaverli dopo aver mangiato la pizza,'*— 'If you sell your children for cheese, you can't get them back after you've eaten the pizza.' In other words, what's done is done. No use wishing she hadn't had an affair with Nathan or argued with Connor at dinner.

Tired of trawling the same regrets, she threw the covers off, wincing as her feet connected with the cold tile floor. She stared out the window into the blue light of dawn. She rolled her neck to banish the stiffness, a series of tiny crunching noises accompanying the movement. Her muscles thrummed with nervous energy. She had to get out of this room.

Rifling through her bag, she found her running shoes and Lycra clothes. Her body needed to move, to exorcise some of these demons through exercise. She tiptoed downstairs, trying to be as quiet as possible. She pulled the weighty front door open, millimetre by millimetre, to avoid the groaning creak that it always made. *Greeeeeeeeeek*, it went, getting more high-pitched the wider it got. She squeezed through a gap just big enough to fit her and tugged it closed, causing another echoing noise. It clicked shut.

Outside, she slipped her headphones into her ears and put on her favourite playlist. Only one thing could snap her out of this kind of mood: Dolly Parton.

She hit play. The beginning notes of *'Jolene'* soared and Stella stabbed fast forward. A song about a red-haired, green-eyed temptress was not going to help her right now, despite it being her favourite song. She hadn't been able to listen to it since Nathan. Instead, she advanced to *'Baby I'm Burnin'.*

After stretching, she set off down the drive. The chilly air felt good against her skin, light just beginning to supplant the darkness. A mile down the drive, she reached the stone lions and turned around.

The familiar beats of *'9 to 5'* played, driving her legs to the rhythm. Her love affair with Dolly started long ago, aged eight. On a charity shop LP, Stella studied Dolly's big blonde hair and motherly smile, thinking she looked like a person who accepted everyone, flaws and all. Dolly wouldn't take away Stella's Christmas presents because she failed to win a competition at school. Dolly wouldn't try to control Stella with comments about how many calories that muffin had in it. Dolly would just love her for who she was.

Stella spent all her pocket money on the album—five whole pence. She popped it on her plastic record player and from the first strains of *'Jolene'*, Stella was hooked. She'd prance around the house using a brush as a microphone with socks stuffed into her shirt. As she got older, she learned more about the singer herself and admired Dolly's story of growing up poor in the mountains of Tennessee and then making it big. People underestimated Dolly because of how she looked, but she shut them up.

Dolly was her go-to woman for all emotional trials, good and bad. Losing her favourite toy. Losing her virginity. Losing at the dance finals (and also when they won). Losing her job. Dolly held her hand through it all.

Her feet hit the pavement, timed to the beat. By the time Stella had run the drive three times, the kinks in her thinking had ironed out. Her conclusion was that she needed to apologise to Connor for her over-enthusiastic defence of marriage. Perhaps she had gone a little over the top. The man was entitled to his opinion, after all. Besides, she actually didn't have strong views about the subject, and now it appeared as though getting a ring on her finger was her main goal in life, which it most certainly was not.

Wiping sweat off her forehead, she climbed the chateau steps and twisted the round iron door ring. It wouldn't budge. She twisted harder. No luck.

It was locked.

She jogged to the back of the building, where soft splashes sounded from the pool. Who was crazy enough to get into that freezing water? She hoped she wasn't about to happen upon the Youngs having sex again.

Stepping around the corner, she ground to a halt. The illuminated water glared blue in the half-light. A figure was doing laps. She squinted, tracking his progress. Chestnut hair made darker when wet, stubbled jaw, tall frame...it was Connor. Without thinking, she jumped behind the wall and pressed her back to it. Running her hand over her sweaty hair, she readjusted her ponytail.

Peeking out, she studied his strong arms as they thrust into the water, pulling his body forward, propelled by his powerful legs. Mesmerised, she watched him switch to a flawless butterfly when he reached the far wall, a stroke she had never been able to master.

Connor finished his laps and pulled himself over the side, water sluicing down his body as he stood. He combed his hands through his hair, squeezing out the excess water. His shoulders rippled as he moved. Stella's eyes widened at his abs, stacked like tightly-rolled cigars Photoshopped by Cuban virgins. Naturally, her gaze dipped toward his tight blue Speedos, vacuum-sealed to his hips, leaving nothing to the imagination. She bit her lip. Connor Knight had a tremendous physique.

An ant nibbled on her ankle, snapping her out of her erotic reverie. She slapped the insect away. *Come on, Stella. Get a grip. No time like the present.* She took an edifying breath and stepped out, striding towards Connor.

He paused when he noticed her, his eyes trawling from her lips down to her sweaty sports bra and bare, toned belly in a way that she found both thrilling and alarming. Finishing his unabashed observation of her, he bent over to grab a towel and wiped droplets from his arms, stomach, calves, thighs... *Jesus, have mercy.*

'Morning, Price,' he said.

'Hey.' She grabbed her ponytail in her hands, fiddling with the strands, and hesitated. Maybe she could just say good morning and disappear inside. But that would make her a coward, and New Stella was no coward. Standing up straighter, she said, 'I wanted to say I'm sorry. I mean...for last night.'

'You don't have to apologise.' He rubbed the towel over his face, wrapped the fabric around his waist, and slipped his feet into a pair of well-worn Toms. She could see goose pimples sprouting over his chest in the cold morning air. For a brief moment, she wondered what would happen if she put her warm hand there.

He walked towards the back entrance of the chateau and she followed. She couldn't help noticing the indent of his spine, the perfect groove to trail a finger down his back. She pinched herself on the forearm to stop herself daydreaming. There would be no finger trailing. None.

They passed through the breakfast room, already set with plates and cutlery.

'No, really. I want to,' she said. 'I guess Liliwen's story put me in a certain frame of mind and—'

'You know what? That's very big of you, Price. Apology accepted.' He inspected a bowl of fruit. Grabbing an apple, he took a bite. 'Glad you realised you were wrong,' he said before sauntering out of the room.

It took a moment for the words to register. Stella squawked, at a loss for a snappy retort. Recovering, she spluttered, 'Wrong?!' and chased him through the door, but was surprised to find he had disappeared. She shouted into the empty air like a madwoman, 'I didn't say I was wrong! Ugh!'

A chuckle echoed from somewhere in the house.

Filled with renewed annoyance, Stella stomped up the stairs to her room, stripped off, and took a long, hot shower. She hadn't *conceded*. Just *apologised*. She tried hard to focus on his habit of irritating her, but, as she slid the soap over her body, she ended up replaying the moment he got out of the pool, the hills and valleys of his muscles revealed by the morning light across his chest. And those Speedos…

With a start, she realised she had finished washing herself ten minutes ago and had been staring into space, her finger idly rubbing her chin. She shut off the shower. As she scrubbed the towel over her legs, she attempted to rationalise her daydreams. Fantasising was okay. Healthy, even, so long as it stayed in her head. Nobody could deny that Connor Knight was a sexy specimen of a man. Even a blind person would be turned on solely by his pheromones.

Racing down the stairs, Stella found she was the first to arrive in the breakfast room. The chef was ferrying dishes from the kitchen to the long buffet table: large bowls of fresh-baked croissants and a tray of gooey French cheese. Eating a good, melty Camembert was a perfectly acceptable replacement for sex, in her opinion.

'Have a good night?' Liliwen asked, sitting down next to Stella at the banquet-style table.

'A bit restless. You?' She leaned over her plate to take a bite of her cheese-laden croissant. Crispy flakes of pastry rained down on the porcelain and stuck to her lips.

'It was lush. You missed a good time.'

'I could hear.'

'Jared acted out *"Hit Me Baby One More Time"* and almost brained himself. Alan got us to guess *Best Little Whorehouse in Texas* in under twenty seconds. And I'm willing to put bets on a game of hide the pickle between either Hannah and Flash or Hannah and Gunner. The heat is *on.*' She started humming the Glenn Frey song from *Beverley Hills Cop.*

Regarding her over the rim of her coffee cup, Stella said, 'You may just be the filthiest older woman I know.' She actually had no idea how old Liliwen was. She seemed sort of ageless.

'Ah, *cariad*! You'd be surprised. Did you know retirement homes are rife with STDs? Naughtiness increases with age, so just sit back and enjoy the ride.' She stirred stewed prunes into her porridge.

'I'll take your word for it,' Stella said, 'And I'll take your bet, too. One pound. My money's on Flash.'

As though they'd been summoned, the boys entered the room flanking Hannah. Gunner carried an open laptop, their heads bent towards his screen. Hannah was giggling with her hand covering her mouth. Stella hadn't heard so much noise coming from Hannah since they'd arrived at the chateau.

The trio sat next to Stella, Gunner on her right, and he put the laptop down on his plate. Glancing over, Stella caught the image on his display: Hannah laid back on one of the chateau beds, in just bra and panties, long legs stretched sensuously into the air. Her blonde hair tumbled over the edge of the bed, her eyes connecting directly with the camera.

'Hmm,' Liliwen said in Stella's ear, 'I think I'm going to win that bet.'

'Wow,' said Stella. 'Hannah, you look...you look...'

'Hot,' filled in Gunner smugly.

'I was going to say confident,' said Stella.

'Thanks,' Hannah said in a clearly audible voice. She smiled.

'Hannah asked me to take some pictures of her after class yesterday.' Gunner scrolled through more images, a whole series of Hannah owning her sexiness.

At the BAPP conference, there'd been a talk where the speaker said boudoir shoots could be a huge confidence boost. Stella herself had never been photographed like this before. With her shyness, it must have taken Hannah a lot of courage to ask Gunner to photographer her. Maybe she'd been in the same lecture.

The experience seemed to have had a noticeable effect on her. 'You should show these to Connor,' Stella said, taking another bite of her croissant. A cascade of flakes fell down her top, lodging themselves in her bra. She looked down towards her cleavage and shook out her shirt, but she could already feel the crumbs trapped between the lace and her skin. If she didn't get them out, then they'd just sit there, irritating her.

'Show me what?' said Connor, who had entered the room just in time to catch her picking crumbs out of her bra. With a playful grin, he walked around the table and put his hands on the back of her chair, leaning over to see Gunner's laptop. Giving up on her quest, Stella knocked back her orange juice, but realised the glass was already empty. Awkwardly, she put it back down. She tried to ignore Connor's clean soapy smell and the fact that she knew what his muscles looked like under his tight black t-shirt.

'Nicely composed,' he said, patting Gunner on the back. Connor gave a few minor comments on body position before getting his breakfast.

His hair was still wet. A few strands had fallen forward over his forehead and she felt the urge to smooth them back. She took a violent bite of her croissant. More flakes fell down her shirt.

The remaining students trudged into the breakfast room, Karen on her phone as always. They could hear worry in her voice as she listened to a story from her mother. After hanging up, she said, 'Mother says the boys are missing me so much and Stu-boo has a stomach ache over it. She says I shouldn't have come.'

Stella warmed towards Karen a little. She knew what it felt like to have a controlling mother.

Standing next to her at the buffet, Connor said, 'Karen, children are resilient. Once you're back, they'll forget you ever left, but you'll remember what you've learned on this course for the rest of your life. Sometimes, you need to do what's right for you.'

All the women in the room melted a little, including Stella. Just when she thought he was a 100% prick, he had to go and say something like that. Karen smiled up at him with gratitude and then unexpectedly threw her arms around him, leaning her head on his chest. 'Thank you,' she said while rubbing her hand over his back muscles.

Liliwen pursed her lips with glee and Stella tore a piece off her croissant.

'Hurry up and eat. Start time's at 8:30 this morning,' Krish announced to the group, tapping his watch face. 'And don't forget, we have a treat after dinner.' He smiled, showing his dimples.

Stella finished her breakfast and returned to her room to clean the crumbs out of her bra in private, wondering what Connor and Krish had in store for them that night.

10

IF SOMEONE HAD TOLD Stella that Connor Knight enjoyed swimming with sharks, it wouldn't have surprised her. Extreme kayaking? Conceivable. Even bungee diving while naked would've barely raised an eyebrow.

But the fact that Connor Knight was a karaoke aficionado? That was a shock.

His third number that night was a near-perfect imitation of Elvis singing 'A Little Less Conversation'. In black jeans, he looked every part the rock star as he gyrated his hips like The King, the click track on the stereo blaring out the music. He didn't even need to look at the words on the screen.

The drawing room had been transformed into a disco, complete with glitter ball hanging from the ceiling and coloured lights flitting across the walls. Bodies shimmied and shook to the music. Next to Stella, Krish twirled Liliwen around in circles. Gunner and Flash took turns grinding with Hannah. Karen, without her phone for once, was pretending to waltz with Jared. In the centre, the Youngs slobbered all over each other as they kissed and swayed. Even Alan had some moves to show off, a unique blend of Fosse meets Kevin Bacon that made Stella think of mating peacocks.

'I used to do a lot of amateur dramatics,' he said to her, as though that explained his singular style of movement. It made her think of her father and his recent interest in the local Shakespeare Society. She hoped his new play wouldn't involve dancing. All of Stella's rhythm had definitely come from her mother's side of the gene pool.

She loved being on the dance floor. For her, it was one of the few places she could truly let go. Her happy place, even after she and Tristan had given up competing.

The song came to an end. Connor wiped the sweat from his forehead with a black towel. Very rock star. 'I've got one more song in me before I turn the microphone over to you lot. It's a personal favourite. Feel free to sing along.'

Caught up in the buzz, Stella put an arm around Liliwen and squeezed as they waited for Connor's finale. At that moment the happiness was overwhelming. She was on the right path, with the right people, at the right point in time. In a burst of magnanimity, she even forgave Connor for their exchange that morning. Who cared if he thought marriage was obsolete? Everyone was entitled to his own opinion.

And then the music started again.

Stella froze as the opening twangs of 'Jolene' punctured the air: once, twice, three times, four. Connor fastened his eyes on her. It felt like minutes. He winked. She stopped breathing. He gripped the microphone and his gravelly, sexy baritone dripped over the lyrics.

Everybody else joined in on the chorus, but Stella's jaw wouldn't work. Gunner and Flash waved their lit-up phones like lighters at a Wembley Stadium concert.

'You okay?' asked Liliwen, squeezing Stella's hand. She barely managed a short nod.

She loved 'Jolene'. Up until recently it had been her song. When they'd go out and a DJ would play it, her crowd would turn to her and she'd oblige by getting up to dance, assuming the role of the titular character, flicking her auburn hair and turning her hips while joining her voice to Dolly's.

But then she became Jolene in real life. The woman who wrecked a marriage. A tear slid down her cheek and she wiped it away, hoping nobody saw.

She rubbed the tears between her fingertips, the water disappearing into her skin, her pain reabsorbed. What was she crying for?

As Connor sang the lyrics she knew so well, Stella realised she wanted her song back. She missed it, like an old friend with whom she had argued over something silly. Nathan had stolen so much from her already. Was she going to let him take this, too? Jolene may have been a green-eyed femme fatale, but she was also confident, alive, a woman with ambition. Besides, didn't the man share some of the blame? Wasn't he weak and disloyal? Why should she be punished for his inadequacy?

The chorus looped around, and Stella's chest lifted as she joined in. She closed her eyes as she reclaimed her song, hips rocking to the beat. She felt lighter, freer, like she had forgiven herself just a little bit. Maybe this was what Ula had meant by *get in the coffin*. Maybe it just meant that Stella needed to be kinder to herself.

Her eyes opened and she caught Connor looking at her over his microphone. He snapped his gaze away. Surprising herself, she experienced a kindling of warmth. Perhaps she had wrong-footed him for once. If there was one thing she could do well, it was dance.

Two hours passed in a jumble of music, gyration and bottles of wine. The Youngs performed '*Summer Lovin'*, which everyone would have found much more entertaining had it been performed by anyone but them. An unexpectedly raunchy rendition of '*I Touch Myself*' followed, sung by Hannah. The ladies in the audience spurred her on with clapping and shouts of encouragement. The once-shy girl seemed like a different person to the one who could barely introduce herself on the first day. Her level of social anxiety made any shyness Stella suffered feel like a doddle, but here Hannah was, being unapologetically herself. Stella admired that. Maybe she was witnessing the birth of New Hannah.

Normally, Stella would avoid karaoke like the plague, but

Hannah's courage inspired her and Stella and Liliwen struggled through 'Dancing Queen' together. It was pitched a lot higher than Stella remembered. It was with relief when the song finished and Krish took the mic, stunning them all with some swoon-worthy Frank Sinatra.

After Alan's particularly energetic and strangely perfect 'Bohemian Rhapsody', Stella needed to cool off. She left Liliwen with Karen and went out to the patio, refilling her wine glass on the way. Outdoors, it was dark and the night air soothed the heat from her skin. She took a steady sip of wine, closed her eyes and tipped her head back, enjoying the sounds of frivolity from inside the house.

'Hey.'

Stella startled. She could just make out the hard shape of Connor on one of the sofas. 'Whoops,' she said, 'I didn't see you there.'

A match flared. He threw it into the chiminea next to him and it instantly caught the tinder inside.

'Feel free to join me,' he said, nodding towards the other end of the loveseat. His lips curved up, as though daring her to do it.

'Sure.' She settled herself onto the cushions, as far away from him as she could on a two-seater. She enjoyed the look of mild surprise on his face. 'You know if this photography stuff doesn't work out, you could have a bright future as the lead in an Elvis tribute band.'

He laughed, a deep sound that made her want to make him do it again. 'You think so?'

'Definitely. I can see it now...white rhinestone suit, little cape, golden sunglasses...of course, you'd have to grow out your sideburns.'

'Alternatively, I could do Dolly Parton in drag. Get a wig...invest in some padded underwear...'

'Oh, I *dare* you. But you never would.'

'Is that a challenge? You know how I find them hard to resist, especially coming from you.' He watched her as he took a slow sip of wine.

She huffed a laugh, suddenly uncomfortable. This felt like dangerous territory. 'I didn't know you were such a fan. Of Dolly Parton, I mean.'

'Ah, my mother used to sing her songs to me when I was little. To help me sleep.'

'That's so cute.'

'But not the later happy stuff. More of the morose early work. You know, the songs that were like "I got pregnant with a man's baby and then he killed me and threw me in the river."'

'Hmmm. That's less cute. Sounds very child appropriate.'

'Well, if you think of most fairy tales, they're actually quite dark. Wolves eating grandma. Mermaids dying. Princes wanting to have sex with dead princesses...'

The way he said sex made it sound so salacious. She swallowed. 'This has gotten very...um, *morbid*. Can we go back to Dolly?'

He chuckled. 'Sure.'

They were silent a moment, listening to Jared murder '*Angels*'.

'You seem to know your way around a dance floor,' he said, taking another sip of his wine.

It pleased her, that he had noticed her dancing. 'Product of a mis-spent youth, I assure you.' The masculine smell of his soap tickled her nose, a scent that she now associated with him. The fire crackled.

He cocked his head to one side. 'So tell me, Price. What made you decide to get into wedding photography?'

'Oh, I just fancied a change from advertising.'

'Ah, yes. The erections.'

'I still can't believe I said that.'

'It's fine. I can 100% believe that you've caused plenty of erections.'

She almost choked on her wine and he laughed. She hoped he didn't see her eyes swoop down towards his disappointingly dormant crotch. Maybe he hadn't been flirting with her with the whole butterfly lighting thing, but this *definitely* felt like flirting. Unwelcome heat ripped through the middle of her.

He continued as though they hadn't just been discussing hard-ons. 'That's quite a big change. I've shot weddings for plenty of advertising types. They always seemed stressed. Was it stress?'

'Sorry?'

'The reason you left?'

Without meaning to, her body shivered strongly enough for her teeth to chatter. The last thing she wanted to do was discuss her less than graceful exit from advertising with Connor Knight.

'Are you cold? There's a blanket there next to you.'

'Oh, great, thanks.' She unfolded it and threw it over her legs. The corner just reached Connor's knee.

'So what was it like? Working in advertising?' he asked. 'I always imagined it would be fun. All those creative types...'

'Oh, you know. It was medical advertising. So, boring actually. How did you get into photography?' She took a sip of her wine and turned towards him, hoping he wouldn't spot her clumsy change of subject.

Stroking his jawline, a fond smile spread across his face. 'That's a funny story. We had a neighbour when I was living in Paris—'

'Ah, that explains the French.'

'Best way to pick up Parisian girls.' He lifted the corner of his mouth.

'You learned a foreign language to pick up girls?'

Pretending to be offended, he said, 'It's good to speak a second language. Wouldn't you agree?'

Remembering how the foreign words sounded on his lips, she agreed wholeheartedly. But she rolled her eyes anyway. He smiled like he knew she found it sexy as hell.

'This neighbour...he looked like a French Santa Claus without the jovial attitude. He always had these gorgeous women coming in and out of his flat. I mean...young, beautiful...never the same one twice. My teenage imagination went wild with what could be going on in there, so every day after school, I'd manufacture a reason to be in the hallway, just so I could listen at his door.'

'...and look at the women.'

He flashed his cheeky smile. 'I won't lie. It was a good place to go through puberty.'

'Ha! Better than deepest darkest Wales, certainly.' She grinned. It felt nice having a regular conversation with him. She liked that he was sharing something about his past with her.

'So one day he sees me polishing our door handle yet again and says, *"Hé toi p'tit con*, come in and make us some coffees" —Are you okay?'

She choked a little when he spoke French. She just couldn't get used to it. 'Yes, sorry. Did you go?'

'Hell, yes. I wanted to see what was going on.'

'And?'

'He was a photographer. He shot modelling portfolios by day and prostitutes in the Montmartre at night. He published a book about it.'

'Sounds like the perfect role model for a teenage boy.'

That laugh again. 'Well, oddly enough, he was. He invited me into his world, full of hot women and soft boxes and darkroom chemicals.'

She could picture it all so clearly. 'So what happened?'

'I started making coffees for him after school. He gradually showed me his equipment and how to set up his lights. Soon, I was assisting him whenever I wasn't in lessons. Sometimes I skipped school to work with him.'

Stella watched his face as he told the story, the bald-faced joy as he spoke about his first teacher and introduction to visual arts. In that moment, she realised that, despite all his unflattering ideas about marriage and romantic love, there was one thing that he adored with all his heart: photography. 'What did your parents think of your new friend?'

'My father was quite focused on his career at the Foreign Office... and other things. He didn't notice until he came home early one day and found me losing my virginity to one of the models.'

'Oh my god! How old were you? Twelve? How did that go down?'

'Actually, I was fifteen.'

'My parents would have lost it. Did he make you stop assisting French Santa?'

Connor sniggered. 'No. Of course not. He bought me a camera and a box of condoms.'

Suddenly she had images of a young Connor in bed with a shed-load of naked French models, all at the same time. Her breath quick-ened. She blushed, thankful he wouldn't be able to see it in the flickering firelight.

The mood had changed. It felt heavier...thicker. But determined to keep things light, Stella coughed politely and pressed on: 'So what happened to the photographer?'

'My father got another assignment, and we moved away.'

'That must have been hard. Are you still in touch with him?'

'No, he wasn't really the staying in touch type. I suppose I'm not either.'

'Oh. That's sad.'

'Is it?'

'I just mean he had such a great influence on you. I imagine he'd be proud of what you've achieved.'

'Ha! I imagine he'd think I'd sold out, shooting weddings. "*Sale gosse*," he used to say—that was his pet name for me. "*Sale gosse*, weddings are the shit on the bottom of the photographic pile."'

'I think it's safe to say you've proved him wrong...'

'I suppose. Huh, I haven't thought about him in ages.' A moment of silence passed. They finished their wine and Connor turned towards her, his knee brushing her leg. She felt a shock that zinged straight to her middle, leaving a flame in its wake.

He was sitting so close to her. Without warning, he reached out and took a piece of her auburn hair between his thumb and forefin-ger. Then he dropped it, as though the action had surprised him, too. Into the awkward silence, he cleared his throat and said, 'Did you know Jolene was inspired by a red head?'

The firelight flickered in his eyes. He was looking straight at her. She laughed, a self-conscious puff of air that hung between them. The mood was shifting again. 'What true Dolly fan wouldn't know that?' she almost whispered.

'She was a bank teller...'

'...That her husband fancied.'

Stella found her breath coming in shallow bursts. Her heart thudded, loud enough that she thought he could probably hear it. Time stood still and the air sizzled with possibility. She tried to remember why this was a terrible idea, but her thoughts had turned to fluff, floating, elusive. His eyes lowered to her mouth. He reached up and ran his thumb down the cleft in her chin and all her nerve endings shifted to that one point of contact. She could already taste his lips. Red wine. She could already feel his stubble against her skin. Rough. Sexy.

If he didn't kiss her soon, her stomach would burst from the frenzied flapping of a million butterfly wings. Was he going to or not? Every part of her felt alive, magnetised. Unconsciously, she leaned forward just a little bit.

He dropped his hand and leaned back.

The moment dissolved as quickly as it had come. Embarrassed, she hid her face in her wine glass and took a sip, only to find it was empty.

He sighed. 'I like you, Price, and your happiness matters to me, so I'm saying this to you as plainly as I can: don't fall in love with me. I'm bad news.' He ran his hand through his hair and turned away, looking into the night beyond the patio like some sort of tortured, Byronic hero.

She blinked. What did he just say? *He* was the one that came onto *her*. He led her on with his story about sleeping with French models and the Jolene stuff and now he was acting like she'd hit on him? Her cheeks burned like she'd been slapped. 'Of all the arrogant, conceited—'

'Well, I owe you a pound!' Liliwen bounded out of the chateau and flopped down on a nearby chair.

'Hey, Liliwen,' Connor said, calm as could be, as though Stella and he had just been discussing the shipping forecasts.

Liliwen tucked her legs under herself. 'There must be something in the air tonight, I'm telling you. You're not going to believe this. Hannah and Flash have gone off together. I thought Gunner would be broken up about it, but no! He and *Karen* have disappeared. I'm going to go to bed before I accidentally fall into Alan's arms.'

Stella cast her eyes down into her empty glass and managed a half-hearted laugh. 'Crazy,' was all she could muster.

Yawning dramatically, Connor stood. 'Actually, I'm going to head off, too. We've got a big day tomorrow. A model who's worked with Ellen von Unwerth for French *Vogue* is posing for us. And the weather is looking sunny, so...good night, ladies.' And with that he left.

As he disappeared into the chateau, Stella exhaled.

Liliwen waited until he was out of earshot. 'Well, forgive me for asking, but what in the name of Catherine Zeta Jones was going on there?'

Grimacing at the thought of what had almost happened, Stella rubbed her temples. All the reasons why kissing Connor Knight would be a bad idea flooded back: his arrogance, his reputation, his philosophies on love, the fact that he was a famous wedding photographer and her teacher, her need to focus right now. The list went on. She refilled her wine glass to the brim. Don't fall in love with him, indeed! The nerve of the man.

She growled and kicked the leg of her sofa with her heel.

'That good, huh?' said Liliwen.

'That was close. Thank God nothing happened.'

Liliwen's pretended to study her nails. 'Oh, yes, love. Thank God you didn't kiss the world's most eligible bachelor since Mr Darcy. What a disaster that would've been.' She gave Stella a pitying look and petted her knee.

'Did you hear him?' Stella dropped her voice to a mocking baritone. '"Don't fall in love with me, Price." Fuck off!'

'You don't have to be in love to have a jolly good time. He's so handsome...'

'But afraid of commitment.'

'He's talented.'

'But has an ego the size of France.'

'He's multi-lingual.'

'But too much of a smooth talker.'

'Listen, pet. Do you want him or not? It's that simple.'

'God, no.'

'Because from what I saw…'

Stella groaned again. Why did every conversation she had with Connor Knight leave her feeling either irritated, anxious, embarrassed or angry? 'I'm not looking for anything right now. I just want to concentrate on my business.'

Liliwen pretended to shoot herself in the head. 'Kids today. Let me tell you, if I were thirty years younger and single, I'd have him trussed up faster than you could say *bara brith*.'

Stella laughed despite herself. 'You're terrible.'

'My Gareth would agree with you. But listen, if you want him, *go for it*. What's the worst that could happen? He says no? When I was fifteen, before Gareth and I started dating, I had it bad for our post boy, Evan. He left school the year before me and I'd noticed him then, but, oh! I really fancied the socks off him in his tight, tight uniform.'

Liliwen paused, lost in remembrance. Stella had to prod her along. 'And…?'

'Right! Well, he never noticed me, so I went on a campaign to change that. I'd take the bus into Tenby on the weekend and send myself saucy postcards from an imaginary beau. "Dear Liliwen, can't wait to see you. Not being able to touch you is killing me. Love, Terry." That sort of thing. I made sure to choose postcards of half-naked women so they would catch Evan's eye. It worked a treat after about a month. Boy, was he hot under the collar when he got to the top of my path, and he got to the top of my path a few times, let me tell you.'

Stella barked with mirth. 'I don't know why I'm shocked, but I am.'

'So was my father when he accidentally found the postcards.'

'Liliwen, you are a dark horse.'

'So have yourself some fun. You're too young to give up on love.'

'I haven't given up on love. I'm just taking a break from it for a while.'

'Well, anyway, bottoms up! *Iechyd da!*'

'*Iechyd da!*' Stella took a deep swig of her wine.

Jared and Alan were singing '*Wannabe*'. Stella put her glass down and pulled Liliwen up. She needed to dance this off. 'It's the Spice Girls, even if Jared is tone deaf,' said Stella.

When they entered the drawing room, Connor Knight was nowhere in sight.

11

By MIDNIGHT, Stella craved bed, legs aching and throat raw from singing. Unfortunately, the rest of the chateau was awake. As Stella performed her nocturnal ablutions, a symphony of weathered bedsprings and animalistic groans punctuated the night. She found herself flossing her teeth to the rhythm of the squeaks. In, out, in, out. Flopping into bed, she covered her head with a pillow, but a pair of earplugs would have been more handy—as well as something to make her forget The Conversation.

'Don't fall in love with me,' she mocked. As if she'd fall in love with somebody so egotistical and self-absorbed. She'd already made that mistake once. As she finally drifted off, she dreamt over and over about almost kissing him, their lips never touching.

She awoke in a foul mood.

Although tired, she suited up and went for another run down the tree-lined drive. Dolly sang as Stella pounded the pavement, pretending she was stepping on Connor's head. She sprinted through *Jolene*'. By the time she finished, she wanted to punch him less. She walked to the back entrance, half expecting to find him in the pool, but the water was still. She ignored her disappointment.

Stella needed the whole incident out of her head. No matter what had or hadn't happened, she still had two days left here, and she needed to learn whatever he had to teach. She just had to let it go.

And then she went down to breakfast.

She was the last to arrive. As she entered the room, all conversation stopped. Only for a second, but she definitely detected a pause that coincided with her entrance. Her mind raced: did they think that something happened between her and Connor? Were they all gossiping about her? Her traitorous cheeks burned as she willed herself to walk over to the buffet.

This was her worst nightmare. Or one of them, at least. She'd been in the industry five minutes and already people thought she was sleeping her way to the top. She absentmindedly put a croissant and some cheese on her plate, but her appetite had disintegrated.

Taking a deep breath, she faced the room. Nobody was paying her any attention. Her shoulders relaxed—maybe she'd imagined the whole thing. Sod's Law, the only free chair was next to Connor. He caught her eye with a strangely friendly grin. 'Morning, Price.'

She frowned.

Liliwen, like some descending angel, called, 'Over here, lovely! I've finished. You can have my seat.'

'Thank you,' Stella said as her friend cleared her plate away.

'No bother, I've got to run upstairs anyway.'

Before she left, Stella clasped her arm and leaned in to whisper, 'Is something going on?'

'You'll see...it's nothing bad. Don't worry,' Liliwen said.

'Strange,' Stella muttered, but at least whatever it was, it had nothing to do with her sex life. Surveying the table, she noticed that half the people were now coupled up. The Youngs, obviously, but also Hannah and Flash, sitting as close as they could get without actually crawling onto each other's laps. Karen and Gunner also basked in the afterglow of intimacy, holding hands and speaking in hushed tones. For once, Karen wasn't on the phone.

'I know,' Jared said from her right. 'It's disgusting. Like Cupid threw up all over.'

A tap on her shoulder.

'Price. A word?'

She turned to find Connor waiting for her, hands stuffed into his pockets. Her pulse quickened. She clamped down on her first instinct which was to jump up and oblige him. But she really didn't want to talk to him. 'I'm eating.'

'Please?' His grey eyes pleaded in an annoyingly endearing way.

Taking a deep breath, she put down her knife. Her stomach fluttered, wondering what he wanted to discuss. Was he going to apologise for last night? Did she want him to? Wouldn't it be better to forget the whole thing?

She followed him into the hallway. Did she imagine it or was everyone in the dining room suddenly quiet again? Maybe this *was* about last night...

Outside, he faced her, and ran a hand through his hair. She held her breath. Here it was. The moment of truth.

'Price, what size are you?'

Of all the things that she might've expected, that wasn't even on the list. 'Excuse me?'

'I need a huge favour.'

The butterflies died one by one in her stomach. This had nothing to do with last night. 'Okay. I'm listening,' she said, mirroring his crossed arms. An apology would've been nice.

'The model for today—'

'The one from *Vogue?*'

'She's called in sick. You're the only person here who could fit into the sample dress.'

What was he asking? Did he want her to *model?* Even her inner people pleaser shook its head at that one. 'Oh, no, no, no. I can't be a— I'm not a model. I'd be terrible.' It wasn't performing in front of people that bothered her. She could dance in front of audiences or present to suits in conference rooms, no problem. But it took preparation. Practice. Repetition. Modelling with no prior experience? No, thank you.

'Well, right now terrible would be better than nothing. But I can tell you for a fact you wouldn't be terrible. Do you know how I know?' he asked. 'Because you just need to listen to my direction and you'll be fine. Do you trust me?'

No, she thought. 'But how am I going to learn if I'm the model? I can't take pictures or write notes. I'm sorry, but I didn't pay five grand to stand around in a wedding dress.'

Connor thought for a second. 'Tell you what. In return for helping out, I'll give you a day of my time back in London. You can do whatever you want with it. Portfolio building. Shooting. Whatever. Deal?'

She bit her lip. The offer was actually extremely tempting. In groups, they had to move at the pace of the slowest member, but one-to-one, she'd learn so much faster. It would also give her time to absorb all the information from this week and ask him follow-up questions.

On the other hand, she didn't feel like doing any favours for Connor Knight. Her gaze wandered back into the breakfast room, where everybody was looking at her. *They know what he's asking*, she thought, expelling a pent-up breath.

Connor got down on this knees and held his arms open. 'Price. Please. I'm begging you.' He looked so earnest, eyebrows raised, eyes pleading in a way she couldn't resist.

From the other room, Jared yelled, 'I'll wear a dress for a day of your time!' The others hushed him.

Sighing under the weight of expectation, she gave in. 'Oh, fine. Get up. Yes. I'll do it.'

'Thank you!' He stood and enveloped her in a hug, lifting her feet off the floor. Stella was suddenly aware of the solid length of him pressed against her body, her skin scorched where they touched. He dropped her on her feet, oblivious to the havoc he just wreaked on her senses, and said, 'The hair and make-up team's in the library upstairs. Why don't you find them and get prepped?'

With that, he hurried back into the dining room. 'She said yes.'

The others answered with whoops and cheers.

WHILE STELLA SAT STILL, studying the spines of dusty French books, the make-up artist pinned her hair into large rolls and brushed various powders onto her face. An hour later, a polished version of Stella stepped into a sheath wedding dress with a dramatic, tulle fish-tail train. Two thin straps held up the lacy dress, clinging to her torso like white chocolate on a strawberry. A line of fiddly silk-covered buttons running up her back took the stylist twenty minutes and many French expletives to fasten. As Stella stood patiently, she spied the dress' price tag resting on the table. She gulped.

From a bag of scuffed white shoes, the stylist pulled out a well-worn size 38 and slipped them over Stella's feet, raising her height two inches. None of the team spoke English; they showered Stella with a cascade of 'C'est magnifique' and 'Très belle'. Examining her over the top of her red cats-eye glasses, the stylist declared, 'Ooh, la la!' which made Stella laugh.

She studied her transformation in the full-length mirror. Her hair had been swept into a loose chignon at the back, a few auburn tendrils curling around her face. The make-up artist had a light touch, Stella's freckles showing through the thin layer of foundation and powder while her eyes smouldered under a dusting of brown and pink. Stella resisted the urge to peel off the false lashes. She hadn't worn falsies since her dance competition days and had forgotten that sensation of having a caterpillar on her upper lid.

And the dress...well, it wouldn't have been her personal choice. She could barely move her legs, and the ex-dancer in her hated clothes that inhibited her limbs. But she had to admit she looked sexy. The neckline dipped between her cleavage, showing off the soft roundness of her breasts. The tight lace accentuated the curves of her body.

For a moment, she imagined this was her wedding day and she was about to marry the man of her dreams—whomever he may be. Her father would be just outside, waiting to walk her down the aisle. Her mother would be wearing some theatrical, vividly-coloured hat that would block the view of guests sitting behind her. Claudia would be eyeing up the groom's men. Stella's lips curved into a smile, lost in her fantasy.

'*T'es prête?*' the stylist asked.

She knew enough French to understand that. '*Oui,*' Stella said, moving toward the hall.

The library lay at the end of a long, dark hallway. As Stella passed under the eyes of oil-paint French ladies, she wondered if their lemon-sucking, strained expressions were also the result of tight corsets and she felt some solidarity with them. Her legs fought like two children jostling for space in a sleeping bag. She wished she had moisturised her thighs before donning the dress, to reduce the friction of skin-on-skin. She was already beginning to chafe. It would only get worse as she began to sweat. She might look like a slick West End production, but on the inside, she was the local pantomime. Could she pull this off?

Strangely, the possibility that worried her most was disappointing Connor. He had put his trust in her to do a job and she didn't want to fail, even if she agreed to it under duress. How mortifying would it be to find out today that modelling wasn't in her skillset?

The hubbub of chatter rose around the corner. Without trying to, she picked out the resonant timbre of Connor's voice. Before wobbling into view, she took a moment to collect her thoughts.

Tits and teeth, darling. Tits and teeth. Tristan's words to her before every dance competition floated into her head. She imagined the squeeze of his hand, sending her his limitless confidence.

She could do this.

As she approached the top of the stairs, she promised that she wouldn't seek out Connor's face first. Unfortunately, her eyes just happened to fall into the middle of the group, where he stood chatting to Gunner. A hush fell. Connor looked up.

Expecting one of his cheeky smiles, she felt confused when he just gazed at her, face blank. If anything, he appeared angry: eyes shuttered and mouth set in a firm line, as though studying her for flaws that might mess up his photographs. Time stretched. She smoothed one hand down the side of the dress and gripped the banister with the other as a flush of heat rose to her cheeks. As her breathing sped up, she realised how difficult it was to draw air in when wearing a ribbed dress.

A wolf whistle broke the spell, courtesy of Flash. Everyone laughed. *Tits and teeth.* She manoeuvred her right leg forward, and placed her foot on the step. She repeated the movement with the left. Then again. Her confidence grew with every step. She was getting the hang of this dress. Adding a hip roll, she held out her arm like a Las Vegas showgirl, earning herself a chuckle from the crowd. *Tits and teeth.* Almost there.

On the last stair, her heel caught on the fibres of the carpet, and she stumbled. Connor stepped forward and caught her by the elbow. The skin under his hand sizzled.

'All good?'

She nodded and he released her, leaving her to mourn the loss of his touch. *Stop it, Stella.*

He turned to the group. 'We'll start at the back of the chateau.' He pointed his fingers gun-style towards the exit closest to the swimming pool.

'Shouldn't we wait for Jean-Luc?' Krish asked as he finished checking over Connor's equipment.

Connor paused in the doorway. 'I forgot about Jean-Luc. Do you know when—'

'*Voilà,*' said a velvet voice.

Stella looked up, straight into the chocolate eyes of sex in a tuxedo. A lean, athletic man with brown skin double-oh-seven'd his way into the room, fondling his cufflinks. He winked and smouldered, '*Allo.* I believe I am your uz-band today.'

'Holy Mother of Charlotte Church,' Liliwen whispered.

'We go?' He offered his arm to Stella.

'*Merci,*' she said, her heart beating a touch faster.

'You look gorgeous. *Très sexy.*' He kissed his fingers and tossed them into the air.

An unexpected giggle escaped her. His overt flirtatiousness and ridiculous good looks made her think of Tristan. She fell into a comfortable space with him as a Tristan replacement, even though she was pretty sure this one wasn't gay. Still, she felt safe enough to be carefree and seductive. '*Pas mal* yourself,' she teased back. He gave a Gallic shrug, as if saying 'Yes, this is true'. He didn't smile so much as simmer, his stubble emphasising his delicious jawline.

Connor put his hands on his hips and raised his voice above the chit chat. 'Anybody who wants to learn something today should follow me.' And whipping around sharply on his heels, he left.

OUTSIDE, another sunny day enfolded them in a mild, but steady spring heat. They had been blessed all week with amazing weather, despite the threatening forecast. Connor led them towards the cherry blossom orchard behind the pool.

Jean-Luc continued to hold her arm to help her navigate the uneven terrain. The stylist walked behind them carrying the fishtail train. The buzz of bees and insects hung in the air, making the back of her neck itch.

Stopping under a tree, Connor checked his camera settings and everyone else followed suit, prepping their equipment. He faced the group as they gathered around him and motioned for Stella and Jean-Luc to stand with the dappled sunlight at their backs. Her temporary husband moved his arm around Stella's waist, holding her close. The pungent tang of tobacco rose from his clothes, overpowering the more pleasant, honeyed scent of the petals above.

Connor cleared his throat. 'Today we're going to concentrate on posing hands. Aside from the eyes, the hands are the most expressive part of the body.' He looked at Stella and Jean-Luc, standing like a couple and narrowed his eyes. 'Stella, can I borrow you for a moment?'

She stepped up and waited for instruction, aware that every eye was on her, including Connor's. It made her feel light-headed—or maybe that was the hair pins sticking into her scalp. She should have told the hair stylist how uncomfortable they were.

'May I touch you?'

The question took her by surprise. Blinking, she sent a silent plea to her cheeks not to betray her embarrassment. He repeated the question. 'Do you mind if I touch you?'

'N-no. That's fine.' Her mouth felt dry. She could really use a glass of water.

Glancing back towards his students, Connor said, 'Always, always ask your models or clients if you can touch them before you pose them. You don't want to come across as a pervert.'

'Gunner, hear that?' Flash joked.

'Ha ha,' Gunner replied.

Connor took a step towards Stella. 'Hands are expressive. They can show tenderness.' He reached up and cradled Stella's cheek in his fingers, surprising her. She could feel the callouses on his palm against her face. Remembering she had a part to play, she raised her eyes to his and, for a moment, their gazes locked together, his pupils darkening as she watched. It was just part of the act.

'Disinterest.' The moment snapped and his touch disappeared as he casually slid his hand into his pocket, twisting away. 'Passion.' He placed his hands on her waist, pulling her towards him and crumpling the fabric of her dress in his fingers. She wondered if he felt the jolt of heat below his belt, too. 'Or sensual.' He raised his hand to her face once again and dragged the back of his fingers slowly along her jawline.

Stella didn't know how much more she could take. Each spot he touched lit up and she hadn't breathed since he started the demonstration. She couldn't tell if she was sweating because of the hot mid-morning sunshine or Connor's attentions. Probably a bit of both.

'Don't ever be lazy when it comes to hands. Here's the difference in a nutshell: this says nothing.' He placed his hand flat against the upper part of Stella's arm, the caress of a robot. Next, he changed the shape of it, adding a slight bend to his fingers, pressing them into her flesh just a little. 'This says "I love you."'

The hairs on her arms stood up. The last man to say that to her had been Nathan and it had been a lie. *Just like now*, she reminded herself keeping her face carefully blank.

He stepped away. Jean-Luc moved in, taking her arm. She smiled gratefully at him, and he blew her a kiss.

'Any questions so far?' Connor asked.

'Can we begin with the passionate hands?' Jean-Luc said, sweeping his gaze across the ladies in the crowd. Liliwen and Karen tittered.

Connor turned towards Stella and Jean-Luc, his gaze snagging on the protective way Jean-Luc held her arm. Stella pursed her lips to stop herself from laughing. If she didn't know better, she'd say Connor was exhibiting signs of jealousy. He obviously liked being the Alpha male and Jean-Luc was encroaching on his territory. This could be fun.

'No. In fact,' Connor tilted his head in thought, 'You know what? The bride is more important anyway. The groom is really just a prop, so why don't you go take a seat,' he gestured towards the sun loungers at the pool, 'and we'll let you know when you're needed. *D'accord?*'

'I am your servant,' Jean-Luc said, bowing his head. Before he left, he leaned over and took Stella's hand in his, placing a delicate kiss on the back of her fingers. '*À plus, chérie.*'

'We don't have all day.'

For the next hour, Stella held pose after pose. Connor crossed her arms, uncrossed one hand and brought it to her face, put the other arm on her waist, and made sure to capture each move on camera. The novelty of modelling quickly started to wear thin. The dress seemed to be shrinking, as though her sweat was making it shrivel. The corset ribs, which hadn't bothered her at the beginning, now dug into the top of her hip.

She also worried that she was beginning to melt. The make-up artist flitted in and out, pressing more powder onto Stella's face.

There must have been at least ten layers of powder by now. As her course mates clicked their shutters, she wished she were on their side of the lens. However, she wasn't, so she should just do the best job she could.

Of course, modelling was a masterclass in itself. Knowing how it felt to be posed by someone as talented as Connor gave her more of an insight into the skill involved. She absorbed the minute changes he made to her chin, her shoulders, her hands, committing them all to memory. To elicit authentic facial expressions, he listed prompts to use, tricks like telling the groom to whisper something dirty in the bride's ear to get a big laugh.

'I do that,' said Gunner. 'It always works.'

It felt intimate whenever Connor pointed his lens at her. Sometimes he would pause before taking the picture, those seconds before he hit the shutter release hanging expectantly in the air. She could feel him studying her through the viewfinder, his dominant eye having free reign to roam over her from head to toe, checking her position. If she were doing it correctly, he would take the picture. If she were doing it wrong, he would lower the camera and coach her into a better pose, sometimes using his hands to manoeuvre her. Always asking permission before he touched her, of course. When he showed her the pictures on the back of his camera, she couldn't believe it was her.

Between set ups, she glanced towards Jean-Luc. He seemed quite happy sprawled on the sun lounger, smoking a cigarette and texting. The stylist stepped into shot to fix the train of the dress and Stella wished she would loosen some of the buttons, just to give her a touch more breathing room, but she was too shy to ask.

All the students were as active shooting her as they had been when working with the professional models. They crowded around Connor, striving to get the same angles. During one set-up, something long and hard appeared between Connor's legs. He dipped his head over his shoulder. 'Alan, mate. Some personal space?'

'Sorry,' Alan replied from the ground. He hunched lower, so he could move his big lens lower, between Connor's knees.

As they each took turns directing her poses, Stella's stomach grumbled. She realised she'd skipped breakfast. At the next break, she'd ask somebody to get her a snack.

'Connor, love,' said Liliwen with a mischievous glint in her eye. 'Would you mind showing us some couple poses now? I think it would be really helpful.'

Karen, Lisa and Hannah chorused their agreement.

Connor sighed. He called to Jean-Luc, beckoning him to return.

Extinguishing his cigarette underfoot, Jean-Luc stood. With the slow, deliberate saunter of someone who knows he is attractive, he ambled towards the group. From his pocket he took out a packet of mints and threw a couple into his mouth. 'Ready for the action, as you say,' he quipped, stopping next to Stella. She was glad to have her *uz-band* back.

'Right then.' Connor shifted his camera to free his hands and motioned for Jean-Luc to stand behind Stella.

Liliwen raised her hand. 'Sorry, Connor?'

'Yes?'

'What if I want to pose the man with his hand on the woman's... you know...her *arse*. How do you make it look tasteful instead of horny?'

'I don't think Stella wants to—'

'No, it's fine. I don't mind,' she said from behind a guileless smile. Liliwen was obviously trying to help Stella realise the dream of screwing a Frenchman. For the fun of it, Stella was happy to play along, even if she had no plans to sleep with anybody. Besides, it seemed to irritate Connor.

Jean-Luc looked delighted.

'Right.' Connor's nostrils flared as he took a steadying breath. 'Remember as I said earlier, the groom is only a prop in a wedding photo. The bride is always the focus. Stella, can you step in front of Jean-Luc and face him?'

She followed his instruction. She would ask for a break after this pose to get a drink and some food. She could feel a hunger headache developing, with the accompanying dip in mood.

'Now, place your hand on his cheek—actually, no. Just off his shoulder.'

He stood back and examined his models, running his fingers over his jawline in thought. 'Price, stick out your left hip and lean to the right. Now drop your back shoulder.'

She tried to do as he asked, but she felt distorted, her body going in one direction and her dress straining to go in the other. 'Is this how it's supposed to look?'

'You're doing it perfectly.'

Much to her annoyance, Stella glowed at his words. She fought with the muscles at the corner of her mouth, trying to keep them from betraying her pleasure at his approval.

He asked the stylist to adjust the train of her dress while he twiddled with the dials on his camera. Stella wished he would hurry up. Her hip was aching.

'Final touches now. Jean-Luc, put your hand *respectfully* on her bottom and bring your lips closer to hers. Like you're about to kiss.' He mumbled this last bit.

Standing back, he pointed the lens at them and shot a few frames. He examined the back of his camera, nodded, and said, 'Okay, got it. You can break the pose.'

Stella sagged with relief. The dress was really starting to chafe and she worried her breasts were going to pop out of the top the way her torso was twisted.

'Wait a second,' Alan objected. 'We haven't had a chance to take the photo yet!'

Ugh, Alan! She lifted back into the pose.

Jean-Luc's smile turned sly as he said to Connor, 'What is that thing you said to do when last I model for you? Whisper *des choses coquines?*' Without waiting for an answer he brought his mouth close to her ear. His hot breath tickled the delicate skin of her neck and she shivered. He tightened his grip. Just loud enough that others could hear, he murmured, *'Je pourrais te dévorer tout cru!'*

Having no idea what he was saying, but enjoying the subtext, Stella erupted in croaky laughter. The shutters clicked like castanets behind her, trying to capture the look of jocularity on her face while her sexy model husband groped her bottom.

Laughing made her remember how parched she was. When was the last time she drank water? Hours ago. The sun was high, despite the shade, its rays hammering down. Her stomach gurgled again. That's right...no breakfast. And the dress was so tight, the ribbing of the corset excavating her skin, and her inner thighs burning, chafed and sweating. She tried to breathe her way through it, but the stale cigarettes on Jean-Luc's clothes mixed with mint on his breath made her head spin. A wave of dizziness washed over her.

Her grip loosened and her head tipped backwards. The last thing she remembered before passing out was Jean-Luc's frantic eyes and his empty hands flailing at the air.

12

STELLA WAS BEING USED as a tug-o-war rope.

At least that's what it felt like. There was also a lot of arguing in French.

Her eyelids fluttered open to find Jean-Luc holding her feet and Connor supporting her under the arms. Connor pulled her one way while Jean-Luc pulled her the opposite direction.

'If you don't both stop right now, I'm going to bang your heads together!' roared Liliwen, despite her diminutive size. 'Jean-Luc, let Connor carry her.'

'Putain.' The French model let go, and Connor gathered her into his arms.

Stella closed her eyes again. If not for the headache, she would've enjoyed letting her head rest against his shoulder, inhaling the warm scent of him. But her head pounded.

'Now take her over to those deck chairs and somebody get her water and a plate of food.' Liliwen seemed to have taken charge. *Brava, Liliwen.*

Connor carried Stella to the pool and laid her gently on one of the lounge chairs. The dress's buttons pressed into her back. Wedding dresses were so uncomfortable. How did women wear them for twelve hour days?

She pushed herself onto her elbows. 'I'm fine,' she tried to say, but it came out garbled.

Jean-Luc kneeled next to her, taking her hand with concern in his dark eyes. On the other side, Connor smoothed a strand of hair off her face.

'Shoo, both of you,' said Liliwen. 'She doesn't need you lot crowding her. I'll sit with her until she's better.'

Exchanging a narrow-eyed glare, Connor and Jean-Luc both peeled away and hovered nearby.

'Are you sure— ' began Connor.

'Go!' commanded Scary Liliwen.

Karen and Gunner scurried onto the scene carrying a bottle of water and a plate of cheese, grapes, and meats. Sticking his hands in his pockets, Connor led the rest of the group back to the house.

Liliwen unscrewed the cap and held the water out for Stella, who glugged it down too fast. The liquid stuck in her throat. She coughed, turning her head to the side to avoid getting the dress wet.

Wiping her mouth with the back of her hand, Stella said, 'I don't remember what happened.'

'Well! It was quite the argy-bargy, let me tell you.' Liliwen offered the food. Stella helped herself, even as her stomach grumbled. 'What's the last thing you remember?'

'Laughing at something Jean-Luc said, then falling.'

'What did he say to you anyway, the dirty sod? Agh! Never mind. Not important. Connor caught you, thank goodness. He didn't have time to move his camera, so it whacked your head quite hard.'

That would explain the sore spot on the back of her scalp. 'And?'

'Jean-Luc grabbed your feet. I suppose he felt bad about not catching you. Anyways, they started arguing. If Connor didn't have his arms full with you, I think he might have punched him.'

'No way!' Stella laughed.

'Is it any surprise after the way they've both been crowing around you all day?'

'Come on. They were not.'

'You're joking, right?' Liliwen felt Stella's forehead to see if it was hot. 'If sexual tension could get a person pregnant, my god we'd all be having triplets.'

'I thought they just had a competitive Alpha male thing going on.'

'Well, it was pretty noticeable. Anyway, I'm sure Alan took a photo.'

Pushing herself up, Stella said, 'I'm feeling better. Shall we walk back to the house, so I can get out of this stupid dress?'

Liliwen offered her arm. Stella shrugged the high heels off and gathered up the train of the dress to avoid tripping on it. 'Let's go around to the front,' Stella said, hoping to avoid walking through the dining room.

The foyer was empty, the only sound the distant tinkle of cutlery and glassware as people ate lunch. The chequered tiles soothed the bottom of Stella's feet after walking across the gravel.

'I'll just go upstairs and sort myself out. I'll meet you in the dining room in ten.'

'Are you sure you don't need my help?' Liliwen asked, concern in her gentle blue eyes.

'I'm good. Thanks.' She didn't want to impose on her friend any more than necessary. Liliwen was probably starving as well.

Stella climbed the stairs, glad to be away from everyone's sticky eyes. Modelling had been fun for a laugh, but she didn't understand how anybody would want to do it full-time.

Inside her room, she dropped the heels and took a long drink from her water bottle. She already felt a million times better, as she caught a glimpse of herself in the mirror on the back of her door. Turning her head left and right, she admired the up-do, which hadn't budged an inch. The hair and make-up artist had done an excellent job.

But that didn't stop the squeezing sensation in her torso. She really needed to get out of the gown. Reaching behind her back, she searched for the zipper. Except there was no zipper, only the row of tiny buttons that had taken the stylist 20 minutes to do up. Determined, Stella reached one hand up her back and the other over her shoulder, but she just ended up dancing in a circle, twisting her legs into her train. She needed help.

The library was just down the hall. Really, she should have gone there first. She hadn't been thinking straight after the ordeal outside. She opened her door and yelped.

Connor stood there, one hand ready to knock, the other holding a plate of sandwiches.

'Price,' he said, handing her the plate. His eyes searched her up and down, checking for damages. Whether to herself or the dress, she wasn't sure. 'Are you okay? How's your head?'

She put the plate on the desk and touched her scalp with her fingertips, prodding the place she had thwacked Connor's camera. The pain had dissipated. 'It's fine. Really. I'm fine.'

'You gave us quite a scare.' He took a step into the room. She found his intensity unnerving. She tucked a loose curl behind her ear, her gaze fluttering to the floor.

He shoved his hands into his pockets. 'Are you going to have a lie down? It might be a good idea...'

'Actually, I was just going to see if someone could help me out of the dress.' She sucked in. 'It's starting to cut off circulation.'

'Oh.' He shrugged. 'I can help you.'

'It's okay. I can just go to the library...'

'Everyone's downstairs having lunch.'

If she didn't get out of this dress soon, she was going to burst the seams. He was there. He could do it. 'All right, then.' Slowly, she turned and let her head fall forward, so he could access her buttons. The door clicked shut and his solid footsteps caressed the tiles as he approached. She fastened her eyes to the bed quilt, concentrating on the swirls of the stitching. That must have taken ages to sew. Exactly how many stitches were there? Must be at least a million. Her breath came faster as she waited for his touch. The intimacy of the situation struck her and the air seemed to thicken. *'Don't fall in love with me, Price.'* This wasn't a good idea.

The brush of his fingers sent goosebumps spreading across her back. Damn her sympathetic reflex system. He must be able to see the tiny peaks. He was probably congratulating himself on his effect. Go, Alpha male.

The first button popped open.

Deep and even with concentration, his breath stirred the air at the nape of her neck. The second button. The third. She caught a whiff of that earthy Connor scent that she'd come to know well.

Ten. She was holding her breath. She put her lips together and exhaled into the charged atmosphere. She wondered if he felt that, too, or if it was just her, making it all up.

Fifteen. Sixteen. She lifted her head and turned to peer over her shoulder. She could see the corner of his t-shirt, the fabric undulating as his hands worked down her back.

Twenty. How many more buttons were there? She didn't know how much more tension she could take. The air hit her back as more and more skin revealed itself. She closed her eyes and crossed her arms over her breasts, tucking her hands under her armpits to make sure the dress didn't fall down.

Finally, the last button popped open at the bottom of her spine. Neither of them moved.

The only noise was their breath, both fast, waiting. Her eyes bored holes into the bedspread.

Tentatively, he touched the skin at the bottom of her back with his fingertips. She sucked in a shallow breath and leaned back into him. As though it was the permission he needed, he slid his whole hand under the dress, feeling the edge of her naked waist. His fingers hovered on her ribcage and grazed the underside of her breasts. Heat followed his touch. He pulled her tight against him, and with a moan, she turned her head, angling her face up towards him.

'Connor…?' she whispered.

His lips met hers. Hesitant at first, but growing more insistent with increasing need. He tasted sweet, like grapes and oranges. Their tongues tangled, crashing into each other and then pulling back and crashing again. He spun her body towards him, marrying his hips to hers. She threw her arms around his neck and pressed herself to him, the muscles she'd spied at the pool firm against her stomach. Her middle felt like a sun, radiating heat. His answering need pressed into her belly. One more erection for Stella Price.

His mouth moved to her neck, first down one side, up the other. Her hand tangled in his hair, pressing his face into her, wanting more of him.

Her heart galloped in her chest, blood sang in her ears. She thought about what Connor had said about hands: how they could betray desire, need, want. Hers showed all of these things as she gripped his shoulders, pushing him towards the sensitive cleft between her breasts.

She couldn't believe she was doing this. On some level, she knew it shouldn't be happening, but, as his lips moved back to hers, for the life of her, she couldn't remember why.

Head thrown back and lost in the sensations, it took her a moment to realise that his kisses were slowing. He nibbled on her ear before pulling away.

'Stella...' he said, using her given name for once. His hands held her waist, pushing her away, so that an inch of air separated their bodies. 'Stella, this can't happen.'

'Hmmm?' she said, still lost in the moment. As her blood and breathing slowed, his words finally registered. She could still feel the imprint of his kisses, the heat of his breath. She shook her head and tried to focus on his face. 'Sorry?'

'This. Us. It isn't a good idea.'

Embarrassment welled up inside her. Of all the things she'd set out to do on this course, not kissing Connor Knight had been at the top of the list. What had happened to her self control?

She pushed him away while pulling up the straps of her dress.

'You're right,' she said quietly, struggling to keep her voice calm and even. 'It's a horrible idea.'

'Stella, I—'

'Sorry, but could you leave? I need to get out of this dress. In private.' It took every ounce of fortitude to look him in the eye and keep her voice from shaking.

'See you downstairs,' he said. Turning, he walked out the door, taking the tension in the room with him.

With a sob she fell onto the bed, struggling to catch her breath. What had she almost done? A few words of praise and concern for her and she'd been ready to jump into his bed. *Idiot.* Hadn't she already learnt her lessons where men like him were concerned? She should have tied a little red string around her finger as a reminder: Connor Knight equals bad. Stay away. She wouldn't make the same mistake again.

And didn't he have a *girlfriend*?!

Trembling, she slipped the dress off and hung it up on the side of her wardrobe, pulling on jeans and a t-shirt. In the bathroom, she ripped all the pins out of her hair and peeled the false eyelashes off, tossing them in the bin. She didn't want any reminders of that morning's antics.

Her stomach rumbled, and she tore into the sandwiches on her desk, chewing with an animalistic fury as she considered her situation. She still had a day-and-a-half of the course left. She would just have to lay low for the next 48 hours, stand at the back of the class, avoid him at meals. After that, she never had to see him again. Except, of course, in London, one day as payment for her modelling. Well, she could just ignore the offer. But by the same token, she didn't want to shoot herself in the foot. Connor Knight was still the best teacher and she didn't have time for mistakes. Like this one.

Just argh! She stamped on the floor.

Finishing the sandwich, she knew she couldn't stay hidden in her room. Liliwen would start to wonder where she was and she didn't want any of the other students to suspect anything. She didn't want them to know how much she had wanted to join Connor's Club, if only just for a moment.

STELLA WALKED into the dining room as casually as she could, trying to slip in unseen.

'Stella!' shouted Liliwen as she came to hug her.

The others stood, chanting Stella's name. She smiled and waved her hand, dismissing their enthusiastic welcome. When they wouldn't let up, she took a small bow, which seemed to mollify them. Everyone went back to their coffees.

She didn't look, but she could feel Connor's presence at the head of the table and knew he was looking at her. She made a beeline for the other end.

'Let me get you a coffee and some biscuits,' said Liliwen, jumping up to find the cafetiere.

As Stella sipped at the bitter brown liquid and nibbled her short-bread, she kept her eyes down, letting the peaks and troughs of the surrounding conversations wash over her. She didn't feel much like talking, which Liliwen and Jared seemed to sense. The Youngs blandly discussed a job they were booked to shoot next month, speaking a little too loudly, the way people do when they think what they are saying will impress those around them. It didn't. Alan was doing a deep dive on lens choice with Connor, who was doing a great job of pretending nothing had happened. Stella tried to ignore his voice, sounding so knowledgeable about focal length. The two pairs of love-birds were having an inane exchange about desert islands and what they would bring if they were stuck on one. When Karen said 'birth control', Stella almost choked. What had happened to the dedicated mother of yesterday?

Somebody's phone rang. Karen checked hers and shrugged.

The chatter went on. Stella rested her head on the back of her chair and closed her eyes for a moment. Alan's voice cut through the air. 'What? Oh my god!' he shouted.

All conversation ceased.

Alan leaned his elbows on the table, phone held to his ear, his forehead propped on his other hand. Even from where Stella was sitting, she could see him shaking.

'Okay,' he said. 'I'll be there as soon as I can.'

He sucked in a deep breath and quickly expelled it, over and over again. Connor rubbed his back. 'Alan, mate, you're hyperventilating. Slow down. Cup your hands over your mouth and breathe.'

Alan followed the instructions. After a minute his inhalations became more steady. 'Thank you.'

Liliwen kneeled next to him, stroking the back of his hand with her thumb. 'What's happened?'

'It's m-my son!' Alan took another large gulp of air, tears springing to his eyes. 'He's had an accident. On his skateboard.' Karen, standing behind him with Gunner, crossed herself.

'Oh no, love. How serious is it?' Liliwen asked him.

Fat tears rolled down his cheek. 'He's in hospital. Concussion. Broken ribs. He's about to have a scan. I need to go.'

'Are you sure you're all right to drive?' asked Connor. 'It's a long way back and you won't get home until past midnight if you leave now.'

Alan squared his shoulders. 'I need to be with my family.'

Stella heard their words as though from a great distance. Poor Alan. He was visibly distraught. It would be dangerous to let him drive alone. And he was her ride. 'I'll go with him.'

Everyone turned to Stella. 'I came with him, so I'll go with him.'

'Are you sure?' Alan wiped snot away with the back of his hand. 'I wouldn't mind the company.'

'I'm sure. I'll go pack while you load your car. Half an hour, max.'

Her eyes briefly met Connor's. She looked away first.

STELLA DRAGGED her empty suitcase from under the bed and tossed her scattered belongings in its general direction. The bra hanging off the desk chair. The neat stack of jumpers and shirts from the drawers. Her dirty laundry huddled in the corner of the bathroom. It all flew through the air, landing in a growing mound of textile.

It was sad that her week in France had come to an abrupt end, but she was relieved to have an escape. Another day and a half in Connor's company would be painful. Just having coffee in the same room had been awkward. Ignoring him while trying to learn from him would have been nigh on impossible. Besides, she was much more prepared to shoot a wedding and run her business than she had been when she arrived. That first day seemed liked another lifetime ago.

Stella threw open the ancient armoire and grabbed the few dresses she had taken the time to hang up. She came to a halt as her eyes snagged on the wedding dress, hanging so innocently from the side of the wardrobe. She petted the lace, allowing herself a moment to indulge in the memories of her kiss with Connor. She shut her eyes. An echo of heat beat between her legs.

Alan revving the engine outside slashed into her daydream. She glanced out the window and saw his estate car parked on the gravel, the other students helping him ferry his kit.

She redistributed her clothes into the two halves of her case. One of the pockets in the divider held a folded square of linen. *Grace*, the embroidery spelled in the corner. She'd forgotten about the handkerchief. She'd give it to Connor as she left. She certainly didn't want to hold onto it.

Slinging her camera bag over her shoulder, she rolled her case across the chateau floor and did a final check of the room. *Au revoir*. She closed the door on her regrets.

By some miracle, there was space for her to squeeze her case in the back of Alan's car, so she didn't have to put it in the footwell for eight hours. Krish, who had been repacking the boot, winked at her.

'I'll take the first shift,' she said, holding her hand open for the keys.

'Wait!' called Liliwen, running out of the house and throwing her arms around Stella. 'You keep in touch, *cariad*. Let's meet up next time you're on my side of the River Severn.'

Tears prickled behind her eyes, and Stella promised to call. She slotted herself into the driver's seat, closed the door, and rolled down the window. The other students had all congregated around them.

Connor helped Alan into the passenger's side and handed him a bag of sandwiches from the chef. 'Let us know when you get back, mate.' He gave Alan's shoulder a squeeze and then looked at Stella through Alan's window. 'Price, I'll be in touch.'

Like a physical touch, she could feel his eyes on her, but she refused to look at him. 'I left the dress hanging in the room,' she said coldly to the dashboard and then, remembering the handkerchief, 'Oh. And I forgot to return this to you.'

She passed the white square to Alan, who handed it to Connor. She snuck a look at him. When he recognised it, the expression on his face surprised her. Stricken. Emotional. *Definitely an important ex*, thought Stella. *Good riddance*.

After seconds that felt like hours, he tucked the handkerchief into his back pocket and gave her one last searching look, stepping back from the car. Stella hit the accelerator. They drove away along the tree-lined road, leaving Chateau Bon Chance and Connor Knight behind.

13

'He did *what?*' Claudia shouted into the phone.

Stella rubbed her ear and replaced the receiver against it, trying to stifle a yawn. She was exhausted after her mad dash across the Channel with Alan. He'd dropped her off at one AM and promised to keep her updated. Stella tried to sleep, but memories of the last five days kept her awake. Whenever she closed her eyes, Connor would be standing in her room with those shielded grey eyes, saying, *'This isn't a good idea'.* The nerve. He'd started the whole thing.

'I think you'd better begin at the beginning, as they say,' Claudia instructed.

So she did.

First, the karaoke. Stella decided not to mention that he'd helped her reclaim *'Jolene'*. Claudia didn't do sentimentality.

Instead, Stella told her about the conversation out on the patio and his arrogant instruction to keep her affections to herself.

'Fucking dobber. What did he mean by that? Like you have any intention of falling in love with him.'

'Exactly.'

Then there was the modelling, Jean-Luc, and all the touching, followed by the fainting spell.

'Yeah, you really should've eaten some breakfast. Modelling can be brutal.'

'Thanks, Liliwen already told me off for being an idiot.'

'Who's Liliwen?'

'Remember that lady I gave my seat to? She's basically *you* in thirty years.' Stella smiled. 'Anyway, that's when he kissed me. Up in my room. After helping me out of the wedding dress.'

'Kinky.'

'It just happened.'

'And how was it?'

Stella paused. On the drive home, she had replayed the kiss over and over while Alan slept. All things aside, it had been the best kiss of her life. Sexy, passionate, grown-up. And with Connor Knight: talented, charismatic, forbidden. If the situation wasn't such a nightmare, it would have been a fairy tale.

But she wasn't going to admit that to Claudia. 'Meh,' she said.

'That's a shame. It's like finding out Chris Hemsworth has bad breath.'

'I'm relieved he stopped.'

'Mm-hmm, you sound *so* relieved,' said Claudia. 'I wonder what your super couple name would be? Stonner? Connella? Actually, you're right. Those are terrible. Forget the whole thing.'

Stella Knight had a nice ring to it. She coughed. 'Am I seeing you next weekend?'

'Um...no. Really busy with shoots.'

'I can do weekdays.'

'I'll let you know.'

They hung up and Stella padded into the kitchen to investigate Tristan's schedule. She could really use his laser-sharp sense of humour and sturdy shoulders to lean on. But, no. The spreadsheet showed he was in Tokyo for a photo shoot. She stomped back to her room, unpacked her suitcase, and climbed into bed, pulling the covers over her head with a groan.

. . .

THE PHONE RINGING woke her up. She looked at the time: 8PM. *Unknown Caller.* Her heart skipped a beat. It couldn't be Connor, could it? He did say he would be in touch. After all, he owed her a day of his time, even though she hadn't yet decided whether she'd take him up on it. Her heart thumped and her stomach fell at the thought, excitement and dread in equal measure.

The ringing continued. She sat up and took a shaky gulp of water. 'Hello?' She tried to sound casual, unhurried and unimpressed all in one word.

'Stella, my lovely! How are you?' came Liliwen's sing-song voice.

Shoulders sagging, Stella masked her disappointment. 'Exhausted.'

'I hope you don't mind. You left so quickly, we forgot to exchange details. I got them off Krish.'

So, Connor definitely had the right number on file. Not that she wanted him to call. 'I'm glad you did. What's that noise in the background?'

'The airport. Thought I'd give you a quick ring to see how you're doing.'

Stella filled her in on the long ride home. She did most of the driving, so Alan could get updates on his son, who had already been discharged.

Liliwen sighed. 'Poor love. We were all missing you last night at the party. Not much of a festive atmosphere, actually.'

'Tell me?' Stella didn't want to seem too eager, but she also really wanted to know.

'Well!' Liliwen began, entering storyteller mode, 'Connor took us off for some more shooting with Jean-Luc and some other model—not a patch on you, my dear, you were gorgeous—so at least we got more training. Even so, everyone was a bit flat that night. Hannah was in hysterics at the thought of Flash going back to the States, so they went off to enjoy their last night together. Gunner and Karen were busy talking about how best to introduce him to her kids. I wanted to yell, "Run, Gunner, Run!" but thought better of it. Jared got drunk and was begging Krish to set up the karaoke machine again. Heaven help us.'

Smiling, Stella pictured it all. She regretted that her time with everyone had been cut short, but helping Alan had been the right thing to do.

'The Youngs—you know, I don't dislike many people, but they really get up my crack, those two—they were going on about adding bridal boudoir to their offering. And Connor said—actually, that reminds me. I had some nudey photos taken once, back in my Miss Wales days. Lord help me if those ever turn up on the Internet. My son would have fits! The photographer had this snake, you see—'

'Liliwen, you were telling me about Connor!'

'Oh! Sorry. Got lost in the memories, as you do. Anyways, Connor said they should do it as it would be a good revenue stream, then Mark Young starts talking about Blake Romero again, you know—that American photographer—and saying how he wanted to go on one of his courses. Connor said he knew Blake and to steer clear of him. Then they started arguing. Like *really* arguing. Connor stormed out and went to bed early. It was all very strange. I suppose Connor really doesn't like this Blake fellow.'

Stella chewed her lip. She had already decided not to tell Liliwen about The Kiss. She wanted to draw a line under the whole thing. The fewer people she told, the less chance of gossip.

'Bollocks! That's my flight,' said Liliwen. 'I'll talk to you soon, lovely. Take care.' Stella sighed. She threw her mobile down and flopped back onto the pillows. So Connor was in a bad mood, huh? Good. She hoped he felt some modicum of remorse. Then again, he could have been cross about a myriad of different things. He probably wasn't thinking about her at all.

Glancing at a picture of Tristan and her from their dancing days on her bedside table, she wished again that he was home. She needed some company.

'Looks like it's just you and me,' she said to her spider plant instead. 'Fancy watching *Bridget Jones*?' She paused, as if expecting an answer. 'No, I didn't think so.'

THE NEXT MORNING, Stella slumped over a bowl of ice cream for breakfast, flipping through the latest issue of *Brides*. She loved inspecting the real wedding section for posing inspiration and checking out the adverts of other photographers—although it also made her realise how much competition existed. How could she make herself stand out against all these experienced shooters?

Stop it, she berated herself. *You can do this.* Whenever she got impatient for results, which was always, her mother would say: '*La gatta frettolosa ha fatto i gattini ciechi*' or 'The hasty cat gives birth to blind kittens'. She had no idea how a cat's haste could cause loss of sight, but the intent was clear: Stella would get where she wanted to be with patience. Build the business. Think positive thoughts. Put it out to the Universe that Stella Price was ready for success.

She turned the page of the magazine and caught her breath. Connor Knight stared back at her, at the launch of a new bridal store. His arm rested over the shoulders of a woman, willowy and gorgeous, with slanted, cat-like eyes and a pout on her bee-stung lips. The caption read 'Connor Knight with girlfriend, Swedish model Galina Svensson.' What was it with Connor and Scandinavian models? Stella sagged in her chair. The woman in the picture wasn't Inga, his date at the conference. Maybe they'd broken up and this was a new girlfriend? How long had they been seeing each other? It couldn't be very serious if he was kissing her in France. Stella grunted. Yet again, she had played the role of Other Woman, albeit unwittingly. An arrow of anger arose, aimed at Connor. Also, Galina meant chicken in Italian. Stella was supposed to be his Mademoiselle Chicken. She closed the magazine and threw it against the wall.

What did she care anyway? She was one hundred percent not interested in him. She had more important things to think about, like how to book wedding clients before she ran out of money. She had pages of notes and ideas to implement from France. She would spend the day writing an action plan. She needed to research venues to contact, organise some styled portfolio shoots, and think those positive thoughts. *Universe, send me a sign I'm doing the right thing.*

But first, another scoop of cookie dough ice cream.

A key clicked in the lock of the flat. Could it be Tristan? His schedule said he'd be home on Friday, but maybe the job had been cancelled.

'Tristan?' she called out, hurrying to tidy away her ice cream dish.

'Is me!'

'Oh. Hi, Ula.' Stella returned to her chair with the bowl and dug her spoon into the gloop.

'Sorry I am coming on Sunday again, but I make lots of filming this week and—eeek!' As she entered the kitchen and spotted Stella, her blue eyes pinged wide. 'What happened to you? Somebody has died?'

Stella wiped her mouth on her lime green robe, bought as a gift by Claudia specifically for its lurid colour. They had a running gag where they bought each other horrible presents. She didn't look that bad, did she? 'Is it my aura again? It's been a long week.'

'It's not your aura. You have eyes like a raccoon and white paper skin. And this robe is like green slimy monster in the *Ghostbusters.*' Ula picked up the crumpled copy of *Brides* from the floor and dropped it on the kitchen island. 'Did something happen in France?'

Everything happened in France. 'Nope. It was great. Really...great.' Part of her wanted Ula to stop questioning her so she could escape to her bedroom. The other part craved the company. She stirred her ice cream.

'I don't believe you.' She clicked her fingers and pointed at Stella. 'I know what is necessary.'

Stella slumped further, too tired for another counselling session with her cleaner.

Instead of inviting Stella to the couch, Ula extracted an iPod from her pocket, chose a song, and pushed the device into Tristan's dock. At least Stella knew where all her extra tips had gone as she said a silent farewell to Ula's faithful old Walkman.

'I'm really not in the mood—'

The opening riffs of Joan Jett's *'Bad Reputation'* sang out from the flat's hidden speakers. 'You need dancing.' Orb-like breasts and hair bouncing, Ula skipped over to Stella and pulled her out of her chair with a strong grip. Stella had no option but to join in lest her limbs get yanked off.

Ula released Stella's hand in order to rock an air guitar. Stella continued to bop up and down, adding a fast flick of her feet. Actually, she did feel better. Ula couldn't have picked a more apt song. Stella had a bad reputation, too, but screw it! Damn the critics. Her father always told her she could achieve anything she put her mind to (and then told her she hadn't tried hard enough if she failed). That was beside the point. Wedding photography was about to get a full dose of Stella Price.

Eyes closed, Stella spread out her arms and twirled. Ula whooped. Stella kicked the slippers off her feet and they careened off the refrigerator. *Universe, I'm ready!*

When the song came to an end, both Stella and Ula were breathless, but smiling.

'Thanks. I needed that.'

'My pleasure. Ah! Speaking of this, I have a surprise for you. Remember I said I would do something nice for you one day?'

Stella recalled Ula promising to set her up with her bodybuilding cousin. *Please, God, no.* She fizzed with positive energy right now and didn't want to have to accept a date with Ula's cousin.

'You've already done enough. I'm much better.'

'My cousin on my father's side...'

Here it comes. She wondered if she could get out of it. Just say no. She prepared her excuses, the usual ones about not dating at the moment, which had the benefit of being true.

'He is a very successful businessman...'

Not the bodybuilder then. Smile pasted on her face, Stella willed

Ula to get to the point. The sugar rush from the ice cream and the high from dancing were beginning to fade. Maybe she should go back to bed—

'And, you see, he is getting married...'

But first she would take a long shower, and—*Wait. What?*

'I told him I know the perfect wedding photographer. A wonderful lady who is always so kind to me.'

Stella's mouth opened, but she couldn't manage words. Was Ula giving her a lead?

'He said to tell you to call.' Ula slid a piece of paper out of her bag and handed it to Stella.

She stared at it. Eleven digits in clear black ink. 'Oh my god, thank you!' Stella launched herself at Ula and gave her a grateful hug. If anyone had asked Stella where she thought she'd get her first wedding lead, she wouldn't have said, 'From my therapist cleaner who dabbles in porn.'

It sounded like the perfect wedding to cut her teeth on. Something small. A traditional family affair. Probably lots of vodka.

She was right about one of those things.

14

On the walk through Kensington, Stella reran everything Connor had said about holding a successful first meeting with a client. They'd sat around the dining room table in the chateau, watching a slideshow about marketing, pens poised to capture every word he uttered.

'Make it about them, what they want. Write down the words they use and then repeat them back when you talk about what you can deliver,' he'd instructed.

Simple. Write things down. Be charming. Make the couple feel like their wedding is the most important thing in the world.

'Come on, Stella,' she muttered to herself, shifting the heavy bag with her new sample album on her shoulder. 'You used to sell drugs for a living. You can book a wedding.'

Three weeks ago, she'd called Ula's cousin, Oliwier, only to get a foreign ring tone. They played a few rounds of phone tag before they managed to schedule a date to meet.

Stella had spent every waking second since then preparing; shooting model brides and grooms in various London locations; designing and printing a sample album; working out a price list; practising her spiel. Afterwards, she planned on sleeping for a whole day.

Stopping on the corner, she checked the map again. The houses in this section of Kensington, near the south entrance to Holland Park, looked like they'd start upward of the £5,000,000 mark. Stella didn't know much about the couple, except their names: Oliwier and Paulina. Her initial chat with Oliwier had been cordial, but short. One thing she did know: she had to book this wedding. Even a small amount of income would help her out and raise her confidence. She needed a win.

She continued walking down the posh street, and stopped in front of the tasteful grey gate at number 69, an elegant property set back from the road. Over the tall, bricked wall, she could see floor-to-ceiling windows and clean, recently appointed woodwork. Stella hastily looked up the address online. This house had last been sold two years ago for the tidy sum of £10,000,000. *Holy shit. Who are these people?* Ula had called him 'a businessman'. Stella supposed she'd find the answer shortly.

Her phone ticked over to 7:00. She exhaled, and hit the buzzer. She posed for the camera, trying to appear friendly and non-threatening. The gate clicked open.

A lily pond in the front garden offered a fleeting glimpse of serenity. She lingered a moment, admiring the jade fountain in the middle. She blinked twice. *Is that fountain a penis?* She immediately dismissed the idea. *Don't be ridiculous. It's obviously a mushroom.* Shaking her head, she walked up the steps to their solid black front door.

She licked her tongue over her teeth to remove any stray lipstick, and gave her hair a shake. *Okay, you can do this.* She pushed the doorbell. A gong reverberated throughout the house, like a Buddhist temple at prayer time.

For a split second, all was quiet in the wake of the gong. And then it started. The barking. A baritone *woof, woof, woof* accompanied by a soprano *yip, yip, yap*. Dogs! Not dogs. Anything but dogs.

The fear leeched into her muscles. Her thoughts zipped back to primary school: a small terrier with vampire teeth, bloody white uniform socks, and the demon's owner, a man with a laryngectomy and a robotic monotone: 'I'm sorry. My dog. Bit. You.'

What had Ula told her about the STOP method? Maybe she could use it here. Was there an R in it for RUN? No. She could do this. Inhaling deeply, she pretended to float above the scene, watching herself on the doorstep. It was sort of funny, really. *Hahaha*. How did she feel? Scared as all hell. Fearful for her life. No! Funny. *Hahahahaha*.

The *woof woofs* and *yip yaps* grew closer. Running really did seem like the best option. Who was she kidding? The hounds would sever her Achilles tendon before she reached the gate.

A scratching noise. Sharp nails on wood. A thump. Stella took a step back.

Locks slid open, a series of grinding noises, clicks and whirs. One, two, three, four...what was this, the Bank of England? The final barrier glided free and the door creaked open, revealing a short, bronzed man holding a chihuahua under one arm and restraining a hulking black Great Dane with the other.

'Holy shit!' Stella said before she could stop herself. She dropped her bag and backed towards a pillar, flattening herself against it.

'Maleńki! Calma calma,' said the man to the woofing dog.

She fixated on the Great Dane's sharp teeth, dripping saliva like a flesh-starved beast. The man flashed a smile so white it was almost blue and said, 'You do not worry. He is friendly. He likes you.'

He'd like me for dinner, thought Stella, unconvinced. Even the chihuahua was licking its lips in anticipation.

'I go put them away. Just a momentito.' He disappeared into the house with the dogs.

Stella peeled herself off the pillar and readjusted her suit jacket and skirt under her coat. Taking a tissue from her bag, she patted her moist forehead and upper lip and picked up her abandoned tote with the album in it. She really needed to practice that STOP method. By the time the man returned, dog-free, she had regained her composure.

When he'd been covered in canines, she couldn't appreciate the garish splendour of his outfit. Now she saw his tight black leather trousers under a loud black and gold Versace shirt, unbuttoned just one place too far to be decent. A diamond stud twinkled in each earlobe while a swathe of golden bling circled his neck. His fashionable, almost indiscernible, stubble seemed stippled on, as if with a sponge and face paint. However, the most noticeable thing about him was the blast of aftershave wafting into Stella's face.

Swallowing a cough, she said, 'Um...hi! I'm the wedding photographer. Stella Price?'

'Stella Price! Beautiful name for beautiful lady. Come. Come. I am Oliwier.' He put his hands together as if in prayer. 'So sorry about Maleńki and Boris. They will not hurt you.'

'He's very...big.'

'Yes, big teddy bear! Do not you worry.'

'Okay...'

She stepped into a hallway paved in sleek porcelain tiles, the colour of a night sky. Two large closets with leopard print doors drew her eye, their busy pattern reflected in a gigantic wall mirror opposite.

'I take your coat?' Oliwier asked.

'Yes. Please.' She shrugged it off and he opened the closet. Instead of hangers, a row of glistening bronze mushroom-shaped hooks sprouted from the wall. Strange. These people obviously had a thing for fungi. Maybe they were dealers in rare mushrooms or something. She reckoned that would be lucrative, but ten-million-pound house lucrative?

As he led her down the hallway, she heard sharp claws hitting porcelain tiles. *Oh no.*

The Great Dane bounded out of the next room, lolloping straight at her. She dropped her bag again and turned herself into wallpaper, her hands rising to shield her face.

'Maleńki! No!' yelled Oliwier ineffectually.

Despite having oversized ears, the dog did not listen. When he reached her, Maleńki stretched to his full height and thumped his rat-sized paws onto her shoulders.

She couldn't even scream. Her eyes watered from the double whammy of the dog's meat breath and Oliwier's patchouli aftershave.

Maleńki examined her. A dollop of drool dripped onto the exposed instep of Stella's heeled foot.

The dog licked her. She clamped her mouth shut to contain a dry heave. Grunting, Oliwier managed to haul the dog off. Eyes clenched shut, Stella contemplated leaving. Now. Screw her bank account. Nothing was worth this level of torture.

But as her breathing slowed and she realised she still lived, another, calmer voice took over: *You can do this. You need this wedding. Go and show him how awesome you are.* This would be the P in STOP: *Proceed* (or *continue* as Ula had written it).

Who could she channel that would make her feel like a winner? A pinch of Claudia for her courage and take-no-nonsense attitude; a touch of Liliwen for her chatty nature and likability; and perhaps even a dash of Connor for his staggering self-confidence.

She stood tall, wiped the dog's saliva from her cheek, and picked up her bag, glancing inside to confirm that the album had survived being dropped twice in the past ten minutes. It had cost her a lot of money and time to put together. She couldn't have it falling apart on her yet.

Oliwier walked briskly back into the hall, hands rubbing together. 'So sorry! He wants to be your friend. Dogs, they are very smart. He knows you no like him.'

'I don't *not* like him...' she lied.

He laughed and waggled his finger at her. She recognised Ula's dimple in his right cheek when he smiled. 'You English. Always so polite.' She didn't bother to correct him and say she was actually Welsh. 'Come, let us get to know one the other.' He winked and twiddled one of his diamond earrings. Apprehension bloomed in her for a whole different reason. Even though the top of his head only reached her eyes and she could probably take him in a fight, she didn't want to get into any awkward situations.

'Walk this way,' he said, swaggering down the dark hallway, hips swaying in a sassy manner. *Interesting.*

She followed. Clearing her throat, she asked, 'Will Paulina be joining us?'

'Ah! No. She is very busy. With the work.'

That gave Stella the perfect opening to ask: 'What is it that you both do for a living?'

'This. That,' he said, flapping his hand dismissively. Why wouldn't he tell her? Was it something illegal? Maybe the mushrooms they grew were on the wrong side of the law.

He led her into a drawing room that could fit Tristan's whole apartment.

At a glance, the decor was traditional with a modern twist: black and white broken up by the occasional splash of bright pink in the form of throw cushions and a massive fuchsia grand piano. Two party-sized black velvet sofas faced each other in the centre, surrounded by various statues, chairs, and jungle-sized plants. It was the perfect room for a cocktail party, a hired pianist entertaining the guests with Elton John covers. On second thought, they could probably afford Elton himself.

'You play?' he asked her.

'No, unfortunately not. It's on my bucket list.'

'Bucket list? I do not know this.'

'Oh, it means things I want to do before I die. You know, like sky diving or travelling the world. That sort of thing.' *Booking this wedding,* she added in her head.

'Ah! Like—' He said something in Polish. Snapping his fingers, he announced, 'I play a song for you, beautiful Stella.' He skipped across the room, skirting the sofas, and sat down at the piano, rolling his neck and cracking his fingers. Hands hovered a moment above the ivory keys before he launched into a note-perfect rendition of the love theme from *Romeo and Juliet*. His whole body moved with the music: left, right, up, down, like a musical serpent.

To say Stella felt uncomfortable as she stood listening to Oliwier serenade her would be a huge understatement. Unable to look at his spasming performance, she took the opportunity to study the room.

The whole right wall was covered in wallpaper showing Victorian characters going about their daily tasks. As she stared more closely at the illustrations, she realised that the people were performing sexual acts: cunnilingus, fellatio, sixty-nine, some light spanking. A blush crept up her cheeks as she averted her gaze to a statue in the corner, a wooden sculpture of a woman with an impossibly long neck. At the base were two rotund breasts, almost testicular in nature. Stella shook her head and looked again. The whole sculpture was both a woman stretching her neck *and* a large penis, like one of those illusions where the viewer sees either the vase or two faces. The ingenue or the crone. The penis or the woman with a long throat.

They hadn't been mushrooms.

Oliwier was still playing. He had segued into *'Sweet Transvestite'* from *Rocky Horror*. Her eyes slid past him to a row of three frames on the wall. Each one featured a set of saucy lingerie with matching sex toy—a tickler, a whip, a spiked collar—presented the way that some people framed their favourite football jersey.

Was this place for real? Could he be the producer of Ula's porn films? A family business?

Stella wanted this meeting to end sooner rather than later. What time was it? She found a clock near the door. The small penis was on the seven and the large penis on the six. Half-past seven and they hadn't even talked about the wedding yet. Nothing she had learned on Connor's course had prepared her for a situation like this. *Maybe he just forgot to cover what to do when your potential client hits on you in his phallic sex den and has the Hound of the Baskervilles as a pet.*

'Excuse me,' she said. He continued to play. She raised her voice. 'Excuse me!'

Oliwier stopped, looking towards her in surprise.

'Sorry. That was truly, truly beautiful, but would you mind if we talked about the wedding?' she said as sweetly as she could.

He threw his hands into the air. *'Tak! Tak!* I get carried away. So sorry.' He scuttled around the sofa. 'Please. Sit. Will you like a drink?'

Actually her throat did feel dry.

'Um, yes, some water would be nice.'

Nodding his head once, he exited the room, leaving her to make herself comfortable. She placed her bag on the floor and sank into the velvet sofa. Behind her, something was snoring. She froze, then carefully extricated herself from the cushions. Kneeling, she peeked over the back.

The Great Dane and the chihuahua laid curled up together on a pillow the size of a classic Mini Cooper, eyes closed, probably dreaming of attacking a red-haired woman. She cursed Oliwier. She thought he had put them in a cage somewhere, which would have been the polite thing to do when there is a guest so obviously scared shitless of dogs.

She crawled off the sofa, holding her breath for fear of disturbing the creatures. Gingerly, she picked up her bags and, following the sound of Oliwier whistling, she intercepted him in the hallway before he could re-enter the sexed-up drawing room. He carried a bottle of Cristal and two glass flutes.

'Champagne? I know you English like the tea, but it is after seven o'clock.'

I'm Welsh! she screamed inside, but, choosing her battles, she said, 'Actually, would you mind if we talked elsewhere? Perhaps the dining room? Somewhere with a table where I can lay out my album?'

He waved the flutes in the air. '*Tak!* Of course.' He turned and led her further into the bowels of the house.

They entered a dining space dominated by an obsidian table that could easily fit 20 people. Chinese vases filled with a florist shop's worth of pink roses lined the spine of the table. Dark, flocked wallpaper covered the walls, thankfully without any copulating couples. It was quite impressive, almost tasteful.

If only they hadn't hung the golden-framed photograph of a naked woman lying in a bed of pink rose petals above the fireplace. Her spine was arched, her legs bent and spread, the model looking straight at the camera with parted lips. Stella hoped that this was the bride, Paulina, and not some random woman. The work itself was stunning, but how could they throw a dinner party with *that* staring at the guests all night?

She squinted at the signature in the corner of the picture and gasped. 'You know Connor Knight?'

'Oh yes, we love Connor. He make beautiful pictures of my Paulina.'

'Why haven't you hired him to shoot your wedding?' She couldn't compete with Connor. Not yet. Why was she even here? Ula must have insisted that her cousin meet with Stella out of some misguided loyalty.

'We did ask, but he is busy during our day. But Ula say you are also very good.'

Ula had never seen any of her work. She'd been oversold.

The distinctive sound of tippity-tapping feet, followed by the trot of a larger mammal reached her ears. *For heaven's sake*, she thought. The Great Dane and the chihuahua sauntered into the room and relocated their nap onto another hair-covered cushion in the corner. They curled up, the smaller dog using the larger one's back as a mattress. It would be cute, if they weren't so goddamned terrifying.

Inhaling a shaky breath, she went through the steps in STOP like a pro. Booking the wedding trumped fear of dogs, at least, for today. She had to secure this job. With great care, she brought out the sample album and laid it on the table, opening it to the first page: a stunning picture of a model bride she had hired. She felt quite proud of it.

Oliwier set the flutes down and got to work on opening the champagne. 'Is she not beautiful?' he asked, blowing a kiss towards Paulina's portrait.

'Yes, it's certainly...different,' Stella said, trying to keep the judgment from her voice. But he must have picked up on it.

'Ah, I forget it sometimes. We do not always have people like you to the house.'

Crossing her arms, Stella asked, 'People like me?'

'You know. How they say...uptight? Proper. *English*.' As he said it the cork exploded from the bottle, liquid spraying through the air.

Stella watched in horror as it settled onto her prized sample album, the one that had just cost her £600 plus extra to get it produced in time for this meeting.

That was it. First the dogs. Then the sex den. And now this. How dare he spill champagne on her book? And how very dare he call her uptight? And how very *very* dare he call her *English!*

'I am *fucking Welsh!*' Stella yelled and immediately covered her mouth with her hands, shocked at herself.

Oliwier froze. The Great Dane lifted its head. The chihuahua raised an eyebrow. Everything was silent except for the champagne dripping onto the floor.

'I upset you,' Oliwier said, putting the bottle down on the table. 'I so sorry. Your book...' He pulled a handkerchief from his back pocket and started mopping up the pee-coloured fluid from the page. With shaking hands, Stella took a pack of tissues from her bag to do the same. At least the print seemed to be okay. Only time would tell if a stain remained on the mounts.

Horror at her unprofessionalism threatened to choke her. 'I'm so sorry. I shouldn't have yelled.'

'No, no, is my fault. I pay for new book.' He pulled out a thick wallet, liberating a wad of fifty pound notes. 'Is good?'

Although tempted, she shook her head no. There wasn't enough damage for a full reprint. She could always just skip over the first page in future viewings. 'It's fine. I think it'll dry.'

'You are sure?' He put his wallet away, and poured Cristal into two glasses.

'Thanks,' Stella said when he offered her one.

'To finding love,' he said, toasting Paulina's picture.

'To finding love.'

'*Twoje zdrowie!*' He clinked her flute and drained his in one gulp. She only wet her lips, wanting to keep her wits about her. She sat down with her back to Paulina and took out a brand new leather notebook. *Right,* she thought, *remember what Connor said: write down the words the client uses.*

'So tell me, Oliwier. What sort of wedding are you planning to have?'

He shrugged. 'Wedding is wedding. I have wedding.'

'Right.' She wrote *wedding* in her notebook. 'Um, is there anything else you can tell me? Is there a theme?'

'Theme is...wedding.'

'Okay. How many guests are you inviting?'

'I think there is one hundred people for day, more come in evening. Most friends, business associates. Some Paulina's family from Złotokłos. I have never met them, so will be first time.'

'Oh, you must be excited. Is your family coming?'

'Only cousin Ula. Rest are dead.'

Stella nodded, keeping her face impassive. 'Right. Okay.' She wrote down *dead* next to *wedding*.

'So how much is?' Oliwier asked with a sweeping gesture towards the album and Stella.

She hesitated. She hadn't expected to start talking money until after they'd gone over the details and she had sold him on her skills and expertise. He hadn't even flicked through her sample album. She said as much.

'Ula say you are the one. Is all recommendation I need.'

'Great,' she said. To buy herself some thinking time, she rooted through her handbag. When setting her prices, she started packages at £1500, but Connor said she should go higher, considering all the hours that go into servicing one wedding client. Taking in the expensive furnishings, she decided to follow Connor's advice.

Sitting up straight, she said, 'Three thousand pounds for the basic package. That's for eight hours of coverage on the day plus a twenty-spread album and two hundred thank you cards.'

Oliwier's face fell. 'Really? Oh.'

Shit, thought Stella. *I went too far*. 'If it's too expensive, I can—'

'Too expensive? Too EXPENSIVE?' He slammed his hand down on the table. 'Is not expensive *enough!* I want very best for my Paulina.'

Stella furrowed her brow, digesting what he said. 'Okay, so you want to spend *more?*' He nodded. 'Well, we can add another thirty spreads to the album?'

'Yes. Yes! Add one hundred spreads!'

'Fifty is actually the maximum number.' Stella did the math on her notepad. 'That brings it to…six thousand pounds.'

'I like it. What more?'

'Um. Well.' She thought a moment. 'Albums for parents! Do you want to give a copy of the album to anyone?'

'Yes, one to Paulina's parents. One to put in each our houses. So that's ten more. And one for each guest, no? People do this, yes?'

Stella's hand began to shake as she took notes. Trying to keep her voice calm, she said, 'Well, maybe not the big album, but I can do miniature versions for everyone. One hundred did you say?'

'Plus the later guests, mostly business associate. About more one hundred people.'

'So two hundred mini albums?'

'*Dokladnie.* Yes.' He looked at his nails and refilled his glass.

'Right. We're at £45,000 now.' Her voice squeaked as she said it. Her heart thumped. *Don't mess this up. Let him call you English all day if he wants*, she thought, suppressing a nervous giggle.

'What more?'

He wants more? 'Ah! We can add in the digital negatives. And… wall art! Do you want some wedding photos for the walls?'

'Yes! Big ones. Hugest size. We have much empty space in Malibu and Sydney houses.'

Stella really wanted to know what these people did for a living. Definitely not mushrooms. Even porn wouldn't bring this level of wealth. Honestly, at this point, as long as it wasn't human trafficking, arms dealing, or cruelty to animals, she didn't care. 'So let's add in ten sixty-by-forty inch acrylics and the digitals. That will bring us to…' She had to take a deep breath, 'Sixty thousand pounds.' She laughed and then clamped her mouth shut, not quite believing it.

'Yes!' He stood up and punched the air. 'Is good! I like it. You like it?'

'I...Yes! I like it.' She couldn't help but smile.

'Is wonderful news. I am so happy you are happy. What is next?'

'Next? Oh, right! I'll need to take a deposit. The wedding is in two months...'

'I give you half now. Half at wedding day.'

'Okay. That'll be fine.' She tried to control her breathing. 'I'll send you the invoice tonight, so you can make the transfer.'

'Oh, no, I pay cash. You wait here. I get.' He jogged out of the room, whistling.

How much cash did they keep in the house? That would explain all the locks on the front door. Tiptoeing to peer into the hallway to check he'd gone, she did a happy dance, running her feet on the spot and punching the air. Sixty thousand pounds! On her first wedding! That was Connor Knight territory. She had to tell Claudia. She had to tell Liliwen. She had to tell the world.

As quickly as the excitement came, it ebbed. She'd just earned £60,000 on her first wedding. That was Connor Knight territory. And she was no Connor Knight, yet. Was she good enough to shoot a wedding like this? This could be the beginning and the end of her new career. Talk about running before she could walk.

Stella sucked in air, breathing out through her mouth. Everything would be okay. She would just have to learn and practice as much as she could in the next two months.

She stopped short. She still had a day banked with Connor in exchange for the modelling. She could contact him and say she needed help. Her need to do well at this wedding superseded any embarrassment. Or did it?

No. She would find another way. The thought of calling him made her nauseous. She just couldn't do it, even for £60,000. Claudia would help her figure something out.

By the time Oliwier's whistling returned, she had calmed down and was sitting primly at the table, album dried and packed.

Oliwier bounced into the room carrying a Harvey Nichols bag. He handed it to Stella. 'Thirty thousand pounds.'

She took the bag and peeked inside. Rolls of crisp £50 notes, secured by rubber bands, lay nestled on top of each other like cans in a pantry. It was more cash than she'd ever seen in one place.

'Count. Please,' he said.

'Oh, I'm sure it's all there,' she said, not wanting to give him time to change his mind.

'No, Miss Stella. You always count when person give cash. Very important lesson of life.'

She took the rolls out and laid them on the table, like she'd just completed a heist. A smoking cigar and a bottle of whiskey would complete the image. Oliwier refilled their champagne glasses and checked his phone while she thumbed through each of the notes one by one. After the first stack, she gained a newfound appreciation for bank tellers. Flipping through wasn't easy at all. She kept losing count and having to start again. Forty-five minutes later, she placed that last bundle on the pile. 'It's all there.' She hoped.

'*Wspaniale!* Good. I am excited about big day with you to make pictures.' He raised his champagne flute. In a mood to celebrate, but not with him, she clinked glasses and finished it.

She replaced the money in the Harvey Nics bag and tried to shove it into her canvas holdall with the album. It wouldn't fit. She would have to carry it separately, through the streets of Kensington, at night. Perhaps she should splurge on a black cab. Riding the Tube with thirty grand large on her lap didn't appeal.

'Ah! Moment! I have some things for you,' Oliwier exclaimed. He ran his eyes over her as though taking measurements and disappeared again.

The Great Dane stretched, upsetting the chihuahua on its shoulder. Stella jumped. She'd almost forgotten them in the excitement. She held her breath, waiting for the hounds to settle again. Actually, the chihuahua was kind of cute in a ratty sort of way.

Oliwier returned, carrying another bag. He thrust it towards Stella. 'Here. These are gift for you. I think they be correct sizing.'

She peeked inside, curious. Lace in a variety of colours filled the bag. She pulled one out, a low-cut red number that didn't leave much to the imagination. She looked at the tag and that's when it hit her. '*Oh, Paulina*! That's who you are.' *Oh, Paulina!*, the globally famous lingerie brand, known for its saucy, risqué designs, was very popular with fashion magazines and the bondage crowd. She had some pieces leftover from her days of trying to tantalise Nathan. Ula really should've warned her.

'Yes? Who you think we are?'

'Frankly, I had no idea.'

He chuckled. 'Well, enjoy. My wishes is they help you find love, also, Welsh Lady.' He double-clicked his tongue at her.

She smiled at all the wild conclusions she'd made over the past couple hours. Mushroom dealers? Porn producers? She realised that, like the chihuahua, Oliwier had grown on her.

Sitting in the cab on her way home with her haul, she thought about what had just happened. Sixty thousand pounds. Her first wedding. Now she just had to become a first-rate photographer in two months. *Gulp.*

15

ON THE DAY of the wedding, Stella wanted to vomit.

As Claudia's classic Fiat 500 rattled down the M4 like an orange tortoise, Stella took a break from reviewing the list of must-have shots sent to her by the wedding planner. Bride getting into dress. Bride walking down the aisle. Bride saying vows. The requirements went on for three pages. Most of them seemed logical. Of course she would photograph the first kiss. What did the planner think she'd be doing at that point? Picking her nose?

Next to her, Claudia sang 'She Works Hard for the Money' at full volume.

Stella closed her eyes and said a silent prayer of thanks for her friend. The moment she'd asked Claudia to second shoot for her, she'd said yes. In return, Stella promised to cook a month's worth of her mother's famous lasagne for Claudia's freezer. That, plus £2000 in cash.

Examining the stuffed back seat, she reassured herself that she hadn't forgotten her camera bag, like the best man re-checking his pocket for the rings. The pristine suitcase stared back at her, carrying her camera and the new lenses she'd splurged on, using her fee.

The nausea subsided. Stella picked up the schedule.

'After the ceremony, he's only given me 20 minutes to get 100 different shots of Oliwier and Paulina.' Not even Connor Knight could do that. When she'd emailed the planner requesting more time, she'd received one line back: *The schedule is my business, not yours.* She couldn't wait to meet him.

The day had dawned dry and sunny, a small miracle after a wet June. *It must be a good omen.* She wiggled in her seat, wishing the cab of the car wasn't so cramped, even though it was still more comfortable than Alan's car had been. The pair of Hunter wellies taking up half the footwell irritated her so she kicked at them. No matter how many times she attempted to move them for some legroom, they wobbled back again.

'Why do you even have these?' she raged. 'I thought you were allergic to the countryside.'

Claudia shrugged, her eyes fixed on the road. 'I flirted with it for a bit…it didn't work out. You can have them if you want.'

Stella threw them roughly into the back seat, narrowly missing Claudia's head.

'Hulk needs to fuck off. Can I have Bruce Banner back please?'

'I know. I'm sorry.' *You can do this*, Stella thought. *You're prepared.*

In the movie of her life, the last two months would be a montage where the heroine works hard to achieve her goals, emerging ready to take on the world. Stella had memorised every note from France, practised posing herself in the mirror, and assisted Gunner with four weddings.

From Connor, she hadn't heard a word. Either he'd forgotten that he owed her a day of his time or he didn't want to see her. She told herself she didn't care. She could do this without him. It just would have been nice if he'd had the courtesy to call.

'We're here.'

The nausea rose again as they drove through the gates of Cliveden, an imposing stately-home-turned-country-hotel with extensive grounds. Or as Claudia called it, 'the place where that Tory fucked a showgirl,' referring to the famous Profumo affair in the sixties.

Their car crawled along the drive, wheels kicking up gravel with a *tik tik tik* that chipped at Stella's frayed nerves.

They entered the forecourt, picking their way around an army of delivery trucks. Claudia parked between a bright red Ferrari and a yellow Lamborghini, her car playing the poor cousin in Cliveden's automobile rainbow.

Stella breathed in and released the air slowly. *You've got this, Price.* Her eyes jerked open when she realised the voice in her head was Connor's. She supposed that made sense. She'd been replaying everything he taught her in France until it became second nature. The only thing she hadn't thought about was The Kiss. Not much, anyway.

'Are you ready?' Claudia asked after liberating their bags from the squashed back seat.

'How do I look?' Stella straightened her black suit jacket and tweaked the collar of her crisp white button-down shirt. Her hair was plaited to keep it out of her face as she worked.

'Like a member of the Secret Service.'

'Just what I was going for.'

Stella chose her outfit carefully, wanting to portray an aura of professionalism and capability. Claudia, in comparison, wore a knee-length dress in bright yellow paired with short go-go boots, dressed more like a guest than photographer.

They lugged their heavy camera bags towards the entrance.

As they walked into the foyer, Stella ducked to avoid getting hit by a rolled carpet borne by two burly men. A team of florists arranged massive flowery masterpieces; another team of black-clad men wore 'Bergdorf Productions' across their backs with the strap line 'Exclusive events for exclusive people.' On the far side of the room, they erected a wall hiding Cliveden's famous carved fireplace behind it. Their drills whirred noisily.

At the front desk, guests checked in among the chaos. Stella sagged with relief when she recognised a familiar face.

'Ula!' Leaving her bag with Claudia, Stella ran over and hugged her cleaner/therapist. She almost didn't recognise her: dressed in a tight peacock-blue dress with matching hat. Even the tips of her hair had switched from pink to blue to match her outfit. Her arms were bare; Stella hadn't realised how defined Ula's arm muscles were. She looked amazing.

'How are you feeling?' Ula pulled back from the hug and rested her hands on Stella's shoulders, massaging them with her thumbs. Stella felt like a boxer about to enter the ring.

'I'm ready. How's my aura?' She hoped her fear wasn't obvious. Both of them were invested in her success today. If she failed, it would reflect badly on Ula, too.

'Orange and yellow today. It's good.' With one final squeeze, Ula stepped aside and motioned towards an unnaturally copper man behind her. 'This is my boyfriend, Ronny.'

'Glad to meetchya,' he said with an American twang, his jaw working overtime on a piece of gum. He had thick veins and a thicker neck, signs that he spent a lot of time in a gym. As Stella endured his assertive handshake, she couldn't help but notice that his forearm was as wide as her calf.

He slipped his arm around Ula's waist, pulling her close. Stella flexed her hand behind her back, hoping he hadn't broken any bones. She needed all her fingers today.

'Ronny is a mega-star personal trainer.' Ula rubbed her palm proudly over his chest. Stella imagined it must be like petting a rock.

'Thanks, babe. I can speak for myself.' With a flick of his wrist, he had a business card in his hand. Did he side-line as a magician? He presented the card to Stella alongside an overpowering whiff of spicy cologne. 'Give me a call if you want to achieve the next level of fitness.'

His eyes were invisible behind reflective sunglasses, but she would bet money that he ran his gaze up and down her body as he spoke. *Jerk.*

'Um, thanks.' Stella abandoned the card in a pocket, wanting this awkward moment to pass. She glanced at Ula with a supportive smile, but she seemed oblivious to her boyfriend's inappropriate behaviour.

'Excuse me. May I show you to your room?' interrupted a Cliveden employee.

Saved by the bellboy. 'I'll see you later, Ula, okay?'

As they walked away, Ronny landed a firm slap on Ula's buttocks. Great, now Stella had another worry to add to her list: Ula's controlling boyfriend. Something about the story Stella had constructed around Ula didn't make sense. Why would she act in porn films and clean houses if she had a successful boyfriend and a cousin who could afford to buy a football team? Stella promised herself to have a frank chat with Ula next time she saw her.

Right now, she had other things to worry about. A fresh wave of nerves crashed over her as she walked back to Claudia.

'Who was that? Looking at him made me want to do a push up.'

'Ula's boyfriend.' Stella crossed her arms. 'Tell me again why I'm not going to crash and burn today.'

'Because I'm standing by with a bucket of water.'

'Uh-huh.'

'Shit, speaking of water, I have to pee. Back in two ticks.' Claudia darted off, leaving Stella alone and conspicuous.

'That's HIDEOUS! I ordered ORCHIDS, not CALLA LILLIES,' an angry voice pierced her eardrums. 'I'll expect a REFUND.'

Stella looked for the source of the complaining. A long-limbed man with bleached blonde hair, wearing a slim-cut beige suit, pink shirt, and a paisley bowtie glided through the room like the lord of the manor. A tail of three assistants in matching grey pencil dresses snaked behind him. Stella's instinct told her to hide, but his head swivelled in her direction. He flicked his eyeballs over her and barked, 'Who are you?'

'I'm the photographer. Stella—'

He grabbed at his chest. 'WHAT are you WEARING?'

'I'm sorry?' Stella replied, looking down at her suit.

'I SPECIFICALLY said in my email that wearing WHITE is FORBIDDEN at this wedding. Bride's orders. This is just hideous. HIDEOUS! Did you read anything I sent you?'

Stella reddened, her temper fighting with embarrassment and her desire to make a good impression. She could hear her mother saying, *'Non castrarti per far dispetto alla moglie'* or 'Don't castrate yourself to spite your wife'. She swallowed her anger.

'Sorry. My mistake,' she said through a fixed smile. She had read all 50+ emails multiple times to make sure she hadn't missed anything. There had been no mention of a 'no white' rule.

He snapped his fingers twice and one of the assistants stepped up. Stella wondered if they each had their own individual snap, like the Von Trapp children. 'Check the hotel lost and found for a blouse. They must have something.' He pulled in a steady breath through his narrow nose and pushed it out slowly through his thin lips. 'Right. Did you get the list of must-haves?'

'Yes. I—'

'And the schedule?'

'Yes, I wanted to talk to you about that—'

'Why are you here so early? The bride won't need you for TWO HOURS yet.' Without warning, he held up his hand and snapped three times. Another assistant stepped forward. 'Remind me to call Frances about the mixologist.'

Was Stella being told off for being early? 'Sorry, I just wanted to be prepared,' she said but he wasn't listening, his attention on his phone. The assistant who had gone to look in the lost and found scurried back, pinching a crimson item between two fingers like a dirty nappy.

'This is all they had.' She tossed it towards Stella.

Stella caught it, finding a red shirt with a high collar, covered in layers of ruffles, two sizes too big. The smell of its previous owner's flowery perfume clung to the fabric along with a faint whiff of body odour on the armpits. 'I'm going to look like a bullfighter.'

The assistant shrugged.

'Beautiful lady!'

At that moment, Oliwier swept down the stairs wearing an open, oversized bathrobe trailing over hotel slippers and tight gold swim trunks. His necklaces glistened over his hairless, oiled chest. Ignoring everyone else, he glided towards Stella and enfolded her in his arms, planting loud kisses on both cheeks. The wedding planner watched with unconcealed surprise. He quickly arranged his features into a pained smile, an unnatural expression on him that caused his facial muscles to twitch.

Turning towards him, Oliwier said, 'Watch out with this lady. She's fucking Welsh. Don't mess it up with her.' He winked at Stella. 'I go now for traditional waxing and massage. See you laters!' Walking towards the spa, he sang *'Ding dong, my balls are going to shine!'*

The sound of the drills broke the ensuing silence. After a few seconds, the planner jiggled his head and screamed, 'MARCUS, WHAT ARE YOU DOING? THAT LOOKS HIDEOUS.' He stalked away.

'I suppose I've been dismissed,' Stella said to nobody, frowning at the polyester blouse in her hand.

Claudia returned from the toilets. 'What did I miss?'

TWO HOURS LATER, Stella stood in front of the Lady Astor Suite, where the bride was getting ready. Her fist hovered above the panelled wood, her tasteful white shirt cuff replaced by garish red frills. Ignoring her bullfighter chic appearance, she focussed her breathing. *Tits and teeth*, she repeated in her head.

As soon as she stepped through that door, she would be in perpetual motion until midnight. This was it. The point of no return. She was the Duke of Wellington before Waterloo. Freddie Mercury before Live Aid. Muhammad Ali before the Rumble in the Jungle.

Taking one final breath, she knocked.

Seconds later the door swung open to reveal an ultra-tanned woman with platinum blonde hair and perfect make-up. Behind her two other women danced to a Whitney Houston song.

'Tak?' she said, which Stella knew meant 'yes' in Polish.

'I'm Stella, the wedding photographer?'

'Oh!' she exclaimed, 'Come in! Come in!' She pulled Stella into the room.

'I am Gosia. Agnieska. Melania.' All wore short silken pink robes with Bridesmaid embroidered on the back. Their hair had been swept into up-dos, eyelashes extended with falsies. Agnieska, the brunette, waved. Melania, whose hair was a deep artificial red, marched towards Stella and took her auburn plait in her hand. 'Look at this colour! Who does your hair? Is it Pietro? How did you get an appointment?'

'Actually, it's natural,' Stella said.

'P-fah! Some women have all the luck.' Melania dropped the braid and drowned her hair sorrows by knocking back a glass of bubbles.

'You want to take pictures of us?' said Agnieska. 'Where is best place? On bed?'

Laughing, they crawled onto the plush blue bed and started posing, their giggling school girl act transforming instantly into sex kitten mode. Their natural smiles disappeared as their chemically-enhanced lips performed what Stella and Claudia jokingly called 'The Chelsea Pout': a supposedly 'sexy' expression somewhere between puckering for a kiss and resting bitch face that made them look like ducks.

'Just give me a moment. I have to prep my camera.'

Exuding an air of calm professionalism while her pulse raced, Stella laid down her bag and unzipped the cover. She picked up her camera and slipped the strap around her neck.

'Is the bride here?' she asked while she prepared.

'She's in the bathroom, getting her face put on. She'll be out soon,' answered Gosia in flawless English.

Stella checked over her camera settings as Connor said to do at the beginning of each set up. After sliding the flash into its shoe, she attached it to the coiled cord from the external battery pack on her belt.

Stella Price was ready for action.

'Okay, ladies, this is what I'd like you to do.'

The next half hour passed quickly while Stella photographed the bridesmaids in various positions. They were eager models, full of suggestions for the shots. On the bed. In front of the window. Outside on the veranda. Individually. Together. When Stella said she needed to get on photographing the bridal details, they all embraced her. As she flicked through the images on the back of her camera, Stella knew she'd made a solid start.

They offered her a line of coke.

'Um, no thank you,' Stella demurred.

While the bridesmaids got high on the bed, Stella rifled through the bags lining the floor, each bearing the names of shops so expensive that she'd never been to them. She found the shoes and garter. Opening the brown cardboard box with Christian Louboutin scrawled across the top in white ink, she unwrapped the shoes carefully. They were off-white and covered in Swarovski crystals with signature red soles. Size 42. A piece of paper fluttered to the carpet and she picked it up. *Mon cheri, I hope you have the wedding of your dreams. Love, Christian.* Stella raised her eyebrows, impressed.

While Stella photographed the shoes and garter, the bridesmaids changed the music to a clubbing mix. Stella noticed that their lacquered up-dos were starting to slip as they bounced to the thumping beat. They would need touch-ups which would take time. She checked her watch, bought specifically for today to keep her on schedule. One and a quarter hours until the aisle.

Next Stella found the gown hanging in the closet. Valentino. Nice. The lacy design flared into a tulle fishtail, reminding her of the dress she wore in France. Stella examined the detailed glass beads sewn into the bodice. That would have taken a long time to sew by hand.

The shot of the bridal dress had to be iconic. She scanned the room for the right place to take a worthy picture; somewhere she could capture the full length.

The veranda doors.

They would frame the dress beautifully, back light making the fabric glow. She had seen similar pictures in Connor's albums. It was perfect.

'Woo hoo!' shouted one of the bridesmaids while jumping on the bed.

Stella carried the dress to the tall glass doors, looking for somewhere to hook the hanger. Nothing. Not even a screw. Chewing her lip, she considered next steps. Noticing the thin gap between the two doors, she had an idea. It only had to hold for a minute while she took the shot. Laying the dress on the velvet sofa, she dragged a chair over. Dress in hand, she climbed up, wedging the metal loop into the slim space between the doors. It stuck. The dress looked gorgeous, exactly as she'd imagined it. She whipped the chair away and picked up her camera. She checked her settings and clicked a series of shots, thrilled at how it all came together.

'Ah! The dress! So beautiful!' exclaimed Agnieska before all three of them appeared in the frame.

'Take picture of us with dress,' ordered Melania, striking a pose. The others followed suit, hugging the dress, hugging each other, pouting. Stella took the shots, wanting them to get away from the gown before it fell down.

'Got it!' she said. 'You can leave it now.'

Melania, who had put her face next to the dress, stepped away. Stella saw a small patch of fake tan on the expensive fabric.

'The dress!' Stella pointed.

'What—argh!' As Gosia stepped back, her up-do snagged on the glass beads, tugging at the gown. The metal hook stayed jammed between the doors, but the slim loops of ribbon attaching the dress to the hanger slipped free. The gown came crashing down, the bodice hanging from Gosia's ruined hair.

The bridesmaids panicked.

'Help me!' shouted Gosia, bending over while Agnieska flapped her hands and Melania hyperventilated.

Stella rushed in.

'Melania, you hold the top of the dress. I'll sort out the hair.'

Carefully, Stella unpicked the platinum strands from the beads one by one. *Everything will be okay*, she told herself. *This can be fixed.*

Agnieska was sobbing now, mascara running down her face.

'It'll be fine,' Stella said, hoping it was true, wanting to calm the frantic bridesmaid before her make-up got anywhere near the dress.

'Paulina is going to kill you,' Agnieska whimpered at Stella.

'Me? But I didn't—'

'WHAT THE FUCK IS GOING ON OUT HERE?'

Everyone froze.

16

THE FIRST THING Stella thought upon meeting Paulina was, *I've seen your orgasm face.*

The second thing Stella thought was that the bride wore her anger well, like the goddess Hera descending from Olympus in a rage. Dark eyes flashed above a flaring, arrow-straight nose. Her plump, chemically enhanced lips pouted in disdain while her dark hair sat high on her head, coiled in a mass of serpentine braids.

The third thing Stella thought was, *Shit, she's tall.* Photographing her next to Oliwier would be like trying to pose Elle Macpherson with Daniel Radcliffe.

Agnieska's cry shattered the moment of surprised silence. Thrusting the dress into Stella's hands, the three bridesmaids scurried to Paulina, all speaking in Polish so Stella couldn't understand. However, she did understand the frequent pointing in her direction; the traitors were blaming her.

'Enough!' Paulina held up her palm. 'You,' she said, stabbing her chin towards Stella, 'what happened here?'

Stella swallowed, unexpectedly on trial. She didn't want to call the bridesmaids bald-faced liars, but by the same token, she didn't want to take the heat. 'It was an accident,' she said. 'I was photographing your dress when they—'

'I have heard enough.' Without wasting a second, Paulina shot off a series of razor-edged commands to the bridesmaids. Melania and Agnieska took the dress from Stella's hands while Gosia disappeared into the bathroom. Stella had no idea whether she had been found guilty or innocent.

'You.'

'Stella.'

'You. Make the bed. It's a mess.'

'Okay…but I need to—'

'We need the bed to look nice for pictures, yes?'

'Yes?'

'So make the bed.'

Obediently, Stella packed away her camera. She checked her watch. Less than an hour until the ceremony and she still needed to photograph the bride getting into her dress and the groom with his best man, as well as introduce herself to the registrar. Under the burden of time, her palms grew moist.

Pulling the white duvet across the mattress, Stella glanced sideways at Paulina, who was inspecting Agnieska and Melania's progress cleaning fake tan off the dress. The bride exerted the command of an army general. Ula really should have warned Stella, but then again, Ula had forgotten to mention Oliwier's wealth and their internationally famous business. She obviously didn't like to share information.

Once the bridesmaids had completed their task to the bride's satisfaction, they hung the dress and hurried into the bathroom for touchups, leaving Stella alone with Paulina.

The bride turned towards the bed and nodded her head curtly. Stella placed the last plump pillow on a pile and looked at her watch again.

'Sorry, Paulina, but we need to get your dress on soon. I—'

'We have plenty of time,' she said in a way that brooked no discussion. Stella wondered what it would be like to work at *Oh! Paulina*.

She would probably be the kind of boss that encouraged staff to work through lunch and made at least one employee cry per day, if not more. An HR nightmare.

Paulina dropped into a downward dog yoga pose, her bottom sticking up in the air and silky pink robe sliding up her back so the embroidered *Bride* disappeared from view. She wasn't wearing underwear. Stella averted her eyes to her watch, which was still tick tick ticking away. She could practically feel her body ageing. Was she the only one who cared about keeping to the schedule?

Yes.

Stella pulled out her phone and texted Claudia: **Hey, have you finished photographing the ceremony details yet?**

Yup! Claudia fired back straight away. **So many hot men down here.**

Those aren't the details we need! Would you find the groom and do his shots with the best man? You have the list. I'm stuck with the bride.

My pleasure.

Stella worried she had just sent a wolf to a sheep's party.

FIFTEEN MINUTES LATER, Paulina still wasn't in her dress. The ceremony started in half an hour. To keep herself busy, Stella slipped into the bathroom for photos of the bridesmaids. The girls had recovered their good spirits, but the residual drugs and alcohol made it hard for them to sit still. They chattered, fidgeting while the make-up artist attempted to reapply mascara and liner, a process that resulted in Melania getting poked in the eyeball.

Stella still had no photos of the bride, who seemed intent on completing the world's most unphotogenic yoga routine first.

Restlessly, Stella paced and ran through ideas for photographing a tall bride with a short groom.

With a quarter of an hour left, Paulina finally stopped her bending and stretching and called for her bridesmaids. Giggling, they hurried into the room, and pulled on their dresses: strapless, bright pink, and figure-hugging with fishtail flares to match Paulina's gown. With their svelte figures and neat hair-dos, they pulled off the look well.

A tingle of anticipation started in Stella's stomach. She was about to photograph her first proper bride getting into a wedding dress. A Valentino no less! This would look great in her portfolio.

'Shall we move over towards the window?' she suggested. 'The light will be nicer there.' In her research, she'd seen many photographs of brides getting dressed bathed in the natural rays of the sun.

For once, the bridal party listened. Stella got her camera ready, but she couldn't see the wedding gown anywhere, just some lingerie on a hanger and a long veil.

Paulina slid on a pair of white pants under her robe and threw the pink silk to the ground, revealing her large breasts.

'Um...' Stella said, 'shall I get the dress?'

'That one is for later,' replied Paulina, as the bridesmaids fastened a white bra around her bosom and attached a collar behind her neck. A long white strap joined collar to bra to underwear. 'This is my own design. My new bridal wear range launches next month.'

Stella snapped her jaw closed and started shooting.

Gosia and Agnieska took two corners of a diaphanous veil and floated it over Paulina's head. After settling the tulle so that it reached the floor at front and back, they pinned it to Paulina's dark braids with two shining diamond brooches from Cartier. The final touch, Paulina slipped her feet into a pair of shiny knee-high white boots. The overall effect screamed bridal sexbot.

At least the light for the photos was really nice.

'CAN I GET SOME SMILES?' Stella asked, posing the bride and bridesmaids on the chaise lounge at the foot of the bed. They all pouted. 'Great.' Stella took the picture. She had yet to see anything approaching a smile on Paulina. Her automatic expression was stony.

'Now, can I have Paulina by herself?'

Stella worked quickly, posing the bride on the bed before taking some further images near a window. The ceremony was in five minutes and she still needed to chat with the registrar. She would have to cut this short, so she reluctantly said she was finished and packed her camera bag.

'Wait,' commanded Paulina. 'I want to see my pictures before you go.'

'Are you sure? They're only small. You won't—'

'I am sure.'

Stella's shoulders sagged. Connor had warned them never to show work-in-progress to clients during the wedding, as it would be hard to see the picture properly on a digital display the size of a postage stamp. However, she couldn't refuse in the face of Paulina's steely expectation.

Pulling the camera back out of the bag, Stella flipped the power switch on. Between the pressure of being late and the scrutiny of the bride, seconds stretched into hours as the bride made noises of disappointment deep in her throat, each one chipping at Stella's brittle confidence. At the point where she thought she might pass out from nerves, the bride said, 'There are one or two I like.'

Stella slumped. She had been proud of those images. As fast as she could, she gathered her things and left, rushing to beat the tears. In the hallway, she leaned against the wall for ten seconds, long enough to take an edifying breath and wipe her eyes.

This was going to be a long day.

She squared her shoulders. *Tits and teeth.* She had a job to do.

With one minute to spare, Stella lumbered down the stairs into the Great Hall, giving the miraculous transformation of the room a cursory glance. Flowers were everywhere. Gone were the period features, red carpets and Chesterfields. In their place, a white tiled floor had been laid, with white chairs for each guest. At the far end, a stage had been built so that everyone could see the couple during the ceremony. A pink neon LOVE sign hung above the spot where the couple would say their vows. A string quartet tucked in the corner performed a classical version of 'Stand by Me'.

She could see Oliwier pacing, dressed in a teal velvet jacket with black trousers and bowtie. He was probably one of the few men Stella knew who could pull off that look. Behind him, the best man massaged the nervous groom's shoulders. In contrast to the groom, the best man towered, his muscular physique filling out the suit and his glossy shaved head glinting under the lights.

'We are already running LATE. This is HIDEOUS.' The wedding planner appeared out of nowhere, hissing at Stella as though she were the cause. Muttering into a headset, he stomped up the stairs.

Stella didn't have time for this. She needed to find the registrar. Connor had impressed upon her the importance of speaking to whomever was running the ceremony, as each one had their own set of unique photography rules. Annoying, but part of the job. At the weddings with Gunner, the celebrants had all been reasonable, one asking that they stay stationary during the vows, another requesting they didn't block the aisle. Fair enough.

As she jogged towards the stage, she searched for Claudia in her bright yellow dress. She checked her watch. 4:05. Where was Claudia hiding?

Up ahead, Stella spotted the registrar and her assistant. The woman's grey hair was pulled into a severe bun in a way that stretched her face, wearing a white blouse over her grey skirt. Apparently, the registrar had been allowed to keep her shirt while Stella had been forced into a red monstrosity.

'Hi, I'm Stell—'

'Are you the photographer?'

'Yes, I—'

'Where have you been? I have another ceremony at five.' She grabbed at a small clock pinned to her collar, as though presenting proof of the time to Stella. 'It doesn't matter. Look, during the ceremony, you can do whatever you want, but no photographs during the vows, signing of the register, or while I'm talking. That constant clicking puts me off.'

That only left the first kiss. 'But—'

'If you break these rules, I will stop the ceremony. Do you understand?'

Stella was getting tired of people being rude to her. She closed her eyes and rubbed her temples. 'Paulina and Oliwier will be disappointed.'

'This isn't a photo shoot. I want the focus on the couple.'

Oh, it will be, Stella thought, picturing Paulina's dress and imagining the registrar's reaction. More sharply than she meant to, Stella asked, 'Can I at least photograph her walking down the aisle?'

'Yes, that's fine.'

'Great.'

Turning away, Stella marched back up the side to search for Claudia. The couple would blame Stella if there were no photos of the ceremony. The thought of facing Paulina's wrath over this made her want to curl up in a ball.

Claudia reappeared from a corridor behind the reception desk. 'Sorry. Toilet again. All okay?'

Stella relayed her conversation with the registrar.

'What a bawbag,' Claudia said. 'I once had a priest make me wait outside during the ceremony. Another reason I quit weddings. What's the plan?'

'I guess we just take pictures of the first kiss. I don't want her stopping the wedding because of me. Can you imagine? Besides, Paulina...' She huffed and rolled her eyes heavenward.

'What's she like?'

'Tall, angry, and half-naked.'

It was ten past. The ceremony would hopefully be starting soon. 'Listen, you stay at the back and get what you can. I'll cover the front. Okay?'

They high-fived.

'Tsk! Welsh lady!'

Oliwier waved at her. She climbed up the stairs to the platform and he gave her an enthusiastic hug. He had a glazed donut look under the lights. Stella could feel the heat as well, with the warm June sun shining outside and all the bodies inside.

'Why do you look like Spanish dancer?' He examined the red ruffles exploding from her jacket.

'Long story. How are you feeling?'

'Me? Good. Excellent. Like tiger!' He banged his chest. Glancing left and right, he dragged her aside and asked, 'How is Paulina?'

Stella thought of the fixed cross expression on the bride's face and her displeasure at Stella. 'Happy as she'll ever be!'

'Good. This is good.'

Oliwier seemed concerned. She was starting to understand that his feelings were easy to read. Happy = Smile. Sad = Frown. Concern = Frown plus creased eyebrows, like right now.

'Why? What's wrong?'

He sucked in some air through his teeth and grimaced. 'Her family.' He nodded his head towards the audience and Stella turned. 'Don't look! They not listen. Paulina tells them she don't want the Polish traditions at wedding. It would be English wedding. And well...' He shrugged. 'Paulina and her mother, they...'

He struggled for the words, so made two fists, bumping them together.

Stella patted him on the back. 'Right. Well. There's nothing you can do about it now. You'll have to let it play out.'

He groaned and nibbled his lip.

'It'll be fine.' She rubbed his velvety arm. 'Now go and get married.'

'How does she look?' A smile lit his face again.

'Amazing.' Paulina did look amazing, just not very bridal. In a way, Stella wished she had this couple's confidence to express themselves so openly. She couldn't help but admire Paulina's unwavering self-belief, so much so that Stella decided to channel Paulina for the rest of the wedding.

'Smile!' she said and snapped a photo of him before turning the lens on the guests. She snuck a surreptitious glance at Paulina's family, who stood out against the sea of couture. The cheery red dress embroidered in colourful flowers and matching headscarf on Paulina's mother contrasted with her dour expression. The way her mouth turned down at the corners gave her a stubborn, unimpressed mien, like she refused to be taken in by any of the frippery. Stella noted the resemblance to her daughter. Next to her sat a short round man with a jolly, ruddy face, the kind achieved by a love of the outdoors and alcohol. He wore a light beige swing jacket edged with evergreen, embroidered to match the mother's dress.

While she watched, the wedding planner's assistant ran down the centre aisle and collected Paulina's father for the bridal entrance.

Stella could see where Paulina got her taste for short men.

Wanting to photograph her father's reaction when he saw his daughter—and more importantly, hers when she saw him—Stella ran up the side walkway, beating them to the main stairway and taking the steps two by two. Out of breath, she waved to the surprised bridesmaids as she summited the last step. Paulina's father followed right behind her.

'We need to get moving,' said the wedding planner. Knocking on the door of the Lady Astor suite, he moved out of the way so the bride could make her entrance.

Stella positioned herself in a spot where she could photograph the father's face. Paulina stepped out of her room in her veil and bikini outfit. A moment of silence. And then two things happened at once.

The father's weathered face crumpled with emotion and fat tears rolled down his cheeks. Snap, snap, snap went the camera.

And Paulina began to yell.

After a tirade in Polish, she turned to the wedding planner. 'I told you I didn't want this Polish traditional clothing and no white. What is this?'

She wasn't proud of it, but Stella experienced a delicious twinge of schadenfreude as the planner took the brunt of Paulina's anger. The berating went on for ages, until the father raised his voice.

'*Tygrysek!*' he yelled. Paulina shut up.

Gosia whispered to Stella, 'It means baby tiger.'

He stepped forward and reached up to grasp Paulina's shoulders. In a deep, authoritative voice he spoke. Stella wished she could understand what he said as Paulina's face grew gradually less cross to the point where she actually wiped a tear from her eye. While the bridesmaids and the planner stood by uncomfortably, Stella captured the moment. At the end of it, he gave his daughter a hug and held out his arm. Snap, snap. Paulina still didn't smile, but it was the closest Stella had seen so far.

'Shall we?' asked the wedding planner through gritted teeth. He spoke into his headset and the string quartet broke off, changing to the opening notes of Madonna's '*Like a Virgin*'. He disappeared down the stairs still mumbling into his microphone.

Stella had everyone pose together for a shot before the bridesmaids started walking. She descended the stairs backwards so she could keep snapping and, at the bottom, Claudia took over so Stella could return to the bride and her father.

It was a strange sight: the Amazon Queen being led down the aisle by a man in the Polish equivalent of lederhosen. The guests gasped as they caught their first glimpse of Paulina. One guest even clapped and said bravo. As the bride processed down the aisle, Stella turned the camera on Oliwier, who stood on a white crate on the platform. He glowed. This was it. This was why she had wanted to photograph weddings. Love, as the neon sign proclaimed above their heads.

The registrar began the ceremony and Stella crouched down next to the stage, itching to take pictures of the action. She watched as Paulina's father pulled out a camera. He crawled into the aisle and snapped away, his shutter release making that sound the registrar had professed to hate so much. Stella looked to the registrar. Would she tell him to stop?

Another guest joined him with her camera. No reaction from the registrar. Stella pursed her lips over her mounting frustration. It was okay for guests to take pictures with their noisy shutters, but not for the hired professional to do so? The hypocrisy wedged in her mind like a popcorn kernel between her teeth as she mourned all the great moments she was missing. An off-colour joke from Oliwier. The bridesmaids' fond expressions. The best man's cheeky eyebrows. Paulina's pouty, unchanging face.

Then Stella had an idea.

She pulled out her phone and shot off a text. Moments later, Claudia joined the other guests in the aisle, taking picture after picture, her yellow dress turning her into a friend of the bride and groom's rather than the second shooter.

With a smug smile, Stella sat back, feeling less angry. Only eight more hours to go. She took a deep breath and waited for the first kiss.

17

THEY WERE HAVING SEX. Loud, headboard-banging sex.

Stella examined her watch. Paulina had disappeared upstairs to change into her Valentino gown almost half an hour ago. The schedule allotted twenty minutes for the change followed by twenty minutes for Stella to get those important post-ceremony photos of the bride and groom. Five minutes of her time had already gone. How much longer could they keep going? The string quartet needed to turn up the volume or else the guests would be treated to the sound of the bride and groom consummating their marriage.

Stella scrolled through the images on the back of her camera to pass the minutes. She couldn't exactly knock on the door and ask them to hurry. Maybe she could get the wedding planner to do it? Wasn't keeping to the schedule his job? But the thought of asking for his help made her skin crawl. She could already hear cries of 'HIDEOUS!' echoing in her head, a word she'd find triggering for the rest of her life.

As the photos from the end of the ceremony flicked by, a bolt of pride made her smile. All in all, it had been heart-warming. Once she'd been allowed to take pictures, she got some cracking shots of guests crying, including Paulina's stoic mother. Stella could see the album taking shape in her head already. Now she just needed the photos of the bride and groom, the linchpin of the whole book.

'Ah, the sound of lurve.'

She startled. Ula's boyfriend, Ronny, sauntered towards her, his white-crescent smile standing out against his saturated tan.

Blushing, she said, 'They're...um...enjoying being husband and wife.'

His lips curved into an arrogant grin. 'Helluva workout, sex. Most people burn about one hundred calories, but the way I do it, you can quadruple that.'

Stella didn't want to discuss calories and sex with her friend's boyfriend while listening to the grunting of her clients. But she politely said, 'Really? How interesting.'

Stepping into her personal space, he plonked his meaty hand on the wall next to her head and leaned in, the pungent soapiness of his cologne diving up her nostrils. She pushed her back into the wall, trying to get as far from him as possible.

'How interested are you?' He twitched his eyebrows.

The sheer mass of his muscular presence sent alarm bells ringing, as did the stench of alcohol on his breath. He could overpower her easily. If she screamed, would anybody hear in this chaos? She could knee him in the balls, but they were probably made of steel, too.

'I'm not interested, Ronny.'

'Really? Because I felt a strong attraction the moment I laid eyes on you.'

As the sounds in the bedroom came to a crescendo, he dipped his head towards her neck and inhaled deeply.

'Mmm. The smell of hard work. So sexy.' He rested his eyes on her lips.

She was about to tell him that was the creepiest way to tell someone she stank, when she heard Ula calling out, 'Ronny? You here?'

He pushed himself back seconds before Ula appeared on the staircase. As she climbed the final steps, he reached into his jacket pocket and pulled out a strip of gum, popping it into his mouth with a calm that Stella found disturbing. 'Just chatting with your friend.'

'Oh,' said Ula, her narrowed eyes darting between them.

Stella gave her a weak smile.

Her face relaxing, Ula said, 'I want to introduce you to some man who needs a fitness trainer.'

'That's what I love about you, baby. Always looking out for my interests.' He grabbed Ula, reaching around her bottom and pulling her towards him. With her body flat against his, he thwacked his lips against hers.

Stella looked down at her camera, wishing this moment would fly away.

Giggling, Ula pressed her hands to his chest and pushed. 'Don't be rude. Sorry, Stella.'

Not trusting herself to speak, Stella shook her head to indicate that no harm was done.

'Come on.' Ula took his hand and pulled him down the stairs. As they disappeared around the bend, he looked over his shoulder at Stella. 'Later,' he mouthed with a filthy wink.

Stella's breath whooshed out. Clenching her fists, she wished she'd slapped him. She needed to shower in disinfectant.

She should say something, shouldn't she? Ula needed to know that Ronny was a sleazy arsehole. How could she be so full of great advice and yet have such horrible taste in men?

Before she had time to explore that thought, the handle on the bridal suite turned. Thank goodness! Finally. She could get on with doing her job and put off thinking about Ronny the Sex Pest.

The door opened. The best man stepped out. He saw Stella and grinned, exposing a couple of gold teeth, while he buttoned up his jacket. 'Hello,' he said, whistling as he skipped down the stairs.

Holy shit, she thought. *Paulina is having an affair with the best man.* What should she do? Should she tell Oliwier? It would break his weird little heart. Maybe she should tell Ula? But what purpose would that serve?

Oh my god. Oh my god. Oh my god. Connor had been right. Weddings were full of hypocrites. At the end of the day, people were rutting animals, ruled by their hormones. Love was a construct invented by romance novelists and people in sales.

The door opened again, interrupting her raging inner monologue. Stella stood up straight and crossed her arms, ready to glare at Paulina with a look of righteous judgement she had learnt from her mother.

Oliwier stepped out of the room. 'Hey, hey, Welsh Lady! Shall we be doing the photos now?'

Stella's mouth opened and closed soundlessly. *Holy shit,* Oliwier *is having an affair with the best man!* But during the ceremony, he had been shining with such love. How could she have interpreted it so, so wrong?

As she began questioning everything, Paulina glided into the hallway behind her husband, cheeks glowing, resplendent in the Valentino gown.

'You. You're here,' she said. 'Good. Where do you want to go for the photos?'

'Um...the lawn?' Stella could barely think. She tried not to picture what had been happening behind those doors, but her imagination was cranked up to two hundred percent.

Paulina linked her arm with Oliwier. 'Excellent. Shall we, *ukochany?'*

IN THE END, Stella managed to hold onto the couple for 30 minutes before the wedding planner tracked them down.

Once she'd managed to get into the flow and stop thinking about their *ménage à trois,* she enjoyed capturing her first portraits of a real bride and groom. Paulina had changed into flatter shoes and Oliwier had on his Cuban heels, shrinking the height difference to four inches. Stella could work with four inches.

First, she took them to the stone stairs outside, which made it easy to even out their heights. Paulina only had two expressions in her repertoire: pout and orgasm face. She had very clear ideas on how she liked to be photographed, barking orders at Stella as she worked. 'Down! Up! To the left! To the right! There!'

It was very off-putting, but Stella did her best to find Paulina's sweet spot.

After the stairs, she had the couple run onto the lawn to get a panoramic shot of them in the expansive, manicured Cliveden grounds.

Next, she grabbed Claudia who had been busy joking with some of the guests and they ran after the bride and groom to photograph them with the stately home in the background. Stella concentrated on the wide shots while Claudia focused on the close-ups.

Stella coached the couple to hold hands and walk slowly towards her, Oliwier slightly in front to minimise the height difference.

'Can I get some smiles?' Stella said again, more out of habit than expecting any miracles.

Step by step, she backed away as they walked forward, Claudia snapping by her side with a telephoto lens. In her heart, Stella knew the shots were good. She grinned behind the camera.

Behind her, the ground unexpectedly dipped and she tumbled backwards, her bottom landing on the soft grass, feet pitching over her head as she rolled. Her instinct to protect her camera kicked in, holding it out to the side. But she didn't fare so well. Her shoulder ached and her right ankle throbbed. Not broken but definitely twisted.

'Welsh Lady!' Oliwier yelled when she went down, but it wasn't a sound of concern that she heard now.

It was laughter.

A sort of barking noise, like a seal choking on its first puff of marijuana. As she sat on the ground, Stella searched for the source.

Paulina's whole body shook with mirth, an actual real smile on her face, as she cackled and pointed at the fallen photographer.

With urgency, Stella looked at her second shooter and sighed with relief. Claudia had her lens trained on the jubilant bride, her shutter releasing over and over, the camera memorising the joyful moment created at Stella's expense.

Oliwier rushed over to help her stand. 'Are you okay?' he asked with genuine concern.

'Fine. Don't worry about me. Really,' she said, despite her sore ankle.

That was when the wedding planner showed up to haul the couple back to the party.

'Did you get it?' she asked Claudia.

'Does the King fart?' She showed Stella the images: beautiful portraits of Paulina, her face creased with joy.

'Phew. She'll probably hate them,' laughed Stella.

'Well at least you know how to get her to smile.'

'Self-harm and embarrassment. I can do that.'

They followed the couple and planner back to the house, Stella limping on her troubled ankle—it had been worth it to get the shots.

As they climbed the stairs to the terrace, Stella detected something amiss. The guests stood silent, as though waiting for a speech, all eyes trained on a scene playing out in front of them: Paulina's parents were barring the couple's progress. Between her mother and father, they held a tray with a loaf of bread, what looked like salt, and two shot glasses. Paulina and her mother locked eyes in an Olympic glaring competition. Oliwier and the father both looked resigned. Stella and Claudia separated and started shooting.

After what seemed like five minutes, Paulina rolled her eyes and grabbed one of the shot glasses, tossing the contents into her mouth. She slammed the glass back down on the tray. Her face immediately convulsed, as though she had swallowed a cupful of lemon juice.

'Ugh! Water!' she spat.

Oliwier whooped and grabbed the other glass, downing the liquid. 'Vodka for me! I am big boss.' He seized Paulina and gave her a sloppy kiss and threw the shot glass over his shoulder. It shattered on the stone.

'Ya-hey!' shouted Paulina's family. The whole atmosphere changed.

From that moment, the vodka flowed. Dying of thirst, Stella picked up a large tumbler of clear liquid off a drinks tray and glugged, thinking it was water. She almost choked.

'GORZKO! GORZKO! GORZKO!'

After the meal and speeches, Paulina's family were chanting again. Every few minutes, when they said these words, the bride and groom had to kiss. Paulina snarled, but Oliwier didn't seem to mind, puckering up and planting one on his new wife's pout with glee.

Claudia and Stella worked the middle of the room, back to back, firing their cameras in opposite directions, a pair of photographic Charlie's Angels. Claudia was in her element. Laughing with the guests, merrily snapping away, and flirting with Filip, the bald, gold-toothed best man/sex toy.

Stella found it harder to relax. As she worked, she pedantically ticked off the memorised list of must-have images. All the formal photography had been completed after the incident with the tray and the vodka. With the help of Claudia and the best man, Stella had managed to gather people for the group shots, although the expression 'herding cats' took on a whole new meaning. The cats had been drunk, exuberant, and not in the mood to smile sweetly for the camera. Stella anticipated having to swap a lot of heads in Photoshop to get one good picture.

After the family came all the friends to photograph with the bride and groom. When Ula and her date stepped up, Stella had to ignore Ronny's hulking presence while she did her job. His slimy, dark eyes bored into her, communicating his thoughts loud and clear. She disliked him intensely. The idea of having to chat with Ula about her taste in men, on one hand felt hypocritical, but also necessary. Ula was such a mystery to her, a mystery further complicated when Stella saw Ula autographing a napkin for Paulina's mother. Why would she want Ula's autograph?

Four hours to go.

Claudia stopped shooting to wipe her arm across her forehead. 'Filip says that Paulina's family is planning to kidnap the bride soon. It's some Polish tradition. The groom has to buy her back with vodka.' 'Paulina will be livid.' That made Stella smile. 'You seem to be getting friendly with Filip, but I should tell you—'

'Fuck. I need the loos again. I don't know what's wrong with me today. Peeing like a drunk after a pub crawl.' Claudia slipped between the tables and down the hallway.

Now that Claudia mentioned it, Stella had to go, too. During her short dinner break, Stella had downed a litre of water, dehydrated from running around in the heat. She hated to think about the state of her borrowed red blouse, which had been acting as a sponge all day. She couldn't wait to take it off and burn it.

Tucking her roller bag in a corner, she kept her camera around her neck, just in case a good shot presented itself. She couldn't remember where the toilets were. Turning down a corridor, she went the way she thought Claudia had gone. Nothing. She continued down another hallway. Just hotel rooms. She stopped and turned back, but the heavy rhythmic pad of footsteps following behind plus the snapping of gum against teeth reached her ears. Stella stopped. Was Ronny stalking her? She ducked behind a thick red curtain hanging from the wall and found that it covered a glass door. Pushing it open, she stepped into the forecourt in front of the hotel.

The courtyard buzzed with activity. A queue of expensive cars snaked away from the entrance, where evening guests handed their keys to the concierge team. Stella jogged towards the bustle. Her ankle still twinged, but she wanted to put distance between her and the door in case Ronny materialised.

As the late evening air cooled her face, she peeled off her jacket to let her skin breathe. The crumpled ruffles of the matador shirt fell limply as she disrobed. She pulled the sodden blouse away from her body and flapped it a few times to encourage air circulation. The thought of putting the jacket on again made her cringe, but she was almost at the final stretch. The first dance would start in fifteen minutes. After that, the cake cutting, bouquet toss, and she'd be done.

Preparing herself to dive back into the fray, she watched the additional guests arriving. Oliwier said they'd invited a hundred acquaintances, mostly business associates. Stella hated being an evening guest. Thankfully, it had only happened to her once. She'd still had to buy a gift and a fancy frock; still had to travel to the venue and stay overnight. She just didn't get to hear the speeches or eat the meal or watch the actual wedding. When—if—she ever got married, she vowed not to have evening guests.

A McLaren discharged its occupants. Followed by a Porsche and a Lamborghini. Behind that a sleek classic grey Mercedes. All those nights watching *Top Gear* were coming in handy.

The Mercedes pulled up and the door opened, lifting like a wing. So cool. She could just see the red leather interior. A pair of long legs swung out, attached to an attractive blonde woman in a short gold-sequinned dress. Two concierges battled each other to help her out of the bucket seat. The woman had the professionally-coifed appearance of a celeb, but Stella couldn't place her. The car's engine rattled noisily as it waited for the concierge to drive it away.

A tall man walked around the far edge of the vehicle. The bright lights of the next car in the queue temporarily made it difficult to see, but when he stepped forward and offered his arm to the blonde, Stella gasped.

It was Connor Knight.

18

STELLA HID BEHIND THE PILLAR, breathing rapid, heart pumping. What was Connor Knight doing here?

The last time she'd seen him, she'd been escaping the chateau after The Kiss. Her stomach flipped, morphing into nausea as the next three hours of her life played out in her mind.

She had to avoid him at all costs. She didn't want him watching her, judging her work, thinking about that day in France two months ago.

And who was that woman? She was neither Inga nor Galina.

Get control, Stella, she thought to herself. *You have a job to do.* Sucking in a deep breath, she put her jacket on, wincing as the humid fabric of the shirt crushed against her skin. She checked the settings on her camera, and dived through the doors.

The Great Hall had been transformed into a disco, with multi-coloured lights and a digital dance floor, currently empty as the guests flocked to the free cocktails. On the platform, a Tom Jones tribute band crooned *'The Green Green Grass of Home'*. Their Tom really did resemble the man himself, his voice a dead match. Hearing the sound of a fellow Welshman gave her the boost she desperately needed right now.

Stella stood a little straighter and scanned for the golden sparkle of Connor's date. At least the sequins made the couple easy to track. She caught sight of them, wending their way towards the bar.

Great, she would stay in this room and wait for the first dance. Plenty of glamorous people to photograph here. She had just started taking photos of the new guests when a hand gripped her arm. She found the wedding planner standing there, his face awash with impatience.

'The Al Thanis want their photo taken outside near the flowers. NOW.'

Why couldn't he ever ask for anything nicely? He turned towards the bar, taking the exact path of Connor and his date.

Her head dropped and she allowed herself a moment of despair. Why couldn't anything be easy? '*O mangiar questa minestra o saltar questa finestra,*' her mother's no-nonsense voice said in Stella's head. 'Either eat the soup or jump out of the window.' Right now, she preferred the window.

The wedding planner led her towards a dazzling middle-eastern couple.

And who were they talking to? Connor and his date. Of course.

Stella swallowed. She should have jumped out of the window because this soup was giving her a stomach ache. The air grew thick and hot. She tried not to notice how well his body filled out his cobalt blue suit. For a second, she remembered those arms...those lips...

Connor spoke and the couple laughed. Still smiling, he turned in her direction. In an instant, his smile dropped. 'Price?' he said. He appeared both confused and angry to see her. His date stepped closer to him and threaded her arm through his, her gaze sweeping over Stella.

What could she say? Something strong and confident. Something that acknowledged their awkward past while asserting her right to be shooting this high-end wedding.

'Hey.'

With no time for small talk, the wedding planner ordered Stella to take the picture. 'Come straight back for the first dance when you're finished,' he said before disappearing into the crowd.

Connor's presence compounded the humiliation of the wedding planner speaking to her like a servant. She wished she could channel her inner Claudia and tell the planner to fuck off, but that would certainly lower her status in Connor's eyes. She could already feel him assessing her performance even before she guided the couple into a pose.

When she finished taking the shots, Connor stepped towards her and opened his mouth to speak. She read the question in his eyes: what the hell are you doing here?

'Sorry. No time to chat. Job to do,' she said before whipping around on her heel and fleeing back to the Great Hall. His fingers plucked at her jacket as she slipped away. She glanced down at the flounces of red spilling from her collar and sleeves. Humiliation: complete.

She had to clear her thoughts. The first dance was about to begin. Guests congregated around the edges of the dance floor. She wondered if Oliwier and Paulina would dance to a Tom Jones song, but, no, the band was heading towards the bar while a DJ prepped her desk. With her background in ballroom, Stella loved first dances, even though people mostly just walked around in slow circles.

She spotted Claudia flirting with the best man again. 'Sorry, first dance time,' she said, tugging Claudia away.

'Did you know Connor is here?'

'I saw him arrive.'

'This wedding just gets better and better.' Claudia laughed.

Stella frowned.

'I mean, worse. Definitely worse.' She hugged Stella. 'Only two and a half more hours. You're doing a great job.'

'Thanks.' They didn't have time for pep talks. 'Listen, I'll position myself near the stage and you go opposite, okay? I move, you move. Attack it from two angles.'

'I love it when you talk strategy.' Claudia saluted and moved into position.

At least Stella sounded like she knew what she was doing.

She found a spot in front of the DJ and double-checked her equipment. Her palms had gone sticky with sweat. She needed a break after the dance.

Overhead a disco ball reflected pink sparkles. Across the floor behind Claudia, Stella saw the dots of light fall on Connor. His arms were folded across his chest. The date leaned her head on his shoulder. Stella didn't want to acknowledge her disappointment, even though she could tell without looking at him, that his eyes were on her. She felt like she was taking her driving test.

As guests crowded around the floor, she crouched, ready to shoot. Her hands trembled. She didn't know if it was nerves from the wedding or anxiety about Connor or just general panic. The lighting during first dances could be tricky, and she didn't want to make a mistake. In her head, she rattled through the steps of the STOP method. The most important thing was getting the shots.

The best man appeared on the dance floor with a cordless mic. Stella wondered if he'd be in the dance, too, and had to purse her lips to stop herself from laughing. The humour helped her relax.

'Please put your hands together for the bride and groom!' he said before folding himself into the sidelines.

Down the wooden stairway at the back of the Great Room stepped an elegantly dressed Oliwier and Paulina. She wore a vintage Hollywood-style dressing gown, white chiffon edged in white marabou feathers that kicked forward and floated back with every step. He wore white PVC trousers and a silk Chinese-style jacket done up to his neck. Paulina's heels increased their height difference to half a foot.

The crowd parted, and the couple swirled onto the dance floor. A Viennese Waltz began; violins chasing bass with some flute thrown in to pick out the main tune. Stella loved waltzes.

Paulina picked up the bottom of her robe and curtsied to Oliwier.

He stepped forward, taking Paulina's hand delicately in his own. They swayed in time to the music before setting off in a circle. Their turns flowed naturally, necks long and graceful. Oliwier was beaming. Paulina led, attempting her own version of a smile. They glided with ease, well-practised in their steps, their love for each other evident as Stella followed them with her lens.

Suddenly, there was a scratch in the music. Oliwier and Paulina separated. Another song began to play. 'Low' by Flo Rida. Definitely not a waltz.

Paulina whipped off her dressing gown and threw it to her brides-maid, revealing a white PVC basque and suspenders underneath. Oliwier ripped off his jacket to reveal his bare tanned chest, criss-crossed by white leather straps and glittering chains.

The real dance began.

As the beat kicked in, Paulina bent over, wiggling her bottom. Oliwier pretended to spank her. She snapped up, popping her body, and skipped around him, trailing fingers over his chest. As she came round, he grasped her by the waist and put his head between her breasts. Pretending to be affronted, she pushed him back, and he clamped his hands around her waist as she dipped back, scribing a slow sensuous circle with her body.

Stella lost herself recording the moment. She could see Claudia across the room, an amused grin plastered on her face while she shot. The routine wouldn't win *Strictly Come Dancing*, but they definitely had moves.

As the chorus swung around again, Paulina sank to her knees in front of Oliwier and mimed giving him a blow job.

Stella's eyes went wide, stuck somewhere between shock and disgust. Her gaze lifted to catch Connor observing her. He had his fist in front of his mouth and his shoulders shook with laughter. Catching her eye, he gave her a supportive thumbs up.

The crowd whooped and yelled, egging the couple on. Flashes burst, as guests shot their own memories of the wedding. Flo Rida sang, and Stella wondered what Paulina's parents thought of this number. She searched for them in the crowd and found them on the side, the father clapping along and Paulina's mother maintaining her signature dour look. Stella clicked the shutter.

Defying the laws of physics, Oliwier lifted Paulina onto his shoulder, stiff as a plank, arms out like an airplane. His jaw clenched, stomach muscles tightening, as he held onto her. For all their sakes, Stella hoped this lift would be over soon. He twirled around a few times and put Paulina back on her feet. Stella exhaled. That could have ended badly.

They struck a final pose as the music finished: Oliwier dipped her and cradled her head lovingly in his hand, gazing down into her eyes. The guests exploded with adulation, jumping up and down, wolf whistling, and shouting bravo.

Across the floor, Connor held out a hand to help Claudia stand from her crouching position. Stella watched out of the corner of her eye as they conversed, each laughing at something the other said. Taking advantage of his distraction, Stella grabbed her bag and escaped through the crowd.

She needed a glass of water and a moment to herself. This wedding had been non-stop and she had to regroup before the final push. The cake cutting and bouquet throw weren't scheduled for a while, so now would be the only time to hide away. She stopped a passing waiter who verified that the iced drinks on his tray were water rather than vodka and took one. Downing it, she took another one before heading off to seek a quiet spot. The day had been intense and exhausting and she just needed to sit down for a moment, where nobody could ask her to take a picture, grope her, or shout HIDEOUS in her ear.

Passing the entrance to the billiards room, she spied Ula and Ronny chatting with the Al Thanis. She hurried past before the Sex Pest clocked her presence. Creepy, imaginary fingers crept up her spine. She had to say something to Ula soon.

She wandered down a deserted hallway and tried a few doorhandles, to see if any would open. She wasn't picky. Any sort of private space would do. Finally, she found one in the depths of the hotel. The room was dark, and cool air hit her in the face. She stepped in, dragging her bag behind, and closed the door. Holding her glass in one hand, she patted along the doorframe with the other, searching for a light switch. Her fingertips grazed a button and she pressed, illuminating shelves full of toilet paper, soaps and shampoos. She had found a housekeeping cupboard.

And somebody else was in there with her. She screamed.

'Shhhhh!' said the Tom Jones impersonator. He sat on an overturned bucket, legs splayed, back resting against a wall of toilet paper, pressing a frosty can of Coke to his forehead.

Clutching her chest, Stella put her glass of water down and leaned on a strut. As the ridiculousness of the situation dawned on her, she began to laugh. He joined in.

'Alright?' he said. 'Sorry. I dint think anyone would come in 'ere.'

She stopped short and blinked. She'd expected a Welsh lilt, not a heavy Birmingham accent. 'Sorry. I didn't mean to disturb you.'

'You the wedding photographa?'

'For my sins.'

'Gary. Gaz for short.' He held out his hand and they shook. 'I've bin hoiding from that bridesmaid. The blonde one.'

'Gosia?'

'Yeah. Right pain in the ass. She keeps trying to undo me trousers. Wants to know if I'm loik the real Tom Jownes.'

Stella pursed her lips and nodded in solidarity. Nothing surprised her at this point.

'I told her nev'rin a month o' Sundays, but she's very insistent.' He sighed and stood up. 'Well, I oughtta get back out there. Another set to do.'

'Break a leg. And best of luck with the bridesmaid.'

'Thanks.' They shuffled to switch places. He opened the door and checked both ways before slipping into the hallway, leaving Stella on her own.

The door swung shut, and she sat on the abandoned bucket. She shrugged off her jacket and undid a couple buttons on her blouse. The water, she drained in one go, wishing she had another. She was sucking on an ice cube when the door swung open.

Connor Knight stepped in. 'Price. You're a hard one to track down.'

She spit the ice cube back into the glass. 'It's been a long day.'

'I'll bet.' His eyes slipped down to the buttons she had undone and she struggled to keep her breathing even under his gaze. He chuckled, a pleasant rumbling sound that came from his belly. A real laugh. 'I am so glad I'm not photographing this wedding.'

She couldn't help but join in. 'You have no idea.'

'Is this your first?'

'Yup.'

'Well, you know what they say: you'll always remember your first.' He cocked an eyebrow at her and half-smiled. She wondered if he was thinking about his French model in Paris.

Crossing her arms, she said, 'Oliwier said he asked you to shoot it.'

'I had a job today that I couldn't cancel. So he invited me to the evening.' He shrugged. 'We get along.'

'He's...unique.'

'Did you go to their house?'

'Um...yeah. So many penises.'

They both laughed. She tipped her head back and made the mistake of looking at his lips, sparking the memory of them pressed against hers. A shot of warmth swirled between her legs and she pressed her knees together. Did he ever think about their moment of passion at the chateau? It had been two months since she'd driven away from him with Alan. No matter how hard she had tried to squash the memory, it surfaced regularly. In the shower. At the super- market. While she was running. In bed.

'How's it going so far?' he asked looking towards the camera sitting on her lap.

'I don't know. Good, I think. But then again, I showed Paulina some of the pictures on the back of my camera—I know, I know,' she said, as he opened his mouth to speak, 'I shouldn't have done it. But she's very...forceful.'

'That she is. What did she say?'

Imitating Paulina's accent, Stella said, *'I like one or two. The rest are shit.* Well, that was the gist of it anyway.'

'Let me see.'

Stella balked like he had just ordered her to undress. Showing him her unedited work felt too intimate.

'Come on. I promise to be nice.'

That didn't actually help. If they were bad, she wanted him to be honest with her. He held out his hand towards her camera and she reluctantly unlooped it from around her neck, offering it up to him.

He flicked through the images on the back, brow furrowed in concentration. His head started to nod as his eyes studied each image for no more than a second.

'These are great, Price. You'll be just fine.'

Relief flooded through her. 'You really think so?'

He handed the camera back to her. 'In all my years teaching photography, do you know how many students I've had, who had never shot a wedding before, with enough raw talent to attack a wedding like this on their first go?'

She shrugged.

'One,' he said.

Stella smiled wide. That might just be the best thing anybody had said to her in her entire life. She sat up straighter. God, she wanted to leap up and kiss him. But she wouldn't.

'Thank you,' she said instead.

The mood in the room shifted and he shoved one hand into his pocket. With his other, he started picking up the travel-sized shampoos lining the shelf to his right. He studied each label and then put the bottle back down again, repeating this multiple times before moving onto the soaps. If Stella didn't know better, she'd think that he was nervous. But that couldn't be. Connor Knight didn't get nervous.

He cleared his throat. 'Listen, I have an apology to make to you.'

Stella sat up straighter, curious to hear what he had to say. 'Okay?'

'I made a mistake.'

Oh my god. Her heartbeat sped up. Was he about to confess that he wished he hadn't stopped kissing her? Even though at the time, she was glad that he did—it prevented her from making a huge error—the idea that he might have feelings for her now didn't scare her the way that it once would have. If she was honest with herself, the possibility excited her. Just a little bit. Although, she didn't know if she could handle it, on top of the amazing compliment he'd just given her.

'Really?' The word rasped out of her dry throat and she wished she had more water.

He hid his other hand in his pocket and even managed to look sheepish, his eyes glued to the floor as he scuffed it with his shiny shoe. 'Yeah, I never should have put you in that position.'

What position had she been in? If she remembered correctly, she'd been facing away from him, then she'd turned towards him so he could kiss her breasts. 'I didn't mind...'

'You were inexperienced. And I took advantage of your kind nature.'

Wait. What?

'It was a lot to ask of you to model for the class that day. I didn't know you hadn't eaten anything and I should have made sure there was water on hand for you. I wasn't thinking straight. I was just... distracted, I suppose.'

Oh. He was talking about the fainting thing, not the kissing thing. She sagged against the wall and pressed her lips together to stop herself from frowning. Of course, he didn't have feelings for her. What an idiot. She wished she could crawl behind the wall of toilet paper and hide from his grey gaze. 'No need to apologise. I actually enjoyed it.'

'Don't get me wrong. You were good at it. Really good.' His words hung in the air as they both studied a pile of tissue boxes.

So that was it? They weren't going to discuss that they'd had their tongues down each other's throats? Maybe he kissed so many women that another one just didn't compute. After all, she had seen him with three different Amazonian blondes since she'd met him: Inga, Galina, and Astrid (as she'd dubbed this latest one).

He propped an elbow on a shelf and leaned on it, crossing his feet at the ankles. 'So I was thinking...I still owe you a day of my time. Are you free a fortnight from now?'

Stella flicked her hair. She wasn't going to march to the beat of his drum. She'd have her day when it was convenient for *her*. But still, she wanted to know what he had in mind. 'I'm not sure. I'd have to check my diary.' *Play it cool.*

'My third shooter for a wedding in Italy has let me down. Do you want to take his place? Big media tycoon's do. Krish'll be there, too. It would be a great experience.'

Shoot a wedding with Connor Knight, the best wedding photographer in the world? In Italy, her favourite country? *Yes, please!* Seeing how he worked would be invaluable. Her whole body wanted to do a happy dance, but she didn't want him to see how eager she was. Instead, she tilted her head to the side and pretended to consider it. 'All expenses paid?'

'Of course.'

She shrugged like she'd be happy to do that or watch Netflix. Whatever. 'Okay, then. I'll come.'

He half-smiled, as though he knew the game she was playing. 'Sure you don't need to check your diary?'

She slit her eyes at him.

Chuckling, he said, 'It's in the Lakes. Beautiful venue. I'll have Krish send you the details and get your flights booked. We're leaving Friday morning, back on Sunday night. That work for you?'

'Of course.'

'Great.' He uncrossed his ankles and stood up straight. 'I better... uh...get back to my—'

'Astrid,' she said and then coloured at the slip up.

'Who?'

'Nothing. Sorry. I meant *your date.*' The shimmering goddess.

'Yeah, me, too.' Stella reached down for her camera bag and unfolded herself from her resting spot. As she stood, the space in the cupboard shrunk and she found herself inches from Connor. She didn't know where to look. So close to him, she could hear the soft regular huff of his breath and smell the pleasant outdoorsy odour of his cologne— different from his usual scent. She hoped with all her might that he couldn't smell her.

Their eyes connected and, for a moment, the wedding, Paulina, Oliwier, Astrid...they all narrowed into insignificance. All that mattered was this small toilet paper-filled room and the two people at the centre of it.

'Uh...I'll go out first,' he said, dropping his gaze and shouldering the door open. 'See you at the airport. Oh, and Price?' He quirked an eyebrow at her. 'Nice shirt. Make sure to bring that with you.'

He walked out. She peered down at her matador outfit. *Olé!* But not even that shirt could quell her good mood. She was going to Italy to assist Connor Knight! She took a roll of toilet paper off the shelf, held it against her mouth, and screamed.

THE CAKE CUTTING PASSED without incident, as cake cuttings do, and before Stella knew it, they were waiting for the bride to throw the bouquet.

Standing halfway up the stairs, Paulina faced the guests and waited for the single ladies to assemble. Twenty or so women gathered. Connor's date stood in the middle, but Stella couldn't see Connor anywhere. Paulina's bridesmaids claimed the front spots. From their energetic bouncing, Stella assumed they'd been snorting coke again. They would be in for a hell of a headache tomorrow morning. Not that Stella had ever done it, but she'd known plenty of people who did in advertising.

I'll shoot the side. You shoot from the back. Stella used hand signals to communicate across the room to Claudia, who saluted. Both moved into position.

Camera to her eye, Stella waited while the guests counted down. 'Ten...nine...eight...seven...' Paulina turned her back to the group. '... three...two...one!'

The bride dipped her knees and flung her arms, releasing the bouquet into the air. It sailed up in a perfect arc. It cleared the heads of the bridesmaids, who tried to jump and snatch it. It sailed over Connor's date. The trajectory descended towards the back of the crowd, towards...

...Claudia!

The bouquet hurtled towards her head. At the last second, she lowered her camera and caught the flowers with her free hand. Stella expected her to laugh, but instead, she pushed the bouquet back into the air, like a grenade with the pin removed. This time, Gosia caught it and, from her gleeful shriek, Stella could tell she didn't mind being the second recipient. The Tom Jones impersonator should beware.

Paulina and Oliwier kissed on the stairs, and Stella snapped one last picture before they disappeared into the crowd. She lowered her camera, letting it hang against her stomach. A feeling of lightness overtook her. *I'm free!* She had survived her first wedding.

Bouncing over to Claudia to celebrate, she was surprised to see her friend wiping a mascara-blackened tear from her cheek.

Stella immediately forgot her excitement. 'Oh my god, Clauds, are you okay?'

'Yeah. Fine. Just a bit of dust.' She batted her eyelids a few times while looking up to clear the dampness.

'For a second I thought you were crying because of the bouquet.'

'That's ridiculous. Why would I do that?' she asked sharply. 'Sorry, I'm just really tired. I'm going to run to the toilet and sort out my face.' Without waiting for a reply, she disappeared down the corridor.

Watching Claudia's departure, Stella hoped today hadn't broken her friend. Stella owed her big.

The Tom Jones band started their last set as she packed her camera bag. The dance floor filled with guests, including Oliwier, who was pretending to swim to *'It's Not Unusual'*. Stella hoped she'd be able to slip away without encountering Connor. They had left things on a positive note, which was where she wanted them to stay.

Claudia reappeared, her make-up tidy. 'C'mon. We have a long drive.' She grabbed a couple slabs of cake from a passing tray.

'Okay. I just have to say goodbye to the bride and groom.'

She left Claudia guarding her camera bag and signalled to Oliwier. He shimmied towards her.

'Hey, beautiful lady! We dance?' he shouted above the music. He pulled her into his arms and began to sway.

Usually she'd be up for a boogie, but the day had left her tuckered out. It was time to leave the partying to the increasingly drunken (and decreasingly photogenic) guests. 'We're heading off.'

'You break my heart. But I look forward to seeing pictures.'

He gave her a hug, with a kiss on each cheek. She hugged him back.

'Wait here for the moment. I have something for you.' Oliwier skipped up the stairs. Stella hoped he would hurry. In the meantime, she peeled off her jacket to release the folds of the shirt. Maybe she should keep it as a reminder of her first wedding. A souvenir. Or maybe she should repurpose it as a cleaning rag.

Oliwier came skipping back down the stairs carrying a green Harrods' shopping bag. He handed it to her and she peeked inside to find stacks of money. Stella had almost forgotten that she was collecting the other half of her payment tonight.

'Thank you!' she said, not quite believing that she held another £30,000. She'd be jittery until the banks opened on Monday. It would be just her luck to get robbed on the one Sunday that she actually had something to steal.

'Is no problem. And we put little present in there for you. For you both. To show appreciation.'

Stella gave him another hug. 'Thank you for trusting me to shoot your wedding. Please thank Paulina, too.'

'Remember—count money before you go. Find me if any problems.' And with one of his cheeky winks, he went back onto the dance floor doing a strange sideways sashay.

Claudia yawned. 'Can we go?'

Their little Fiat was still holding court between the Ferrari and Lamborghini. They packed their bags into the back seat and climbed into the car, slamming the doors on the noise of the party.

Stella opened the Harrod's bag to count the money, but she saw something sitting on top of the piles of cash. She reached in and pulled out two lacy items with pink tags.

Handing one to Claudia, Stella held up the thank you gift from her first wedding couple. 'Lovely. A pair of *Oh! Paulina* crotchless panties. Just what I've always wanted.'

Claudia pulled the elastic on hers, zinging them at Stella's head. 'Leave it to you to book the craziest fucking wedding in the world.'

19

PULLING HER SUITCASE, Stella passed through the sliding doors at Heathrow terminal five. Krish had instructed her to meet them at the benches near the British Airways check-in. As she approached, she saw two men sitting next to each other, legs crossed casually, newspapers held up to obscure their faces. Both papers were seven days out-of-date. She was well acquainted with their contents.

Stopping in front of them, she crossed her arms and tapped her foot. 'Har dee har har,' she said. 'Very funny.'

Connor lowered his copy of the *Daily Mail* and pretended to be star struck. 'Why, Krish, can this be the photographer from that wedding I was reading about?'

Krish looked over the top of his paper. 'Why, yes, I believe it is.'

'Can I have your autograph?' asked Connor in a horrendous American accent.

She swiped at him playfully. 'You have no idea what it's been like. My phone's been ringing off the hook with journalist requests.'

'Are you kidding?' Connor said, folding up his paper and tucking it into his carry on. 'I've been in this business almost fifteen years and I've never achieved this level of notoriety from one wedding.'

'I'm just lucky, I suppose.'

It had all started a few days after Paulina and Oliwier's wedding. A journalist from the *Daily Mail* had contacted her, having heard from a guest that the celebrations were worth a feature. He was after some of the professional shots, to be published with credit. She phoned Oliwier to ask permission and he involved their publicist. She sent off the edited images to their PR, who took care of everything, and Stella received a nice payment from the newspaper for use of her work. She would never have known how to negotiate that without the help of the publicist.

On the morning the coverage came out, she excitedly went to the corner shop to buy a copy. It had landed a double-page spread. The picture she'd taken of Paulina on the sofa in her 'wedding dress' occupied a good part of the right page, next to a shot of the couple outside Cliveden.

What she didn't expect was a snap taken by one of the guests from the first dance. It showed Paulina performing imaginary fellatio on the groom. In the background, the photo captured the moment Stella's face had slipped. Her disbelieving features were in perfect focus behind the dancing couple, her eyes wide with shock, her mouth in a disgusted grimace. Since then, her phone had been ringing off the hook with interview requests. *The Sun* had run the picture with a red circle around her and a caption saying, 'Oh No! Paulina!'

She hadn't accepted any of the calls, despite the lure of payment. It felt like a breach of trust with her clients. She had, however, gained thousands of new Twitter and Instagram followers.

Claudia thought it was hilarious. The perfect end to the perfect wedding. Liliwen had sent her a text saying '**You go, girl!**' and her parents had phoned to make sure she wasn't traumatised, although she could tell her father found it amusing. He probably bought multiple copies of every paper where she appeared, to share them with his Shakespearean acting friends. After promising to say a rosary for the sinning couple, her mother said, '*Non tutte le ciambelle riescono col buco*', meaning 'Not all the donuts come out with the hole.' Perhaps her mother's point was that, even if wedding didn't turn out as expected, at least she still had a donut.

THEY FLEW business class to Malpensa. As they descended into Milan over the white-tipped Alps, Stella wallowed in the joy she always felt when she landed in Italy. It was a second home to her. Summers spent with her mother's family outside of Venice were some of her happiest memories. Her heart skipped along with the wheels as they bounced on the tarmac.

Exiting the plane, the familiar muggy July air enveloped her, along with an instant slick of sweat. She adjusted her sunhat and fanned herself. With luck, it should be marginally cooler in the Lakes.

After the brief minutes of Italian heat, the air conditioning inside the terminal was a welcome relief, hitting her like an icy shower. She smiled at the young, tanned immigration agent as he checked over her passport and he returned her grin, saying, *'Benvenuto, signorina.'* He winked. Connor cleared his throat behind her.

At the baggage carousel, most of their luggage appeared in the first round, except for one bag of Connor's expensive equipment. The same baby seat passed them twice before Connor decided to seek some help.

An airport attendant stood nearby, leaning on a trolley. He scrolled through his phone, unlit cigarette hanging from his mouth.

'Scusi,' Connor said in the British version of holiday Italian, 'One of my bags is missing. It's *molto importante.'* He pointed towards the empty carousel. The volume of his voice had increased like that would aid understanding. Stella stifled a smile.

The older man grunted, *'Non capisco,'* and returned his attention to his phone.

'I need your help. I—'

'Connor?' said Stella.

'Yes?'

'Allow me.' She stepped forward and gave the attendant the full beam of her smile. In perfect Italian, she said, '*Mi può auitare per favore. Il mio amico ha perso una delle sue borse e ne abbiamo bisogno per un matrimonio che dobbiamo scattare. Ci potrebbe aiutare a trovarla?*'

His face lit up and he flashed a surprisingly white smile at her. '*Certamente!*' he said and asked her some questions.

Finally, he pointed towards a sign marked OVERSIZED a few carousels away. She could see the corner of Connor's hard black case, hiding behind a bicycle bag.

'*Grazie mille,*' she said and turned to Connor. His eyes were wide with astonishment.

Eventually, he said, 'You kept that quiet.'

Giving him a cheeky half-smile, she shrugged. 'It's good to speak a second language. Wouldn't you agree, Knight?' She walked towards his bag, feeling his gaze on her back.

He chuckled. 'Touché.'

She caught Krish rolling his eyes.

A driver met them outside and drove them to Lake Como. On the way, Connor debriefed them on the couple getting married. 'Margaret Rooper and William Nightingale, owner of Nightingale Media Group. They publish titles for niche markets. In fact, they publish a few photography mags.'

'I know NMG,' Stella said. 'They print a handful of medical press, too. My first ever advert that I wrote appeared in *GP Times*.'

'Erectile dysfunction?' Krish joked.

'Herpes, actually.'

'Charming,' said Connor. 'Guest list is around the 200 mark, with a lot of society names. The Roopers have estates all over Scotland. She's got her own PR firm—I assume that's how they met. Krish, you know what you're doing.'

'All good, boss.'

Turning to her, Connor continued, 'Price, your job is to shoot details. Wide shots of the rooms before guests arrive, close ups of flowers, that sort of thing. Have fun with it. There is absolutely no pressure on you to photograph any of the guests, unless you see something worth shooting or you want to practise.'

'Check,' she said, glad he was treating her the same way he treated Krish: friendly, but professional. They were obviously on the same page about their kiss; they should pretend it never happened.

'Schedule wise, we'll drop our bags and have a quick bite, then recce for the couple shoot on Sunday. There's a dinner for guests tonight, but, Price, you don't have to come to that. They only need us for a couple hours anyway.'

He reached into his carry on and pulled out a folder. 'Here are the timings for the day and important numbers, etcetera.' He handed them each a schedule. 'Weather looks good, although there may be thunderstorms late on Saturday night. Wedding starts at 4:00. We'll go to the venue around 1:00 to check it out, then Krish and I will move on to the hotel where the couple and guests are staying. Price, you'll stay at the venue to work on details. Any questions?'

She shook her head, lips pressed together. She must have looked nervous because he reached out and gave her a jocular pat on the leg. 'Nothing to worry about.'

Her leg tingled where he had touched her, but she ignored it. Just because they had chemistry didn't mean she had to warm up her Bunsen Burner. She would do what she should have done with Nathan: disregard her feelings and concentrate on her goals. She was in Italy to learn. Most photographers would kill for this opportunity. She would focus on that, channelling her inner Paulina who was the most determined, driven woman she knew.

Connor settled into his seat and disappeared into his phone. She stared down at the schedule. The groom's name tugged at her memory. William Nightingale...had she ever met him? She was familiar with the company, but something about the name niggled at her brain. Shrugging, she tucked the schedule into her bag and watched the passing Lombard countryside, trying hard not to notice how nice Connor smelled.

. . .

TWENTY MINUTES LATER, they pulled up in front of their boutique hotel, a yellow palazzo situated in a quiet part of Como's Old Town. A bellboy sprinted out to help with their luggage while Connor checked them in. Stella breathed the clean lake air and gazed at the sand-coloured Italian architecture that made her heart sing. Even the cracks in the walls were charming. The entry doors were huge, built for giants instead of Italians. She spied a Vespa here and a Vespa there, each of them rusty and at least 20 years old. Towards the end of the road, a green cafe awning shaded a handful of half-occupied outdoor tables. Her stomach grumbled.

They agreed to meet in 30 minutes for lunch. Opening the door to her suite revealed a magazine-worthy room with a private, walled balcony. Stella laid down on the king-size bed, falling into the creamy duvet with a soft whoosh. It came as a surprise that they were staying somewhere so nice. She assumed they'd be in a cheap pensione. *I guess Connor Knight doesn't do cheap*, she thought with a smirk.

She changed into a light blue sundress, pairing it with strappy sandals, perfect for exploring a hot city. She applied extra sun cream and grabbed her wide-brimmed hat – redheads and bright sunlight didn't mix. It must've taken longer than her allotted half hour because someone knocked on her door.

Opening it, she found Krish in shorts and a t-shirt. 'Connor sent me to see if you were ready. Whoa!' Keeping his feet outside the door, he leaned in for a quick ogle at her room. 'You won the room sweepstakes. Mine is tiny. And you have a balcony! My room looks over the street.'

'I'm happy to switch, if you want,' she said, smiling to make sure he knew she meant it.

'Nah. It's fine. We'll barely be in them anyway.' He checked his watch. 'Ready? We don't want to keep The Boss waiting. You know how he gets about time.'

Did she? Not really.

'Yup.' She stood and grabbed her handbag and sunglasses.

At the bottom of the stairs, Connor was typing into his phone while he waited. They decided to get *panini* at the café down the road.

'Why is it that I could make this same sandwich back in London and it wouldn't taste this good. I mean, it's literally just bread, red peppers, and mozzarella,' Krish said, ordering a third one. 'What? I'm a growing boy,' he defended himself at Stella's sideways glance.

'Quality of the ingredients,' Connor said, licking oil off his fingers.

After they finished, Krish rubbed his stomach. 'I think I may have eaten too much.'

'You think?' said Stella.

'Boss, if you don't mind, I need to lie down. Is it okay if I skip the recce?'

'That's fine, mate. We can handle it. Right, Price?' Connor slapped her on the back like mates at the pub and grabbed his sunglasses.

God, he looked good in sunglasses. Like, Tom Cruise in *Top Gun* good. Stella gave herself a mental shake.

'Shall we?' he said.

His camera hung around his neck. The way he carried it was so natural, like he had been born with it there. He held the grip lightly in his right hand while his left swung free. She had a ridiculous urge to reach for him. Instead, she strangled her bag strap firmly in two tight fists.

'So what's the plan?' she ventured.

'We, my friend, are getting on a boat.'

AT THE MARINA, shimmering yachts bobbed in the gently undulating water. They found a Venetian-style taxi, oiled mahogany gleaming in the sun, and Stella negotiated with the driver to take them to Bellagio, a town across the lake. The driver said he would throw in a tour of the coastline for an extra thirty euros. She translated for Connor and he said, 'Why not? Ask him if he can also show us some picturesque docks, too. For the shoot.'

The boat sped away from the lakefront. Connor and Stella reclined on a white leather bench at the back, the wind licking their skin, providing relief from the heat. She had to keep her hand on top of her head to hold her hat in place. A smile creased her face. She looked over at Connor. He was smiling, too, as he observed the scenery. He took a photo and their eyes met for a brief moment as he lowered the camera.

Although there was a foot of space between them, as the boat rode the waves, his knee fell towards hers. She could feel the hairs on his leg brushing her bare skin. She shivered.

True to his word, the driver pointed out some attractive docks that Connor could use for his photographs of the bride and groom. He cut the engine in front of the Villa del Balbianello, a baroque building right on the water. Its light walls reflected the afternoon sun, surrounded by a verdant garden with huge trees that reminded Stella of broccoli. She translated the driver's words for Connor: 'It was a Franciscan monastery in the 13th century,' followed by a long list of former owners. At the end, he added, 'Tell your husband that James Bond's *Casino Royale* was filmed here.'

'He says—'

'I got the gist,' replied Connor. Her cheeks flamed. Hopefully, he only understood the second half of the sentence.

'*Andiamo al Bellagio?*' the driver asked.

Bellagio was even more gorgeous than the Old Town. The water seemed clearer here, with stronger tones of blue. They pulled up to the dock and paid. Through Stella, Connor asked if the driver would be available on Sunday morning to take them on the shoot. They agreed a cash price, place, and time to meet and exchanged details.

'That's one thing done,' Connor said as they climbed out of the boat. He extended his hand to help her. It was probably her imagination, but she thought he hung onto her a second longer than needed.

Together, they strolled into the town, a pastel candy box of houses: pink, yellow, peach, cream, all topped with orange terracotta tiles. Connor wanted to check out the view at the top of the town. They ambled up the cobblestone stairs leading to the vista, no mean feat in the humidity. Around every corner, a viable spot for photos presented itself.

'Will your bride want to do this in her dress?' Stella asked, remembering the inhibiting bridal dress from France.

'They're paying me a lot of money to get these shots. They have to put in the work if they want something truly spectacular.' A touch of arrogance crept into his tone.

They found the spot above the town and he held up his camera. 'Model for me?'

Smirking, she replied, 'Sorry, I only work with Jean-Luc.'

Connor cut his eyes at her.

She gave him a playful punch on the arm. 'Of course. What do you want me to do?'

He asked her to stand against the salmon-coloured wall. 'Tilt your head back just a little...there, stop...now part your lips...just breath though them...good.'

The shutter released.

Sliding into Teacher Connor mode, he gave her a lesson in photographing subjects in full sun versus shadow. A personal lesson from Connor Knight in the Italian Lakes. Gunner and Flash would be dying of jealousy if they knew.

He directed her into a few more poses before he let the camera drop, wiping his forehead. 'I think it's *gelato* time, don't you?'

'I thought you'd never ask.'

They didn't have far to walk for a *gelateria*. She ordered a cone with *limone* while he wanted *cioccolato*.

'It's too hot for chocolate,' she protested.

'It's never too hot for chocolate.' He pretended to take offence.

They walked towards the water. 'You know,' he said licking up a sugary drip heading towards his hand, 'you're different when you speak Italian.'

'How so?'

'You get very...animated. You use your whole body to talk.'

She laughed. 'You should see my mother. She can say an entire sentence in a gesture. You're right though, the Italian blood comes out more when I'm speaking it.'

'Hmmm. It's very…'

Sexy? Alluring? Captivating?

'Spunky.'

Spunky?

She couldn't see his eyes behind his sunglasses, but the corner of his lip twitched in a mischievous way.

'So your mother is Italian and your father is…?'

'Welsh, born and bred. Married forty years and still going strong.' The temptation to remind him of the longevity of her parents' marriage proved too much. She hid her smile behind her cone. Reaching sea level, they claimed a bench overlooking the water. Stella's photographic eye identified at least ten amazing spots to capture the couple with the lake in the background, which meant Connor could probably see fifty. The bride and groom would be spoiled for choice.

'I was actually born in Italy,' he said, nudging her leg with his knee.

She popped the last bit of cone into her mouth. 'Really? Where?'

'Rome. We were only there for a few years. I don't remember it. My father got transferred to Cairo, then Islamabad next.' A brief frown passed over his features.

'Oh, yeah, you said he worked for the foreign office. That must have been exciting.'

'It had its ups and downs,' he said, staring at the mountains across the lake.

'Where else did you live?'

'Barbados—that was fun. Istanbul. And Paris. You've heard that story. After, I moved to London and started my business.'

'Do you have any siblings aside from your brother?'

'Nope. Just Michael. Eight years younger.'

'Wow, that's a big age difference. Are you close?'

'Yes and No. He was ten when I left to start my career. They moved to Oslo and I saw him when I could. You know how it is, in the early days of building a business. He turned out just fine, though. Oxford grad. Lawyer. I'm the black sheep.'

'I don't believe that.' They were silent for a moment. Wanting to keep him talking, she asked, 'Where do your parents live now? Is your father still in the service?'

'Armstrong was in Bangkok last time I checked. I don't know if he'll ever retire, he loves it so much.' He looked at her. 'And...my mother died in Islamabad.'

She inhaled in shock. 'I'm so sorry.' Without thinking about it, she reached out and put her hand on his forearm.

'It was a long time ago. She died giving birth to Michael. Pre-eclampsia.'

A suspicion germinated and she asked, 'What was her name?'

'Grace.'

The name on the handkerchief. It had been his mother's. It had been an extreme act of generosity for him to give it to her on the awards night. He hadn't even hesitated. That's also why he'd looked so distraught when she'd handed it back to him in France. Her heart ached. 'You...you must miss her a lot.'

'I do.' He nodded and looked at his feet. Her hand was still on his arm, her thumb absently rubbing back and forth. 'She was a pretty special woman. Funny, kind, beautiful. I remember the parties she used to throw. I'd hide under the table with my imaginary dog, Cyclops, and just watch all the different people walking past.'

Without meaning to, she laughed. 'Sorry. Imaginary dog?'

He dazzled her with a cheeky grin, more natural and unrehearsed than the half-smile he usually served up. 'Too much?' They both threw their heads back with laughter.

Realising where her hand rested, she withdrew it, tucking a piece of hair behind her ear. She looked towards the clocktower. The time was 4:30.

His expression turned serious. 'Listen, I know we never talked about—'

'Shit! Connor! What time do you need to be back at the hotel?'

'Five o'clock?' He glanced at his watch. 'We've got to go!'

Bolting for the docks, they scrambled to find a taxi. He seemed agitated and quiet on the way home, no doubt worrying about being late. Inside she was kicking herself. What was he about to say to her when she'd interrupted him? Apologise for the kiss? Tell her he was involved with someone? Tell her he wasn't involved with someone, which was worse. Now, she'd never know. The moment had disappeared.

When they arrived at the hotel in the nick of time, he threw a curt 'see you tomorrow' over his shoulder before running to his room. Krish was already in the lobby in his suit, ready for the dinner.

'How's your stomach?' she asked.

'Better. How was the recce?'

'Fine.' She wished him good luck and escaped up the stairs.

After ordering room service for dinner, she spent the evening cleaning her equipment and preparing for the day ahead. She memorised the schedule, trying to work out how she knew the groom. God, wouldn't it be horrible if he'd dated Claudia or something like that?

As she settled into bed, inhaling the calming scent of lavender in the air, it came to her. She remembered exactly how she knew William Nightingale. And Claudia had nothing to do with it.

THE NIGHT she met William Nightingale, she had a fight with Nathan.

'I've been waiting two hours,' she said in a rare moment of standing up for herself. 'You could've at least texted me. It's inconsiderate.' It wasn't the first time he hadn't been punctual, but it was the first time she'd decided to let him know it bothered her. Sometimes he kept her at his beck and call, like she didn't have a life outside their affair.

'Sorry, babe. I couldn't get away. Jeanette was supposed to be going to a friend's tonight, but she got a cold and decided to stay home. Had to go buy her some Night Nurse and all sorts of bullshit. Good news is, I told her it would be a late one.' As he kissed her on the neck, she translated his words: *there'll be time to fuck at your flat before I have to go home.*

He ushered her into the taxi. 'You look beautiful, by the way. I'll be the luckiest man in the room tonight.' As usual, her anger thawed when he showed her affection.

That night, he was taking her to a private members' club in Mayfair. She was excited; she'd never been to one. She had visions of plush seating, beautiful people, and erudite conversation.

Plus, he was introducing her to one of his friends. It felt like a step towards a better future. One where they didn't have to sneak around.

Their taxi pulled up outside the club, and Nathan held the door open for her. The club didn't look like much from the outside. Just a short green awning over a bouncer guarding a red velvet rope. He nodded to Nathan—obviously a regular—and let them enter.

They descended a dark stairway into an equally dark club. It wasn't as big as she'd expected. The bar occupied one corner with low-lit booths carved into the walls. The smell of stale cigars assaulted her senses. The clientele seemed to be old men, mostly middle eastern, all of them drinking alcohol, and young blonde women caked in make-up wearing obscenely short dresses. A decrepit-looking man at the bar ogled her legs over his tumbler of whiskey, and she tugged at the hem of her own dress uncomfortably.

Nathan led her to a booth in the corner, where a couple had already arrived. The man had an overbite and a bald spot like an island in a sea of receding hair. Nathan introduced him as William Nightingale, his college roommate. The girl's name...Stella couldn't remember. It definitely wasn't Margaret.

The night was tiresome. The champagne flowed, but Stella didn't have much in common with the girl, and Nathan and William talked about people she didn't know. Still...wasn't it a step in the right direction? Meeting his friends?

In the early hours of the morning, she and Nathan stumbled back to her flat and she'd suffered an unsatisfying, drunken fuck before he left.

The whole night hadn't been very memorable and she'd duly forgotten it.

Three months later, the award ceremony happened.

IN HER HOTEL BED, Stella tossed and turned, trying to ignore her growing dread.

What if Nathan and Jeanette were at the wedding?

Chances were high. William and Nathan had been close. He might be the best man for all she knew.

Her stomach clenched and her sheets grew wet with sweat. The last time she'd seen Nathan and his wife was at the awards. He hadn't even been there when she collected her things from the office or negotiated her severance. Like a coward, he'd left it to the financial officer.

She could just imagine the unhappy reunion. It would certainly ruin the wedding, reflecting badly on Connor, and she didn't want that at any cost.

She couldn't go. She'd find a reason to stay at the hotel. She could blame it on food poisoning or bad cramps. Something. Anything.

She. Could. Not. Go.

But Connor had put so much trust in her. She couldn't let him down. Plus there was the expense of bringing her to Italy. It was an amazing opportunity to witness the world's greatest wedding photographer shooting a real life wedding. Nathan had already ruined her last career. She'd be damned before she let him ruin this one.

Stella had spent her life letting other people's desires and actions affect her decisions. Finally, she was doing something for herself. No man, especially not a small one like Nathan Bastion, would ever have that kind of power over her again.

Even so, maybe she should tell Connor the situation and let him decide. That would solve everything, but then she'd have to come clean about Nathan. She'd rather eat insects for a week. She thought about their time in Bellagio yesterday. They were becoming friends. If Connor knew about her affair, it would colour his opinion of her.

Besides, the slim possibility existed that all this worry would be for nothing. Maybe Nathan and Jeanette wouldn't even be there. And if they were, Stella wasn't the main photographer. She could hide away in the shadows all day, a photographic vampire. Connor said she didn't have to interact with the guests if she didn't want to. Well, she didn't want to.

What would Paulina do? Paulina wouldn't let any man get in her way. What would Claudia do? She's say screw it, just do it. What would Liliwen do? She'd laugh and tell her a story about some sexual conquest she'd had before she got married.

Feeling resolved, Stella finally climbed out of bed. Like a zombie with a caffeine addiction, she drank espressos from the machine in her room until she felt vaguely human.

By the time she was done showering, it was almost 11:00. Discounting her secret service-style shooting suit, she reached instead for a sleeveless navy linen dress she'd packed as an alternative. It was still classy and professional, but much cooler. The air was already thick with heat.

She slathered herself with factor 50 and put on the dress, twirling her hair into a messy bun. She covered her under-eyes in concealer and hoped it wouldn't melt.

Downstairs, she sat in the garden with a magazine she was too nervous to read and her camera backpack. In her head, she played out everything that could go wrong today. It always ended with Stella in tears and Connor angry. She hoped she was doing the right thing.

Drawing a deep breath, she watched a dove land on an olive tree branch. It must be a sign. If Nathan and Jeanette did turn up and see her, perhaps enough time had passed that they could all be mature adults about it. After all, Stella could have pressed charges for assault and she hadn't. That should count for something.

Krish tapped her on the shoulder and she jumped. 'Ready for lunch?'

'Yup,' she croaked, picking up her camera backpack and ditching the magazine.

Misreading her anxiety, he said, 'You'll be great. Once you get going, the day'll pass quickly. I promise.'

'Thanks.' A smile limped onto her face to hide the cyclone of her thoughts.

They joined Connor in the hotel restaurant. She did the Italian thing and hid her tired eyes behind big sunglasses. It didn't matter anyway. Connor was in Boss Mode and, therefore, focussed on the job at hand. He rattled off the schedule one more time. They synced the clocks on their cameras, so that when Krish merged the different image streams in post-production, they'd fall along the same timeline.

After lunch, they bundled into a taxi. The driver zipped along the curvy coastline with the over-confidence of someone who regularly drove that route. Stella gripped the door tightly. It did nothing for her nerves.

As they pulled up to the venue, Stella gasped; it was breathtaking. It sat right on the water, commanding views of green hills tumbling into the lake on the opposite shore. To the north, water flowed as far as the eye could see, disappearing into misty, distant mountains. The two-story villa was a mix of yellow and pink, with mustard shutters on the windows, surrounded by manicured gardens.

She tagged along anxiously behind Connor and Krish as they walked the grounds, from the villa to the boat launch, down the tree-lined path to the massive concrete balcony where the ceremony would take place, and back again. What she wanted was for them to leave, so that she could find the seating plan and search the guest names.

Just when they were about to do that, the wedding planner, a petite brunette woman with a clipboard, found them and started flirting with Connor. They'd apparently worked together in the past. From their banter, Stella wondered if working was all they'd done. She pressed her lips together and tried to ignore the sudden niggling jealousy. Great, that's all she needed in addition to everything else.

After the planner hobbled away on impractical heels, Connor noticed Stella biting her fingernails. 'I've seen your work. You have nothing to worry about.' He patted her paternally on the back. The ball of dread in her stomach expanded.

Finally, Krish and Connor were speeding off in a boat to the couple's hotel, leaving her alone.

She waved goodbye. As soon as they disappeared from view, she spun and ran towards the villa. She headed for the lower courtyard, a large square space paved with grey stone and surrounded by naked ivory statues of men striking athletic poses.

The seating plan would usually be written out and propped on an easel, but she couldn't see one. The only thing she could see was a lemon tree with hundreds of tags hanging from it.

Suspecting the worst, she went over and grabbed a tag at random: *Lord Alfred Tottington, Table 6* it read in a curly font.

Shit. What a ridiculous thing to do. What was wrong with a simple board listing everybody's names? The guests would spend half the drinks reception trying to find their table assignment. The wedding planner obviously hadn't thought this through, another strike against her.

Leaving her camera on a nearby table, Stella got to work. Lady Elspeth Granger. Olivia Wadsworth-Pinkly. John Smythe III. Estonia Fenton. If she weren't awash with anxiety, she would have found the names hilarious.

'Can I help you?' cut in the voice of the wedding planner like she'd caught Stella rifling through her jewellery box.

Stella forced a smile and turned to greet the woman who had made her life more difficult than it needed to be.

She was regarding Stella with suspicious eyes, clutching her clipboard like a shield.

'Hi, I'm Stella, remember? Working with Connor Knight? I was just admiring your table plan. So...clever and unique.'

'Oh, do you think so?' The woman's demeanour changed immediately, losing the pinched bitchy look. 'I thought it would be different. I matched the colour of the paper stock to the creamy ecru of the statues and had the font hand-designed based on a plaque inside the villa.'

'Wow, that's a lot of thought.' Stella felt bad for hating her. She obviously took great pride in her work.

'Please take lots of detail shots. This wedding is going to look superb in my portfolio.' In the distance, Stella heard the sound of a helicopter overhead.

The planner perked up even more. 'Must dash! That's the cake arriving from London.'

Stella couldn't even fathom how much that must've cost. She waited for the planner to disappear before continuing her frantic quest. As her neck started to ache from leaning sideways to read the tags, she unfortunately found what she was looking for: *Nathan Bastion, Table 3.*

Blinking, she stared at the name. *No, no, no, no, no.* Hope dissolved into a rising tide of panic. Adrenaline shot through her, even though, deep down, she'd expected this.

Breathe.

She closed her eyes.

Breathe.

She felt herself leave her body, looking down at the scene.

Breathe.

Slowly she examined her symptoms. *Well, her pupils are dilated, she's sweating. Limbs can't move. But other than that, she's perfectly fine. No blood. No broken bones. She's alive. No physical danger.*

Over the next few seconds, she came back to herself and found that she could move again. She picked up her water bottle and emptied it in one long gulp.

You can do this. She regulated her breathing and weighed her options. The list was very short. She couldn't run. That would just make her look foolish to Connor and Krish. That left hiding. When the guests arrived, she would make sure she stayed out of sight, use all these naked statues as cover.

And if hiding didn't work...well, she'd deal with that if it happened. No use getting wound up about something that might not occur. She had a job to do.

Squaring her shoulders, she slung her camera over her neck, slipped her arms through her backpack, and headed towards the balcony to take pictures.

. . .

AN HOUR LATER, she heard shouting. *'Stanno arrivando!'* The guests were arriving.

She'd already scouted the perfect place to hide near the dock. The guests would alight from their boats and ascend a set of stairs before walking down the tree-lined path to the balcony.

At the top of the stairs, a row of nude statues would conceal her. Stella hid behind Neptune, popping her head out once in a while to see what was happening. She knew she could have stayed in the villa until the guests were safely seated, but a small part of her wanted to see her adversaries. Had they changed? Had he lost any hair? Had Jeanette had any more surgery? In her head, her mother warned: *'La troppa curiosità spinge l'uccello nella rete',* basically 'Curiosity killed the cat' but the Italian version talked about pushing birds into nets.

As boat after boat expelled passengers onto the dock, Connor and Krish arrived. While Krish stayed below to photograph the guests, Connor climbed the stairs. At the top, he swivelled his head, looking for her. She peeked out, and he waved her over. Reluctantly, she left her cover, keeping a firm eye on the emptying boats.

'Anything exciting happen while we were gone?' he asked as he scrolled through pictures on the back of his camera.

'What? No! What could possibly have happened?' she whispered, like they were in a library.

He stopped scrolling and skewered her with his grey eyes. 'You okay?'

'I'm fine.' She coughed and then said in her normal voice. 'I'm fine. Just a...a frog in my throat.'

'Right.' He picked up his camera bag. 'Well, I'm going ahead. See you later.' He gave her one last concerned look and sped off.

She exhaled and resumed her position behind the statue.

Her eyes tracked each guest. Some 30 boats came and went before she saw his salt-and-pepper hair, windblown from the water taxi ride.

He reached up and flattened the wayward strands. *Always concerned about appearances,* Stella thought. Behind him tottered Jeanette, dark hair sprayed rock solid, a lime green fascinator perched on top to match her outfit. Probably Chanel. They hadn't changed one bit.

'Stella?'

She jumped. Krish was standing behind her.

'You okay?' he asked, laughing.

'Fine! All fine!' She giggled like a maniac. An anxious highly-strung maniac. Glancing towards the steady stream of guests, she clocked Nathan and Jeanette on their way to the balcony.

'All right.' Krish said warily, examining her sideways. 'I'm going to the ceremony. Want to join?'

They headed off together. Nathan and Jeanette led about 50 metres ahead. Stella kept her eyes glued to them, ready to hide if necessary. Jeanette turned her head, saying something in Nathan's ear. Stella squeaked and jumped behind Krish's six foot plus frame.

'What? What's wrong?' Krish asked, on alert for some imminent threat.

'Um...just a bee,' she said, stepping cautiously out from behind him and swatting the air.

'You gave me a heart attack.'

'Sorry. Highly allergic.' She wasn't allergic to anything, although being this close to the Bastions was bringing her out in hives.

When they arrived, Stella stayed back, next to the stairs where the bride would descend. Krish went closer to the guests, aiming to capture pictures from alternate angles to Connor, who was stationed at the front near the floral canopy. Stella watched as Connor hid his kit bag and raced up the centre aisle, past Stella, and off towards the dock where the bride would soon alight. As he jogged past without a glance, Stella tried not to reminisce about the toned muscles she'd seen in France. He moved with such power and grace—

No, no, no. If she needed a reminder of why this train of thought was a bad idea, Nathan was sitting 20 metres away.

Remembering that she was supposed to be hiding, she ducked down behind a large stone urn. From there, she could just make out the bride's light blue speedboat docking at the jetty. Minutes later, Connor came backwards down the path as he photographed the bride in her stunning Vera Wang dress, holding her father's arm. When they'd almost reached the mouth of the stairs next to Stella, Connor zipped ahead to shoot the bridal procession. Stella could hear the rustling of the guests as they turned as one in her direction. She pulled her shoulders in to make herself smaller.

When she heard the guests resume their forward-facing position, Stella chanced a peek around her urn. Nathan and Jeanette with her bright lime fascinator were sitting on the right, on the groom's side. Hiding toward the left, Stella could take pictures while obscuring herself at the same time.

She snapped close-ups of the women's colourful hats, wide shots of the congregation in front of the breath-taking Como scenery, and a fun portrait of an old man who had fallen asleep in the back row. Towards the end of the ceremony, before everyone made an exit, Stella scurried to hide in the villa until all the guests had filtered into the lower courtyard. Through the open window, she could hear the buzz of conversation. 'Mags looked lovely. Don't you think?' 'Ya. Stunning. Just stunning.' Stella bit her lip. Nobody would be saying that about the groom. He had even less hair than the last time she'd seen him and the overbite was still his most prominent feature.

Connor and Krish would be busy shooting family photos, followed by the hero shots of the bride and groom after the ceremony. She peeked through the window and spotted Jeanette's practically fluorescent fascinator among the crowd. Peeling away from the wall, Stella skirted the edge of the courtyard while holding her camera bag next to her face, and jogged back towards the ceremony balcony.

Halfway down the tree-lined alley, she found Connor directing the bride and groom as they strolled towards him, hand in hand, gazing lovingly at each other.

'Now smile!' Connor yelled out. 'And kiss.' From taking his class,

Stella knew Connor was waiting for the moment just after the kiss, when people smiled genuinely at each other. That was the money shot.

He acknowledged Stella with a nod and kept shooting. Krish was already taking alternative angles of the couple, so she decided to make herself useful and photograph Connor at work, in case he could use them for promotion.

They went inside the house to utilise the ballrooms' painted ceilings. She watched Connor work: methodical. Creative. Brilliant. Where a normal person would just see a wall, he'd see an opportunity for art. A slash of strong sunlight through the window, became a feature in a graphic, geometrical image using shadow play. Between the rapport he maintained with the couple, chatting to keep them at ease, and his artistic vision, she could understand why he was the best.

God, his talent was sexy. She stepped on her own foot to squash the thought.

After they finished, the bride and groom returned to the drinks reception with the photographers and Stella veered towards the empty upper courtyard to shoot the wedding breakfast set up.

At 6:00, it was time for a rest while the guests ate. Krish sat down in the break room with a tired huff, pulled out his laptop, and began downloading Connor's memory cards. The waiter brought in a tray of bottled water. Stella picked up two and rolled them over her face and neck, she was so hot.

When she looked up, Connor was watching her.

He leaned back on the sofa and closed his eyes. He must be exhausted after running around on this sweltering day. He'd removed his suit jacket a while ago, leaving him in a white Oxford with the sleeves rolled up. Even simple clothes looked good on him.

After they ate, the tension in her body receded. The wedding was halfway over and it should be easier to dodge Nathan and Jeanette as it got dark.

Stella shuffled to sit next to Krish. He was sorting through Connor's images and marking options for the slideshow. She loved seeing what Connor had shot at the hotel that morning. There was a brilliant portrait of the bride alone, standing at the end of the swimming pool with the panorama of the lake behind her. She was in the centre of the frame, which was almost perfectly symmetrical with the mountains angled behind her. Her hands, body language, expression —everything was exact. Connor Knight didn't make mistakes.

By the time they stood to get back to work, the air had grown cooler. Connor stretched, arms high in the air, his back cracking.

'Ouch,' Stella said. 'That didn't sound good.'

'I basically pay for my chiropractor's kids' education. This job is not great for the back.'

They loaded themselves up with their bags and cameras.

With his clipped, professional voice on, Connor turned to her. 'Price, you go shoot the cake.'

When she found the cake in the lower courtyard, she could understand why they wanted this one. Whereas Paulina and Oliwier's cake had been a more traditional, layered tower, this cake was art. It was completely covered in white chocolate. The maker had moulded the statues at the villa in white chocolate and piled them with roses until the confection tapered into a peak. How much had it cost to fly it to Italy? It would have needed refrigerating the whole way. Hopefully they'd cut it soon. Even though it was evening and the sun was going down, the cake was already sweating in the mellow warmth.

She picked up her camera and took close ups of the chocolate statues and a wide shot with the backdrop of the lake and mountains. She found a chair and took one from the top, angling down on the confection. The chair wobbled a little and she had to lean backwards to avoid tumbling onto the table. *That was close.*

Climbing down, she put the chair back and surveyed the table to see if there was anything she'd missed. She noticed a funny smell. She sniffed the cake, wondering if it was coming from there. Then it hit her.

'Stella Price.'

Vanilla and gardenia overwhelmed her senses and she closed her eyes, awaiting the usual rush of anxiety.

'Hello, Jeanette,' Stella said, turning to confront Jeanette in all her lime-green glory. A trickle of sweat careened down the side of Stella's face, having nothing to do with the heat.

'I couldn't believe my eyes when I saw you cowering behind those statues.' Jeanette's words slurred, her Essex origins peeking through. 'So…you're photographing weddings now?'

'Yup.' All the tools Stella had for controlling anxiety disappeared from memory.

'Is fucking the groom part of your service? A USP? I'm sure William would be up for it. He's always been a letch.'

Ouch. Stella felt the verbal slap. Ironically, it helped to calm her down.

Jeanette said, 'I always wondered what I'd say to you, if I saw you again.'

That makes two of us. Breathing deeply, she could feel control returning. 'For what it's worth, I'm sorry. I wish it'd never happened.'

'If wishes were horses…or is it fishes…?' Jeanette swayed towards her, but Stella had nowhere to go. The mega-expensive cake was at her back. Alcohol wafted on Jeanette's breath.

'He's *mine*. He'll always be *mine*. No matter how many of you ginger whores he fucks.' Specks of spittle flew from her perfectly-lined mouth.

The sharp edge of the table pressed into Stella's bottom. She skirted around the perimeter to put more space between Jeanette and her, so that they faced each other, the cake between them.

'Please, let's not do this here. It's in the past,' Stella said.

'You may have moved on. But I haven't.'

Jeanette gripped the table for stability. Stella's eyes flicked to the precarious white chocolate confection.

A nasty smile curved Jeanette's lips. 'Your new boss is a dish. Are you sleeping with him, too?'

Stella realised that her panic may have passed, but the danger hadn't. 'He's not my boss,' she said. 'And no.'

'It would be such a *shame*, don't you think? If you knocked over this cake. Do you think he'd get angry?' She reached out and poked one of the statues. A chocolate arm fell to the table.

'Jeanette. Don't.' Stella's heartbeat screamed in her ears. 'I've already paid for what I did. Trust me.'

'Trust you? I don't think so.' Jeanette grabbed the edge of the table, lifting two legs off the ground. In opposition, Stella pressed down on it.

'Please don't do this,' she begged. Their eyes met and time slowed down. She could see the moment that Jeanette decided she was going to follow through: her black eyes hardened into slits, the wicked smile shifted into a snarl, and she started to lift the table.

'Is everything okay here?'

Stella could have kissed Krish in that moment. He walked towards them, as if approaching rabid animals.

Jeanette dropped the table. The cake wobbled a moment, then settled. She spun around, changing from an angry harpy to a woman in complete control, and flashed a bright smile at Krish. 'All good. We were just admiring the cake.' She reached over and picked up the arm that had broken off. To Stella, she whispered under her breath, 'Watch your back', before popping the arm into her mouth and retuning to the wedding, head held high, hips swaying, Stella assumed for Krish's benefit.

They both stood without speaking until Jeanette disappeared from view. As soon as she was gone, Stella grabbed her stomach and closed her eyes. She began to hyperventilate.

In a few strides, Krish was next to her. He rubbed her back. 'Just breathe. Breathe.'

He continued to soothe her until she calmed down.

'I'm okay now. Sorry. And thank you. The cake also thanks you.'

'Holy shit. What was that all about?'

She sighed. She had to tell him. 'I had an affair with her husband. It didn't end well.' Surprisingly, saying it out loud in such a matter-of-fact way loosened her tension.

He whistled. 'Wow, that...' he paused to think of the right words, '...really sucks. Is that why you've been jumpy all day? I thought you were just nervous.'

'Please *please* don't tell Connor,' she whispered, tears springing to her eyes.

'I promise I won't, but if anything else happens, you should really tell him yourself. He'll understand.'

She nodded, swallowing hard.

'Have you finished photographing the cake?'

'Yes,' she said and showed him the images on the back of her camera.

'Those are really good. Why did I come here? Oh, yeah. The bride and groom want a quick ride on a boat with Connor to get some pictures with the villa at dusk. You and I are going to cover the guests while he goes. Will that be okay?'

She thought about it for a moment. She supposed there was no point in hiding anymore. Nathan was such a wimp, he wouldn't approach her in front of all the guests for fear of a confrontation.

'Let's go,' she said.

CONNOR HAD ALREADY LEFT when Krish and Stella arrived at the upper courtyard. She used her long lens, to keep as much distance between her and the guests as possible, but she still registered the moment Nathan first saw her. He did a double-take, stared at her a moment, then turned his attention back to his conversation, as though she meant nothing.

The rest of the wedding went smoothly. The speeches were mildly amusing; the cake cutting gloriously uneventful (the bride didn't notice the missing arm). Stella shuddered to think about an alternate reality where Jeanette had flipped the cake off the table. For the first dance, the bride and groom moved around in a slow circle to a Frank

Sinatra song. With fondness, Stella thought about Paulina and Oliwier. They had probably ruined her for all other wedding dances.

By 10:30, Connor was saying his goodbyes to the bride and groom and confirming their plans for the morning. She watched as the bride grabbed both sides of his face and kissed him full on the lips. The slideshow of images after the speeches had been a big hit and she had cried at almost every image. Stella would cry, too, if she were Margaret: despite her slightly hooked nose and lack of a chin, Connor had made her look like a supermodel. After the show, he had been hugged by most of the bride's family. The groom's eighty-year-old grandmother had pinched him on the bum. She said loudly, 'I may be old, but I'm not blind.' Stella wondered if Connor had to deal with a lot of inappropriate man-handling at weddings. Of course, there were all the rumours about him sleeping with bridesmaids. She saw the wedding planner whispering in his ear as she hugged him and slipped a piece of paper into his hand. Maybe not rumours, then. Stella frowned.

Connor and Krish went to load the taxi and Stella made a detour to the toilet. She had been holding it for hours, afraid of running into Jeanette again. However, at that very moment, Nathan's wife was dancing inappropriately with the best man.

After, she snuck into the break room for one last peek at the lake through the open window. It was fully dark now. She couldn't see the stars, as clouds had started to gather, but the lights of the towns on the coastline sparkled as though stars themselves.

'Hello, Stella.'

She froze. *Not now*, she thought. *I was almost done.*

'Hello, Nathan,' she said through gritted teeth and turned towards him. He stood in the doorway, one hand in his pocket and the other holding a glass of what she knew would be whiskey. The more expensive the better.

'I couldn't believe it when I saw you earlier. You look amazing.' His eyes travelled up and down her body and he stepped towards her. She was glad to report his compliment left her cold. 'So tell me. What *are* you doing here?' He slurred and swayed, stumbling in her direction. He put his glass down on a sideboard and loosened his tie.

'Working.'

He barely considered her answer before leaping towards her, grabbing her by the arms and pushing her against the wall. He pinned her with his body. 'I've missed you, babe,' he whispered sloppily in her ear before smashing his lips to hers.

21

STELLA HAD ALWAYS IMAGINED that if she were assaulted by a man, she could handle it. She was strong, young. She took self-defence classes at the gym. A knee to the groin or a poke in the eye and she'd slip away.

The reality was different.

Nathan pinned her against the wall, holding her firmly by the wrists. She yanked her arms, but he was just stronger. When they'd been together, he'd visited the gym regularly, not enough to gain Connor-level definition, but apparently enough to disable her.

His lips attacked hers, sour wine on his breath. She turned her face away. That, at least, she could do. Her knee was trapped beneath his leg, and when she tried to swivel away, he pushed against her harder.

She tried to use her voice, choking, 'Nathan! Stop. I don't want this. I don't want you.'

'C'mon, babe, for old time's sake.' His slobbery kisses slid down her neck.

She almost screamed, but the sound caught in her throat. If she screamed, it would bring everybody running, and that would hurt Connor's reputation. Perhaps that should be the last thing on her mind right now, but she couldn't help considering it.

She gave her hands another yank. Nathan held them in a vice as he moved towards her mouth. Staring at the open door, she willed somebody to walk by.

Almost as soon as she thought it, Connor stepped into the room. He paused, his face going from calm to rage in the time it took for Nathan to groan her name.

'Help!' she sobbed.

One second Nathan was touching her. Then he wasn't.

Connor threw Nathan to the ground. Grabbing him by the shirt, Connor lifted Nathan's prone form inches off the floor and pulled back his arm, ready to punch.

'No! Connor,' Stella said, wrapping her hands around his flexed bicep to hold him back. 'He's not worth it.'

Chest rising and falling rapidly, Connor stayed rigid. Eventually, he relaxed his arm, but kept hold of Nathan's shirt.

'If you *ever* lay hands on her again, I will end you. Do you understand?' Connor growled. She had never seen him so angry. Veins stood out on his neck, his lips pulled back in a snarl.

'Mate, you got this all wrong,' Nathan said. Leave it to Nathan to try to charm his way out of this situation. 'We're old friends—'

'If you know what's good for you, you'll stop talking.'

Nathan stopped talking.

Connor dropped him, and Nathan slid along the floor until he was a safe distance away. He stood and flicked his shoulders to resettle his dress jacket and his dignity.

Stella followed him with her eyes, her thoughts in turmoil. How had she ever loved this man? How dare he touch her? How dare he even think about her? She had shouldered all the consequences from their affair. Despite saying he loved her, Nathan took everything from her: belief in herself, faith in her own judgement, her career, and even her favourite song. She was tired of flagellating herself over what had happened. It took two people to have an affair.

She wanted her self-respect back.

As she stepped towards him, Connor reached out and gripped her elbow. His touch fired through her veins and she struggled not to react. 'I've got this,' she said. They held each other's gaze for a few seconds, communicating a million things through subtle movements. Without words, she asked him to trust her. Finally, he nodded and dropped his hand.

Approaching Nathan, who was smoothing back his ruffled hair, she said, 'Let me make something clear. I don't love you and I never want to see you again.'

Nathan straightened his tie. 'Stella, babe—'

If only he'd kept his mouth closed, perhaps what happened next wouldn't have happened at all. Before she knew what she was doing, she wound back her arm and punched him. He stumbled backwards.

'Fucking fuck,' he said, cradling his face. 'You bitch.'

She gave a short laugh. Her knuckles stung and her lips ached from his attack, but other than that, she felt nothing. Maybe this was what Ula meant by *get in the coffin*. Maybe she had to exorcise her self-loathing. It seemed a fitting funeral for the turmoil of the past ten months.

'Goodbye, Nathan,' she said, turning away.

Connor stood behind her. As she raised her eyes to his with a self-satisfied smile, she didn't know what she expected. A high five? A 'you go, girl'? A quip about being the female Rocky?

But no. Instead, his brow collapsed into a frown, his grey eyes turned stormy, and his lips pressed together in a firm line.

'You all right?' he asked, his voice gruff.

Smile falling, she nodded.

'Good. Let's go.' He stepped back, picked up her camera bag like it weighed nothing, and turned towards the door.

As she followed him down the low-lit hallway, tension emanated from his body. She realised that he didn't know who Nathan was, didn't know any of their history, didn't know how triumphant she felt right now. She would have to tell him. A lump rose in her throat.

'Connor, that man—'

'We'll talk later.'

Swallowing, she watched his shirt undulate over his tense, broad shoulders. This was a new side of Connor; she was used to him being in control of his emotions. Unflappable. Any jubilation she had at vanquishing Nathan slipped away. A sudden pressure behind her eyes took its place, sending a solitary tear down her cheek. She swiped at it. Did Nathan have the last laugh? Had he robbed her of Connor's friendship?

In front of the villa, Krish was waiting in the taxi. Connor opened the door for Stella and she crawled inside. He didn't follow.

Passing the bag to her, he addressed Krish. 'Take her back to the hotel. I'm going to walk. Just bring all the equipment up to your room and I'll get it in the morning. Six-thirty in the lobby, yeah?'

Krish agreed and Connor shut the door, rapping the roof to let the driver know he could go.

She still felt too shocked to speak. She wanted to explain to Connor what had happened. Turning her head away from Krish, she fixed her eyes on the window, swallowing a sob.

'Are you okay?' asked Krish.

Nodding and attempting to smile, she willed away the tears, but the effort of seeming fine was too much. One tear plopped onto her cheek. Then another. Within seconds her whole face was wet.

'Hey, hey,' he said, pulling her head onto his shoulder. 'Don't worry. I'm sure it'll be okay.'

'Will it?' She told him what had happened.

He listened, nodding with sympathy. 'You know it wasn't your fault, right?'

'I know. But still... Connor seems really angry. I could have ruined the wedding. His reputation—'

'If I know Connor, I'm pretty sure that's not what he's thinking right now.'

Pretty sure isn't 100% sure, she thought. The whole scene kept replaying in her mind. The look he gave her after she hit Nathan. Raw.

Hard. She wished she had never come along on this stupid wedding. If only the third shooter hadn't fallen ill. Except....

'Have you ever had a third shooter at weddings with Connor before?' she asked Krish.

'No, this is the first time. Actually, you've been a real help. It's usually me who has to run around like a headless chicken trying to get all the detail shots, plus being on hand to assist Connor. It's been great having you here.'

She smiled weakly while her thoughts free-falled. So Connor had lied to her about the third shooter. But why? Why not just ask her to come along in payment for her modelling session in France? Two hours ago, this discovery might have thrilled her, but now it just made her sad. Any friendship that she'd been fostering with him was over.

A loud crack of thunder sounded in the distance.

As they got out of the taxi at the hotel, fat raindrops began to fall.

'You go inside. I'll get the equipment,' said Krish.

'No, I can help.'

Together, they carried all the bags to the lift. The rain was getting heavier. Where was Connor?

'Thanks. I'll take it from here,' Krish said. 'Are you going to be alright?'

She nodded. 'Good night. See you in the morning.'

SHE TOOK THE STAIRS, hoping to expend some of her pent-up energy. In her room, she peeled off her sweaty dress and showered, to wash off the memory of Nathan's hands. Under the water, she worried about Connor. Losing his good regard scared her more than the encounter with Nathan. He wasn't content with ruining her old life; he had to ruin this one, too.

Towelling herself dry, she looked out the glass doors at the deluge. The thunderstorms in this part of Italy tended to be short but hard, necessary to lower the temperature of the sun-baked land. She pulled on her ivory camisole set, the satin clinging softly to her damp skin, and plaited her hair. Outside, the rain was pounding onto the balcony. She threw open the doors.

The cool, misty air hit her skin. Leaning against the door frame, she raised her gaze towards the sky. Should she text Connor, just to make sure he got back safely? She pulled out her phone to check how long it took to walk from the villa to their hotel. About an hour. He should be back soon. What if he'd been hit by a car? It was dark and wet out there and Italian drivers were all in their own personal Formula One race. She'd wait five more minutes before sending a message.

Perched inside the balcony door, she closed her eyes and replayed the events of the whole trip in her head, from their boat ride to the wedding, minus her encounter with Nathan. She thought about how brilliant Connor was. How easily he talked with couples and made them feel comfortable in front of his lens. He was funny and intelligent, despite his... interesting views on marriage. She thought about the way his whole face lit up when he smiled and how she lit up inside when she made him laugh.

He was nothing like Nathan Bastion. Seeing them in the same room, next to each other, it was clear to her that Connor was the better man in every way.

She opened her eyes as the rain stopped.

How much longer could she deny that she was seriously attracted to Connor Knight? Even back at the BAPP conference, she felt a pull towards him on stage. At the time, she thought it was just the draw of celebrity, but, no. This was more than that.

What was she going to do about it?

Lightening suffused the sky. The hairs on her arms stirred in response, standing on end.

A knock on her door cut through her thoughts.

For a moment, she worried it might be Nathan, that he somehow figured out where she was staying. But it would take more courage than he possessed to come looking for her. Perhaps it was Krish, checking on her? She walked slowly to the door and placed her hand on the knob, breathing in and out before turning it. Hope fluttered in her stomach.

The door swung open to reveal Connor, leaning his hands on either side of the frame. Water dripped from his hair and clothes onto the tiles. His white shirt clung to his chest. He sought her eyes with his.

'Connor?' She itched to reach out and place her palm against his beating heart, but she didn't know where they stood. Her stomach twisted at his expression. No sign of anger at all; only a raw look filled with an emotion she couldn't identify.

'I wanted to kill him,' he said, so low she almost didn't hear. 'I've never felt that before. If you hadn't stopped me...'

'Shhh. It's okay.' She took a small step towards him.

He dropped his hands from the doorframe and straightened to his full height. She couldn't tear her gaze away from his.

'Tell me to leave and I will.' His eyes burned into her, grey and molten at the same time.

It took a moment for his words to penetrate her thoughts. Leave? No way. She would gaffer tape him to the bed if she had to. 'No. I-I want you to stay.'

He took a step towards her. The air between them undulated with electricity. Her eyes dropped towards his middle and she saw his need already bulging against his trousers. She glowed. One more tick for Stella Price. It made her feel powerful, brazen, desired.

His hand lifted and hovered next to her cheek, not touching. All the nerve endings in her body migrated to that cheek, willing him to close the gap. She held her breath.

'May I touch you?' he asked.

She swallowed and nodded.

Connor reached towards her and dragged his finger softly down the side of her face. She leaned into it, her lips parting. Her breathing shallowed, as though anything heavier might blow the moment away.

His thumb settled in the cleft of her chin where he gently stroked the dented skin. Up and down, slowly, on repeat. She'd always had a love/hate relationship with that feature, but right now, it was her favourite part of her body. As his own breath deepened, his thumb entered her mouth and she wrapped her lips around it, grazing it with her teeth as he pulled it back out again. He trailed it down her neck, towards her breasts.

Her entire body burned. If he didn't kiss her, and soon, she would faint with need. Foreplay was nice, but Stella needed more of him.

She grabbed him by the shirt and pulled his lips down to hers.

A chuckle rumbled deep in his throat, as though he had won the game of Who Could Hold Out Longer. But within moments, nobody was laughing. His fingers slid into her hair, and her hands travelled to his waist, tugging him further into the room. He kicked the door closed. Rainwater soaked her satin camisole as he pressed himself against her.

'I've wanted this,' he said, his mouth grazing her ear.

'Me, too.'

When she said it, she knew it was true. From the moment their fingers touched during thumb wars, fighting their attraction had been like wading through treacle. As his lips moved down to her neck, she shivered, languishing in the joy of having his hands on her body.

Pulling back, he peeled his suit jacket off before finding her lips again while she got to work on his shirt buttons. She remembered his toned body next to the pool at the chateau, the muscular physique. As she undid the last button, it was like unwrapping a present that she'd been wanting for months. *Merry Christmas to me.*

She stepped back while he shrugged off his shirt and threw it on the floor. Arms free, he reached for her waist. She raised her arms, anticipating that he would take off her camisole. But instead, he slid his fingers into the waistband of her shorts and hooked his fingers over the elastic. He pulled down on them while kneeling in front of her. Once she'd kicked the bottoms away, he repeated the action with her knickers, working them down her legs.

Stella silently thanked the gods of hair removal that she'd been for a bikini wax the previous week.

When her panties had been discarded, he rested his fingertips on the sensitive skin behind her knees. Slowly he glided his hands up the back of her thighs. She bit her lip. It took everything she had not to moan his name.

The seconds stretched. As his hands continued their journey, he leaned forward and kissed her on the inner thigh. She almost melted into the furnace burning between her legs. At this point, it wouldn't take much to push her over the edge. She grabbed his shoulders and squeezed, signalling him to go on. He looked up at her with a devilish grin and moved his mouth upwards.

Outside, the rain began to pour.

In one fluid motion, he stood up.

Stella reached for his zipper, but he was there first, removing his trousers at speed. Instead, she divested herself of her top, eager to feel all of him against her naked skin.

'God, you're so beautiful,' he said, his thumbs rubbing the curve of her waist as his eyes drank her in. Those words on his lips almost undid her.

He was even more magnificent than she remembered, ridged with hard-earned muscle. She placed her hands against his chest. It was covered in the perfect amount of hair, not too much, not too little. She leaned forward and kissed the skin over his heart.

A clap of thunder sounded outside. Taking her hand, he pulled her towards the private balcony and into the pouring rain. The water cooled her hot skin. They stood together as small rivers snaked down their bodies. For a moment, the fact that she was here, on a balcony, in the rain, in Italy, with Connor Knight, struck her as insane. She smiled. If this was insanity, then sign her up. His mouth wandered towards her breasts.

Next thing she knew, he had picked her up and was carrying her to the bed. He laid her down, the duvet soaking up the water from her skin. He disappeared for a moment and she felt bereft until he reappeared with a foil square in his hand.

Her mouth twisted in an amused smile. 'You're prepared. Were you a boy scout or something?'

'Price, I was *never* a boy scout,' he said as he ripped open the packet and rolled it on.

After that, there were no more words.

22

As though the storm had never happened, the first rays of morning light tickled a cloudless sky. It was 5:55 AM. Connor's alarm would ring in five minutes. Until then, Stella wanted to feel his arms around her, marinating in these last few moments of being in bed beside him.

Because this would be the first and last time.

In the hour since she awoke, Stella realised two things. The first was that Connor Knight snored. Not the loud kind that sounded like the prelude to sleep apnoea, but more of a gentle huffing snort. She found it cute.

The second was that she couldn't start a relationship with him.

It wasn't the sex. That had been great. So great that it made all her past lovers look like fumbling pre-pubescent boys. So great it made her wonder how many women he'd practised on before her.

They'd made love three times, Connor's supply of wallet condoms seemingly bottomless. In between, they'd acted out almost every scenario pictured on Oliwier's X-rated wallpaper. Before they'd fallen asleep around two in the morning, they'd christened the shower. She'd never felt so dirty while getting clean. In a good way.

At some point, they'd stopped long enough for her to tell him about Nathan, leaving nothing out. Connor had listened without judgement, stroking her hair as she spoke and kissing the bridge of her nose where Jeanette had hit her long ago. With every telling, Stella felt less and less controlled by her past. Ula would be proud of her.

Stella had fallen asleep sated and content.

However, at 5:00, her eyes popped open. What had she done? How could she repeat the same mistake, especially when she'd expressly forbidden it? She had stopped blaming herself for what happened with Nathan, but the effects of the affair still haunted her. She couldn't go through that again. And hadn't Connor himself warned her off falling for him?

In her head, the story was already written. When people found out, they would talk about her. She could already imagine what they'd say: 'That's one way to get free photography tuition' or 'She didn't waste any time.' Connor, of course, would come through unscathed. Men were seen as conquistadors, but women pinned as whores. Her memory lingered on an interview that she'd attended after the awards incident. Within minutes it was clear that the creative director, a paunchy man in his fifties with leering eyes, had only requested an interview to see if she would dish the dirt on Bastion...or something else. As she passed the front desk on her way out, the receptionist had coughed the word *slut*.

And Connor...he would grow tired of her. She would disappoint him. Or another Scandinavian model would catch his eye. Something would make him realise that she wasn't worth loving. On top of that, there was his opinion on monogamy and marriage.

Don't fall in love with me. I'm bad news.

The alarm rang.

Behind her, she sensed his body stirring in more ways than one and she decided to put her misgivings aside for a little longer. They still had some time left. He stretched and she turned to face him, her skin tingling in response. She tangled her legs with his. Until they left this bed, she would be his lover.

'Morning,' he said, bending down to kiss her.

'Morning yourself.' The sight of his handsome face so close to hers made her heart beat faster. Ending this would not be easy.

'Sleep well?'

'Well enough. You?'

'Well enough.'

She thought they were being awfully polite when all she could think about was him being inside her again. Perhaps she should offer him a cup of tea. The precious seconds ticked away. To move things on, she pressed her body into his and said, 'Shame about the shoot this morning.'

His lip curled into a half smile. 'I can shower fast,' he said as he flipped her onto her back and rolled on top of her. Magically, another foil wrapper appeared in his hand. *Seriously*, she thought, *where is he getting all these?*

As he lowered himself onto her for the last time, she abandoned herself to him.

STELLA ALWAYS LAUGHED at movie scenes that started with a copulating couple throwing themselves back onto the pillows, panting like they'd just run a marathon. She thought that never happened in real life, though Claudia insisted that it happened to her all the time.

Yet here she was, after a frantic fifteen minute session with Connor, feeling like she'd just finished an aerobic workout. She wondered if she should stretch her hamstrings.

Kissing her on the nose before pushing himself off the bed, Connor said, 'Time to go.'

'Are they meeting us at the marina?' The space next to her felt empty. It took everything she had not to pull him back.

Despite the lack of sleep, Stella felt excited about this morning's shoot. She'd get to see Connor Knight doing what he did best—well, *second* best after last night—without the pressure of a wedding schedule. It would be a great learning experience for her and she'd be able to eke out her time with him before they went their separate ways.

'Ah,' he winced, 'I meant to tell you last night, but got a bit distract-ed.' He threw her a cheeky sideways glance as he stood up, completely uninhibited by his nakedness. 'Margaret wants to bring her make-up artist along for touch-ups. That's five people on the boat, one of them in a big dress, so there won't be space for you. I'm so sorry.'

'Oh. Okay,' she said, unable to keep the disappointment from her voice.

'If it's any consolation, I'd much rather stay here.' He disappeared into the bathroom and she heard the sound of the shower turning on.

Her phone beeped and she automatically reached for it on the bedside table. Who was texting her at this time? Probably her mother. It was Sunday, after all. Stella read the message, from someone named Valentina V: **Looking forward to seeing you on Wednesday. I've been waxed and polished and the new boobs are amazing. Vx**

It was Connor's phone. She dropped it back onto the table like it had burned her. She hadn't meant to read it, and now that she had, she really wished she hadn't. Nausea blossomed in her stomach. Who was Valentina? Was she 'Astrid', his date at Oliwier and Paulina's wedding? Or someone else. Did Connor have a girlfriend?

Stella wanted to vomit. When he had come to her room last night, she had stupidly assumed that he came to her free of commitments. Suddenly their night of passion didn't seem so special. It felt filthy and wrong.

He came out of the bathroom, hair wet, wearing a fluffy hotel robe, and looking sexy as hell. Her traitorous nipples hardened at the sight of him and she covered herself with the sheet. Her body was now firmly off limits to him. How could she have been so stupid, again?

As he gathered up his wet clothes off the floor, she thought about his limitless condom supply. Had he brought them with her in mind?

A picture of the petite wedding planner flashed behind her eyes. It seemed sex in Italy had always been on the cards for Connor.

She huffed an unimpressed laugh, and he looked up at her. 'All okay?'

'Yeah. Fine.' She couldn't bring herself to ask about the text message and Valentina. First of all, he'd think she'd been snooping. Second of all, he had to leave to meet the bride and she didn't want this conversation rushed, condensed into a handful of seconds. She would bring it up later.

He gave her a quizzical look and sat next to her on the edge of the bed. 'Look, I really am sorry about the shoot this morning. I know you're disappointed.' A yawn overtook him. For a moment, Stella felt bad for him. He had to bring his A-game to a bridal shoot on four hours of sleep. Then she remembered he had cheated on his girlfriend with her and her heart hardened.

Seemingly oblivious to the tempest brewing inside her, he said, 'We should be back around one or so. We'll have a quick bite and then head to the airport. I've organised late check outs, so no need to hurry.' He leaned over and briefly kissed her nose before picking up his phone and wallet off the bedside table and walking to the door.

She stayed stubbornly quiet, wondering if he'd notice.

'So…I'll see you later,' he said with a wink and left.

As the door slowly clicked closed, she stared at the space where Connor had been and the first tear fell.

JUST PAST ELEVEN, Stella took a long shower to wake herself up. Her eyes were puffy and she felt sluggish, even after the extra time in bed.

The sluicing water reminded her of last night, the memories bringing equal parts pain and pleasure. Even drying herself off made her think of him. Every sensation evoked a whisper of his hands: the soap, her towel, her robe. All her nerve endings craved his touch. She hoped it would ebb with time.

Bitterly, she wondered if Connor paid for Valentina's amazing boob job.

Anger fizzled up in her again and then melted away, replaced by sadness. She didn't want her memory of last night ruined because, in all other ways, it had been perfect. She wanted to pickle it and put it on a shelf, look at in years to come and remember that time she had an actual vaginal orgasm during sex.

Stella donned another sundress and packed. As she stood in the doorway with her bags at her feet, her gaze caught on the messy bed. She imprinted every detail onto her brain: the black and white tiles, the balcony, the smell of lavender. With a tortured sigh, she stepped into the hallway and let the door click closed behind her.

Downstairs, she checked out, leaving her bags with the valet. Her thoughts were in turmoil. She needed a change of scenery to help her sort herself out.

Wide-brimmed hat firmly in place against another hot day, she left the hotel, aiming for the waterfront. She wanted to breathe as much clean lake air as she could before returning to London.

As she sat on a bench and stared at the luxury boats bouncing on the waves, she thought about last night. *'I've wanted this,'* he said to her. But since when? Was it since the thumb war? Or France, when she modelled with Jean-Luc? Or when he saw her at Oliwier's wedding? Yesterday? When did he start wanting this?

Because for her, she knew it had been from the beginning. In typical Stella style, she had entered the photography industry and immediately gravitated towards the one man she should least get involved with. Claudia had been right not to trust her. What had she said? *'I know how you get horny around authority figures.'*

Also, Stella had to remember who she was dealing with: a man who hung out of helicopters for his promo shots. A man who had a girlfriend named Valentina with excellent boobs. A man who allegedly slept with bridesmaids. In France, Jared the King of Gossip said he'd heard that Connor once scored with a mother-of-the-bride.

Commitment didn't seem to be his strong suit.

Taken or not, that wasn't the kind of man she could trust. She wanted more for herself. Her affair with Nathan had at least taught her that.

But then there was the Connor that she had come to know. He might be arrogant, but he was also witty, loyal, smart, generous, and so talented. And that face...a wave of heat washed over her as she remembered sitting on it.

Her eyes squeezed shut. No matter how much she had enjoyed their brief, steamy affair, the fact of the matter was that Connor Knight was beyond her, in more ways than one. Aside from being unavailable, he was too big of a personality for her. Too famous. If she allowed herself to be pulled into his universe, she wouldn't be able to shine at the same frequency. He burned too bright. Right now, she felt like a very dull star. Maybe one day she would ascend to his heights, but that moment felt far, far away.

She frowned, sad at this realisation. Even if he was free, why would he want *her*?

A handsome man pushing a bicycle ambled past. *'Sei più bella quando sorridi,'* he said with a wink. *You're more beautiful when you smile.* Like it was her duty as a woman to decorate his world with her facial expression. She wanted to tell him to go fuck himself and felt surprised when the words actually slipped out of her mouth. He scowled at her.

Stella stood and continued walking along the waterfront, towards an older married couple strolling hand-in-hand, eating gelato. She faltered. She wanted that one day, somebody to share her life. Connor's words came back to her: *'Marriage is obsolete.'* She frowned again. The sooner she got home, back to her life and away from this place, the better.

Glancing at her watch, she noted Connor and Krish would return to the hotel soon. She wanted to be there before them, ready to go. On the way back, she stopped to buy sandwiches for everybody. With the bag of panini on her lap, she sat in the lobby and waited.

Her leg jiggled and she bit her lip. How would Connor act towards her? Affectionate? Distant? Professional? And what about Krish? She hoped Connor hadn't told him about last night. It wasn't that she didn't trust Krish; she didn't trust anybody. Except Claudia, Tristan, and maybe Liliwen.

The wait was killing her as the clock ticked towards 1:30. Part of her wanted Connor to come piling through the door and take her in his arms whereas the greater, saner part of her wanted him to act like nothing had happened. She herself would be taking the latter route. Playing it cool. Cool as a cucumber. Cool and the Gang.

She heard them before she saw them, Connor's warm laugh reaching her ears. They entered the lobby with their camera bags, talking rapidly.

'I couldn't believe it when she almost fell off the dock,' Krish said, grinning.

'That's exactly why I have insurance.'

'Great shot though. Worth it.'

The two of them were high on the shoot they'd just had. Stella felt left out.

'Hey, Stella, you okay?' said Krish when he noticed her.

Connor's head whipped up and they locked eyes. His lip curled into a smouldering half smile. 'Hey.'

She had to look away. *He has a girlfriend*, she repeated over and over to herself. 'Yeah, great. Um, I've got sandwiches,' she said, holding up the bag while her cheeks reddened. Inside, she wanted to shrivel and die. She didn't feel remotely cool. *Why not just say I carried a watermelon and be done with it*, she thought.

'Great! Sandwiches!' said Krish as he took the bag and bounced over to a table. He rifled through the contents and held one out to Connor.

'I'll have it in the car. I still have to pack.'

Krish peeled back the crinkling paper and bit into the ciabatta. 'My bags are already down here. Thought you'd've packed last night.'

'Too tired.' Connor's eyes grabbed hold of Stella's.

Her blush deepened. She couldn't look at him without remembering what his lips had done to various parts of her. She took off her sunhat and fanned herself.

With a self-satisfied grin, Connor excused himself and went upstairs.

Stella released a lengthy, frustrated breath, and beat down the part of her that wanted to follow him up there. The invisible thread of awareness that connected their bodies almost strangled her. She'd need to cut it. Move on.

The good news was that Krish seemed oblivious to the overwhelming sexual tension. The bad news was that this was going to be an excruciating journey home.

23

I NEED to talk to you. Call me, Stella texted Claudia as soon as the plane landed.

Connor had slept at every opportunity since they left the hotel, which suited Stella just fine. Maybe he was trying to avoid her. Or maybe he was exhausted after getting four hours sleep because of their massive shag-a-thon, followed by a big shoot. She tried not to linger on why he was tired, but the memories overtook her in waves, electrifying her body.

The closer they got to home, the more her resolve hardened. Last night was a one-off. Perhaps she just wouldn't ask him about Valentina. In a way, she didn't matter. Whether he had a girlfriend or not was inconsequential: a relationship with Connor would be a mistake regardless, for all the reasons she'd been repeating to herself since leaving the hotel. Forget Valentina. Forget Connor.

To help her maintain her distance, she'd spent most of her time at the Malpensa terminal either in the toilets or the duty free. She bought Claudia a magnet featuring a close up of the David's penis and a block of Parmigiana cheese.

As they exited arrivals at Heathrow, she was relieved to see three cab drivers holding signs, one with her name. Krish had organised a mini-cab home for her, alone.

The six of them walked to the parking garage and took the lift to the second floor. Stella kept her eyes on the ground. Connor stood next to her. She could feel his presence in every part of her. His coat brushed against her, and it took all her willpower not to jump into his arms.

Outside the lift, Krish gave her a brotherly hug. As his arms held her, she noted that he was a really great hugger. 'Great job and I'll be in touch about transferring the images, yeah?'

Stella squeezed him, holding on a few seconds longer than necessary. She knew what was coming next. Already, she could sense Connor hovering nearby.

Releasing Krish, she pivoted towards Connor. Before he could put his arms around her, she stuck her hand out into the no-man's land between them. 'Well, Connor, see you soon,' she said, sounding business-like.

His eyebrows fell into a confused V and he hesitated. Stella flicked her eyebrows twice towards Krish, hoping Connor would get the hint. With an amused smile, he stepped towards her and took her hand in his. 'Price. I'll call you.'

Hands entwined, he rubbed his finger on the inside of her wrist, on top of the sensitive network of veins. She almost melted. Her lips parted involuntarily and she took in a sharp breath. The dips and plains and calluses of his hands were so intimately familiar that she could probably draw a picture from memory. How could a handshake feel so sexual?

To cover up her emotions, she pumped his hand up and down and released it, turning to follow the driver. It took everything she had to walk away.

As soon as she sat safely in the car, she dabbed her eyes with her sleeve and checked her phone. Nothing. Claudia hadn't replied. Stella fired off another text and waited five minutes. Nada.

She needed to talk to Claudia. Now. Her friend had been known to leave her phone unattended for hours. It was Sunday night, so she was probably taking a bath or watching TV. Stella decided to take a chance.

'Excuse me,' she said to her driver, 'can we go to Richmond please?'

THE TAXI DROPPED her off in front of Claudia's flat at the top of Richmond Hill. Stella always felt a frisson of good-natured jealousy whenever she visited Claudia. Her parents had bought her flat as an investment property decades ago and now Claudia was buying it from them month-by-month, at today's market price, of course. Claudia figured she'd inherit it before she fully paid it off.

Her flat looked out over the Thames Valley, the only rural view protected by an Act of Parliament, with the arterial river snaking its way through a plush green landscape. Admiring it, Stella feel like she had stepped inside a Turner painting.

Stella pressed the bell to Claudia's flat firmly, as the button had a tendency to stick. She waited to be buzzed in. Nothing happened. Maybe Claudia wasn't at home. She'd been so busy lately; could she be at a shoot?

Stella pressed it again.

Inside, the thud of heavy footsteps descending the stairs echoed and a shadow loomed larger and larger as it approached the glass. The door swung open.

Magnus Fiennes appeared, wearing boxer shorts and a shirt that read 'Posh men do it best'. He pushed his floppy hair out of his eyes.

Stella's mouth fell open and she nearly tripped over her suitcase.

'Ah. You're not the pizza man,' he said.

'And you're not Claudia.'

'Er... no.'

Backing away, Stella said, 'You know what? I'll just phone her. It seems like a bad time...'

'No, please, do come up. I know she wants to talk to you.' He picked up her suitcase and stepped aside. She hesitated a moment before sidling past him, up the stairs toward the flat she knew so well —and the friend she didn't know as well as she thought.

She tried to process what was happening. What was Magnus Fiennes doing here? Claudia claimed she hated him for being 'the biggest twat in photography'. She'd specifically said, *what happens at convention, stays at convention.* Turning up in suggestive statement t-shirts and underwear was definitely not 'staying at convention'.

They entered the flat and Magnus closed the door.

'Sweetie?' he called out.

Sweetie? Claudia was somebody's *Sweetie?*

'Is the pizza here? I'm fucking starving. I think I could eat one all by my...self.' She entered the room and flinched when she saw Stella.

Momentarily losing the power of speech, Stella's eyes bulged, struggling to take in what surely was an optical illusion. Her friend, her best friend, who she'd known for ten years, had come down the stairs wearing a tight black tank top.

And there was a small bump over her belly.

'Oh,' said Claudia.

'Wow,' said Stella.

'Um.'

'Wow,' repeated Stella. She closed her eyes and reopened them, just to make sure she wasn't hallucinating. 'Wow.'

'You can stop saying that.'

'Wow.'

Claudia arched an eyebrow.

'Sorry. It's just...wow.'

'Have a seat. Sweetie?' Claudia said, turning to Magnus, 'would you get Stella a glass of water? Or something stronger?'

'Water is fine.'

'My pleasure,' he said, eyeing them both nervously before fleeing the room.

Stella took a seat on Claudia's white suede Heals sofa. She remembered when they'd bought it, whacking the whole ridiculous amount on a credit card along with the designer lamp that hung over them like a graceful swan.

'So...*sweetie?*' Stella began.

'What? It's ironic.'

'It's certainly *something.*'

'You're surprised,' Claudia said.

'Um...*yeah.*'

Magnus came in with the water. He had taken the time to slice lemon for each of their glasses and lay out some biscuits on a plate. He'd also put on some jeans.

'Sorry I've been so distant lately,' Claudia said.

'I can see why.' Stella reached for a biscuit, realising she hadn't eaten any dinner.

'Just hear me out.'

'Okay. I'm listening.' She crossed her arms and waited, all thoughts of the reason she'd come by in the first place miraculously taking a back seat. Claudia got full marks for distracting Stella from Connor Knight.

Claudia started talking, as though she'd been keeping the words in a box. 'Well, as you know, it all started at BAPP. It was supposed to be a bit of fun. Trust me, I was as surprised as anyone to find out what a magnificent beast he was in the sack.'

'Thanks, sweetie,' Magnus said as he brought in a bowl full of crisps and left it on the table.

'My pleasure, sweetie,' Claudia replied. Stella pressed her lips together. This sweetie stuff was a lot to take in.

'But then we broke up, just before that crazy fucking wedding.'

Stella remembered the out-of-place wellies in Claudia's car. 'Why did you break up?'

'Because I told her I loved her,' supplied Magnus as he came back in with a bowl of olives.

'Let's say I was *confused* by my complicated feelings for him.'

'Basically, she loved my posh arse and "couldn't fucking believe it", to use her words.'

'And then I realised I was pregnant...'

'...With *twins*,' Magnus called over his shoulder as he returned to the kitchen.

Stella didn't think her eyes could get any wider, but they did. She wasn't sure of the appropriate reaction. Was Claudia happy about the state of events or in shock or...? Stella, herself, was in shock.

'So, it was all a bit unexpected and hardly felt like something I should mention, as I was just having a laugh. But that's all changed and now...we're getting married.' She held up her left hand and laughed, her face wrinkling with glee. Sidetracked by the belly, Stella had failed to notice the magnificent diamond gracing her friend's slender ring finger.

'Oh my god. That's...that's great. Congratulations!' She leaned in and kissed Claudia on each cheek. 'So...when's the big day?' Stella asked while holding Claudia's hand to lavish her whopper of a jewel with the appropriate amount of attention.

'Oh, quite soon. Before the babies come at the end of December, so October, I think. His grandmother would have a fit if we waited.' Dropping her voice, Claudia said, 'God, his grandmother is a fucking battle axe. I'll tell you another time.' Then she mouthed, 'She hates me.'

Stella knew there were other questions she should be asking, but the biggest one was: *how did I miss this?* Her best friend was having a life-changing love affair and Stella had completely failed to spot the signs. Had she been so involved in her own drama that she'd been a bad friend?

'I'm so sorry,' Stella said.

'It's not that bad...yet. I've only had morning sickness a few times. Although sometimes I can't remember my own name. These pregnancy hormones are wild.' Lowering her voice, she said, 'Seriously, I'm like a rutting cat. Poor Magnus's dick is going to fall off at this rate.'

'No, I mean...I'm sorry for not being there for you.'

'Please, Stells. Don't be ridiculous. I didn't tell you.'

'But I should've known, you know? Like...I should have had a hunch...a spidey tingle...or something...'

'Pfff.' Claudia flapped her hand in dismissal. 'Well, you're here now. And there's something else.'

'What? You're not moving to Thailand, are you?'

'No, no. Nothing like that. I want you to be my maid of honour.'

Stella placed her hand over her heart. 'Of course! Oh my god, yes!' She threw her arms around Claudia, careful not to squeeze too hard. Happy tears gathered behind her eyes. This was a big life moment: her best friend getting married, asking her to stand with her, never mind the babies. Stella's emotional cup runneth over. She wiped at her eyes as she pulled away. 'Do I get to organise your hen do?'

'Yes and I'm going to want strippers. But first, we're having an engagement party in five weeks. August 28. You'll be there?'

'I wouldn't miss it for the world,' said Stella, punching it into her phone diary. 'The twenty-eighth is in six weeks.'

'Ugh. Whatever. My brain is all over the place. Yesterday, I couldn't remember the word for, um...uh...'

'Toilet roll,' Magnus filled in as he presented a beautifully arranged tray of tapas.

Claudia snapped her fingers. 'Yes, toilet roll. All I could think was "arse wipers".'

He sat down on the sofa next to her. She grabbed the olives and snuggled into Magnus's chest like she'd been doing it for years. His hand rested comfortably on her stomach. Smiling, she plucked an olive from the bowl and popped it into his mouth. As he chewed, he nuzzled into Claudia's dark head.

Who were these people?

Stella felt an odd sense of displacement, like the taxi had accidentally dropped her off in an alternate universe. She had never seen Claudia so content. Even the flat was tidy, which was bizarre. Claudia usually thrived in mess. There were no piles of magazines. No clothes on the floor. From what Stella could see of the kitchen, it appeared clean. No stack of dishes waiting to be washed. Magnus was obviously a good influence.

The buzzer rang.

'Golly. That'll be the pizza, I hope,' said Magnus as he extricated himself and dashed down the stairs.

Leaning towards Claudia, Stella squeezed her hand and said, 'You look happy, Clauds.'

'I *am* happy if you can fucking believe it.'

'May I?' Stella reached towards Claudia's tummy.

'Of course, rub away. See if a genie comes out.' They both laughed as Stella patted the bump. It was small, but firm. She couldn't believe two little humans were tucked inside.

Chewing, Claudia asked, 'Why are you here, anyway? How was...um...uh...'

'Italy?'

'Yes! All I could think of was "Pasta Land".'

Stella opened her mouth, but held back the words. This was Claudia's moment. Stella had already missed so much in her best friend's life and she didn't want to water down Claudia's joy with her tales of woe.

'It was great,' Stella said. 'I bought you a penis magnet and some cheese.'

IN THE TAXI HOME, Stella still couldn't get her head around it all. Claudia Monroe, her best friend, was pregnant and getting married. And she wasn't marrying some bohemian foreign circus performer or a tantric sex practitioner; she was marrying Magnus Fiennes, a man who probably had Buckingham Palace on speed dial.

As she left Richmond, however, her own problems pushed their way to the surface and her thoughts returned to Connor. She wanted to talk about it, but lacking Claudia and Tristan, who was in South Africa, it looked like her spider plant would be getting an earful. Perhaps she should meet Ula for a coffee, get her take on things.

It was almost 10:00 by the time she got home. The delirium of sleep would be welcome.

Inside the flat, she threw her keys into the bowl, greeting the picture of Tristan in his underwear with a tired smile. Walking into her bedroom, she dumped her suitcase and camera bag, and slumped on the bed.

She could smell something. Onions? And hear something, too. The gentle whir of the microwave plate rotating.

Sitting up, she called, 'Hello?'

No answer.

It couldn't possibly be Ula, could it? It was late even by her standards.

Stella got to her feet, grabbed a rolled up yoga mat, and held it over her shoulder like a bat. She tiptoed down the hallway. The microwave pinged.

Just as she was about to jump into the kitchen, Tristan stepped into view, wearing track suit bottoms and an apron that proclaimed *Kiss me, I'm Welsh!*

He jumped, almost dropping the dish of steaming sausages and mash. 'Bloody hell, Stells.'

'Tristan!'

'What were you going to do with that? Down dog me to death?' He put his plate on the kitchen island.

Discarding the mat, she threw herself at him, leaping into his arms and tying her legs around his waist.

Chortling, he hugged her back. 'Surprise! I take it you missed me?'

'You have no idea.'

24

THEY TALKED FOR HOURS.

Sitting at the dining room table, her tiredness forgotten as the red wine flowed, she filled him in on everything since they'd last properly hung out—which they realised had been before France.

'So tell me...where've you been? I need to live vicariously through you.' Stella leaned her elbows on the glossy white surface and rested her head in her hand.

'Darling, it's all dreadfully tedious,' he answered, tucking into his dinner. 'Five-star hotels, photo shoots, fashion houses, catwalks and so many blow jobs...*yawn*. You know modelling: it's a lifestyle, not a life. If you've done one Versace campaign, you've done them all.'

Stella had heard this speech before. It was complete rubbish. Tristan loved his job. 'How long do I have you?'

'Beginning of September, then I'm off to Fashion Week in New York.' He sipped his wine. 'But let's talk about you. Are you still doing this wedding photography nonsense?'

She crinkled her nose, pretending to be insulted. Unlike her father, Tristan meant it in jest. 'It's not nonsense. I'm serious about it.'

'It's not exactly high art, darling.'

'You sound like my dad. I'll have you know that there are amazing

wedding photographers out there. You're just a fashion snob.'
Imitating his manufactured posh accent, she crooned, 'If it's not
Bailey, it's bollocks.'

'Well, yes, this is probably true.'

'Remember, the photos I took of you for my A-levels landed you
your first modelling job.'

'Fine, fine. I'm sorry. I'm sure you're brilliant, like you are at everything you do.' He held up his glass and nodded his head in deference.
'Speaking of, didn't I see you in the *Daily Fail*? I had to stay in some
awful four-star in Singapore and they kept delivering it to my room.'

'Yup, that was me.'

'You looked ghastly. Almost didn't recognise you.'

'I was only photographing the wedding of *Oh! Paulina*. You know
her?'

Tristan rolled his eyes. 'Know her? I avoid her like the plague. She
keeps trying to hire me, but I've told my agent under no circumstances. Too trashy.'

Insulted on their behalf, she said, 'She's a pretty amazing woman.
And her husband isn't so bad either. He's crazy, but I like him. Did you
know he's Ula's cousin?'

'Ula? Our cleaner Ula?'

'How many Ula's do you know?'

'You'd be surprised.' He drew a sharp breath. 'Do you think she was
planted here? As a spy?'

Although it wouldn't surprise Stella if spying was in Ula's bag of
tricks, she said, 'For what? To report what brand of butter you use
when you're in London?'

'Well, it's possible,' he sniffed. 'That reminds me. She left a note.
She's gone on holiday to Poland.'

'Oh.' Stella hadn't managed to have a chat with their possibly porn-
star cleaner since the wedding. She still needed to warn Ula about
Ronny.

Leaning towards her with a salacious grin, Tristan said, 'So...any
wild sex parties while I've been gone?'

'No...' She bit her lip and her cheeks grew warm.

'What? What?! Tell!'

'I did have sex. Not here. In Italy.' She covered her face with her hands.

'I always thought you'd end up with an Italian. Who was he?'

'Not Italian. British. English. Sort of...my mentor?' She winced as she said it. Tristan already knew all about her past romance fails.

'I thought we weren't doing that anymore.'

'We're not. But Connor is...hard to resist.'

He narrowed his brown eyes, as though trying to access a memory. 'Hold on. It's not that bloke from the helicopter photo you sent me?'

She nodded.

'Well, that's understandable then. You're only human.' He filled his fork with mashed potato. 'Was it just sex or something more?'

'Just sex. A one-off...as far as I'm concerned.'

'Good girl. And as far as *he's* concerned...?'

'I don't know. I *think* he has a girlfriend. Or many girlfriends. I mean, every time I've seen him with a woman, she's been someone different...but the same. Tall, stick-thin models who are completely vacuous. No offence.'

He waved it off. 'Well, there's no problem then.'

'Right?'

'I had a filthy night with this Argentinean cowboy—'

'I mean, I don't want a relationship right now. I'm not going to let a man derail me again, you know?' Her eyes beseeched him to agree.

He reached out and touched her hand. 'Darling, I completely get it. Relationships would get in the way of our careers. We're only in our twenties, after all. We have our forties for monogamy,' he said with a shiver.

'Hear, hear.' She clinked her glass against his and took a large gulp. It felt so good to have Tristan home. He'd reinforce her choice to treat her night with Connor as a one-off. Tristan understood where she was coming from. Even more than Claudia, he had witnessed her horrible love affairs since the very beginning, aged sixteen: losing her virginity to one of their rival dancers the night before a big competition. Note: it didn't end well, though it did feel better than sex when they beat him to the title two years later.

Tristan and Stella chatted until midnight. He roared when she told him about her confrontations with Jeanette and Nathan and how good it felt to get him out of her system. By the time she returned to her room, tipsy, but content, she was determined in her course of action with Connor.

So why couldn't she stop thinking about him? And when she picked up her phone and read:

Thinking about you. Chat tomorrow? C

Her heart did a little flip.

THAT FIRST WEEK, Connor texted three times and left two messages. One asked if she was free for dinner. She replied with some lame excuse about meeting with a client (imaginary) and ignored the rest. On his Instagram, which she checked religiously, she saw that he posted a picture from her short-lived modelling career in France. The photo made her catch her breath. She looked like a bold, sexy version of herself. The way her eyes stared confidently down the lens, lips parted with a gentle smile, inviting the viewer to look closer. Was that how he saw her? Under it, he'd written: 'The best part of beauty is that which no picture can express. *Frances Bacon.*' She shivered. Was he trying to send her a message? He seemed to be pursuing her pretty hard which made her wonder...had she been wrong about Valentina? Suddenly, she wanted nothing more than the opportunity to ask him about it and kicked herself for not doing it in Italy when she'd had the chance

She waited for another text from him, but it never came. She felt too embarrassed to reach out to him. She convinced herself it was for the best, even as her insides twisted. Her photo was also deleted from his Instagram.

Stella knew she had acted badly and it made her look ungrateful for everything he'd done for her. But after a few days, she began to believe again that it had been the right decision. *'Per vivere felici bisogna fregarsene del giudizio degli altri'* — 'To live happily, you have to be heedless of the judgment of others.' Her mother hadn't said that one. Her mother's epitaph would probably read: *what would the neighbours think?* No, this one Stella had seen on a bathroom wall at an Italian restaurant.

She couldn't allow herself to think about how Connor might be feeling. Every time she imagined it, her heart lurched and her back muscles knotted with tension, so eventually, she learnt to rein in those thoughts for self-preservation. Anyway, according to his Twitter feed, which she also checked every day even though she knew Krish was the one running the account, Connor was criss-crossing the globe, shooting weddings in Scotland, Bali, Germany, New York. He'd probably already forgotten their tryst.

So, she threw herself into work, while hanging out with Tristan and planning Claudia's hen party.

From the thousands of images she and Claudia had taken at Paulina's wedding, Stella managed to whittle them down to 1500. She rolled her eyes when she saw one of Claudia's shots with Oliwier smiling manically in the foreground and Filip peeing into a flower pot, blurry in the background. That one would not be going in the album.

The process of choosing album images and retouching them took her two weeks and multiple late nights. When she called Oliwier to schedule an appointment to present her work, his phone rang with a foreign tone. Before she could hang up and text instead, he answered.

'*Halo?*'

'Oliwier, hey! It's Stella.'

'Ah, my Welsh Lady! How are you?'

People laughed and glassware tinkled in the background.

'I'm fine. Listen, I won't take up much of your time, I just wanted to know when I can see you and Paulina? I need to show you the album design before I send it to print.'

'We are so busy...we will not be needing meeting. I am trusting you. Just send for printing.'

'Are you sure?'

'Yes, yes. No worrying.'

They hung up, the memory reappearing of Paulina looking through the images on the back of the camera and not liking much of anything. But she also couldn't force them to have a meeting with her. She would just have to do a meticulous job.

After spending two entire days examining every image to make sure she hadn't missed anything, she sent her first ever full wedding album to print. Nausea consumed her as she paid for the order, including all the extra album copies. It made a big dent in her bank account, but at least she could check it off the list. Later that night, she celebrated with Tristan.

'This calls for Cristal, darling,' he said, which Oliwier would've approved of. They got horribly drunk, pushed all the living room furniture aside, and re-enacted their favourite dance routines from days past.

Besides that, Stella had returned from Italy to an answering machine and inbox full of wedding enquiries, thanks to all the recent newspaper articles. It corroborated the saying: 'There's no such things as bad PR'. She had a business.

Everything seemed to be heading in the right direction, except for one thing: no matter how much she tried to forget him, Connor's face and voice loomed large in her thoughts. She replayed their night together constantly. The guilt from fobbing him off ate at her. Maybe she could have handled it in a more adult fashion. But she knew herself. If they'd met, she would have ended up in his bed again. It was as simple as that. His planet would pull her into his orbit and she'd find it hard to pull loose again. She didn't want to get attached to somebody who didn't have the same life aspirations as her. She'd always wanted to get married one day.

Yet underneath it all was a niggling voice scolding her that she'd never given him a fair chance, that she had been stupid to let him get away.

She really wished Ula was around for another session on the couch. Unbelievably, her impromptu therapy had worked. Stella had jumped into the coffin, held it closed, and the spectre had disappeared. Or at least shrunk considerably. The problem was: Stella needed Ula's help with her next issue.

So she texted her. Thankfully, she replied right away: **What is the problem?**

It took ten minutes to write out the entire litany of events from Italy, including Nathan, her night of wild passion, and her decision to ignore Connor's texts.

What Stella wanted to hear was something like: 'That sounds like a sensible decision. You're doing what you need to do to protect yourself from future heartache and further mistakes.'

What she got was: **Are you crazy?** She sounded just like the niggling voice.

Stella frowned, taken aback. She read the rest: **You need to learn to do hard things.**

She decided not to point out that she had done the hard thing; that's what got her into this mess. But that wasn't what Ula meant.

Ignoring him WAS hard, Stella replied.

Ula zinged back: **You are letting fear run your life. You need to move on :o) xxx**

That annoying, sinking feeling when she knew somebody was 100% right melted through her body. Not for the first time, she wondered how Ula could be so wise, yet date a scumbag like Ronny. Life was full of contradictions.

She walked into the kitchen, frowning.

'Oh my. That's a face I wouldn't want to meet in a dark alley. What you need is a party,' said Tristan.

'I thought that's what we've been doing.' They'd already been out clubbing two nights that week. She reached into the freezer for ice cream.

'Well, I've had an invitation and I need a presentable plus one.'

'To...?'

'A wedding. Well, more of a shindig for their London friends. They already tied the knot at her family castle. You may have seen it in *Hello.*'

'You know I don't read *Hello.*'

'Snob.'

'I'm the snob. Ha!'

'Anyway, it's for Fleur and Tecumseh Smythe-Webster.' His deep voice caressed the words, meaning that Stella was supposed to be impressed that he'd been invited.

'You're making that up.'

'I swear I'm not.'

'Tecumseh? Is he native American?'

'No. Just pretentious parents. Anyway, should be a good bash. Stormzy might be performing.'

'Who's that?'

'You're joking, right?'

She stuck her tongue out at him. 'Okay. Why not? Sounds like fun.'

25

STELLA SHIMMIED IN THE MIRROR, watching green sequinned strands dance in the light. The dress had been an impulse purchase from Selfridges. She'd wanted to wear something she could move in, as Tristan and she always enjoyed tearing it up on the dance floor, and this one fit the bill: an emerald halterneck with a low back and a skirt cut on an angle from mid-thigh to knee, leaving her hips free to swivel. The dangling threads of sequins covering the dress elevated it from boring to brilliant and the colour complimented her vibrant auburn hair, which she left hanging down in voluminous waves.

Laughing, she felt properly sexy for the first time in ages. She'd even worked out how to apply a smoky eye based on instructions torn out of a magazine.

'Stells Bells!' Tristan greeted her in the hallway. 'You. Look. Fab-u-lous,' he purred, gesturing for her to twirl with his pointer finger.

'You're not so bad either,' she said, straightening his bowtie. He wore a midnight blue, single-breasted tuxedo tailored like a second skin.

'Oh, stop it. This old thing?' He held open his jacket to reveal the lining: a loud Vivienne Westwood print.

'Flashy,' she said.

'Oh, just wait til you see my new toy.' In the parking garage, he led her to a green vintage Jaguar and held the door open for her. 'Do you like?'

'What happened to the Porsche?' she said as she dropped into the tan leather bucket seat.

'Too gauche.'

'Of course.' She rolled her eyes and away they roared, the grizzly sound of the engine echoing off the walls.

Stella was looking forward to the wedding celebration, especially because she wouldn't know anybody there. She needed a knees-up tonight. The past week had been brutal. Oliwier and Paulina's entire album order had arrived on Wednesday and Stella had spent the ensuing days checking over each album rigorously, repackaging them, wrapping each box in paper and branded ribbon, and shipping them to Oliwier and Paulina's house.

A sense of relief washed over her as the courier took the boxes. She wanted to celebrate. With a knot in her stomach, she realised the one person she wanted to celebrate with was Connor. He would be so proud.

Had she done the right thing turning away from him?

Tristan swore. 'Ugh. Papparazzi,' he said as they approached the art deco facade of Claridges Hotel.

She peered through the windshield and clocked a bevy of middled-aged photographers cordoned off beside the entrance. Tristan yanked on the parking break and the car slammed to a halt in front of the valet.

'Smooth,' Stella said, glad she was wearing a seat belt.

'It's a classic car. We're lucky the brakes work at all.'

The valet opened the door for her. She grabbed her clutch and hoisted herself out as elegantly as she could from the low seat. The last thing she wanted was a picture of herself in the tabloids with her knickers circled in red. Thankfully, she didn't have to worry: although flash bulbs were going off, the paps were crying, 'Tristan! Over here!' All lenses were trained on him.

When he finally joined her at the entrance, she pretended to look at her imaginary watch.

'All part of the job,' he gritted through his teeth as he smiled at another photographer and showed off his Swarovski-encrusted skull cufflinks.

They walked through the foyer and into a candle-lit anteroom boasting a huge floral centrepiece. They hadn't taken two steps when a woman in a tight yellow dress shouted 'Tristy-Baby!' and launched herself at him, planting loud air kisses near his cheeks. She immediately started listing the places they might've last seen each other. Was it the yacht party in Monte Carlo? The premiere in Cannes? The fashion show in Madrid? Stella studied a wall sconce. A waiter across the room carried a tray of champagne in antique glasses, so she excused herself despite Tristan's pleading eyes and peeled away toward the drinks.

As she picked up two glasses and turned, a flash bulb went off nearby. She turned toward the person behind the camera.

'Krish?' she said at the same time that he said, 'Stella?'

'I almost didn't recognise you.'

With a sinking feeling, she asked, 'Is Connor here?'

Krish looked down at his camera, as though embarrassed. How much did he know about what happened in Italy? From the panicked expression in his eyes, she guessed everything.

'Um, yeah, he's here somewhere. He's in a foul mood though. I'd stay away.'

'Why?'

'He's tired. Been working non-stop for weeks. Plus he hates this kind of gig. We shot their actual wedding in Scotland and she emailed the studio at least three times a day in the run up to ask how long we thought her veil should be and which shade of slightly different pink lipstick we thought would photograph better.'

'Nightmare.'

'Between you and me, I also think she has a crush on Connor. Happens a lot with him.' He squinted at her with concern.

She nodded, hoping he wouldn't catch the flash of pain in her eyes. 'Anyway, gotta go. I'm supposed to be on the lookout for celebs.'

Before he could zip away, Connor's voice asked, 'Hey, Krish, do you have an extra card on you? Mine's almost full and—'

Krish stepped aside, leaving Connor and Stella facing each other. Krish's eyes ricocheted between them and he excused himself.

Stella's heart flipped. It flopped. Her breath caught and her stomach floated like a balloon. The entire rest of the room disappeared and it was just the two of them, gazing at each other, his eyes surprised and stormy. She drank in the sight of him: his handsome face, the full lips she missed kissing, the thick chestnut hair that she had run her hands through, the eyes she wanted to gaze into while they talked about all things life and photography. In that moment, she realised that the past four weeks had been an exercise in futility. Nothing would change one, significant fact.

She loved Connor Knight.

'Hi,' she said shyly, hoping against hope that he would gift her with his devastating half smile, that he would forgive her.

He frowned.

The air rushed out and the atmosphere in the room crashed around them, the sound deafening.

'Darling, there you are.' Tristan walked up to Stella, and Connor's expression darkened even further, eyes bulging slightly and mouth disappearing into a thin line. Tristan took one of the champagne glasses from her and drained half its contents. 'That Edwina is a terrible bore. When I tap my face with two fingers, that means save me, all right? Come on, let's find some interesting people.' He put his arm around her waist like it was the most natural thing in the world. 'Oh, sorry,' he said, noticing Connor and his camera. 'Did you want a picture?' He struck a pose next to Stella.

Connor pulled on his collar, like it was too tight. She went to introduce them, but her mouth had gone dry, making it hard to form words. Before she could take a sip of lubricating champagne, Connor sharply raised his camera to his face, snapped a photo, and walked away. Stella blinked, spots dancing across her vision. When it cleared, she looked around, trying to locate him, but he had disappeared.

Tristan put his mouth against her ear. 'Ding dong. I can see the appeal of the career change now.'

She pushed away from him. She needed to find Connor and set him straight about her and Tristan. She searched the foyer, frantically pushing past the glamorous people, not caring about the bitchy looks. But he was nowhere to be found.

Coming back to Tristan, she took his arm and pressed her forehead against his shoulder, fighting tears. 'That was *him*,' she said, her voice catching.

'Well, fuck me. If I'd known he was that hot, I would have told you to go for it.'

That was the last straw. Uncontrollable manic laughter bubbled up inside her.

'Let's get you to the bar.' Tristan patted her hand and led her away, cackling, into the main ballroom.

THE PARTY WAS ALREADY in full swing and a burlesque act had just finished onstage. Pretty young things were dancing to club songs in one half of the room, while others gathered around the pink Perspex bar. Some guests disappeared into a side room, where a casino had been set up.

As soon as they entered, she sensed the almost imperceptible movement of hundreds of eyeballs swivelling towards them, as if expecting some long dead relative to walk through the door. From the non-stop barrage of air kisses, it swiftly became apparent that Tristan was a popular person.

The manic laughter after Connor's snub had faded rapidly, replaced by agonised contemplation. As Tristan introduced her to people with names like Yaya and Preston, she replayed the meeting with Connor in her head, trying to figure out if he hated her completely or whether there had been any cracks of forgiveness in his steely facade. Thankfully, none of the other guests Tristan presented to her seemed the least bit interested in asking her questions, leaving her free to obsess quietly.

Connor had treated her like she meant nothing. All the easy camaraderie they had built up had been destroyed by her treatment of him after Italy. What had she been thinking? Why couldn't she have realised this four weeks ago? Why had she listened to Tristan, a self-proclaimed bachelor whose goal was to sleep with someone from each country before 30? Now Connor would always think of her as that ungrateful woman who tricked him into teaching her, slept with him, then ignored his texts. She had to agree with his sentiment in France: couldn't she do *anything* like a normal person?

She wiped away a rebellious tear. She was so stupid. He had told her, point blank, not to fall in love with him. And what had she done?

Every time a flash went off, her head flicked in its direction, hoping to catch a glimpse of him. After half an hour, she had a neck cramp and a headache.

'Excuse me,' she said to Tristan and the person currently conversing with him. Blair? 'I've got to visit the ladies.'

Tristan tapped his cheek with two fingers, but she ignored him, taking her drink and leaving to find the toilets.

She sat in the cubicle with the seat down, trying to come up with a plan. What would Ula tell her? *You need to learn to do hard things.* She sighed. There was only one way to attack this: find him, explain herself, and apologise. Tell him she'd made a mistake. Beg if she had to.

After fifteen minutes, she took a deep breath and stood. She walked out of the ladies, determined to find Connor, and banged straight into him.

'Ow!' she said as his camera bashed into her hip.

He grabbed her by the shoulders to steady her, but dropped his hands as soon as he saw who it was, like she had skin of fire. Her arms tingled where he had touched her and her hip throbbed, but both were overshadowed by the thud of her beating heart.

This would be as good an opportunity as any to execute her toilet cubicle plan.

'Connor, I—'

'Let me stop you there, Price. You made your choice. I'm a big boy. I've already moved on.'

'Please will you—'

'Can't talk now. Busy,' he said, brushing past her, into the men's room.

Anger rising, mostly at herself, she yelled out, 'You can't avoid me all night!'

'Watch me!' came the muffled reply.

She briefly considered following him into the toilet, but two men went in after him. 'Ugh!' she grunted as she slapped the wall with an open palm. *I've already moved on,* he'd said. Her heart squeezed.

She stomped back to the ballroom and found Tristan standing with a group of women. They were all laughing at some joke that probably wasn't very funny.

'Stells!' he greeted her as she joined him. 'Let me introduce you to—'

She was not interested in talking to anyone. 'I need a drink,' she said into his ear. 'Now.'

He must have recognised the desperate, serious note in her voice because he made excuses and steered her towards the bar. On the way, he stiffened, 'Oh, shit—turn left. I slept with that guy.' Stella saw an attractive, muscular man with spiky blonde hair and the hint of a large tattoo peeking over his collar.

'Nice,' said Stella.

'Not nice. He fired me from an editorial job for *GQ* when I didn't call him back. Totally awks.'

They found a free spot at the bar, Stella standing to block Mr GQ from seeing Tristan while he ordered cocktails involving umbrellas.

'Why didn't you call him?' she asked, a drop of displeasure leaking into her voice.

'What? Oh, it was just a casual thing. Well, I thought so anyway.' He picked the umbrella out of his drink, toasted her, and sipped from the straw.

Stella kept her drink on the bar. 'So you just used him for sex and then discarded him. And you're surprised when he's angry.'

'I thought he knew that show was one-night only. Anyway, what's your problem?'

My problem is that you gave me shit advice, she thought.

'I just think it's rude and insensitive and beneath you to act that way. He's a person, too, you know. With feelings.' *I've already moved on* echoed in her head.

He tilted his head to the side and studied her, eyes narrowed. 'Okay...what's going on, Stella?'

Before she could answer, a shrill voice cried out, 'Tristan! So glad you could make it, darling.'

Stella turned to find the bride, Fleur, standing behind her in a figure-hugging white dress. Next to her stood Connor, exuding discomfort as he tried to look anywhere except at Stella. The bride was holding his arm possessively. She let go for a moment to give Tristan a kiss on each cheek.

He tried to introduced Stella. 'Fleur, this is my—', but Fleur wasn't interested.

She cut in: 'Darling, I simply must have a picture with you. Connor, be a dear?' Stella stepped out of their way as Connor took their photo, Tristan gifting the camera with the wicked grin for which he was famous.

Afterwards, the bride continued to chat—something about her upcoming honeymoon clearing landmines followed by two weeks of relaxation on a beach somewhere. Stella was only half listening because she was busy staring pointedly at Connor, willing him to look. He clenched his jaw, a vein throbbing on his forehead, eyes fixed on the back of his camera as he scrolled through images. Her foot tapped. She could feel her temper rising the more he ignored her.

Her foot tapping increased in pace. He zoomed in on a picture, squinting as if trying to examine the bride on a microscopic level.

Finally, as Stella hovered on the verge of kicking Connor in the shin, the bride pulled him away to photograph her with more guests. Stella downed the rest of her cocktail and ordered another.

'Is it getting hot in here or am I standing next to Mount Etna?' Tristan asked.

'What?' she practically shouted at him.

'What is going on with you?' Tristan asked. 'You have a face like a slapped arse and your skin has gone all blotchy. It's highly unattractive.'

Stella looked into the eyes of her oldest friend and sagged. 'I'm sorry, I'm just in the unfortunate situation of being in love with that photographer.'

'The one you've been ignoring after having hot, passionate sex in Italy?'

'Yes.'

'Oh, you poor darling,' he said stroking the back of her head with pretend comfort.

'Stop it!' she said, pulling away. 'I'm serious. I'm in love with him. I've made a huge mistake. I ruined everything by not talking to him after Italy. Now he just thinks I'm some…maneater who ditched him after getting what I wanted. I've tried to corner him, but he's really angry. I don't think he's interested anymore.' The words ended in a sob.

Tristan rubbed her back. 'And then he sees you with a devilishly handsome specimen like me and is—understandably—jealous…yah, that sounds like he's not remotely interested.'

'Come on. What are you saying?'

'He's green as Kermit's ballsack, my dear.'

'No way. He's not *jealous*. He's *angry*.'

'Oh, honey. Trust me. If there are two things I can tell about a man, it's when he wants to shag me and when he's jealous. And unfortunately your Connor isn't the option that I would like.'

'He explicitly told me *not* to fall in love with him.'

'Well, a man can change his mind, can't he? Maybe I just make him insecure.'

That made Stella laugh. She couldn't imagine Connor being insecure about anything.

'Now that I've seen him in the flesh, the thing I want to know,' Tristan began with a serious frown, 'is how is he in bed? I bet he's got a dirty trick or two up his sleeves...'

'Tris!' She blushed.

'You're right. You're right. I'm sorry.' He paused for a moment. 'But just for reference, is it more of a pickle? Or are we talking English cucumber? Perhaps a small aubergine?'

She punched him on the arm.

'Okay, so what are you going to do about this?' he asked her.

'What can I do? He won't talk to me.'

'Well, in that case, you need to make him take notice. You need to show him the Stella Price I know.'

'And who's that? A pitiful newbie who makes atrocious life decisions?' She rolled her eyes and laughed.

He thought for a moment and, in a rare demonstration of seriousness, said, 'The Stella I know is a champion, a fighter. Remember when I wanted to quit dancing? We kept coming so close to winning, but could never break into that top spot. It was you who made me keep going, "Give it one more year, Tris," you said. "Give it one more year with everything you've got and we can do it. If we quit, we'll always regret it." And then we won.'

'Life seemed so much simpler then.'

'You're right. Life can be a hard bitch. But do you know whose voice I hear in my head whenever I feel like something is too difficult, or I want to quit?' He paused until she looked at him. 'It's yours, Stella.'

She had tears in her eyes. Her shoulders slumped. 'I haven't felt like myself in ages. I slept with a married man. I knew it was wrong and I did it anyway.' *I deserve everything bad that's come to me.*

Reading her thoughts, he said, 'You can't beat yourself up over that for the rest of your life. Hell, if I prostrated myself over every married man I slept with, I'd never get up.' He handed her a cocktail napkin and she dabbed at her eyes. 'Stella. If he wants to be jealous, then let's make him jealous and be a little bit wicked while we do it.' His eyes slanted towards the dance floor. 'Do you remember our cabaret dance?'

She followed his gaze. 'The rumba? I-I think so. You?' She began to feel lightheaded at the thought of what he was proposing.

'Well,' he held his hand out, 'let's find out.'

She bit her lip. Tristan was right. Connor was used to seeing her as the damsel in distress. The student. The one who needed direction and guidance. Well, that wasn't her. Stella Price was a grown woman. A champion, as Tristan reminded her. She may have had a bit of a dip, but she wasn't the sum of her bad decisions. She decided to do it, not to make him jealous as Tristan suggested, but because it was time for Connor Knight to see who she really was.

She took his hand. 'Let's go.'

They clutched each other like giddy school children about to break the rules and walked towards the dance floor. Tristan left her a moment, to check with Fleur if she minded them stealing the lime-light temporarily, but she thought it sounded marvellous. He approached the DJ and slipped him a £50 note to play *'Wicked Game'*, next.

Together, they stepped into the middle of the dance floor, swaying to the current number while they waited for theirs to start. Adrenaline raced through her veins, that familiar sensation she used to have before performing. Part of her wanted to flee, but she stayed put. She glanced towards Tristan. His face had already assumed that glazed look of concentration. She knew from experience that he was going through the moves in his head, counting out the beats. He gave her hands a brief squeeze. 'Tits and teeth,' he whispered to her and she smiled.

Breathing deeply, she rolled her shoulders and tipped her head from left to right, back to front.

Something told her to look up. Her eyes found Connor's. He stood on the edge of the dance floor, camera in hand. Their gazes held for a second before he broke away. Suddenly, she wasn't sure this was such a good idea.

The song ended.

This was it. The moment of truth. Too late to run now. She inhaled, shutting out the world.

Their song began.

The first sexy twangs of *'Wicked Game'* filled the room. They snapped into action.

Tristan's arms closed around her, his hands moving languidly up her body, starting at her hips and finally coming to rest on her face. He gripped her head and looked into her eyes with theatrical lust. She remained there for a moment before disengaging from him, like she was trying to get away. He grabbed her by the hand and whipped her back, her leg lifting up to hug his thigh. He pinned her leg with one possessive hand while she slowly dipped back, her arching spine scribing a circle in the empty air, her breasts pressing upwards, hair hanging down.

By the time Chris Isaak's vocals started, the other dancers realised something special was happening. They parted to make a large circle, leaving space for the two ex-champions to perform. When they did their first lift, the audience broke into rapturous screaming.

For Stella, it felt good to be inhabiting this body again. Her confidence grew as they flowed through the routine, hitting step after step, if not perfectly, then at least commendably. Tristan clasped her hand and she ducked her head under his arm, turning so that her back was to his chest. They swayed back and forth like one person, hips glued together, before he twirled her out in a graceful arc, letting her hand go, so she could turn a few times on her own before coming back to him. Chris Isaak's sultry voice caressed each word, lamenting thwarted love.

She concentrated on the story behind the dance. Rumba wasn't just about putting a string of movements together; there needed to be a reason. A motivation. The emotion had to show on their faces or the dance wouldn't land. In their teenage years, they had listened to the lyrics and come up with a tale about a firefighter who had lost his lover in a fire. It wasn't going to win an Oscar as a storyline, but it helped them create personas to inhabit while performing.

That wasn't the story she was acting out now. In her head, she imagined Connor's hands on her. She thought about how he didn't want to fall in love with her, how she didn't want to lose him.

They executed a perfect 'New Yorker': holding hands in the middle and facing the same way, they stepped forward and presented their other hands high in the air. Then they repeated it in the other direction, moving at pace.

After that, it got really sexy.

Stalking away from Tristan towards where she had last seen Connor, she looked up to find he was still there. She rocked her hips back and forth, closing her eyes and swirling her arms above her head before swivelling down towards the ground and back up again. Connor seemed to have forgotten he was ignoring her. She pierced him with her eyes as she stood up again, moving her hands over her body. He stared at her, transfixed, camera forgotten. Tristan grabbed hold of her from behind and whipped her around so she was facing him again. She glued her hands to the side of his face, then slid down him, her back leg stretching on the floor behind her, before he yanked her up into his arms and she wrapped her legs around his middle while he twirled in a circle.

Her favourite part was coming up. The showstopping move. A difficult leg extension while the backup singers crooned about breaking hearts.

Tristan supported the bottom of her spine as she leaned back, lifting her leg provocatively into the air. At the top of the move, her hair hung down towards the floor and her pointed leg was aimed like a gun at the chandelier. She counted three as she held the pose—three seconds that felt like an eternity as her muscles thrummed. And then it was over. She snapped back to standing, holding Tristan as if for dear life. She gazed at him with unrequited love shining in her eyes, turned, and walked slowly, seductively, away.

The music ended.

Applause and wolf whistles drowned out the sound of the next song starting up. She smiled at Tristan and he enveloped her in a hug, lifting her off the ground.

'I'm going to need physio for a month after that,' he said through his smile.

'Me, too.' She laughed. 'Thank you.'

'Come on, Stells. You can always count on me to put you back on your feet.' He squeezed her one more time and released her.

'Sev-EN!' someone in the crowd yelled, imitating Len Goodman from *Strictly Come Dancing*.

'Are you kidding me?' said Bruno Tonioli, the ex-*Strictly* judge, in his thick Italian accent. He stepped out from the crowd and rushed towards Tristan. 'That was a ten! A masterpiece! It was like a little slice of heaven. I'm feeling all hot and frisky now.' He looked Tristan up and down. 'Here, take my card. We need to talk.' With a wink he went back to his friends near the bar.

Stella stepped away from Tristan, leaving him to deal with his fans as they surrounded him. She scanned the room for Connor.

He was gone.

The dance floor overflowed. She pushed her way through, graciously accepting compliments along the way. One woman tried to hug her and a man slipped her his number, but she ignored them, continually moving forward. Finally, she popped out into the ante-room where fewer people were congregating. She skirted around the flower display, head swivelling around to see if Connor was there.

She spied Krish, packing away Connor's equipment into black canvas bags.

'Krish!'

'Stella! Wow! That was something else. I didn't know you could dance. When did you learn to do that?'

'A long time ago. Listen, where's Connor?'

'He had to leave. A headache or something.' From the way he said it, she knew he was lying. 'We're finished anyway. I'm just going to drop off our stuff at the studio.'

'How long ago did he disappear?'

'A couple minutes...?'

'Thanks.' She slipped off her shoes and took off at a run towards the front doors, bursting onto the street where the paparazzi still waited. They raised their cameras; a few clicked off shots, just in case she turned out to be someone famous. Most of them went back to smoking their cigarettes. She turned one way, then the other, scanning the pavement for Connor. She couldn't see him.

A movement across the road caught her eye. A gull-wing door cruised upwards.

There he was, sliding his coat off and throwing it into his old-school Mercedes—the same one she'd seen him drive to Oliwier's wedding.

She ran towards him. A bike swerved around her, the rider swearing. 'Sorry!' she cried.

Connor's head whipped towards the commotion. He stalked around the car and shouted, 'Are you crazy?'

'Connor,' she said as calmly as she could.

'Are you trying to get yourself killed?' he continued.

'Connor!' she roared to silence him. 'He's gay.'

'What?'

'He's *gay*.'

His face crumpled in confusion. 'Who? The cyclist?'

She rolled her eyes. 'The guy I was dancing with. The one I went to school with. He's gay. As in, doesn't like girls.'

He leaned back onto the car. She could tell the moment that the meaning of her words penetrated. He looked at her.

'And also, I'm really sorry. I shouldn't have ignored your texts. I was just trying to protect myself after...you know. Nathan.' She hated saying his name. 'I didn't know what to think. You were always with Inga, or Galina, or Astrid...'

'Who?'

'You know…all your blonde models…and who's Valentina? I saw her text that morning in Italy…'

He scrunched up his nose. 'Valentina Vavilvek? My client?'

'Your…client? Well, why was she texting you about her boob job at six in the morning?'

Understanding dawned on his face and he said, 'She was in Dubai at the time. She always texts at weird hours. And we had a photo shoot in the diary a few days later. She likes to do a new boudoir shoot whenever she gets work done. The joys of being the bored wife of a billionaire.'

'Oh.' Well, now she felt like a prize nugget. She took a step closer to him. 'Just tell me: are you free to be with me?'

The storminess in his eyes had been replaced by something else. Something intense. She had never noticed it before, but there was a small speck of green on the right, just above his pupil.

He put his hands on her waist and pulled her towards him. 'How can there be anyone else, when you're all I can think about?'

Her heart grew three sizes in less than a second.

Without warning, he kissed her with all the pent-up frustration of the past few hours. She swayed, pressing her body against his the way she'd been dreaming about since Italy.

A symphony of catcalls started up across the street, the bored paparazzi enjoying the free show. Stella broke away and blushed, hiding her face in his chest, while Connor waved to them. She admired his ability to charm everybody.

Taking his hand, she pulled him so that the open gull-wing door blocked them from view. 'I feel like an absolute idiot.'

'Well, I'm not going to disagree with you.' He gave her that half-smile she'd been dying to see.

'So…' she began. 'You weren't *jealous*, were you, Connor?'

'What? No.'

She raised an eyebrow at him.

'Okay, maybe a little bit.' She stepped on his toe. 'Okay, horribly. Didn't actually know what jealousy felt like. Now I do.'

'You've never been jealous before?'

'I've never had anyone worth being jealous of.'

Her pulse quickened at his words. Could he have feelings for her, too?

He pushed her back to catch her eye. 'So what do we do now, Price?'

Running her fingers through his hair, she grabbed a handful at the nape of his neck and pulled. 'I'm going to get in that car with you and we're going to drive to your place.'

After she collected her bag from inside, they climbed into his car and zipped through London towards his warehouse flat in Shoreditch.

A few minutes after falling through his front door, they were in bed.

And she didn't leave his flat for three days.

26

ON THE SECOND DAY, he shot her.

It was mid-afternoon and they had just finished refuelling themselves with pizza and a bottle of red wine. She was washing the dishes when Connor put his arms around her and nuzzled her neck. She revelled in how comfortable they'd become with each other. Flipping the tap off, she spun and engaged him in a deep kiss, her whole body fizzing with the memory of what they'd been doing for the past day and a half.

He slid his hands underneath her bathrobe and pulled her closer. She had lost count of how many times they'd made love. More than ten, less than a hundred. She thought he might be attempting to add one more to the tally when he said, 'I want to photograph you.'

It took her a moment to understand. 'Who? Me?'

'Yes, you, Price. Who else do you think I mean?'

Connor had already photographed her twice: once in France with Jean-Luc and then again in Bellagio. She wondered if being together would change the way he directed her, make it somehow different. 'Okay. I don't have any clothes here, though.'

He nibbled her shoulder. 'What I have in mind doesn't involve clothes.'

'Oh. Right.' *Definitely different, then.*

'Is that okay with you?' He put his finger under her chin and gently tipped her head, so that she had to look at him. 'If it's not, that's fine. No pressure. I just want you to see yourself through my eyes. How beautiful I think you are.'

Her insides melted. If she was honest, the idea excited her. The notion of surrendering herself to his artistic vision felt sexy and a little bit kinky. She knew that if anyone would do a good job of it, Connor Knight would. And besides, she was curious to see his vision of her.

'Okay. Let's do it.'

He smiled and kissed her on the nose. 'Great. It'll take me half an hour to set up.'

'I'll take a quick shower then.'

Standing under the rainfall-style nozzle, she tried not to get her hair too wet. Afterwards, she towelled herself off and put the robe back on. Having just imbibed half a bottle of red wine, she brushed her teeth with her new toothbrush; he kept spares on hand. She wondered if he had any body lotion, so she opened the cupboard door, only realising as she scanned the contents that it might be an invasion of privacy. What if he had a tube of haemorrhoid cream? Or wart medicine? She shut the door quickly, but not before she saw a half empty, industrial-sized box of condoms. A Christmas present from his dad?

A small voice in the back of her mind wondered how long he'd had the box. Should she check the expiry date? Still, it was obviously a good thing that Connor practised safe sex. She knew she wasn't sleeping with a monk.

After splashing some water on her face, she double checked her teeth before flicking off the light.

In the corner of his apartment, Connor had set up a small studio. A dark olive painted backdrop hung against the brick wall, its bottom edge trailing on the bare wooden floor. For this shoot, he had pulled out the big guns: his chunky Hasselblad camera, imposing atop a sturdy tripod.

Connor was screwing a large softbox to one of his Broncolor lights when she came out.

'Are you going to butterfly light me?' she joked, worrying the belt of her robe with her fingers.

'No. I'm going for a softer look. More natural. Why?'

'Remember...it's what you said to me? At the BAPP conference...?'

'Oh, yeah.' From the way he said it she suspected he didn't remember. She knew it. She was right to accuse him of hitting on her with a line. He obviously used it so often that he couldn't remember specific instances.

She would bring it up another time, when he didn't look so deliciously distracting in his navy tracksuit bottoms and nothing else.

'So where do you want me?' she asked, hugging her bathrobe, feeling shy.

Without replying, he walked unerringly in her direction, maintaining eye contact until he stood in front of her. Taking her hand, he pulled her towards the backdrop, stopping when they were facing each other in the middle of the space. Still looking at her, he asked, 'Are you ready?'

'Ready as I'll ever be.' She wet her lips.

He untied the belt around her waist and pushed the robe to the floor, so that she stood naked in front of him.

Stella felt exposed, even though he had seen her like this many times in the past 48 hours. She crossed her arms in front of her chest, wanting to hide some small part of herself. He caught her hands and lifted each one to his mouth in turn, kissing the soft skin on the inside of her wrist.

'You're beautiful,' he whispered. 'You don't ever need to hide from me.'

She nodded, her heart singing at his words. Maybe she would forgive him for the whole butterfly lighting thing.

He went to stand behind the tripod. Now it was just her, in a big bare space, in front of Connor. Awkwardness permeated her usually graceful limbs, like she'd just grown an extra arm and wasn't quite sure what to do with it.

'I know what you need.' He picked up a nearby remote and hit play. The beloved first strums of 'Jolene' sang through the room.

Stella laughed. 'You know, I never told you, but you returned this song to me.'

That heart-lifting half-smile. 'How so?'

'After Nathan...I thought I'd become Jolene, the red-haired, green-eyed marriage-wrecker. I couldn't listen to it for ages, which really hurt because it's my favourite song.' She sat on the antique wooden stool in the middle of the set, forgetting her nudity for a moment.

'But then you sang it...in France...and I realised that I couldn't let him take her from me. And his wife...Jeanette...she was no innocent victim either. The pair of them didn't deserve my song. I wanted it back.'

The camera clicked and the flashes flared as he captured her. 'Hold that expression.' He took a few more frames. 'Stunning.' Stella knew that would be a good picture, channelling the fire of Jolene.

For the next three hours, he photographed her, expertly guiding her into pose after pose, telling her how extraordinary and beautiful she was. Eventually she began to believe it. When he said it, it sounded like he really meant it; not the casual off-the-cuff remarks Nathan used to make, weaponised compliments designed to keep her in his thrall. The self-consciousness melted away as she got used to being his model. Similar to when he'd photographed her in France, she could feel the caress of his eyes on her skin through the viewfinder, but this time, she allowed herself to revel in it. To feel sensuous. She started suggesting poses herself.

Eventually, they abandoned their set for more casual locations and he picked up his lighter, more portable Canon camera. She arranged her body on his sofa, on his bed, on the floor, in the bath. For a brief moment, she wondered if he photographed all his girlfriends, but she pushed the thought away. He was here with her now.

. . .

LATER THAT NIGHT, they lay in bed, his laptop on his legs as they scrolled through the images.

It was a masterclass in technique. As he flicked between frames, she could see how a slight change in the angle of her head or a gentle parting of her lips, could completely transform a photograph and make one superior to another.

And the way he captured her...she looked strong, confident, and full of life. She could let him take her picture all day long, every day.

They tapped through the images, selecting their favourites. Hers was one of her lying on her side on the sofa. He called it 'La Maja Desnuda.'

'It's a painting by Goya,' he explained. 'Hanging in the Prado in Madrid. Have you been?'

She admitted that she hadn't really travelled much, mostly just the UK and Italy. She let it hang in the air, hoping he'd offer to take her to see it. A mini-break to Spain, together. It would be fun. A couple activity.

He didn't say anything.

Instead, Connor saved the image as a low-resolution version and sent it to her on email. His inbox flashed up on the screen briefly as he did it, full of bold messages he had yet to read. A hot rush of guilt shot through her for monopolising him so much when he obviously had work to do.

He snapped the laptop closed and put it aside. Laying back on the bed, he gathered her next to him, her cheek resting on his chest.

'Tell me something about yourself,' she said. 'I feel like I don't know a lot about you.'

'What do you want to know?'

'Well...what about your family? You mentioned you had a brother?'

'Michael. He's an international human rights lawyer.'

'Is he as handsome as you?' She had noticed he didn't have any family photos up in his home. The only pictures on his walls were iconic originals by famous photographers like Man Ray and Cecil Beaton. He had an extensive collection.

'Oh, he's much better looking. And he's gay. Maybe we should set him up with your friend, Tristan?'

'Oh god, no. Don't you like your brother? Tristan is a man-eater of the first degree.'

Connor chuckled. 'Yes, probably not a good idea. Michael is the bleeding heart type.' That surprised her. She thought the Knight boys would both be confident, testosterone-filled beasts.

'What about your father?' she asked.

He smirked. 'My father is one of a kind. A real character.'

She waited for him to say more. When he didn't, she prompted, 'Did he ever remarry? After your mother?'

Connor snorted. 'No, never. Although he loved her, Armstrong wasn't really cut out for marriage. He was more of a girlfriend—or two or three—in every port type.' She detected admiration in his voice.

'Oh.' Stella was starting to see where Connor got his low opinion of the institution: straight from the source. She could imagine his childhood now, a string of women coming in and out of his father's bedroom, a new nanny every few years when they moved countries...Connor and Michael had no consistent female influence. No motherly love. It made her sad.

Rising onto her elbow, she decided to change the subject. 'Tell me about your childhood dreams. What did you want to be when you grew up?'

He glanced at her and took a strand of auburn hair in his hand, twirling it with his fingers. 'Do I get to ask you anything or is this the Connor Knight Inquisition?'

'You already know about me. I want to know about you.'

'Hmmm. Well, when we lived in Cairo, I wanted to be an archaeologist. My earliest childhood memories are visiting ruins in Egypt. At the time, rules were lax and we could pretty much climb over ancient statues.'

'The young Indiana Jones.'

'Well I swear to God, I met the prototype for Indiana Jones in Giza. There's a picture of me somewhere—my dad has it, I hope—I'm sitting on the lowest stones at the base of the pyramid with some guy wearing a brown leather coat and a fedora.'

'That's hilarious. I've only ever met one archaeologist and he was short and fat.'

He chuckled before going silent. 'You know, the ancient Egyptians had a belief. They said that when a person passes from this life, he dies twice: once physically and once when his name is last uttered on Earth. That's always stuck with me.'

'Do you think that's why you work so hard now? To leave some sort of legacy?'

He squinted his eyes, as though gazing into the past. 'A legacy, yes. That's a good word for it. I want the Knight name to mean something. I suppose being a wedding photographer is one way to achieve that.'

'Really?'

'Well, albums with my name engraved in the back will be passed down from generation to generation. People will be speaking my name for years after I'm gone.'

'You know that's not the only way to leave a legacy…'

'Oh? Does the other way involve staying in bed with you for a week? Because if yes, I'm up for that.'

'No.' She swatted at him playfully and said, 'It's not just about the artefacts of our existence. Legacy can be about how you interacted with people—were you kind? Thoughtful? Did you treat others with respect? Then of course there's having a family, children to carry on your name…'

He made a disdainful face and shrugged. 'I'm more focussed on my art.' He pointed outside the bedroom door, towards his photography collection. 'I want people hanging my work on their walls, admiring it, long after I'm gone. To me, that's legacy.'

'Hmmm.' She commanded her facial features to remain neutral. She didn't want to show how much his reaction to the words *family* and *children* had shaken her. With his upbringing, would Connor Knight ever be ready for a relationship? Even though she loved him, was she just setting herself up for more heartbreak? Would this end up the same as her affair with Nathan: with a detached boyfriend promising a life that would never materialise?

She sighed. Connor tucked his fingers under her chin, stroking her cleft with his thumb, and lifted her face to look at him. 'Penny for your thoughts?' His fingers swooped lower, where he began to draw idle shapes on her breast. It made it hard to concentrate.

Well, she couldn't tell him what she'd actually been thinking, so she fumbled for something else. 'You're going to get on really well with my parents.'

His idle drawing went still and she felt his body tense for a quick moment.

Stella groaned inside. Why had she said that? A great way to scare off a commitment-phobe is to talk about meeting the parents. *Idiot!* Then again, maybe she'd done it on purpose, to test the waters. Either way, she rushed to cover it up. 'Anyway, I'll be out of your hair soon. I've been summoned to the family seat this week. My father's retirement project was joining the local Shakespearean society and he's making his debut as Prospero in *The Tempest*. Lord help us all.' She wasn't looking forward to it—AmDram Shakespeare wasn't known for its excellence. But duty called. Four days at home meant four days of avoiding their questions and lying about why she'd left advertising. Her stomach flipped. She'd be a nervous wreck by the time she returned to London.

Remembering Connor's stacked inbox, she said, 'It's probably for the best anyway. You have to get back to work. I can't stay here forever.'

Tell me you want me to stay, she begged silently, crossing her toes.

He rolled her onto her back, pinning her arms. The feeling of his skin against her body was becoming precious to her. She would miss it when she had to leave.

'This is the best bloody holiday I've had in ages. I wish it didn't have to end,' he said, lowering himself to meet her lips.

She wanted to ask him so many things. What did he mean by *end*? *'End'* as in *until next time* or *'end'* as in *so long and thanks for all the fish*? If this was a break from his daily life, was she just a holiday romance? How did he feel about her? Did he want her to be his girlfriend? The number of times she'd almost said, 'I love you' in the past 48 hours frayed her nerves. She definitely didn't think Connor was ready to hear that and she didn't want to make the mistake of pushing too hard, like she had in the past with other boyfriends—just before they broke up with her.

So she didn't ask any questions, surrendering to the moment instead. The answers could wait another day.

27

THE SUN WARMED their skin through the steel-framed windows next to his bed. She made a mental note to suggest he invest in black-out blinds for the future. Assuming there would be a future.

They enjoyed a lazy morning, involving more exploration of each other's bodies and breakfast in bed. She was impressed by his omelette-making skills. Her mother always told her to choose a man who could cook. Stella was contemplating the idea of moving her train home to Friday instead of Wednesday. If she did, then she could still see Liliwen as planned on Friday night and it would minimise time spent with her parents. But would Connor want her to stay here longer?

She yawned and her chin tingled. She rubbed at the skin. Connor hadn't shaved since they'd crashed into his flat on Saturday night, tearing at each other's clothes. Watching her, he said, 'I should shave, shouldn't I?'

'Much as I love you with the Don Johnson five o'clock shadow look, that might not be a bad idea.' *Shit* – she accidentally said 'I love you', but it was in the context of an eighties TV show, so hopefully, she got away with it.

'I'm going to grab a shower while I'm at it. Listen, my neighbour texted to say he needs a parking permit. They're in the drawer next to the oven.'

'Which neighbour? The one from Coldplay?'

In the same breath as proclaiming that he wasn't impressed by celebrity, Connor had filled her in on the many famous people living in his building.

'No. David. I think he's in tech.' He climbed out of bed, confident in his nakedness. She enjoyed looking at him and wondered when he found the time to work out with his hectic schedule. Connor opened a wardrobe and rifled through the neatly folded clothing. He threw a Nirvana t-shirt and some running shorts towards her. 'In case my neighbour shows up.' He winked.

'Do you have a cleaner?' she asked.

'Yes, why?'

'I just couldn't imagine you folding all those shirts.'

He pretended to scowl. 'I'll have you know that I'm an expert shirt folder.'

The corner of her mouth lifted in disbelief.

'Okay, you got me,' he said, pulling on a pair of tracksuit bottoms. 'She comes tomorrow morning. We better go out for a few hours while she's here. She short sheets the bed when she's jealous.'

Stella smiled. It made her happy that he wanted her there tomorrow—even though she had a train booked for Wales in the afternoon. Although a frown soon chased it away as she thought about how many times his cleaner had cause for jealousy. She pulled on the clothes.

Padding into the open-plan kitchen, she checked the drawer for the permits. It contained a random collection of junk: matchbooks, pens, a half empty box of Tic Tacs, a single cufflink. A folded place card from a wedding breakfast caught her eye. 'Dr Amelia Taggart' it read in cursive font. Opening it revealed a mobile number scrawled in blue pen.

'Huh.' Looking around to make sure Connor was still in the shower, she dropped the card in the bin. Then she felt guilty. What if Amelia Taggart was a specialist doctor and he'd gotten her number for a friend who suffered from some rare, but curable disease? She picked it out of the bin and returned it to its original place. Before closing the drawer, she located the parking permits scrunched up at the rear.

She was about to sit down on his sofa with an article about retouching armpit skin in the BAPP magazine when she heard a sharp knock.

Standing and smoothing down her Nirvana t-shirt—the one with the naked baby floating in a pool—she crossed the flat, grabbed a parking permit, and rolled back the heavy wooden door.

Jared, her classmate from France, waited in the balcony hallway, pink polo shirt buttoned up to his Adam's apple. Behind him, the pitter-patter of a light August rain filled the central courtyard.

'Stella! What're you doing here? Are you having a portfolio review, too?' He stepped over the threshold, put down his case, and hugged her. As he released her, his eyes flicked over her casual clothes.

'Um...um...yes, a portfolio review! With Connor. After you. I'm just a bit...a bit...early!'

Of all the people to turn up at Connor's flat, Jared was the most likely to tell everyone he'd found her there, practically naked, playing house. He would spread rumours not out of spite, but just because that's who he was. She couldn't let that happen. Her stomach somersaulted. Gossip had already destroyed her reputation once.

If she just stuck to her story, she could nip this in the bud.

At that moment, Connor strolled out of the bathroom, waist wrapped with a small, almost indecent-sized towel, water droplets clinging to his buff chest, like a model from an Imperial Leather advert.

Stella bit her lip and glanced at Jared, who seemed torn between fainting from desire and orgasming with glee.

'Shit, Jared, was our appointment today? So sorry, mate. I totally forgot. I've been, uh, busy.' Connor's eyes brushed over Stella. There was no hiding the grin on his face. 'Give me a second and I'll just get dressed.' Oblivious, he disappeared into the bedroom.

The door closed.

Jared turned towards her with a delighted smirk. 'So you've had your *portfolio* reviewed, have you?' The sing-song way he said portfolio told her there was no maintaining the charade.

She crossed her arms over her chest 'Fine! You caught us.'

'Oh my god, Stella! How? When? And please don't skimp on the details. I want to hear them *all*.'

'Jared, *please*. You can't tell anybody, okay?' She grabbed his sleeve, pulling him towards the kitchen to put some distance between them and Connor's bedroom.

'Of course not. What do you take me for?'

An incorrigible gossip, she thought. 'I'm serious, Jared. Tell. Nobody.'

'I'll keep schtum…if you give me one salacious detail. Anything. Just one.'

'That's ridiculous. I don't kiss and tell.'

He pulled his mobile phone out of his pocket and began typing a text.

'Fine. Fine! Um.' What could she tell that wouldn't be too embarrassing? Dropping her voice to a whisper, she said, 'He's really good at talking dirty in French.' The previous evening, they'd held a contest to see who could arouse the other person in a foreign language. Both of them won.

He squealed. 'I bet he is. *Voulez-vous coucher avec moi?*'

'Shhhh!'

'One more. Just one more.'

'No. I've fulfilled my side of the bargain, now you fulfil yours.'

Pouting, he said, 'Fine, but we're having lunch soon.'

'Fine.' She'd manufacture a way to get out of it later.

The door to the bedroom opened and Connor emerged in teacher mode, professional and focussed, ready to review Jared's pictures.

Stella wished she could cover Connor with a dust cloth and keep him to herself just a little while longer. Jared had well and truly brought her back to reality.

After making them each a cup of tea while Jared spread his work across Connor's billiards table, Stella retired to the bedroom. She leaned against the closed door, resisting the urge to bang her head against the wood.

'Shit.' Despite Jared's assurances, she didn't trust him. Telling Jared not to gossip was like telling a cow not to moo. In France, she was guilty as anyone of laughing at his stories, some even at Connor's expense. If she could go back in time, she'd impress upon Jared that gossip is hurtful, even when it seems benign.

But she couldn't. And now she was going to be on the receiving end, yet again.

One thing she did know: she wasn't ready for this to be public, not until she was sure of Connor's feelings. Was this a fling? It didn't feel like one to her, but she'd been wrong before. Other questions vexed her. Why did Connor have 'his' and 'hers' bathrobes when no one else lived here? Why did he have a stash of extra toothbrushes and an endless haul of condoms? How often did his cleaner get jealous? Who the fuck was Dr Amelia Taggart?

Connor Knight didn't seem like a man searching for a monogamous relationship.

Her sparkly green sequinned dress caught her eye, hanging over a chair near the dresser. Perhaps it was time to get back to her life. She had been cocooned at Connor's for three days. As nice as it had been, she had responsibilities, like a business to run.

With that in mind, she took her phone out of her clutch and turned it on. She had switched if off when they left Claridges.

The first thing to pop onto her screen was an image from Tristan: Mr GQ, half-naked in their kitchen. **Whoops!** She rolled her eyes. She hoped Tristan wasn't going to mess it up again while knowing that he most definitely would.

Second, a message from Claudia dinged, asking if Stella wanted to come over for a movie and could she pick up a mango and some hot sauce on the way.

Meanwhile, Liliwen had sent a random picture of a young red-headed girl in traditional Welsh costume sitting astride a sheep. **Made me think of you. Looking forward to Friday. x**

Finally, Stella saw she had a missed call from Oliwier. A thrill of excitement momentarily eclipsed her misgivings about Connor. She called her voicemail, looking forward to hearing Oliwier's reaction to the albums.

'Hello, beautiful Lady.'

Her senses tingled. His voice didn't sound as jovial as it usually did.

'Thank you for books. So many books! But I am having problem. Paulina say she not happy. She want to be retouched more.'

More?! Stella had spent hours—*days!*—making sure Paulina shone in every photograph. She looked amazing even without the Photoshop; Stella had merely enhanced her: a skin smoothing here, a tuck there. Any more and she'd look fake. Most women would be elated to resemble Paulina in those albums. Of course, Paulina wasn't most women.

'She is wanting to see you to discuss on Wednesday at 10am.' He left the address of the *Oh! Paulina* headquarters in Kensington. 'Bye-eeeee!'

Stella stared at the phone. What was she going to do? Reprinting the whole order would cost thousands, and she would lose a hefty chunk of her profit. In hindsight, she should have printed one album and gotten that approved before she printed the whole order. A rookie mistake.

And now she had to have a meeting in person with Paulina—a woman who absolutely petrified her. What a nightmare!

Stella needed that money. She had a list of things to buy for her business: a more powerful Mac, an Eizo screen, a Wacom tablet. If she had to retouch another wedding using a mouse, she'd end up with

Carpal Tunnel. Somehow, she'd have to convince Paulina not to demand reprints. But how? Stella's automatic response was to agree with people and do what they wanted, even to her own detriment. What honeyed words could she employ to convince Paulina the albums were fine? She doubted that even channelling a combination of her mother, Claudia, Liliwen, Tristan and Connor would help her now.

Stella wasn't above begging.

Tiredness overwhelmed her. Aside from a physically demanding few days, the emotional load was starting to take its toll. She couldn't deal with this right now. She turned the phone off and stuffed it into her bag.

Retreating to the bed, she pulled the covers over her head and curled up in a ball.

A COUPLE HOURS LATER, Connor kissed her awake.

'You can come out now. He's gone.'

She blinked at the early afternoon light, her head foggy. For a moment, she considered pulling Connor into bed, but the memory of Oliwier's call crashed over her, making her sit up.

Connor regarded her with concern. 'All okay?'

'No, actually. I had a call from Oliwier saying they aren't happy with the retouching in the albums. *Eleven* main albums and *two hundred* mini-albums.' Her voice rose at the extent of the problem.

He took her hand and stroked the skin. 'It's okay. Did he approve the artwork?'

'Well...yes...sort of...he told me he trusted me to do a good job. "Just send for printing" he said.'

'And did you get that confirmed in an email?'

'No,' she squeaked. She pulled her hand away and covered her face.

Connor took a deep breath. Her cheeks warmed with embarrassment at having cocked up so badly on her first wedding. He must think her a novice. 'It'll be okay. Have you spoken with them directly?'

'Not yet. She wants to see me on Wednesday morning.'

'It'll be fine.'

'You don't know Paulina.'

'Actually, I do know Paulina.' Of course. The picture in the dining room. 'She is a desperately insecure woman hiding behind a tough exterior. She's difficult, but you can reason with her if you approach her the right way.'

'Maybe *you* could. She hates me.'

'How could she hate you? You're adorable.'

He took her hand again and kissed the back, but Stella wasn't in the mood to be coddled. She put her hand against his chest. 'I can't right now.'

After a short pause he asked, 'Do you want me to talk to her?'

The temptation to say yes stuck in her throat. It would be such an easy out and she had more confidence in his ability to turn it around than hers. But she couldn't do it. She needed to learn how to stand up for herself, solve her own problems.

'No, it's my mess. I'll clean it up.'

'I understand.' He rose from the bed, heading towards the door. 'Why don't I whip up some dinner? Our cook in Barbados taught me how to make a mean Bajan Macaroni Pie. I'm sure I have all the ingredients...'

Stella squeezed her eyes shut. It had been fun playing house, but she needed to know what Connor actually thought about the future.

'Connor, what is this?'

'What is what?'

'This. Us!' She waved her hands around: *everything*.

He shrugged. 'I don't know what this is.' Returning to the bed, he sat down next to her. 'I have fun with you. Isn't that enough?'

She threw the covers off and paced the room. 'The problem is, Jared is going to tell everybody that he saw me here. That we've been —' She waggled her eyebrows. 'Everybody's going to be talking about me.'

'So let them! Who cares what people say? They talk about me all the time.'

'Yes, but you're a man. It's different for women. After my affair with Nathan was outed, *I* was the one who lost her career, not him. Me, they called a whore while he was Lothario.' She paused. 'Do you know what they say about you?'

'No.'

'That you regularly sleep with bridesmaids!'

He crossed his arms.

'And Jared! In France he told us that you once seduced a mother-of-the-bride.'

'To be fair, she seduced me.'

She couldn't tell if he was joking. 'You are NOT HELPING.'

'Price...Stella...' he said, pushing himself off the bed and grasping her by the shoulders. He stared calmly into her eyes, which only annoyed her more. 'Can't we wait and see where this goes? You'll have to bear with me...I've never had a relationship that's lasted longer than three months.'

Three months?! That did not make her feel better. She did not want to be his training wheels.

Rubbing his hands down her arms, he said, 'Let's just take this slow.'

Angry heat flushed through her body. She didn't want to *take it slow*. If she was going to put her heart and soul into this relationship, she needed more than *take it slow*. She had more to lose than he did. Before she knew what she was saying, the words rushed out of her. 'I don't want to take things *slow*, Connor! I love you!'

She clapped her hands over her mouth.

Fuck.

His mouth pressed into a grim line and his eyes narrowed. The hands that had been caressing her arms stopped dead. Her heart plummeted to her toes as nausea unfurled in her stomach.

The silence stretched.

'Um.'

Stella frowned. The man spoke two languages fluently and that was all he could muster in response to *I love you?*

She'd done it again. Pushed him too soon. Her body started to tremble. She needed to get out of there, give them both space. A lot of space.

Suddenly going home seemed like the perfect idea: even if her family drove her crazy, there was still something comforting about Italian proverbs and motivational mantras, righteously delivered by people who loved her.

'I have to go.' Her heart aching, she tore herself away from him and picked up her things.

Visibly shaking himself out of it, he crossed his arms. 'What are you doing?'

'I need to think, Connor. I can't think when I'm near you.' She stepped towards the door and he blocked her way.

'We...we should talk.'

'I think I've said too much and you've said too little, so...' Hot tears were gathering behind her eyes and she wanted to leave before they erupted.

'I just told you that I wanted to take things slow...'

'Great! And I'm going to leave, so you can take things just as slow as you'd like.'

'Stella, come on.' He reached for her and she flinched away from his touch. His expression turned steely. 'I'd like to point out that I'm not the one who keeps running away.'

'I'm not running away,' she said, even though she totally was.

Connor huffed and looked out the window. Turning back to her, he held up a closed fist and pointed his thumb up like a hitchhiker. 'Stella Price, I demand a rematch. I win, you stay and we talk; you win, you go.'

She could tell he was trying to bring some levity back into the situation, giving her that almost irresistible half-smile of his: confident and a little bit cocky. Did he think this was a joke?

Tempting as it would be to continue holing up with him practising

315

positions in the Kama Sutra, she had to make the adult decision for once.

She wrapped her hand around his fist and kissed his thumb. 'Silly games won't solve this problem.'

A look she couldn't decipher fell across his features and he pulled his hand back as though she'd burned him. 'I don't like games either,' he said in a flat voice. He turned away from her and exited the room.

28

ON WEDNESDAY AT EXACTLY 10:00AM, Stella sat across from Paulina in her office. Behind her a wall of supermodels stared back in various poses of orgiastic pleasure as they showed off their *Oh! Paulina* lingerie. It was slightly intimidating.

'How was the honeymoon?' Stella asked, making small talk. After her scene with Connor yesterday, this was the last place she wanted to be, but life went on.

'Invigorating.' So far, Paulina hadn't said much as she slowly looked through her wedding album, writing notes as she went. Today she wore her sable hair down, paired with a tight, red dress printed with tiny skulls and a belt that looked like a chain. Stella wondered if Paulina looked at her closet that morning and chose the most daunting ensemble she could find.

Paulina's desk was shiny and white, covered in sketches and spreadsheets. When Stella arrived at the Kensington address, she didn't know what to expect from Paulina's place of work after seeing their home décor choices. She pictured a lot of nervous employees, tiptoeing around for fear of upsetting the Boss—like in *The Devil Wears Prada* but worse. Paulina, Stella thought, would probably have a male PA. She imagined him walking around the office like Maggie

Gyllenhaal in *The Secretary*, a yoke around his neck and that week's forecast in his mouth.

She was almost disappointed when Paulina's PA turned out to be a fifty-something named Dotty who offered Stella a hot beverage when she arrived. She declined. Her hands were shaking too much to handle heated liquids.

As Stella watched Paulina's notepad filling up, she tried to formulate a plan, but came up blank. She had no idea what to say. Her *modus operandi* was to do as instructed, make people happy, don't challenge. Don't say the wrong thing. Connor's face after she told him *I love you* floated through her thoughts. She pushed it away. She couldn't think about him right now. She had a job to do.

What magic words would get Paulina to change her mind? Stella smoothed a hand down her light pink pantsuit and straightened her shoulders. Ula's voice whispered in her ear, reminding her of the STOP method to calm her anxiety.

Stella dragged a deep breath in and out.

Reprinting all the albums would cost exactly £13,460. She had worked it out. Aside from teaching her an expensive lesson, that would make a huge dent in her bank account. Her father would have a fit if she told him about this.

She already felt embarrassed that Connor knew about her *grand erreur*, as he'd say in French. Then again, making mistakes was human. As was love. And she was very, very human. If he couldn't handle loving her, warts and all, then—

'Right,' said Paulina.

Stella jumped and knocked over her suitcase. She planned to go straight to the station to catch the train to Wales after this. Paulina closed the album and shuffled the pages of her notes.

'Come.' Paulina waved her over to stand next to her. Her perfume, an expensive mix of jasmine and rose, swirled around Stella as she leaned over the desk.

Paulina flipped to the first picture of her. 'Look, here. My waist looks too wide. You can nip it in a little.'

Caught up in her personal drama, Stella had forgotten to bring a notebook. 'Sorry, Paulina. May I borrow a pen and paper...please?'

With an annoyed sigh, Paulina reached into her desk and pulled out a pad and pen, both branded with the company logo, and gave them to Stella. 'You can keep it.' She turned to the next page in the album. 'This one. There needs to be more shadow under my chin to make my jaw look more defined. And here, my knee caps look fat.'

Stella nodded along and wrote down Paulina's remarks as quickly as she could. They went on and on. 'Liquify my legs. Remove this hair. Tan my arms.'

With every single self-criticism, Stella could feel her despair rising. Paulina didn't need all these changes. They wouldn't make a big difference to the pictures, but they'd make a huge difference to Stella.

By the time they reached the end of the album, Stella had filled half the notebook with unnecessary instructions. How could she convince Paulina the changes weren't needed?

She returned to her seat and tucked the notebook into her bag. Now was her chance. She had to plead her case before she left this office or else she'd never forgive herself.

What would Claudia say? What would Liliwen say? What would *Dolly* say? Stella could feel the panic rising as her mind went blank. She tried her hardest to channel somebody, *anybody*, as her thoughts slid over each other. She could see Paulina's expression darkening, her eyes growing bored. Manicured fingers tapped on her desk.

'Stella. Speak. You obviously want to say something.'

Paulina knew her name? That surprised her after being referred to as 'You' for the whole wedding.

Drawing a breath in through her nose and out through her mouth, Stella attempted to still her thoughts. She repeated the exercise.

As her mind calmed, one question suddenly occurred to her, one she'd never asked herself before: what would *Stella* say?

If she wanted to get Paulina to change her mind, Stella would have to speak from her heart, based on her own experiences. That would be the only way to make her arguments sound authentic and persuasive.

Sitting up straight, Stella lifted her chin and opened her mouth. *Here goes...*

'Paulina, in my opinion you don't need any of these changes.'

'Excuse me?'

Stella hurried on. 'You can try to please everybody, but you never will. Trust me, I know. I've been trying my whole life. I understand that you think you have to maintain appearances because of your work—you're a strong, sexually confident, independent woman with an international business and you're worried to let anyone see weakness. But the thing I've admired about you since I met you was how you are so unapologetically yourself. I would kill to be more like you. So why is this any different? Maybe nobody has told you this lately, so I'm going to say it: you're beautiful just as you are. I didn't over-retouch you because you don't *need* it. I look at those images and I see a woman who is already perfect *because* she lets people see her authentic self and says, "Fuck you. That's who I am."' Stella stopped talking, out of words. She had shocked herself by saying all that to Paulina, whose facial expression hadn't changed.

Stella believed every word she'd said. Paulina didn't need to be Photoshopped until every line on her face was smudged out of virtual existence and her features blurred into each other. She was *The* Paulina, after all.

Going in for the close, Stella puffed up her chest and asked, 'So what do you say, Paulina? Shall we leave the albums as they are?'

STELLA SKIPPED off the train at Cardiff Central, still high after her meeting. She had done it! Paulina had agreed to leave all the albums as they were. Not because of Stella's impassioned speech, which Paulina had actually rolled her eyes at, but because when she was on the cusp of saying no, Stella pulled out her trump card: 'If you leave the albums alone, I'll get you Tristan Hughes for your next campaign.' She had already gained clearance from him to make the exchange earlier that morning, after a lot of begging. Stella didn't know for sure if it would work.

But Paulina had practically drooled.

As the train whizzed towards Cardiff, feeling like she could take on the world, she'd even texted Connor: **Paulina issue sorted. Sx**

He'd texted back straight away. **Great news.**

No Cx.

Although it made her sad, not even that could dampen her feeling of achievement. She had gone to bat against Paulina and *won*.

At the exit from the train station, Stella saw her father and waved.

As she approached he boomed, *'We are such stuff as dreams are made on, and our little life is rounded with a sleep.'*

'Let me guess...*The Tempest?*'

'That's my girl,' he said as he wrapped his freckly arms around her. She sank into the hug, relieved to be home. True to form, Bill Price was dressed in a light blue polo and white shorts, like he was about to play tennis, despite the fact that he'd never picked up a racket. Stella smiled; that was her mother's influence, right down to the impossibly bright white trainers. Some things never changed.

Bill took her wheelie case in one hand, his other arm thrown around Stella's shoulder as they walked to his convertible. 'Good journey?'

'Great!'

'I hope you brought your business plan. I want to see it,' her father said. 'You can't be lazy when it comes to these things.'

'I know, dad.' Thirty seconds. That was how long it had taken before he brought it up.

'Businesses that fail to plan, plan to fail.'

Stella grunted in frustration. She was actually doing pretty well and didn't need his criticism right now. In fact, she didn't deserve it either. 'You know what, dad? My business is actually doing great. I made £60,000 on my first wedding, which is practically unheard of for a new photographer, and I've got another few jobs already booked.'

'That's all very well and good, but—'

'But nothing, dad! Can't you just say *well done* and trust that I know what I'm doing? You've been training me all my life for this. I have it in hand.'

Bill paused and threw a furtive glance towards her. Stella could practically hear his thoughts: *who is this person?*

He cleared his throat. 'Well done, Stella girl. And it's not that I think you can't do it, it's just that I worry about you. I want to help.'

'Okay. Helping is fine. Criticising is not, agreed?' He nodded. For the rest of the drive to Penarth, Stella answered her father's many questions about her new business.

They pulled into their drive and warmth spread through her at seeing the beloved bricks and mortar of her childhood. La Casa Price was beige paint and brickwork with boring square windows, more traditional than others on the street, but she loved it. Many summer nights had been spent on the balcony atop the garage, looking out over Bristol Channel towards the distant coastline, wondering where life would take her.

Angela was watering shrubs in the front garden, made up as though expecting a visiting dignitary. Her auburn hair, once a similar shade to Stella's, was faded to a lighter coppery tone. She was chatting with a twenty-something man, tall with hunched shoulders and hands shoved deep into his pockets.

Inside the car, Stella groaned. 'Dilwyn.' She hoped that his crush on her had gone away. It was painful for all parties involved.

'Actually, he's matured a lot,' said Bill. 'His moving business is taking off. Your mother is helping him with the accounts and he already has two vans and a Luton, with plans to buy more. Smart kid. An entrepreneur.' In Bill's eyes, that was just about the best thing anybody could be.

'Do you think mum is trying to set us up again?'

'Don't be ridiculous. He's not Catholic.'

Neither am I, she thought guiltily. *And neither are you!* Despite the fact that Bill was an atheist, he and Angela had one of the strongest marriages she had ever seen. *The heart wants what it wants...*

Her thoughts returned to Connor. Like a physical need, she wanted to know what he was doing right now. Editing photos? Preparing for a wedding? Thinking about her…?

Lost in her own head, she didn't notice Angela's approach. Stella jumped as the car door flew open and her mother exclaimed, '*Ma che cosa indossi?* That colour looks horrible on you.'

'Nice to see you, too, mamma.' Let the criticisms commence!

'Come, come. I made my famous lasagne for dinner.' She walked into the house, followed by Bill with Stella's bag.

Sucking her lips, Stella hid her laugh. Her mother's famous lasagne was a running joke, being the only dish Angela Price ever made. Her mother was the only Italian in the world that couldn't cook.

She climbed out of the car. Dilwyn was hovering near the shrubbery, motionless, a lone player in a game of Freeze Tag.

'Hey, Dilwyn. How are you?'

He turned towards her, cheeks aflame beneath his short beard. 'AlrightStellayoulooknice.' Crush intact, then.

'Thanks.' They stood awkwardly for a handful of seconds that felt like minutes. Finally, Stella said, 'Well, see you later!' and followed Angela through the door.

Upstairs in her old room, now painted a subtle lilac, Stella put her bag in the corner. As soon as she'd left for university, her parents had redecorated the room for guests, removing her Hot Gossip posters and shoving Stella's belongings into the closet. Throwing open the closet doors, she ran her hand over the sparkly dresses saved from her competitive dancing days. Would any of them still fit? Probably not. They'd been tight at the time. Her hand came to rest on a frilly pink lace and taffeta dress she had worn when her class hosted an American-style Prom. It looked like a Disney princess had sewn it with the help of rodents. Her tastes had definitely improved.

Before heading downstairs for dinner, Stella glanced out her window. She had missed this view. The waves crashing over distant coastlines and seagulls bleating had never failed to cheer her up. Connor and London were miles away. She could think here.

. . .

OR SO SHE'D THOUGHT. Two days later, she packed for an overnight stay at Liliwen's, exhausted from her mother's constant chores. Angela had allowed her exactly one evening of relaxation before the work kicked in. So far, they'd weeded the garden, painted the shed, planted seeds for spinach and radishes, strung up the onion crop, and cleaned the car.

She didn't even have her evenings free: for dinner the first night, Angela invited Father Marco, who wanted to know whether she preferred mass in London or his mass.

The next evening, Dilwyn came over for Pictionary. Stella wanted to go for a long, solitary, soul-searching walk along the coast to agonise over Connor, but no. Instead she had to suffer through Dilwyn's abject horror when he accidentally drew a flower that resembled a vulva. Stella's father called him Georgia O'Keefe for the rest of the night.

When her mother inevitably asked Stella about her love life, she said she wasn't dating anybody right now, to which Angela had replied with an Italian gesture. And when her father had asked her to explain again why she'd left Bastion, Stella had developed a timely headache and left the room.

Her trip to Liliwen's was a holiday from her holiday. She couldn't wait.

Zipping up the small holdall she'd borrowed from her father, she checked her phone for messages. Nothing. Connor said he didn't want to play games and neither did she, so she swallowed her fear and sent him three simple words: **I miss you.** Would he reply?

She'd like to know she was at least on his mind.

Maybe she wasn't.

'THIS IS QUAINT,' Bill said, taking in the immaculate stone cottage set back from the road with a meticulously tended garden. It looked like a postcard. A collection of wind chimes tinkled gently in a tree next to the front door, accompanied by clucks from the brood of chickens on the lawn. Stella frowned; chickens made her think of Connor. Then again, everything made her think of Connor.

She waved as her dad drove off. She felt like she was in secondary school again, going to a friend's house for a sleepover, except this time she didn't have to hide the wine.

At the front door, she barely knocked before it swung open. 'Stella!' cried Liliwen, breaking into a bright smile, as they hugged. 'Ah, lovely. So good to see you. Come in. I see you've brought refreshments.' Liliwen closed the door behind her and showed Stella into the house.

She was immediately struck by the homey feel of Liliwen's cottage. The hallway was lined with family portraits, a mix of shabby chic frames showcasing different milestones. A picture of Liliwen's son as a baby hung next to one of Liliwen and her husband, probably in their 40s, dressed as Sandy and Danny from *Grease* at a party. Another photo showed their boy on his first day of school, wearing his smart grey uniform. Above that was a black and white picture of Liliwen in her Miss Wales days.

'Wow, Liliwen, you were *bangin'*!' said Stella, putting on her best Welsh accent. In this picture, Liliwen looked like a Hollywood starlet, her platinum blonde hair expertly coifed, her skin dewy with youth. She was wearing a sash that said *Miss Pontypridd*, smiling saucily for the camera.

'Ah, those were the days. When my breasts were as pert as my attitude.'

Going from picture to picture, Stella absorbed the timeline of Liliwen's perfect life.

'It looks like you've had a great time.'

Liliwen feigned being insulted. 'I'm not dead yet! Still many years to go, thank you very much.'

'You know what I mean. It just looks like you and Gareth have a lot of fun together.'

'Well, as photographers, we know pictures can lie. But we've had our moments.' Leading her up the stairs, she said, 'Come, let's put your things in the guest room. I've made us some supper.'

'Will Gareth be joining us?'

'Heavens, no. I kicked him out for the night. He's at the golf club with the boys.'

'Thank God. I have so much to tell you.'

'Then we'd better get started!'

Wine flowing, they chatted all through the roast lamb and potatoes. 'Did you hear about Karen and Gunner?' Liliwen asked. 'They're getting married!'

'No way! Are you invited to the wedding?'

'No, of course not. But Karen and I write on the email sometimes.'

Stella sipped her wine. 'Well, good for them.'

'A toast to Karen and Gunner,' Liliwen said before draining her glass. 'You know, it reminds me of the time I had a little affair with my friend's brother when I was fifteen. An older man! I won't tell you what we got up to at his bedsit. But it involved a lot of whipped cream.'

Stella almost spat out her wine. 'Liliwen, for a woman who's been married to one man most of her life, you really packed in the experiences. I feel like I haven't lived at all when I hear your stories.'

'Speaking of vicarious living, I think it's time you told me about you and Connor.'

Stella struggled for words. She hadn't mentioned anything about it. 'How did you...?'

'Jared, of course.'

Effing Jared. Sighing she said, 'I can't think about anything else.'

'I can imagine,' she said, winking.

Stella tapped her with her foot playfully under the table. 'You're terrible.'

'So what's his place like?' Liliwen asked. 'I bet it's a right old bachelor pad.'

'I suppose so,' Stella said, picturing his space. 'It's a big warehouse flat. Not a lot of furniture.'

'I bet he's got a billiards table.'

'Yup.' Images of lying on the green felt while Connor nibbled her inner thigh flashed through her mind. She moved on quickly, filling Liliwen in on everything since Italy.

The little O of Liliwen's mouth got wider as Stella talked. Wrapping up with Jared's visit and the aftermath, she said, 'So I just blurted it out and you should have seen his face. Like I told him I was an alien or something. I'm just not sure he's ready for a relationship.'

'Did he say he isn't ready?'

'Well, no. He said he wants to take it slow.'

'Sounds sensible.'

'Sounds noncommittal!'

'Sounds like you're coming up with excuses not to be with him, lovely. Are you sure it's *him* who's not ready...?'

'Maybe love isn't enough! Maybe he's not built for commitment! I don't want to get hurt.' *Again*, she added in her head.

'You know, this reminds me of—'

'Liliwen!' Stella held out her hand, begging her to stop. 'Is this going to be another tenuously-related story with a dubious sexual moral? Because if the answer is yes, I'm not sure I can handle it right now.' Stella laughed and took another sip of wine.

'No, no, nothing like that. What I was going to say was, it reminds me of a tough decision I had to make once. About whether I wanted to be with Gareth. When he cheated on me. Just after I had Rhys.'

Stella drew in a sharp breath. 'Oh, I'm so sorry, Liliwen.' Reaching out, she took her friend's hand.

'I'm over it now. That being said, if I did ever see that Mary again, I'd probably still bash her one. Except she's dead, so...'

Stella gasped.

'Oh no, I didn't do it! Cancer, it was. But anyway, that's not the point. He cheated on me. With his *secretary*, of all people. And I was angry. I mean *really angry*. One night I kicked him in the goolies so hard he had to spend a week in bed. There I was, trying to deal with a newborn and, in hindsight, probably some post-natal depression, and he let himself be seduced after some silly office party. I was livid, I tell you.'

'So...why did you stay with him?' She didn't want to admit it, but she hoped it might give her some insight into Jeanette. Why didn't she ever leave Nathan when he was constantly cheating on her?

'I won't lie, it was hard. Forgiveness felt like I was letting him get away with it. Giving him permission to do it again. But in a way, even though forgiving him made me more vulnerable, it also made me stronger. See, when I really thought about it, I couldn't envision life without him. Punishing him would have been punishing me, and I had Rhys to think of. Gareth was my best friend, and I loved him with all my heart. And he was truly sorry, poor love. He fired the woman right away. Labour laws weren't what they are today.' Stella didn't point out that things hadn't moved on as much as Liliwen thought. 'Anyway, he cried so hard, begging me to stay, I thought he was going to burst a vein, and that was before I kicked him.'

A tear trailed down Stella's cheek. In another place and another time, Liliwen had been Jeanette. Guilt rose up in her, even though they weren't talking about her affair.

'Ah, lovely, don't cry. It's in the past.'

'I'm sorry. It's just...God, life is hard, isn't it?'

'Everybody has a sad story because...well, because that's life. It's imperfect and deliciously messy and sometimes shit happens. But if you don't throw yourself into it because you're scared of getting hurt, then you'll never know the other side: the joy. The surprise. The sheer wonder of being alive.'

Stella was well past gentle tears now. She extracted her hand from Liliwen's and cast around for something to wipe her dripping nose.

'Just use your serviette, lovely, it's fine.' Liliwen refilled her wine glass. 'Listen, everybody does things that they regret. But it's how they move forward that's important. Gareth has been the picture of loyalty ever since, and we've had a good life together. I made the right choice.

Besides that, he knows I have a particularly sharp pair of sheers in the garden shed, should he ever wander again.'

They laughed, and Stella blew her nose loudly into the napkin.

As Liliwen cleared the dishes, Stella considered everything she'd just heard. Her chin quivered with new tears as the usual shame and guilt rose inside her again. She couldn't help it. They were her constant companions, no matter how hard she tried to move forward. She realised that *getting in the coffin* wasn't a one-time occurrence—it was more of a recurring, continuous action.

Liliwen returned with a tub of ice cream and two spoons. 'I've got dessert! Hope you don't mind—Oh, lovely! What's wrong?'

Taking a deep breath, Stella said, 'I have my own story to share. And I hope you don't hate me when it's finished.'

The words fell from her lips. Confessing to Liliwen was harder than telling Ula or Krish or Connor because Liliwen had been the wronged woman. Stella was Liliwen's Mary.

She listened. She didn't interrupt. She let Stella get it all out and when it came to the end and Stella was standing on that stage with a bloody nose and her heart breaking, Liliwen said, 'Thank you for sharing this with me. I can imagine it took a lot of courage after what I just told you.'

'Do you hate me?' Stella was having trouble finding a clean corner of her napkin to use.

'Of course not, lovely! Why would I do that?' She got up from her chair and put her arms around Stella. 'As I've said to you before, everybody has their own story. We're all human. Surprise! You are, too.'

Stella could feel her heart heal just a little bit more at Liliwen's words. Giving that seat to her at the BAPP conference had been one of the smartest things Stella had ever done.

'But coming back to you and Connor...this is a new relationship. You can't let all this past pish-posh get in the way. If you love him as you say, then wait for him to catch up. Maybe he will. Maybe he won't.' She shrugged. 'But in the name of the glorious Shirley Bassey, give the man a chance. Just because he didn't say I love you right away, doesn't mean he never will.'

Perhaps she was right.

As Stella lay in Liliwen's guest bed staring at the ceiling beams, she replayed her time with Connor in the context of what Liliwen had said. So, he didn't say *I love you...*yet. So far, he hadn't done anything to make her doubt his commitment to trying. The three-month-thing, toothbrushes, robes, and his bottomless condom supply suddenly seemed like insufficient reasons to push him away. Even his opinions about legacy and his reticence about children could be something to discuss further down the line. After all, it wasn't him who had run away after Italy. The real problem was her own insecurity. Her past, not his.

She needed to take a leap of faith and wait for him to leap in after her.

Remembering his touch made her skin tingle and heat flower between her legs. His smile made her breath quicken. She missed talking to him, watching him work. She had never met anybody who affected her like Connor Knight. And he always made sure she orgasmed first, the sign of a true gentleman. Had she been unfair to him? She already knew Connor was no Nathan. And she couldn't spend the rest of her life avoiding people who might hurt her. Giving Connor the power to hurt her wasn't weakness. It was strength.

Damn it, Ula and Liliwen were both right. She had to move on.

And if Stella was going to do that properly, she needed to start being honest with everybody in her life. Including her parents.

In the small hours of the night, she finally fell asleep, a decision beginning to form.

29

STELLA AWOKE with a sore head and a two-part plan: first, come clean to her parents about why she'd left Bastion. Until she did that, this lie would control her life and she wouldn't be free to start a new relationship. And second, give Connor the space to grow into their relationship in his own time.

If she hadn't already ruined things.

After a delicious late breakfast and a tearful goodbye from Liliwen, her father drove her home, reciting his lines from *The Tempest* the whole time. *'Now my charms are all o'erthrown, And what strength I have's mine own, which is most faint.'* She watched him as he steered the car and prayed that he wouldn't freak out when she told him the truth. That he'd still love her despite the fact that she'd done a bad thing. Reaching out, she rubbed his arm, wanting to bottle up this last moment when he still thought of her as his innocent little girl.

Angela was watering the flowers again when they arrived home. In the passenger's seat, Stella closed her eyes and inhaled. No time like the present. She'd already put it off for ten gut-wrenching months. If she didn't tell them soon, she'd develop an ulcer. Better to get this over with than let it hang over her head for even one more day. She had made the decision. She needed to act.

Despite her resolve, her limbs felt heavy as she dragged herself out of the car. This wouldn't be fun. 'Mum, dad. Can we speak inside, please?'

Her mother took one look at her face and stopped the hose. 'Stellina, what's wrong?'

'Please, mum. Inside.' Without waiting for a response, she went into the house, dropping her bag at the bottom of the stairs. She stepped into the fancy living room, usually reserved for visits from religious figures and members of the WI. It felt like the most appropriate place to deliver bad news. Her parents shuffled in and sat side by side on the dusky rose Chesterfield sofa.

'What's this about?' asked her father.

Stella looked to the picture of the Pope on the wall and began, 'I need to tell you both something. And you aren't going to like it.'

'*Dio mio*, she's taking drugs. I told you this would happen in London. Everybody does drugs in London.' Angela swatted Bill's shoulder, as though he had personally supplied them.

'*Mamma*, I'm not doing drugs.'

'You're pregnant.' She covered her face with her hands.

'I'm not pregnant.'

'*Amore*, let her speak.'

Stella made a fist, digging her nails into her hand. She could do this. With a deep breath, she began, 'You know how you keep asking me why I left Bastion? Why I switched to photography? Well, it wasn't because I fancied a change.' She stopped. Both her parents had gone unnaturally still. She couldn't believe she was about to do this.

Pausing for just a moment, she savoured the last few seconds *before they knew.*

Eyes on the floor, she finally said as fast as she could, 'It's because I had an affair with my married boss and ended up losing my credibility in front of the whole industry.'

Her mother crossed herself. Her father crossed his arms. Nobody said a word for what seemed like an eon. Dinosaurs were born and died in that silence. Finally, Angela said, 'We raised you better than that, Stella.'

She flinched. From an early age Angela had impressed upon her daughter the seven deadly sins, lust always the first one on the list (although Stella didn't really understand what it meant until her teens). Stella could feel hot tears building behind her eyes, her usual shame clawing up her throat. Her mother would probably cut her off, excommunicate her from the family, excise her picture from the albums. Stella would have to see her father in secret from now on, if he didn't hate her, too. She'd never be allowed back to this house. Life as she knew it was over.

Before Stella could say anything, her father commanded in his best CEO voice, 'Tell us what happened. All of it.'

And so she did.

It took a full hour for her to reveal the whole saga, starting with the affair. As the truth spooled out of her, her entire body relaxed in a way that it hadn't after telling anyone else, including Liliwen. Despite their angry faces, Stella knew she'd made the right decision. When she told them about the award ceremony and Jeanette, Bill exploded with a list of expletives that caused Stella to jump.

'You need to take them to court. They can't just get rid of you like that.'

'Dad, that's the last thing I want to do.'

'Well, it's clear to me what needs to happen next,' said Bill, clasping his hands and leaning forward. 'You need to come home. London is obviously a toxic environment.'

'Yes,' agreed her mother. 'I think this is for the best. You can play with your photography here until you decide what to do next.'

Stella couldn't believe her ears. Their solution was to take control of her life again. This was the whole reason she'd moved away in the first place. Old Stella might have at least considered it, but New Stella had her own plans. New Stella was tired of letting fear of what others thought rule her life.

'Mum! Dad! I am *not* moving back here. I have a life in London.

Friends...' —a lover? Perhaps she wouldn't mention that. They could only handle so much in one day— 'For the love of God, you have both been trying to control me for years. Mum, I started dancing because of you. But I stopped for *me*. Dad, I went to university and studied biology for you. Now I'm finally doing photography for *me*. I don't need you to save me. I'm a grown woman and I can stand on my own two feet.'

Her parents seemed shocked into silence by her outburst.

With a dramatic sigh, Stella walked to the sofa. 'Shift over.' She motioned for them to make space for her in the middle and sat down.

'I'm really sorry that I disappointed you, but I'm only human and I make mistakes. Do you...do you still love me?' A tear escaped down her cheek.

'Stellina, of course we still love you. You're our baby girl.' Her mother put an arm around her and rested her head on Stella's shoulder.

'As you from crimes would pardon'd be, Let your indulgence set me free.'

'Um...does that mean you forgive me?'

Bill laughed. 'Yes, of course I do. But I think the question I need to ask is do you forgive me? I never meant to control you. I just wanted the best for you. I never realised...'

'Dad, don't worry. Nothing to forgive.'

They all hugged on the couch and Stella could feel the tightness she'd been carrying with her for so long, easing. *'La verità ti rende libero'* — 'The truth will set you free,' she thought, not sure where it came from but pretty sure it was the Bible. Maybe the lid on that coffin could finally be nailed shut now.

Stella's phone rang and she pulled away to check, thinking it might be Connor. It was Claudia. Stella let it go to voicemail.

'So what's your plan, Stella?' asked her father. She smiled. He just couldn't help himself.

Almost immediately, the phone rang again. Now, Stella was concerned. What if something was wrong with the babies? 'Sorry, I have to take this.'

She walked out of the room and sat on the stairs. 'Hey, Claudia.'

'Why the fuck are you in Wales?' she blasted down the airwaves.

Stella drew her eyebrows down in confusion. 'Because my father is playing Prospero.'

'I don't even know what that means. It's my engagement party tonight. Didn't you put it in your diary?'

Stella dug her free hand into her hair. 'What? No—it's next Saturday.'

'No! It's *tonight*!'

Quickly checking her phone diary, Stella said, 'No, you definitely told me next Saturday.'

'Shit. I got it wrong. Fucking hormones.' And she started to cry.

This completely freaked Stella out. Claudia never cried. 'Shh, don't worry, I'll figure it out. How did you even know I was here?'

'Magnus told me.'

'How did Magnus know?'

'Connor told him.'

'Why was Magnus talking to Connor? I thought they hated each other.'

'I have no idea. Fuck!' she wailed into the phone.

Stella winced at the panic in her pregnant friend's voice and stood up fast. 'Shit. Shit. Shit.'

'Language!' called her mother from the fancy sitting room, where they could hear the whole conversation. Her father would be so angry with her if she didn't come to his play. On top of the bombshell she'd just dropped on them, she wouldn't be winning any daughter points. But on the other hand, she couldn't let Claudia down. Stella was the maid of honour. She'd already somehow missed that her friend was pregnant and in love. Stella felt like she had to step up in the friend stakes.

Claudia actually whimpered. 'You *have* to come tonight. I can't do this without you.'

It wasn't like Claudia to sound so vulnerable. Stella made up her mind. This was just one of those hard moral choices that life threw up sometimes. In this case, being a good friend trumped being a good daughter. 'I'll be there. Text me details.'

They hung up and moments later a message pinged with the address of the venue: a club in Belgravia, 7PM-midnight.

Stella banged her head against the wall. She didn't know what would make her father more upset: her confession about Bastion or missing his play. Plastering a smile on her face, she turned towards the sitting room. 'Daddy,' she said sweetly, 'you know how one of the major themes of *The Tempest* is forgiveness. Well, I have one more thing to ask of you...'

IT WAS all hands on deck. Stella researched trains. Angela checked on buses. And Bill investigated car rentals.

All of them came up empty handed.

Stella rested her head on her hands on the kitchen table. 'Great Western is running replacement rail services today. I wouldn't get back to London until midnight.'

'*Porco miseria!* We just missed the bus and the next one isn't until 6:00.'

Bill said, 'Car rentals are a no-go. I suppose those Visit Wales tourist ads have been really effective.' He nodded with respect.

Glancing at her watch, Stella stood. 'I'll call Liliwen. Maybe she can take me.'

But she had plans. 'Ah, sorry, lovely. I would if I could. Sounds like a right laugh. But Rhys is bringing over his girlfriend tonight. We think they might have an announcement.'

'Oh, fingers crossed!' Stella said before hanging up.

Despondent, she stared at the neat row of unused cookbooks, hoping that Jamie Oliver or Nigella Lawson might supply an answer. How was she going to solve this? Did she know anybody else who could help? On top of the cookbooks, she saw the edge of the big notepad they'd used for Pictionary the other night. Snapping her fingers, she sprinted out the front door and ran to their neighbour's house, knocking with urgency.

'Dilwyn! Dilwyn!'

He answered, his face colouring when he realised it was her. 'AlrightStella?' he mumbled.

'Are you busy for the rest of the day? And are any of your vans available to rent?'

BY THE TIME he retrieved his Luton from its parking spot at the industrial estate, it was 3PM.

'The aircon is broken, but it's the only one I have free today.' Boosted by the power of purpose, he'd recovered his ability to speak around her. The long journey would be that much less painful.

Before climbing into the cab of the truck, Stella hugged her parents, thanking them for their understanding.

'Break a leg, dad!'

'Give Claudia our love and congratulations,' said Angela. 'Tell her I'm glad she's not having the babies out of wedlock.'

After fastening her seatbelt, Stella pulled out her mobile and sent a text to Connor, saying she was on her way back and could she stop by after the party. Stella had already wasted enough time away from him; she didn't want to waste any more.

Soon Stella and Dilwyn were hurtling down the M4 as fast as the clunky Luton could go. It shook with the effort of maintaining 70 miles per hour.

She checked her phone for a reply from Connor. Nothing.

Before leaving, Stella had packed in a hurry and run through the shower. Browsing the dresses in her teenage closet, she realised only one fit. At least her prom dress had Lycra inside. It was sleeveless with a sweetheart bodice, complete with big pink bow—more suitable for a sixteen-year-old than a woman in her late twenties.

Getting to Claudia's party by 7PM was worth a little embarrassment.

They made good time over the Severn Bridge, then past Bristol and Bath. As they approached Swindon, traffic started to slow thanks to an accident on the other side. They lost fifteen minutes.

Still no reply from Connor. Maybe he was working. Or maybe he had changed his mind. Maybe he didn't want her anymore.

No. She couldn't think that way. Stella needed to trust her instincts, and her instincts told her that Connor was special—in the same way they had told her that Nathan was not. She remembered the gut-churning guilt that consumed her the whole year she had been with him. She thought it was heartburn and had scoffed Rennies like candy. If she'd been thinking clearly, she would've heeded the signs.

Well, she would heed them now: she believed in her relationship with Connor. Who cared if people knew about them? It was nobody else's business. As long as they understood each other's hearts, that was all that mattered. A self-deprecatory chuckle bubbled in her throat: to think she had believed it was Connor who didn't want to commit when it was her all along, pulling away from him.

'What's so funny? I could use a laugh,' said Dilwyn, eyes blinking wide at the road.

Stella looked at the man playing her knight in shining armour today. She had never noticed it before, but he had quite a sweet face: candid blue eyes, dimples, and lips that smiled more than frowned.

She turned down the radio for a moment. 'Thank you again for doing this. I really appreciate it.'

He kept his eyes on the road. 'It's no problem. No plans tonight anyway.' After a pause, he said, 'Living in London, you wouldn't understand how hard it is to meet people back home. I don't like any of this Internet dating faff and I'm too shy to approach women at bars, so...'

Those were the most words he'd ever spoken to her. 'You'll find someone. Any girl would be lucky to have you.'

His face brightened. 'You really think so?'

'Definitely.'

'So what are you doing down in London anyway? Was it something in advertising…?'

'I'm a wedding photographer.' Stella braced herself for the usual reaction. *You must be poor!' 'My uncle is a photographer.' 'I bet you've got a camera that takes great pictures.'*

But what Dilwyn said was, 'That sounds lush. I bet you've met some interesting people doing that.'

Stella paused. She thought about how much had changed in the past year and all the people who were now part of her life. Magnus, who had captured her friend's slippery heart. Liliwen, now a good friend. Krish, Jared, Gunner, Karen and all the others from the course (except the Youngs). Even Oliwier and Paulina, who taught her that love comes in all different shapes. And of course, Connor.

'Actually, yes,' Stella realised, 'I've met some really great people.'

Dilwyn quietened after that, having used up all his conversation, so she turned up the radio. If they continued at this rate, they should get to Belgravia by 6:55.

Passing the junction with the M25, the motorway narrowed. The GlaxoSmithKline pharmaceuticals building waved to her like a flag from her past, reminding her briefly of Nathan. She stuck two fingers up at it.

And then they hit traffic.

30

THEY FINALLY PULLED up outside the club at 8PM. Stella had bitten her nails to shreds. The building's art deco facade was illuminated by pink tungsten up-lighters and chatter and music spilled from the open windows. Stella was relieved guests were still arriving.

'Let's pull around the corner, so I can change.'

They found a loading area. She sent a message to Claudia to describe her location and Dilwyn climbed out while Stella pulled on the frothy pink dress. As she forced her feet into satin heels, the cab door swung open.

Claudia clambered in, hurling herself onto the faux leather driver's seat. A high-waisted white baby doll dress hid her stomach, paired with shiny go-go boots.

'What the fuck are you wearing?'

'I know. But it's the only thing I had at my parents' house.'

'Here.' She handed Stella a make-up bag and told her to turn towards the window, so she could do up the zip and run a brush through Stella's wind-tangled hair. 'There's something I need to tell you. Connor is coming later.'

'What?!' She groaned. Glancing down at the pink prom gown, she wished she wasn't dressed like an extra in a John Hughes film. Well, nothing she could do about it. Stella dug through the make-up bag for mascara, spilling items on the seat in her haste. 'I love him, you know.'

'Yeah. No shit.' Claudia finished brushing Stella's hair. 'There's some hairspray in the toilets, if you want to keep the frizzies down.'

'Great. How do I look?'

'Like a fancy bottle of Pepto-Bismol. Shall we go? Magnus's grandmother will have a fit if I'm absent too long.'

'She sounds like hard work.' Stella stuffed her discarded clothes into her suitcase.

'You have no idea.'

They popped out of the truck, Stella wobbling on the tight, satin heels. Dilwyn loped over to them. 'Alright?'

'Who's this?' Claudia asked, looking him up and down. 'Cute dimples.'

'This is Dilwyn, my saviour.'

'In that case, you must come to the party,' said Claudia, using the excuse to rest her hand on his arm, feeling his muscles. Stella had never noticed them before. They must be from helping people move.

'No, you're alright,' he protested, rubbing his eyes. 'I'm exhausted. I'm going to the nearest Travelodge and collapsing.'

'If you're sure…'

'I'm sure. I don't think it's my kind of party,' he smiled shyly.

Stella threw her arms around his massive frame and gave him a crushing hug. 'You saved me tonight. Thank you.'

'It was nothing,' he said. She couldn't see his face, but she knew he'd be blushing.

He hefted himself into his seat and the truck sputtered to life. Stella and Claudia walked around the corner arm-in-arm and entered the club.

'YOU'LL KNOW A FEW PEOPLE,' Claudia said as the bouncer asked their names. 'I'm the fucking fiancée,' Claudia reminded him as she pulled Stella past.

'Half the guest list couldn't make it at such short notice, which I think was the Old Bag's plan. Fewer people to witness our "great shame". Most of them are friends of Henrietta's anyway. That's the grandmother.'

'Of course, it is,' laughed Stella. 'She couldn't be named Judy. Or Pam, could she?'

'The family call her Bunny. I can't bring myself to call her that. Quick, you sort yourself out in the toilets. I'll meet you inside.'

They parted ways. In the ladies', Stella sprayed down her fly-aways and ran a finger under her eyes to remove wayward specks of mascara. A toilet flushed behind her and a woman emerged with half-pink hair and a matching dress.

Stella startled. 'Ula!'

Ula screamed and washed her hands before hugging Stella. 'I am so happy to see you.'

'What're you doing here?'

'Ronny is the personal trainer for the groom and his friends. I saw your assistant from the wedding is the bride and I wondered if you would be coming.'

The news that Ula was still dating Ronny sobered Stella. She took Ula by the shoulders and swallowed. 'Ula, I—'

A phone started ringing. 'One second. Halo?...Yes, yes. I'm coming now.' She hung up. 'Sorry, it's Ronny. He wants to know where I am. Thinks maybe I'm flirting with another man.' Rolling her eyes, she laughed. 'He can be so funny.'

She turned to go, but Stella grabbed her by the wrist.

'Ula, that's not funny. It's controlling.' Inhaling a deep breath, she said, 'I need to tell you something. I'm sorry I didn't say anything sooner.'

TEN MINUTES LATER, Ula was on a mission. Stella watched as she threaded through the crowd in search of Ronny. When she found him, she pulled him towards the entrance.

Stella followed them outside, even as her eyes searched for Connor. When would he be arriving? She had no idea what she'd say yet. Something that would make Tom Hanks and Meg Ryan sigh. Something she needed more time to come up with. But right now, she needed to help her friend.

When she caught up with Ula and Ronny, they were standing down the road, towards the spot where Dilwyn had dropped her off.

'I am tired of this, Ronny. We're breaking up.'

'Baby, what's going on? What'd I do this time?'

If possible, his tan seemed even darker and his lying teeth even whiter, gum snapping. Stella approached and his face twisted into a sneer. 'Oh, it's you.' Realisation crept across his face. 'I see what's happening here.'

Stella went to speak, but Ula jumped in. 'What is happening is I have caught you too many times. You hit on my friend at my cousin's wedding. Big mistake.'

'Baby, that's not what happened. I didn't hit on her. *She* came onto *me*.'

Gasping with disbelief, Stella again opened her mouth to speak, but Ula said, 'No, Ronny. She's a good person. You are a liar. She told me what you said about counting calories during sex.' She turned to Stella. 'He's always counting. It's ridiculous. He records it on his Garmin watch.'

The veins in Ronny's forehead and neck throbbed and he stepped towards Stella. 'Tell her you're lying.'

Instead of feeling intimidated, Stella kept her breathing regular, standing her ground despite the adrenaline. She knew exactly where to hit him. 'Ronny. My best friend is marrying your best client. Half your base is made up of his mates. All it would take is a word from me and—' she snapped her fingers. 'Gone. Do you understand?'

She could see the thoughts galloping across his face: shock chased by disbelief chased by anger. His lips curled into a snarl and he grabbed Ula by the wrist. 'We're leaving.'

'You're hurting me,' cried Ula as he tugged her arm.

'Let her go!' shouted Stella, seizing Ula's other arm. 'Think, Ronny! You're making a mistake.' She tried to get through to him, but he had gone past reason.

He stepped towards Stella. 'Fuck off, you fucking cunt!' Ula cried out as he pulled her from Stella's grip. Ronny turned. That's when a fist came out of nowhere, connecting with his face with a crunch. He let go of Ula and cradled his nose. The fist followed up with an upper-cut, connecting with the bottom of his jaw. He fell over.

Dilwyn waggled his injured hand. 'Alright, Stella?'

Ronny was crawling to his feet, blood pouring from his nose and murder in his eyes. He roared, 'I'm going to fucking kill you!'

But before he could charge Dilwyn, two burly bouncers with fore-arms even thicker than Ronny's ran out of the club, immobilising him with a choke hold.

Ula and Stella both turned their attention to Dilwyn. 'You forgot some of your make-up in the cab,' he said, brandishing Claudia's golden mascara wand. Stella could have kissed him in that moment. Ula did.

Dilwyn's blue eyes bulged and his arms flailed. Ula crushed his cheeks between her manicured hands—pink nails matching her hair and dress. By the time she separated her lips from his, Dilwyn had turned purple.

'Come,' Ula said, ignoring the drama of Ronny and the bouncers. 'Let's find some ice for your hand.' She pulled him into the club.

Stella followed, shaking her head. As she watched Ula and the captive Dilwyn disappear into the crowd, she realised she still hadn't unravelled the mystery of what Ula did for a living. But right now, she had her own mission to fulfil.

She found Claudia talking to a woman in a flowing bohemian dress. Claudia introduced her as Lada Lovechild, a newborn photographer from Manchester. Stella couldn't concentrate on the conversation, her mind occupied with thoughts of Connor and what she would say to him, so she hid behind a glass of champagne, searching the room.

The place was packed. If this was half the guest list, Stella wondered how many people had originally been invited. A jazz band played on a red-curtained stage, the perfect background for the conversational buzz. Uniformed staff handed out canapés and drinks on silver trays.

'That's HIDEOUS! Change it at once.'

Recognising the voice of the wedding planner, Stella spit out her champagne. 'You're kidding me,' she hissed at Claudia.

'Sorry, he's apparently the best. Bunny insisted.'

Stella glanced over her shoulder to see him harassing one of the waiters for his loose bowtie. Nothing to do with her. She chuckled at the magnitude of her relief.

'This night is full of surprises,' Stella said. Claudia laughed more loudly than Stella expected. It wasn't that funny.

At the edge of the room, a flash went off. Her breath caught. Was it Connor? 'Who got the honour of doing the photos?' Stella asked.

'Krish, of course. Trained by the best. Don't tell Magnus I said that.'

As Stella scanned the room for the face she loved, she spied an older woman on a sofa in the corner, dressed like Dame Maggie Smith in *Downton Abbey*. Two other women with matching looks of disdain sat next to her.

'Is that Bunny?'

'You mean the woman who looks like she orgasms when she hears *"Jerusalem"*? Yeah, that's her.'

They giggled.

'Sweetie!' Magnus appeared and kissed Claudia. 'I've been looking for you everywhere. I want to introduce you to Bongo, my old cricket chum. Oh, hallo, Stella!'

Had he become even more posh since she'd last seen him? She laughed as he pecked her on both cheeks. 'Hi, Magnus.'

His eyes widened at the pink frilly number that Stella was sporting.

'Don't ask, sweetie,' warned Claudia.

'Stella!'

She looked up and spotted Krish coming towards her.

He embraced her with one arm. 'You're looking, um, jubilant.'

'Dress to impress,' she replied, holding the skirt out and shaking her ruffles. 'Is Connor here?'

'Not yet. He had another job to finish first.' Flourishing his camera, he said, 'Why don't you pose with the couple?'

Stella stood on one side of Magnus, Claudia on the other. Krish fired off a few frames.

'Now one of just the two of us,' Claudia commanded. She put her arms around Stella and squeezed for all she was worth. 'I'm so happy you're here,' she whispered in Stella's ear.

After Krish went to photograph some new guests, Magnus pushed his hair out of his eyes and said to Claudia, 'Bongo?'

'He can wait. I haven't seen Stella in ages. I'll find you in a minute.'

Magnus kissed her forehead and left them to chat. Claudia exhaled.

'Oh my god, Stella, what am I doing?'

Stella led her to a free sofa. 'What's wrong?'

'He has friends named Bongo and Minxy and Spuds.'

'Really? What do they call Magnus?'

'Ugh. Maggot. Don't ask me why.' With sudden emotion, Claudia whispered, 'For Christ sake, he's played polo with Prince William. We are worlds apart.' A tear trembled in the corner of her eye.

'Aw, Clauds,' Stella said, surprised by this rare show of fear from her fearless friend. She drew her head to her shoulder. 'If anyone can show him a more righteous path, it's you.'

Sitting up and flapping her hands at her face to dry it off, Claudia said, 'Sorry. These bloody hormones.'

Her brows creasing in concern, Stella took Claudia's hands in hers and said, 'I haven't seen you together a lot. But I get the feeling that there's true love there. In some crazy way, you two make sense.'

Claudia wiped her nose on the back of her wrist. 'Come with me to meet this Bongo fellow. I don't think I can do it on my own.'

'I'm always here for you, Clauds.' They tipped their foreheads together.

While Claudia suffered the introductions, Stella hungrily pinched some canapés from a waiter. Scanning the room for Connor, she spotted faces she recognised from the BAPP conference and a clutch of university friends.

It was approaching 9:00 now. Where was Connor? She should have asked Krish for his ETA. She turned to Claudia and said, 'I'll be back. I'm just going to the toilets.'

Claudia grabbed one of her frills and said, 'Not quite yet.'

'Why?' Stella asked. Her friend shifted her eyes towards the stage. A new performer was settling down in front of the microphone with guitar in hand. Stella had to do a double-take. Big blonde hair, tight pink dress, huge boobs...it was Dolly Parton!

'Oh my god!' shouted Stella. But Dolly's lips were slightly too big and her height twice real Dolly's size and, even with the expertly applied make-up, Stella could tell an imitation when she saw it.

'Is that a *drag queen?*' Stella asked Claudia.

Claudia looked at Magnus. Stella saw them exchange a secret smile.

The drag queen pulled the mic close and said, 'Hello, London, how y'all doin' today?' Except it wasn't a sweet Southern voice that she heard.

Behind her, someone said, 'Bloody hell! Is that *Connor Knight?*'

Stella squinted at the drag queen and that's when she saw that it was unmistakably Connor. Those cheekbones and those eyes— despite the false lashes and excessive blue eye shadow—were definitely his.

She leaned toward Claudia. 'What's going on?'

Pursing her lips, Claudia pretended to draw a zipper across her mouth and threw away the key, very pleased with herself.

Unsure what was happening, Stella crossed her arms and waited. For a man that was so handsome, he made a terribly ugly woman. Why was he dressed like that, hilarious as it was?

'We're here tonight to celebrate the love of two great people...well, one great person and Magnus.'

'Knobhead,' said Magnus standing next to Claudia.

Connor's lip lifted in a half-smile and he continued, 'Somebody I love dared me to do this, so I'm here to sing a song about a flame-haired woman who knows exactly what she wants. Mademoiselle Chicken, this one's for you.'

Did Connor just say he loved her in front of this entire room? Stella's knees weakened and she grabbed onto Claudia's hands for support.

The pink sequins on his dress flashed in the spotlight as he strummed the first notes of 'Jolene'. Of course, Connor could play the guitar.

He began singing, that same sexy, gravelly voice that she'd heard in France, but this time every note plucked at her heart. As he sang about Jolene's red hair and green eyes, his eyes sought hers and, when he found her, he winked and she smiled at him, a world of promise about what they'd be doing later in her gaze.

Not only had he helped her reclaim her song, he was now giving it a whole new meaning for them. Tears pricked at her eyes.

The audience sang along on the chorus and Stella joined in. Connor strutted around the stage like the lovechild of Bob Dylan and Lady Gaga. He'd really missed his calling when he became a photographer.

She watched his fingers flying over the strings of his guitar and remembered the feeling of those fingers on her body. Her dress suddenly felt a little tight.

With disappointment, Stella realised he was nearing the end of the song. She could listen to him forever. If his words were anything to go by, maybe she'd get the opportunity to do just that. She heard Connor change the lyrics to: 'I'm the only one for you, Jolene'.

Stella threw her head back and laughed.

As he crooned the final words, the guests screamed for more, the applause deafening. 'Connor, we love you!' They began to chant his name, but Connor had other ideas.

He bowed, drinking in the adulation for a few moments, and put down his guitar. His grey eyes searched for her again and settled on her face.

'Hold this,' she said to Claudia, handing her the champagne flute. Almost as one, Connor and Stella started moving towards the stage steps.

Stella could only think of one thing: kissing his luscious pink-lipsticked mouth.

'Excuse me. Pardon me.' All the photographers in the room seemed to have congregated at the bottom of the stairs, wanting a piece of Connor. She pushed through the bodies, earning herself a few filthy looks, until she stood in front of him.

He grinned at her. 'Bonjour, Mademoiselle Chicken.'

'I'm feeling oddly attracted to you right now,' she said, reaching up and placing her hands against his boobs.

'I could say the same to you.' He grabbed hold of the frills at her waist and pulled her towards him.

She picked some blonde tendrils of artificial hair off his mouth before sliding her hands behind his neck and pulling his head down to hers.

Around them, she could hear whispers: 'Who's that? Who's Connor Knight kissing?' Their voices faded as she focussed on the man in her arms. Their kiss deepened and she struggled to remember that they were standing in the middle of an audience. Laughing, she reluctantly pulled away.

'Ti amo,' she said, rubbing the tip of her nose along his jawline.

Next to her ear, he whispered. 'Je t'aime.' He stepped back and looked into her eyes. 'Forget all that stuff I said about going slow. And sorry I didn't say I love you back. I'm an idiot and you caught me unawares. I messed—'

'Shhh. It's fine. It doesn't matter. Also, you have lipstick all over your face.'

'Thanks. You, too.'

They kissed again.

The noise in the room crept into her consciousness and they broke apart. A DJ took over the musical entertainment and the guests thronged onto the dance floor, ready to throw some shapes after Stella and Connor's romantic show. Already, the photographers were on their phones, racing to break the news on Twitter. Stella didn't care.

Taking his hand, she pulled him towards Magnus and Claudia. 'I assume you knew about—' She proffered her hand towards Connor's sequined dress.

Claudia shrugged and started shimmying.

Magnus said, 'Frankly, I would have paid good money to see this, but Connor did it all for free.'

'Maggot! Maggot!' called his grandmother, approaching them with her head held haughtily in the air. 'What's going on here?'

'It's just Prince Harry having a bit of fun, Bunny,' he said loudly, apologising to Stella with his eyes before leading his grandmother back to her sofa.

Stella threw her arms around Connor, tossed her head back, and laughed. Connor tried to nuzzle her neck, but the large wig got in the way.

'Mind if I take this off?'

'This is crazy,' she said, as she helped him take out the pins holding it in place. 'How did you even come up with this?'

'I called Magnus because...well, because I wanted some advice. He was marrying your best friend, so I thought he might be able to help me out.'

'And did he?'

'No, he was completely useless, but he did invite me to this party and mentioned you'd be here.'

'But I was in Wales? How did you know I'd get back in time?

'Stella Price, you are one of the most determined, thoughtful, loyal, and exasperating people I know. A little geography wouldn't get in your way. And you texted me, remember?'

Happiness shivered through her. She could get used to seeing herself through his eyes.

'Still...why *Dolly*? I mean, a conversation would have sufficed.'

He stared into her eyes, emotions simmering in the grey depths, although it was hard to take him seriously with so much blue eye make-up on. 'Because I realised that I needed to show you, publicly and beyond a shadow of a doubt, how I felt.' He brought his hand up to caress her face. 'This is all new and you're going to have to bear with me while I feel my way. I can't change my past, but I want you to be part of my future.'

Stella swooned. Did he have a scriptwriter?

With a wicked grin, he added, 'Also, you challenged me. You already beat me at Thumb Wars—albeit dubiously. I couldn't let you win again.'

'Hmmm. Is that how it's going to be?'

'That's definitely how it's going to be,' he said.

Her body thrummed, mind buzzing.

Around them, the other guests danced to *'Celebration'* by Kool & the Gang.

'C'mon, lovebirds,' Claudia interrupted. 'You're making me feel sick and I've had enough of that the past few months.'

Connor laughed and twirled Stella, both of them styling it out in their horrible pink dresses. As he caught her at the waist and dipped her, Stella was relieved to find that—as well as being a talented photographer, a great singer, and a thoughtful lover—Connor Knight was also an excellent dancer.

EPILOGUE

TWO YEARS LATER

STELLA UNWRAPPED the glittery paper to find a throw pillow printed with her and Connor's faces under the headline, 'Getting hitched!'

'I love it,' Stella said to Claudia. 'It's horrendous.'

'Aw, thanks.' She smirked, wrinkling her nose.

Placing it on the four-poster bed, Stella continued her pre-wedding to do list by rolling the garter up her leg—a present from Oliwier along with a box of risqué bondage-wear as an apology for not being able to make the wedding. He was busy opening a new store in Hong Kong with Paulina.

Noticing the time, Stella took a deep breath and asked, 'How do I look?'

Claudia ran her eyes over the ivory floor-length tulle gown with long, sheer sleeves and plunging neckline. A crown of flowers encircled Stella's head, her auburn hair hanging freely down her back. 'Frankly, you look hot, Mrs Soon-to-be-Knight.'

'I haven't yet decided if I'm taking his name...'

Claudia Fiennes rolled her eyes. 'Shall we?' They linked arms and exited the farmhouse, joining Stella's father outside.

Krish raised his camera and photographed her dad's reaction to seeing his baby girl.

'Stella.' Bill choked on the words. 'You look beautiful.' He hugged her tightly and wiped tears from his eyes. The camera clicked.

Together they walked into the woods where Stella Price would marry Connor Knight.

They'd decided to hold the wedding in the forest near where Connor's mother had grown up. That way, she could be with them in spirit.

The wedding planner had done an amazing job, stringing lights among the trees and creating a stunning arch of white flowers and greenery where they would say their vows. On either side of the hessian-rug aisle, she had arranged vintage pews for the guests to sit on. It was a forest fairy tale.

As they approached the ceremony, Stella put her hand over her stomach to calm her nerves. She inhaled and exhaled to control the lingering nausea. Her father patted her arm.

They passed a tall oak at the back of the pews with a sign saying 'Family Tree' hanging from some twine. She grinned at the pictures of their nearest and dearest stuck to the bark: a photo of Angela and Bill as bride and groom; a portrait of Connor's mother, Grace, holding baby Connor in her arms. In a separate frame, Armstrong and Michael showed off a fish they'd caught in the fjords of Norway. Wedding photographs of grandparents and great-grandparents added history to the collection, the paper getting browner and the expressions sterner the further back they went in time.

Finally, Stella, Bill, and Claudia stood at the top of the aisle. Stella clutched her bouquet of wildflowers, inhaling their calming scent. A single musician with a guitar sat near the front, playing an instrumental version of 'I Will Always Love You'. Claudia went first, in her figure-hugging russet-coloured dress. It had taken her over 18 months, but she'd lost the baby weight from carrying the twins, Lucan and Jack—the former name chosen by Magnus, the latter by Claudia.

Waiting under the canopy, Stella spotted Connor in his tailored grey suit. As always, when she saw him, her breath caught. She still pinched herself when she remembered the weekend he took her to

Madrid as a surprise and got down on one knee in front of 'La Maja Desnuda'. The security guards had come running when they heard the hysterical British woman shrieking and crying.

Somewhere along the way, Connor had decided marriage wasn't such a bad idea after all.

Stella lifted her foot and took her first step towards the rest of her life.

THE SPEECHES CAUSED a lot of hilarity. Bill talked about young Stella and the first time they met Connor. Angela had sat him down in a chair, Italian Inquisition style, and grilled him about why he thought he deserved her daughter. When she was satisfied with most of his answers, she squeezed his cheeks and told him she knew people who could make his life difficult if he messed up. Michael, Connor's brother and best man, managed to roast him without using a single borrowed joke or mentioning any ex-girlfriends. Stella was overjoyed to hear a story about ten-year-old Connor in Barbados, when he accidentally drank a glassful of rum and spent the afternoon singing Elvis songs to tourists on the beach.

Claudia brought tears to everyone's eyes when she ended her speech with, 'You're the only person I'd ever drive off a cliff with, Stella. I love you.' Motherhood had made her more sentimental.

Connor spoke about when he first fell in love with her. It might have been when she challenged him to a thumb war. Or when she claimed to be responsible for half the middle-aged boners in Europe. Or perhaps it was when she was hiding in a closet after photographing the world's most X-rated wedding dance. 'Whenever it was,' he concluded, 'today I am lucky to call you my wife. Now and forever.'

Angela broke out in sobs. Armstrong Knight, or as Stella liked to call him, the Silver Fox, pulled out a clean handkerchief and proffered it to her mother with a flourish. Stella could see where Connor got his charm.

Afterwards, the party started.

Before heading upstairs to change for their first dance, Stella waved to Dilwyn and Ula, who were tying the knot later that year. Dilwyn's confidence had grown since they started dating. He had shed his lost puppy look and now exuded an air of assuredness. Her parents put it down to the fact that business was flourishing, but Ula probably had a lot to do with it.

Stella giggled at the fact she used to think Ula was a porn star. When Stella had finally asked, Ula laughed and explained, 'I am a You Tube influencer. My channel, it shows older women to...how do you say?...reclaim sexuality. I review sex toys, help them to understand where their clitoris is. That sort of thing.' The erratic schedule was due to her neighbour, who filmed her segments when he wasn't on set as a camera operator. 'He was cheap,' she said. When she eventually got her own equipment thanks to Stella's tips plus some sponsorship deals, Ula turned up to clean regularly, every Wednesday at 10AM, until she decided to move to Cardiff to be with Dilwyn. 'I can work anywhere.' And because she enjoyed cleaning as it gave her 'time to think', she now cleaned Stella's parents' house.

Angela had no clue about Ula's main work. Or so Stella thought. On her last visit to Wales while looking for a hot water bottle in Angela's bedside drawer, she'd shrieked when she found a sex toy Ula had reviewed on her channel. Stella had tried to erase the memory.

Next to Dilwyn and Ula at the bar, Stella noted with distress that Michael and Tristan were hovering together and Tristan had his charming face on. Michael looked like a softer, blonde version of Connor. She had warned Tristan that Connor's brother was off-limits, but he probably took that as a challenge. Since winning the last series of *Strictly Come Dancing*, his ego had gone stratospheric.

Further down the bar, Magnus and Bill were drinking beer and arguing politics.

Liliwen ran by with Gareth in tow. 'This wedding is absolutely fabulous.' Under her breath, she asked, 'Are you headed upstairs for a quick one?' She gave Stella a light slap on the bum. 'Go for it, lovely.'

Upstairs, Stella and Connor shared a long-anticipated kiss before changing into their tango outfits. She had spent months teaching him a sultry Argentine number for their first dance. As with everything Connor did, he picked it up handily. Countless times, they'd had to take a break from the lesson to work off the sexual tension in bed. Or wherever they happened to be at the time.

She slipped out of her wedding dress and hung it on the wardrobe. They would spend their first night as husband and wife in this room, but right now, it looked like a suitcase had exploded. She stepped into the white tango dress with the slit up one side and asked Connor to zip it up.

'Are you nervous?' he asked as he spun her around.

'I always get nervous before I perform. I'm not like you, entertaining a crowd without fear or preparation.'

He chuckled and continued buttoning his black shirt. 'You'll be great.'

Biting her lip, Stella decided it was now or never. 'Connor?'

'Yes?'

'Did you happen to see Lada Lovechild downstairs?'

'The newborn photographer? Yeah, I think she was helping herself to the Pimms.'

'We've become quite friendly lately.'

Connor threaded his cufflinks through his buttonholes, small platinum discs engraved with C & S. 'She's great. Talented.'

Stella persevered. 'It's just that I need to speak with her. About a shoot.'

'Yeah.'

'For us.'

Connor stopped tucking in his shirt. He turned towards her slowly. 'What are you saying?'

She looked at him, eyebrows raised.

His face broke into a wide smile. 'When?'

'Around January.'

In less than a second he had her in his arms and was kissing her all over: lips, neck and shoulders. She took his hand and placed it on her belly.

'Well, I'm not going to be able to concentrate now,' he said, stroking her stomach through her dress.

'Put on your game face, Connor Knight. We have a first dance to do.'

'Yes, boss,' he saluted her and they went downstairs, hand in hand.

As they glided through the moves, hitting only a few minor snags, Stella took in the faces surrounding them, of family and friends, old and new. What a journey it had been and what an exciting adventure she had in front of her. Although the dance would probably only get them a score of seven from the imaginary judges, as she looked at her new husband, she knew that their future was a definite ten.

THE END

COMING in September 2023

F-Stop!

Connor's assistant, Krish Kapadia, decides to start his own photography business. But when his feisty ex-girlfriend, talented videographer Francesca March, turns up at a wedding, Krish has to decide between the life he thought he wanted and her.

PRE-ORDER TODAY

HOME BY MIDNIGHT PUBLISHING

ACKNOWLEDGMENTS

This book was a labour of love, my love letter to the photography industry, and a project that kept me sane throughout the tumultuous Covid years. For that, I will always be grateful.

There are so many people I need to thank. To my first reader, Anais Hamelin, who suffered through reading a shitty first draft and corrected all my bad French. To my J Team Coven – Jayne Rice, Joanna Lyons, Jessica Popplewell, Juno Goldstone, and Farrah Riaz – your support, your close reading, and your suggestions have made this book what it is. Jayne, you are one of the first people who reads anything I write and it's stronger for it.

I'm lucky to have not just one, but two writing tribes. During lockdown, I stumbled into a 6-month course with Curtis Brown and met a crazy cast of characters. To all the CBC Henrietta Spuddle gang: Jen Hyatt, Barbara Whitfield, Edward Crocker, Pip Swan, Paula Jones, Abhi Parasrampuria, Heidi Gallacher, Stacey Thomas, Lisa Nathan-Goucher, Hannah Sutherland, Daniel Allen, Alice Sutton, Cathryn Campbell, and Samantha Quinn. All of your enthusiasm and great critique during the course helped to make me a better writer. And I have to give a shout to our fantastic tutors, Simon Wroe and Cathi Unsworth.

To my editor, Amy Borg, who made sure I wrote the book I wanted to write and, to Bailey McGinn, who created the amazing cover and saved me from the depths of despair.

This book would have been impossible to write without the years of friendship and mentoring that I had from a huge cast of people in the photography industry. First off, Jerry and Melissa Ghionis – thank you for taking the time to talk with me about your adventures in wedding photography and for your unerring support. You are the original photography rock stars. To my mentors: Damien Lovegrove, Martin Grahame-Dunn, Damian McGillicuddy, David Anthony Williams, Dennis Orchard, Kelly Brown, and David Edmonson. What you all don't know about photography isn't worth knowing. To the Super Awesome WPPI crowd, the karaoke scene is for you guys. I specifically have to mention Terrie Jones from the SWPP for all the hard work she's done for the Society (the real life BAPP), as well as Sanjay Jogia, Natalie Licini (the chickens are for you), Selena Rollason, Melissa Love, Angela Adams, Bella West, Magdalena Sienicka, Giles Christopher & Abi Cockroft, Faye & Trevor Yerbury, James Musselwhite, Renato Taveres, Veruschka Baudo, and Marte Lundby Rekaa.

Thank you to Glen Bryan, original member of the Penge dance team on *Come Dancing*, for being my ballroom guru and psychology guru. Katy Thomson, for many things, but in this case for telling me about her life as a diplomat's brat. Amy McWade, thanks for the Brummie. Ceri Morgan and Sandra Atherton, thanks for listening to me waffle on about these characters during our lockdown walks. My appreciation to everyone who talked to me about their anxiety. You know who you are.

To all the Sarahs in my life: Thank you to Sarah Gillman for the never-ending support. Sara O'Keefe, thank you for all the advice. Sarah Boggio, thank you for being my cheerleader and the best auntie. Sara Finke, for helping me name Ula – I know you'll get that psychology degree one day. And finally to Sarah Edmunds, for saying that I wanted to be the Jilly Cooper of photography. Look what you started!

To my agent, Katie Greenstreet: thank you for believing in me.

Dolly Parton, thank you for the inspiration and continuing to be one of the most decent people on this earth.

To my dad for reading my sexy book, correcting my bad Italian, and generally being the best dad a girl could have. To my mom and Aunt Nancy, thanks for the writing genes. To Faith, thank you for taking good care of my dad. To Anne Hughes, for checking my Welsh and for being the best crazy mother-in-law (in a good way). To Meri, who gave me a love of reading: you are missed.

And last but not least...my family! To G and H, I couldn't do any of this without you both. I love you with all my heart. And to James, for reading all my pages, supporting me, and being better than any romantic hero I could ever dream up. Still having the time of our lives.

SIGN UP TO MY NEWSLETTER

In my monthly newsletter, I share book recommendations, snippets about my writing life, news about upcoming releases, photography tips, and the occasional competition.

Sign up at JuliaBoggio.com.

ALSO PLEASE LEAVE A REVIEW

Whether it's on Goodreads, Amazon, or a Facebook reading group, please take a moment to leave a review. You have no idea how much we authors appreciate them.

ABOUT THE AUTHOR

Originally from New Jersey, Julia moved to London in her early twenties. She worked as an advertising copywriter until discovering her love of photography on a 6-month trip around South America. She started a wedding photography business which received some great PR when her own *Dirty Dancing*-themed wedding dance went viral on YouTube. She appeared on *Richard & Judy* and *The Oprah Winfrey Show*, where she danced with Patrick Swayze. In 2009 she opened a luxury portrait studio and has photographed everyone from the Queen to Queen, the band. After 15 years as a photographer, she returned to her first love: writing. Julia lives in Wimbledon with her Welsh husband, two children, and an oddly possessive cat.

Sign up for Julia's newsletter at JuliaBoggio.com.

f facebook.com/juliaboggio
🅾 instagram.com/juliaboggio
♪ tiktok.com/@juliaboggiowriter